PRAISE FOR DEIDRE KNIGHT'S PARALLEL SERIES

Parallel Heat

"Twists and turns abound . . . sensually intriguing."
—Romance Junkies

"Knight's unique perspective and clever plotting make this story and this series something to savor!"
—*Romantic Times BOOKclub*

"[Deidre Knight] has cleverly created some great and complex characters. Everyone seems to be hiding something, whether it's intentional or not . . . in this fantastic paranormal series." —Fresh Fiction

"Great pacing, action-packed plotting, and a truly imaginative take on the dizzying intricacies of alternate realities." —BookLoons

"In a novel that eclipses the first, Deidre Knight creates a compelling cast of characters in a unique sci-fi romance." —Wantz Upon a Time Book Reviews

"Beautifully crafted . . . like a blank canvas, richly layered with mood, atmosphere, and vibrant details. This unique world that Ms. Knight has created will capture the hearts of fans." —Romance Divas

continued . . .

"A unique plot, with twists and turns that leave you guessing . . . a fantastic paranormal tale of the redeeming power of love."
—*USA Today* bestselling author Susan Kearney

"At times humorous, at others heart-wrenching, but always compelling, Deidre Knight offers readers a fresh, wonderfully creative glimpse at the complexity of human decisions. What a page-turner!"
—Gena Showalter, author of *The Pleasure Slave*

"A unique and sensual story about honor and duty and the power of love. Compelling characters, complex world building, fascinating alternate realities, and riveting love scenes."
—Catherine Spangler, author of *Shadow Fires*

"This book swept me off my feet. A fantastically original, smart, and sexy adventure—*Parallel Attraction* delivered everything I want in a story!"
—Susan Grant, RITA-winning, bestselling author of *Your Planet or Mine?*

"A compelling debut by Deidre Knight. Her world building is intriguing, with her exploration of the two people and the time travel twists . . . an entertaining, enjoyable read." —Evolution Writers Book Reviews

ALSO BY DEIDRE KNIGHT

Parallel Heat
Parallel Attraction

PARALLEL
SEDUCTION

Deidre Knight

A SIGNET ECLIPSE BOOK

SIGNET ECLIPSE
Published by New American Library, a division of
Penguin Group (USA) Inc., 375 Hudson Street,
New York, New York 10014, USA
Penguin Group (Canada), 90 Eglinton Avenue East, Suite 700, Toronto,
Ontario M4P 2Y3, Canada (a division of Pearson Penguin Canada Inc.)
Penguin Books Ltd., 80 Strand, London WC2R 0RL, England
Penguin Ireland, 25 St. Stephen's Green, Dublin 2,
Ireland (a division of Penguin Books Ltd.)
Penguin Group (Australia), 250 Camberwell Road, Camberwell, Victoria 3124,
Australia (a division of Pearson Australia Group Pty. Ltd.)
Penguin Books India Pvt. Ltd., 11 Community Centre, Panchsheel Park,
New Delhi - 110 017, India
Penguin Group (NZ), 67 Apollo Drive, Mairangi Bay,
Auckland 1311, New Zealand (a division of Pearson New Zealand Ltd.)
Penguin Books (South Africa) (Pty.) Ltd., 24 Sturdee Avenue,
Rosebank, Johannesburg 2196, South Africa

Penguin Books Ltd., Registered Offices:
80 Strand, London WC2R 0RL, England

First published by Signet Eclipse, an imprint of New American Library,
a division of Penguin Group (USA) Inc.

First Printing, April 2007
10 9 8 7 6 5 4 3 2 1

Copyright © Deidre Knight, 2007
All rights reserved

This one is dedicated to my soul sister, Angela Zoltners. Not only does she have a cool last name, but she's a wonderful friend and reader. Thanks for loving Scott and Hope as much as I do. Lots of love!

ACKNOWLEDGMENTS

As always, there are far more people to thank than I can ever properly acknowledge, but I'm going to give it my best. If I leave you out, know that I'm still grateful, but sometimes forgetful!

First and foremost, my family's support allows me to chase all my crazy dreams. Judson Knight, my husband, and my precious daughters, Tyler and Riley Knight, share with me this journey. I love you very much!!

My sister and agent, Pamela Harty, is not only my best friend, but the best agent I could possibly have.

Our office staff at the Knight Agency keeps me sane during every workday: Julie Ramsey, Elaine Spencer, Jamie Acres, Lolita Love, thank you from the bottom of my heart.

My good friend Rae Monet proved invaluable in providing FBI lingo and details (who knew you had a flying armed form? Now I do!). Likewise, Brenda Novak was supremely helpful by answering countless e-mails about diabetes. Bless you, dear, for all the good information.

And, as always, my heartfelt appreciation and thanks go out to my terrific editor, Anne Bohner at NAL, who nurtures my confidence and skill by giving me freedom as well as strong encouragement. Thank you!

Thanks to Kara Welsh and Claire Zion and all the wonderful publishing staff at NAL. Your belief in me makes me want to truly shine for each of you.

Mambo thanks to Nancy Berland, Elizabeth Middaugh, Kim Miller, and the rest of the fabulous Nancy Berland Public Relations crew! You guys rock my world.

Prologue

The day was almost done, the scorching sun sinking hard beyond the line of mountains and pillars of smoke. In every direction that the soldier looked he saw one thing—destruction. The cities were long gone, the men and women with them; places that had once seemed invincible when he'd first stepped on Earth now lay decimated. New York, Los Angeles, London—annihilated by missiles intended to protect America and the free world, turned upon the humans by their bloodthirsty enemies: creatures that had devoured humanity after traveling from their own planet, millions of light-years away.

Nothing remained but dust and stone and ash. And death. So much death that Jake Tierny was gagging on it. But that was why this mission was the most critical one he'd ever undertaken, and this after a near-lifetime of soldiering. Earth's future depended upon his actions in the next few hours. Humanity's future depended on it, even as the universe did, because if their enemies could not be stopped on this human battlefield, then they never would be. They would move on to a new planet, a new race, devouring the inhabitants like the locusts they truly were.

Jake pushed past a mud-encrusted tent flapping in the heated wind, and shielded his eyes against the setting sun. He had come to tell his king and queen good-bye; after he used the mitres to travel back in time to that critical day—the one day they knew could turn the tide of war and stop their enemies—he would never come back.

Kelsey had returned hours earlier, explaining how their once-protector, Marco McKinley, had forced her to operate the mitres, allowing him to travel backward ten years in time. His queen was nothing if not tough, hardened by years of battle at her husband's side, even as she had the nurturing heart of a mother. Marco's final betrayal had hit her particularly hard, and she'd been in seclusion ever since, quiet inside the temporary home she shared with Jared, their king. No regal splendor marked their tent, no royal flags or banners. Theirs was just one more in a long series of shabby lean-tos erected two days earlier along the edge of Mirror Lake.

So it all ended here. The final battle—the greatest and most futile one—where they would turn their few remaining guns on the Antousians and have a last showdown. The OK Corral, alien style. Jake smiled; he liked that image of an Old West standoff here in the true American West. Too bad he'd miss it. He knew it would be one glorious sight to see.

"My lord," he called out, clearing his throat as he stood outside Jared's tent, waiting to enter.

Muffled sounds came from within: the soft, feminine voice of his queen followed by Jared's familiar deeper one. "Come in."

Jake dipped his head low, his broad shoulders barely clearing the entry as he pushed his way inside. Kelsey knelt on their pallet, her eyes swollen from crying. *Don't blame yourself! No one could have stopped McKinley, not with that much hatred driving him to do what he did!* He wanted to say that, but swallowed the words; his human queen would never buy his easy absolution.

He offered Jared a crisp salute. "Commander, the forces have massed along the lake's southern rim," he said. "Our scouts say attack will come after nightfall."

Jared gave a thoughtful nod, never looking up from the grimy battle plan spread on the table before him. The man had fought his way through more skirmishes than any forty-year-old soldier should have realistically survived. And yet here he sat, his long black hair silvered by maturity and hardship, his face scarred by years of captivity at their enemy's hands.

"We're no match for them, not this time." Jared's voice was more weary than defeated. "They will kill the lot of us."

"And so it will end," Jake agreed solemnly.

"And so it ends." Jared met his gaze meaningfully, his one blinded eye half-closed, the other trained on him intensely.

"Unless we mount a counterstrike."

"Go on." Jared nodded for him to continue.

Jake stared at the ground between them, praying that his commander would go for his very radical strategy. "You're right about today—this will mark our final defeat," he answered at last. "And that's why my plan is our only choice."

Jared glanced up, surprised. "What do you have in mind?"

"I know how we can open a door, sir." Jake knelt, placing a fist over his heart. "And I'm the one to do it."

"Tell me of this plan, Jakob." His one good eye narrowed intensely.

"I'm going to use the mitres, my lord. I'm going to chase McKinley back in time—and stop him, sir. I'm going to kill the bastard before he can accomplish his goal."

Chapter One

The woman wrapped in his arms was a stranger, just another human he'd sniffed out at a local bar; together they'd ridden in silence to this small motel. The room key was scuffed, with a numbered tag attached, and as he inserted it into the flimsy lock, his hand shook.

She leaned into him, giggling. "Give it to me."

"Got it," he mumbled under his breath as she made an unsuccessful play for the key clutched within his hand. She was tipsier than he was; after all, he'd spent too many nights prowling for women and drinking not to hold his liquor well. More than that, the woman could barely see. She wore eyeglasses with lenses thicker than the ice coating on his car windshield, and she'd stumbled several times on unseen slick patches in the parking lot. She was so loose in her steps, actually, that he'd had to grab hold of her, steadying her, an excellent excuse for pushing up behind her much smaller and extremely feminine body. A maneuver he planned to repeat once inside the privacy of their room.

As one they burst through the door, fumbling and grabbing at each other's bodies wordlessly. She was just a wisp of a thing, so small that it was easy to drive her up against the papered wall and pin her there. She wrapped both her surprisingly strong legs about his waist in a V shape, locking him within the warmth of her muscular thighs.

Damn those tight jeans of hers, he cursed, struggling

to unzip them as he kept her suspended between his body and the motel room wall.

To the right of her, his gaze landed on a framed photograph of a cowboy out on some lonesome stretch of road, just another slice of this Wild West life. In his own strange way, the universe had plunked him here in Jackson, Wyoming, as one of the very last of the true cowboys—a nomad, a wanderer without a real home anymore. No wonder he sought to pleasure himself endlessly with her kind.

With his mouth he took her, not bothering with gentleness. From the first moment he'd spotted this one across the bar he'd been unable to control his lust for her. His most base urges, the ones that drove him to mate with human women, came gasping their way to the fore, unrelenting in their need as he palmed first one breast, then the other through her cashmere turtleneck.

She thrust her tongue inside his mouth, tasting of bourbon and salty peanuts. So sweet. So perfect. He deepened their kiss, flicking his tongue against hers, warring for domination in a battle he was doomed to lose. She had him completely already—more than any of the other human women he'd brought to this same dingy, drafty motel so many times before.

Breaking apart from her kiss, he slid both hands beneath her bottom, cupping her and pushing her back against the wall even harder. She weighed so little, it was easy to wedge her there; her thighs tightened their locking hold about his hips as she settled into the ride. Her hands closed about his lower back, grasping hard, pulling his shirt free from his jeans until her sweaty palms met his even sweatier skin.

"What's your name?" he whispered against her cheek, licking her face with the tip of his tongue. She smelled of fresh snow and some perfume he couldn't name; she tasted of his future, his past, everything he'd ever wanted in a human mate.

"Hope," she answered huskily, unwrapping one leg, but he stopped her, catching it.

"Don't!" he cried, louder than he intended, and she lolled her head against the wall, staring at him. Though not really; her eyes didn't seem to fully focus on him, and she'd already ditched the glasses.

"Okay," she told him softly, "I won't," and hitched the leg back about him in another locking embrace.

He gasped, pressing his forehead against hers as he drew in a steadying breath. "I want to do wicked things with you, Hope," he admitted in a thick voice. His heart hammered so rapidly he was certain she could feel it.

She surprised him by laughing, a soft, husky sound that caused his groin to tighten like a hard fist. "Good," she said after her laughter faded. "Because I want to do wicked things with you too. Really wicked things."

It was the only invitation he needed, and he rushed ahead, releasing her momentarily. He separated her from her jeans easily, shoving them low about her hips, then peeled down her silk panties until all that remained between their two hungry bodies was his own damned jeans. His hands trembled as he struggled to free himself from the pants while keeping a firm grasp on her.

"Here." She planted a salty kiss against his lips. Then in one fluid gesture she'd unsnapped and unzipped his pants, pushing them down gracefully. "Wow, Commando," she teased, almost as if it were a pet name for him, not an observation about his absent underwear.

It was how all his people dressed, but naturally he didn't volunteer that fact. Or that he was a different species than she, for that matter. No, she didn't need to know about his sordid genetic history, his hybrid DNA or any of that. Talk about a cold shower on their thrumming, driving lust. She just needed to get how bad he wanted her, nothing else.

He slid his arms about her, swinging her away from the wall, and with just two steps they collapsed into a heap on the bed, she spread flat beneath his much larger body.

The bedsprings jostled and bounced as he settled atop her, both their feet dangling off the end of the bed. She was small, almost too small to lie beneath his bulky frame, so he struggled to be gentle. But it was tough to go slow, and when she gave a nod of silent assent, he knew not to hold anything back. With a satin-smooth gesture, he sheathed himself inside her warmth and wetness. She gasped, her gray eyes watering, then said nothing more; she held on to his shoulders as if her life depended on it, and he got a pretty good idea that she wasn't in the habit of this kind of thing.

The jostling of the bed became a rocking, forceful creaking as the two of them thrust and ground their way deeper and deeper. She rolled with him, landing awkwardly atop him, their hips still locked together. He was deep inside of her still. So deep, and he ached to go deeper. With a careful gesture she moved into a straddling position, her gaze never leaving his, though he wondered how much she really saw, her eyes seemed so dazed and unfocused.

"Hope." He moaned, arching his back beneath her movement. She had hold of him in the most intimate way, so slick and grasping, unrelenting. "Gods help me."

She bent low, trailing sloppy kisses across his jaw. "Your name, Commando." She panted in his ear as he pummeled into her again and again. "Tell . . . me your name."

For a moment he couldn't speak; he was that blind with need for the human. Her petite body fit perfectly atop him—a position he almost never wanted. Control. Domination. They were his sexual trademarks. But this woman? Gods, he would give her his very soul.

"Scott." He gasped, feeling her tease him toward the edge. *So close, so close. Gods! Gods, too . . . much! Gods, she's the one! Gods!*

Call me S'Skautsa, sweet love. Call me husband, mate. . . .

"Call me Scott," he nearly shouted.

Then his eyes flew wide open and he was suddenly quite awake.

*   *   *

"Gods!" Scott shouted, sitting up in bed too fast—so fast, in fact, that it caused a lightning-bright flash of pain behind his eyes as he moved from his dream state into a waking frame of mind.

Where the hell am I? He squinted in the half darkness. The hospital, he remembered with a thick, heavy feeling in his heart, and jerked the sheet back over his legs, aware that he had one massive hard-on.

Guilt and fear closed in on him. He'd been dreaming about Hope Harper again—and such real dreams he'd have sworn he'd lived them before. Only he hadn't.

Slipping a hand between his legs he stroked himself shamelessly, needing the release he never seemed to reach in his sleep. Hope had taken him to the very brink, and then . . .

He'd landed here, awake and more than slightly aware that the woman of his dreams was a virtual stranger. *Then why doesn't she feel like one? She feels like someone I've loved all my life.*

For almost a week Scott had been in a drugged-up, pain-riddled daze, after having both of his legs shot out from underneath him during a massive battle against the Antousians at Warren Air Force Base. The drugs had to be the true source of the dreams; at least, that was what he told himself, because the alternative was much more disturbing.

He was lucky as hell that he hadn't been killed there on the base. If not for Hope, he never would have made it out alive. The FBI linguist had dragged him to safety beneath a truck chassis during the firefight to end all firefights, then followed him back here to the hidden safety of his king's mountain fortress.

Of course, Hope was pretty damned convinced that if not for her, he never would have been shot in the first place, but he knew better. Only at her side had he found the will to make it out alive at all. It had been her belief in him that had fired his resolve to survive, not just after he was wounded, but beforehand, too, during his days of captivity at the base.

Sinking heavily into his hospital pillows again, Scott wondered why the human hadn't returned to visit him. It had been hours—days, maybe? He wasn't even sure, not with the gauzy haze of the medication obscuring details, and the drumming, endless pain in his legs. The medics promised he would walk again, that he would recover completely, but in the half darkness of his hospital room he'd begun to have his doubts. And with the doubts, the rampant fears had come. He was a soldier and a leader: Without full command over his body, what good would he do his king? He would become a sideline liability. A tactical strategist, but not an active participant. And he'd rather die than become useless, someone whom his soldiers pitied and his king politely deferred to. Hell, what was the point of that kind of life?

Hitting the call button, he intended to grill the medics for the full truth. They owed him that much, for damned sure.

"Yes, Lieutenant?" The shift nurse poked her head inside the doorway of his room.

"These drugs don't work worth shit." Fumbling with his handheld medication control, he jammed at it angrily. "This planned torture or something?"

"You've slept for hours already." The nurse walked toward his bedside, her military-issue boots tap-tapping on the tile floor. "You should wake up and eat a little."

Dillon collapsed into the pillows, totally exhausted already. He didn't want to eat; he wanted to know why Hope hadn't returned to visit him.

"Women," he muttered, his eyes sliding shut. The sound of the bedside chair scraping the floor surprised him, and he glanced up to find that his nurse had plopped right into the thing.

"I take it you're talking about someone other than me?" She laughed. He hadn't seen this one on shift before; maybe she was new enough not to realize what a badass he could be. All the other rotating medics and nurses steered clear of him like he was an Antousian gorabung. "Or are you just talking women in general?" she pressed.

"Hope Harper." He grunted. "The human . . . she came to visit me a few days ago."

She stared down at his chart, barely masking a smile. "Oh, her. Is she denying you pain meds?"

He scowled. "What's your name, medic?" he demanded gruffly, sizing her up from top to bottom. She wore her uniform with a bit of attitude, not pressed and starched like it should be.

"Shelby Tyler, sir."

"Nurse Tyler, you do know who I am, right? Nobody erased your memory as to my role within this army?"

Again the blond-haired woman laughed, shaking her head. "Of course I know exactly who you are, Lieutenant. You're not only His Highness's top military adviser, but you're a hero to us all. I meant no disrespect; it was just a joke. You looked like you could use a laugh about now."

He growled, but said nothing more, and Shelby blew out a sigh, growing serious. "Listen, sir, I know you're in a lot of pain, and I know that human has you in a fit. So why don't you just talk about it? I'm good at listening."

"Good at listening." He cut his eyes sideways at her. "You a psychologist too?"

She smiled, but didn't answer at first. "No, but I've been in love a few times myself."

Bolting upright in bed, he grimaced with pain. "I am not in love with that woman! I barely know her—"

"Uh-huh." She tapped his chart with a pen, sounding wholly unconvinced. "Barely know her, sure."

"I met her a week ago. That's it."

"Then what do all those dreams mean, sir?" she asked with a perfect tone of innocence.

"How do you know about my dreams?" He twisted the bedsheet in his hands.

She leaned forward, meeting his gaze seriously. "Because I've been your night nurse since they brought you in here, sir, and I know you've been having some serious—perhaps amazing—dreams about 'that woman.' So why don't you stop denying it and talk to me a little?''

Well, damn it all to hell. Had he been mumbling in his sleep? Apparently. With a face flushed hot from embarrassment, he decided on evasive maneuvering. "You have a Southern accent. What on earth is a Refarian medic doing with an accent like yours?"

Her smile faded some. "I spent my first five years here in our Texas facility."

They exchanged a mournful, knowing look. "I see," was all he said. None of them liked to talk about the Texas incident.

"So, yeah, I guess I picked up a bit of an accent." She forced a smile. "Sure didn't mean to."

Shelby's bedside manner did distract him from his larger troubles, and her accent was—much as it pained him to admit it—almost cute.

"Now, are you going to tell me about those dreams of yours or not, Lieutenant? 'Cause it's two in the morning, and it's going to be a long shift otherwise."

"Is that why you backed off my meds?"

"You needed to wake up a little, sir. That's all. Besides, you missed Hope Harper's last three visits."

He studied the ceiling tiles so she wouldn't see how the news that apparently Hope had visited him while he slept—repeatedly—made his heart race. Unfortunately, he couldn't control the monitors beside his bed, and their previously steady beeping accelerated like mad. He raked a hand through his disheveled hair, willing his heart to cease its rapid palpitations.

"Look, next time she comes . . . wake me up, all right?"

"Are you sure you don't prefer those dreams?" Shelby ventured silkily. "Because from the sound of it—"

"Wake me up," he commanded, assuming his voice of leadership.

"Got it, sir." She stood and pulled down his sheet, which he immediately jerked back over himself. After all, he was totally naked beneath the thin material, and he wasn't exactly prepared for his nurse to see him in the buff.

"I have to check your bandages," she reminded him, reaching yet again for the cover and giving it a staunch tug.

This time the cool fabric rose like a ship's sail, then popped back with a crisp salute, totally exposing him. But Shelby never looked at his groin—or any other part of his anatomy, for that matter—training all of her attention on gently unfastening the dressing on his right thigh.

As she bent over him, her brow knit in concentration, it occurred to him that she fit the profile. His profile: She was small, compact, and had fabulously large breasts. His taste for her type—in the human variety—had been nearly insatiable, as he'd chased them almost endlessly in the bars around Jackson and Teton Village. Even Jared had recently remarked on his need for human women, and Scott had absolutely no defense for his actions. It almost seemed like some sort of compulsion written into his hybrid DNA, as if that part of his genetic map that read "human" drove him like a randy missile to seek the females of humankind for mating.

Yet nothing in him was stirred by this blond medic's proximity, her beauty, nor even his own sheer nakedness, and it wouldn't have been even if she were human. The inescapable fact was that his love of petite, fair-skinned blondes had now been directed toward one specific and very particular human woman: Hope Harper. And now with the sensual dreams of her kicking in like his sought-after pain meds, it didn't seem he had a chance in hell of curbing his attraction toward the woman.

He was lost to her already. Completely. He only

prayed that time and his injured body wouldn't prove him a fool.

"I've been dreaming about her as my wife," he whispered into the half darkness, staring at the top of Shelby's bent head. "And other things . . . since I was a prisoner at Warren."

He wasn't sure why he suddenly felt like confessing, or why he yearned to tell this stranger his secrets, but relief fell over him like a soothing blanket of protection.

She nodded, continuing to inspect his wound. "Kinda strange, isn't that?"

"It's got me all tangled up inside."

Shelby reapplied the bandage, gently covered him with the sheet, and then collapsed into the seat beside him again. "Yeah, well, that Hope really is something else," she agreed with a bob of her head. "A real piece of work, that one."

He frowned, not sure what she meant. But he didn't have to ask, either, because she quickly continued, "I mean, it's like she doesn't even realize she's almost blind. She just pops down here every few hours, determined to see you, but doesn't even worry about herself. I'd be worried if I couldn't see where I was going around this place. Wouldn't you?"

An inexplicable melancholy came over him then; he'd thought talking to Shelby would ease his murky feelings of desire and longing for Hope. Now all he felt was that somehow Hope was going to get hurt here, in the midst of a war she had no real part in.

"She's a real character, all right," he replied dully, trying to ignore the frisson of fear that chased over his spirit.

"And I can tell she really cares about you too," Shelby said. "It's her feelings for you that keep pulling her back down to this place."

This caught his attention. "Why do you say that?"

"Well, last time she came she kept asking me questions about you—would you be able to walk for sure, were you in pain. I could just tell from talking to her that she really felt for you."

Something began niggling at him, and he didn't like it. "Tell me that you didn't mention my dreams."

Shelby grinned and didn't answer except to shrug.

"Nurse Tyler!" he roared. "Tell me you didn't say anything!"

"Oh, just that you kept calling out for her—I had to mention that one little thing."

"Leave. Now," he gritted, turning away from her. He wasn't sure if he wanted to have the woman publicly shot or if he wanted to kiss her out of gratitude. Because at least if Hope knew he cared for her, had been asking for her, then that meant she might keep coming back. And it might mean that she'd understand how he'd already grown to care for her, even after so short a period of time.

"I'll just check you again in a bit, but don't worry, sir."

He cocked a curious eyebrow, daring to glance at her one more time. "About what?"

"It made Hope happy when I told her that. 'Cause she blushed like crazy when I said it."

She wasn't the only one; Scott's face burned hot over this entire discussion. "What exactly have I been doing in my sleep? Are you intuitive or something?"

"Nope, you're just loud."

He braced for the worst. "Loud . . . um, how?"

She patted him on the arm. "Apparently you're quite loud in bed, sir. That's what I meant. And apparently that's exactly what you keep dreaming about."

Scott shook his head, closing his eyes. "You're dismissed," he managed to say, although his voice wavered much more than he would have liked. Somehow this medic from Texas had known exactly what he was dreaming, and he doubted he'd been nearly as loud as she claimed. Intuitive or empathic or whatever she might be, he was transparent as a snowflake to the damned nurse.

Chapter Two

Hope hit the button on her bedside clock, and its mechanical voice stated, "Two fifty-three." With a weary sigh, she flopped back onto her small cot of a bed. The Refarians didn't trust her yet, at least not completely, so they'd given her lousy quarters down in the belly of their main base, right next to some enlisted guy who stayed up half the night playing what sounded like an alien version of poker.

In fact, from what she could tell, the soldiers they'd bunked her up with were basically no different from the guys she'd known growing up on half a dozen army bases scattered around the globe. Well, with one major exception: They weren't from this planet. And most of them had golden-red skin, almost Native American in appearance. A few random soldiers she'd seen seemed blond and fair-skinned, but they were the exception, and her failing eyesight might have misled her about their appearance anyway.

The soldier who had the quarters next to hers was rowdy as all get-out: played his music too loud after hours, and was generally an inconsiderate slob. Like now. There was a sudden uproar of laughter, some shouting of male voices, and that did it for her. She reached around on the dark floor, feeling in the blackness for her shoe, and hurled it at the wall. "Hey! Shut up!" she yelled.

If you lived with the soldiers you had to act like one.

In response, somebody banged on the wall and shouted at her in Refarian; then there was some general whooping that she chose to ignore.

She rolled onto her side, held her pillow over both ears, and focused on sleep—something that had evaded her ever since she'd arrived at this alien compound. Well, correction: Sleep didn't evade her; restful sleep was as elusive as her fading eyesight.

She chalked it all up to the dreams. Ever since being drugged back at Warren, she'd been continuing to dream of Scott Dillon. Sometimes he was her husband; sometimes she was pregnant; often they were having dimension-shattering sex. Literally—since apparently what she kept dreaming about and seeing was from some alternate reality. That was how the only other human in the compound, Kelsey Wells, had explained it to her in the most rational, logical tone. Yeah, it made total sense!

It was as if she'd chosen to step into a living *Twilight Zone* episode the minute she'd hopped on that transport with Lieutenant Dillon—a decision that had upended her world completely. And it definitely didn't help matters that her eyesight issues were taking a decided turn for the worse. The altitude up in this corner of Wyoming was even higher than back in Denver, where her degenerative retinopathy had already been sliding her into darkness at an accelerated rate.

Maybe this wasn't the right thing after all, she thought, loneliness choking her. *Maybe I should have never stepped into something I knew almost nothing about.*

But she'd made a professional career of walking into the unknown, since that was pretty much what working for the FBI translated to. This situation in the alien compound was no different; it was also the right choice after witnessing the Refarians defend humanity when Warren Air Force Base had come under attack. No way was she consigning herself to the outside of this particular alien conspiracy, not now that she understood the stakes. It didn't take a genius to realize that Earth was in serious danger.

More noise erupted next door, and enough really was enough already. Leaping out of bed, she tugged on a borrowed pair of jeans, tossed on a military-issue T-shirt, and stormed into the narrow hallway to find utter darkness. She stood there, listening to the hiss of some sort of equipment. A radiator? A weapon? With her fingertips she felt her way along the corridor wall, locating the door of her neighbor.

She lifted her fist and banged hard. There was mumbling from within, then sudden light, blurred and covered with black spots—the same ones that always marred her fading vision. A tall figure loomed over her, which wasn't that hard when you were only four-foot-eleven.

"Listen, buddy"—she jabbed at the air with her fingertip—"it's almost three in the morning."

A husky laugh was her answer, then a surly, "Look, human, you're on *our* base. This is our home on *your* outpost, so deal."

She tilted her chin upward, summoning a look of defiance. "Yeah? Well, get this—I work for the FBI. Want me to have your license plate called in sometime?"

In half a heartbeat she heard the click of a weapon engaging. "Wanna say that again, human?" Tough Guy threatened. But from behind him a softer feminine voice called out, "Taggart, lay off of her. She just got here. And she's on our side."

The smaller figure stepped into the arc of light. "Sorry about that," the woman said, and, slipping an arm about her shoulder, led Hope back toward her own room. "I'm Anna, and he's a nutcase. I'll see if they won't move you tomorrow so you can get some sleep."

"Not my fault humans need to rest all the time!" Taggart complained to Anna, then slammed his door behind him.

Hope could have cried from gratitude. "I shouldn't have baited him."

"Actually, you should have." Anna laughed as they

reached Hope's room again. "He deserves every bit of it."

"That's what I thought."

"Listen, are you all right? Is there anything you need?" Anna asked, following Hope into her darkened quarters.

Hope dropped heavily onto the side of her cot. "Just to see someone—anyone—who can help me figure out what I'm going to do around here. I've been to visit Lieutenant Dillon a few times, but . . ."

"He's not doing very well," Anna finished, her voice clipped and formal. It seemed to be the way this alien spoke once away from her soldier comrades next door.

"I'm worried about him," Hope admitted. "Have you heard anything more about his prognosis? The medics won't tell me a thing."

"He's going to recover, but physical therapy will be required. And time. Lots of time."

"Scott's my only friend in this place, Anna. He's the reason I came at all because I knew he was on the right side of things."

And because I felt drawn to him for reasons I couldn't begin to understand, she wanted to add, but swallowed the words.

"Well, Lieutenant Dillon is nothing if not on the right side of things," Anna said with a quiet laugh.

"What's that mean?"

"I'm crazy about the lieutenant, even though he rides us hard. He's a good leader to all of us."

Crazy about him? Crazy how? Hope wondered, slightly panicked, but shoved the emotion aside. "Is he a high-ranking officer?" she asked coolly. "I mean, he's only a lieutenant, right? I'm not sure what his position is."

"So, they really haven't told you anything, have they?"

"Only about the mitres. Kelsey said that some sort of alternate dimension was created by the same device that

wiped out all the Antousians back on Warren. That
there were . . . side effects. But nothing about the
lieutenant."

"Well, we don't have the same rankings you're accus-
tomed to. Anyone in higher authority is called 'lieutenant.' Actual hierarchy isn't so much a part of our system,
so that's the rough English translation. The equivalent,
if you will."

"Then is he high up the chain?" Hope's heart suddenly sped to a rapid tempo. At last! Some answers
about the literal man of her dreams.

"He's second in command below Commander Bennett
over the entire Refarian military."

"Wow, didn't see that coming." Hope shook her head.
She'd known he must be important from the deference
the night nurse showed him—either that or the woman
had a major case of the hots for the man, one of the
two. But one of their military chiefs? That she hadn't
guessed at all.

"Do you have any idea what he looks like even?"
Anna asked her seriously. "I mean, can you see much?
You wear those thick glasses."

Here we go again—someone thinking I'm helpless, she
thought. "He has black hair and dark eyes and fair
skin," she answered evenly, happy to show Anna just
how capable she was despite her vision problems. "He's
about six feet tall, and I gather that he's pretty darn
good-looking."

"How do you know all that?"

"I still see some; it's just blurry."

Anna shifted beside her. "No, about the good-looking
part—how can you tell that much?"

*Yeah, like I want to tell you that I keep dreaming he's
making love to me in about five hundred different physical positions, making me scream his name at the top of
my lungs and giving me such world-shattering orgasms
that I can hardly recover once I wake up.*

Hope snorted. "Don't ask."

She was thinking of the dream where Scott took her home from some bar to a motel room and had her up against a wall. That one seemed to recur most often, and always left her panties wet when she woke.

"Well, for the record, Scott Dillon is extremely handsome. Every single woman in this camp has a thing for him."

An ugly shot of jealousy rang out in Hope's mind. "Oh . . . well, so then he must have plenty of women." Her voice sounded falsely peppy, too breathless.

Anna patted her shoulder and walked toward the open door. "Oh, he has plenty of women, but not around here."

"Why not?" Hope asked in surprise.

"Because there's only one kind of woman our good lieutenant likes, and that's your kind. Blond, petite, buxom, and"—Anna paused at the door—"human, Ms. Harper. Very, very human."

The dreams folded about her in the same way they'd been doing for the past week, muted and vivid. Surreal and immediate, everything at right angles and at odds with itself. Scott was in their tent this time, pressing warm kisses against her very pregnant belly. He trailed his fingers over the warm, itchy skin there, having pulled up her sweater. Occasionally he would nuzzle her; sometimes he'd lave her belly button with his tongue.

They were terrified; it hadn't been a good or safe pregnancy so far, not with all of her health challenges. Now, late-term, those complications were revealing themselves for what they were: the ravenous jaws of death, unrelenting. Unmerciful. Too much for either of them, or their baby, to take.

"I have to go for help; you know it." He leaned his cheek against her full, rounded stomach. "It's time, and we can't do this by ourselves."

"I'm strong enough." But her argument was faint. Scott knelt by her side, shaking his head.

"If I don't go now it will be too late." He leaned over her, kissing her softly on the lips. "I don't want to leave you, not now."

"Then don't!" She lifted a weak hand to his shoulder. "We'll be all right."

He seemed about to reply, but then turned toward the tent entrance where a dark figure had stepped in beside them. A doctor perhaps? Someone to deliver the baby? She'd never seen the man before in her life, and Scott raised his pistol, leaping to his feet right over her where she lay.

"Drop your weapon!" Scott shouted, and the dark, hulking stranger lifted both palms.

"I mean no harm." His voice was rich and thick and deep. "I can help her."

Scott circled the other man, glancing up and down his form, and then, as if in slow motion, turned back to face Hope. "Trust him," he said softly. "Trust Jakob Tierny. Go with him when he appears."

Hope struggled to sit up, shouting, and found herself not in the tent, but right within her small cot of a bed down in the bottom sector of the Refarian's Base Ten.

Trust Jakob Tierny. She had no idea who that man was, or why Scott would be urging her to go with him. What she did know, however, was that when they'd been on Warren, he'd spoken to her in a dream then, warning of Earth's imminent attack. And his words had been totally true.

Hope shook her head, thankful that the poker game next door had apparently ended, and wondered—almost prayed—*Who is Jakob Tierny?*

Chapter Three

Chris Harper's supervisor eyed him warily. "You have no evidence whatsoever to support this theory of yours." Special Agent Blake Miles leaned back in his chair. "Those barracks were decimated, and that's our last ID on your sister."

But his twin had survived the blast; Chris had known it from the beginning of her disappearance, having felt their familiar, humming connection. And today he'd actually sensed Hope reach toward him.

"She's alive—gotten in over her head, but I know she's okay. Well, at least okay enough to still be breathing and walking somewhere on this planet of ours."

Blake was a friend, had been for a few years now, and it was that cautious blend of comradeship and professionalism that cast a shadow across the other man's face. "What proof, Harper? You've got to give me something solid here, anything, and I can run it up the pole. But hoodoo spooky voodoo? I can't do a goddamned thing with that."

Chris raked a hand through his spiky hair; like every other guy within the bureau he followed the unofficial "look." He could recognize a fellow agent anywhere; the uniform was nondescript, yet obvious to anyone inside their FBI-tainted tent.

"I don't have concrete evidence," Chris tried to explain. "It's just the way she and I have always known each other. We're connected."

Blake shifted folders on his desk, shaking his head. "Then we're stuck. Not one thing I can do to help you."

Chris leaped to his feet, pacing the small office. "Do you have a body? Do you have any DNA evidence that she died back there at Warren?" He eyed his boss, raising his eyebrows meaningfully, but of course no answers were forthcoming. "Maybe you do, and you can't say. Maybe it's all need-to-know, but I don't think so. I'm betting that you don't have shit to make your case that my sis died in that blast."

"We're chasing bigger leads here, Harper. Come on! Do you really think headquarters cares what happens to one of their linguists? They're only interested in pinning down this Refarian leader, Jared Bennett. Anything else is a waste of time in their minds."

Chris ceased his pacing, planting both hands on Blake's desk. "And what if I told you that my gut says that she's totally tied up with Bennett now? What would you say then?"

Blake assessed him carefully, leaning back in his government-issue chair. "I'd say that you'd better have more to go on before asking me to go to D.C."

"You've listened to the tapes of her with Scott Dillon. You heard their conversations. She was taken in by that alien. Hell! She decided to help him. You don't think she wouldn't have gotten embroiled in this mess?"

Blake chuckled, giving a knowing shake of his head—he knew Hope better than most of their fellow agents in this office, because he'd been briefly involved with her a year earlier. Although their relationship had hit an almost immediate dead end, Chris had always suspected that Blake still had feelings for her.

Blake gave him a grudging grin. "I think Hope would chase her ass around the moon if she thought she could stir up trouble," he said. "That sister of yours likes to prove her mettle. Her illness seems to demand it."

Chris folded both arms over his chest, nodding. "There you have it. She's in this thing, Blake. In it deep and crappy. It's totally her style, but she's put herself in the line of fire this time, and no matter what we think about what transpired at Warren"—every one of them who'd been there that day agreed that the Refarians had saved their asses—"she's not where she's supposed to be."

Blake tapped his desk. "What're you gonna do, Chris? I need to know so I can plan accordingly."

He rubbed his eyebrow, thinking. He hadn't the first idea of a good strategy for finding his twin, but he did know she would eventually contact him. "Sit and wait. That's the only thing I can do—that, and be ready when she gets in touch. Her cell's been off ever since, but I'm sure she's got it, and eventually she'll power up that bad boy. We can triangulate her position when she does."

And she'd reach for him; in their oddball, shared way of talking inside their minds, she would eventually get in too deep and try to connect with him. Chris knew it beyond anything else that had happened over the past few days. His sis could never disconnect from him for very long.

"I'm not reporting a thing back to headquarters." Blake stared past him. "We'll wait and see what she does."

Chris nodded. "We'll see what she does, sure, but I already know what she's gonna do. At least eventually. And that's contact me. When that happens, we've got our lead right to those alien soldiers and to Jared Bennett."

Scott was a beautiful man when he slept. In fact, he was beautiful all the time, and Hope didn't have to be fully sighted to realize that fact. She didn't dare touch his face, but as she kept watch over him during his sleep—obviously a prolonged nap, since it was about lunchtime—she did risk feeling his arm, just sliding her fingertips up and down the warm skin. His arms had silky hairs on them, and she pictured how they must be black, like the hair on his head. As she stroked higher she felt bulky, hard muscle; his was a soldier's body, hardened from battle and training. Not the pretty-boy bodies you would see in a gym. She could tell just from feeling him that he'd pushed himself against every limit he could find, and for a long time. The results were that he was lean and hard and absolutely gorgeous.

She stood, bending over him. It was too dark in the room to make out any details about his face, but she sure did try. She deigned to stretch one fingertip and touch his mouth; he had a full, lush bottom lip and a thinner top one. A man's mouth, but with a touch of succulent danger, that hint of softness that betrayed so much hardness to back it up. She pushed her face just a tiny bit closer, catching his scent, and ached for her lost eyesight. Just to be able to see him . . . well, she'd do anything to know what he really looked like. So she did what she could, and that was lean in just a little bit closer.

And right when she had her face within a few inches of his . . . he moaned. Loudly, shifting his hips around beneath the bedsheet, and for a split second she froze like some thief in a spy movie caught in the bank vault. Slowly she began to back away, but her sweater didn't budge at all; stupidly, she'd managed to catch it on his bedrail, and so she found herself trapped, leaning right over him.

Scott practically purred, releasing a soft groan that was a slow, sensual sound of pleasure. "Oh, yeah, sweetheart. Yeah, *yeah*." His voice grew much louder, and he moaned. "Yeah!"

She heard his hips rustling beneath the sheet, then swore—absolutely swore—she heard him stroking himself. The man was a sexual freaking dynamo; if he did this in his sleep, what was he like when he was awake?

"Hope." He sighed her name, his rhythm beneath the sheets increasing. "Oh, Hooooope, oh, yeah. Love it, umm."

She clamped a hand over her mouth. *Oh, my God! Oh, my God! This is* me *he's having sex with!*

Glancing all around in panic, she tugged and tugged

on her sweater sleeve, but it just wasn't going to come loose. She could jerk it apart, but he'd probably wake up and realize she'd been hovering over him while he was practically having an orgasm all over her name.

His bed creaked loudly beneath him, the sheet sliding and moving—Scott sliding and moving along with it. He began thrusting his hips, and Hope burned with an erotic mixture of lust and embarrassment.

Was he having that dream about the wall? That was her particular favorite, the way he pushed her up against it, kept her suspended, her legs wrapped about him. She sighed dreamily, but then suppressed a giggle upon realizing that, yeah, he probably was dreaming about that damn wall. In fact, he was obviously having a mind-bending sexual experience—with her, no less—while she basically witnessed the whole thing. It was totally messed up.

All right, I've gotta do something about this. I'm stuck here; he's loose right there, and he's going to bust me for watching him once his sexual fireworks go off.

Stepping as far away as she could—which was only about two steps backward—she let her sweater sleeve stretch as much as it would, then gave one more tug, and it ripped free. And so did Scott's shout.

"Hey! What's going on?" He barked the words as if he were shouting at his troops.

"You were asleep." She sank into the seat beside him, masking her face; she sat perfectly straight, hands folded in her lap.

"Hope?" She could hear him raking a hand through his hair; then the sheet rustled. It was as if he were trying to figure out what had happened.

Finally, he chuckled low in his throat, a husky, sensual sound that made her nipples tighten. "Was it as good for you as it was for me?"

"Excuse me?" The flush on her face intensified like mad. She folded her arms across her chest, shifted them, and then folded them again.

He gave an amused snort. "I'm told I'm loud in bed,

that's what. I'm assuming—based on your completely guilty posture—that you were more than slightly aware of my most recent dreamland escapades."

"I didn't mean to be," she admitted quietly, beginning to giggle.

He laughed too, a faraway sound in his voice. "Some dream about being in the berth of a battle cruiser, standing in front of this giant window, looking out at the stars. Your hands were splayed against the glass, I had you from behind"—he sighed, and she got the idea he was demonstrating—"just like this. . . ."

She waved a hand to get him to shut up. "I haven't had that one yet; how about you let me just discover it on my own? Okay? Sounds perfectly fabulous."

His bed creaked, and his voice shifted. "We lived these visions and dreams—you do realize that, right? That they're from a parallel world, an alternate future. We have this weapon, the mitres, that allows for time travel. It also opens dimensional space, and it's been used twice recently."

She nodded. "I know; Kelsey explained it to me. That you had someone come through time from the future, and that he changed things, events. She said that this future we both keep seeing doesn't necessarily exist—not now that your people have changed things with the mitres."

"Man, you're good; that's better than I'd have explained it myself, and I've been inside the damnable thing."

She leaned back in the chair. "I'm not saying I totally get it; it's just my take on what she told me."

"Essentially, my dear Hope, we were amazing, rockhard, and unstoppable lovers in our future. We were. But that's another version of ourselves, those future selves, who lived those things. Whatever happens between us from here on out"—he reached out and stroked her hair—"that's still to be determined. It's up to us, but personally I'm all for bringing that future to pass."

She shook him off. "Oh, good grief! You have just

way too much sexual self-confidence." She rubbed at her burning cheeks. "That must come naturally to your species or something."

He kicked at the covers. "Nah, it's just me and my basic love of sex. Why not love it? It's a fabulous indulgence when the rest of my life is all fighting and war and strategy. Sex with a good woman . . . well, it's one of the best pleasures in life. More to the point, I particularly love bedding human women whenever I can."

"You're making me feel so special." She actually felt a little bit hurt.

He jerked in the bed, coming back to himself. "Hope, I'm not saying you aren't special."

"You're saying you love bedding my species—any female of my kind."

He sighed, all his sparring and repartee gone. "You need to know about my past; I figured I had to be honest, so you would know, not catch it around here as rumor or hearsay. I've been driven—and seriously I do mean driven—to couple with human women. I've begun to think it's some kind of strange mating urge."

She gulped. "A mating urge? What do you mean?"

"Look, we'll talk about all of this later. But my past is my past, Hope—just like those images are some alternate kind of past, something our other selves lived before. But right now I'm talking with you about here and now and what you mean to me."

She caught his hand as he stopped stroking her hair, and pressed it to her cheek. "Tell me what I mean to you."

"You saved my life, Hope, for one thing, but it's way more than that—and it's more than how well I'm getting to know you from these dreams and images."

She finished for him. "We have a baby in the future." They'd talked about it at Warren, but she wasn't sure he remembered. "I saw you kissing my stomach."

He caressed her cheek lightly with the backs of his fingers. "I know . . . I saw that too. I even heard her name. Leisa. That was my mother's name."

"Have you actually seen our daughter in any of those visions?" Her throat went dry; she'd yet to see their baby girl, and if he described the child, she knew she would probably burst into tears.

"Not yet." His voice grew quiet, pensive. "And maybe that future isn't necessarily what we're going to live, but what I guess I'm trying to tell you, Hope, is this—we're not in an ordinary dating scenario here. I don't see or feel a lot of reason to go slow. I want to get out of this crap hole as soon as I can, and make love to you for real. I want to show you what I can do to you, how I can make you scream my name, and more than that, I want to get to know you, really know you."

Well, there wasn't a lot a girl could say to argue with that plan. Except he had to get well and give it time, and she knew he didn't want to do that. "You've got to heal up first, Scott." She slipped a hand onto his forearm, stroking the soft tickling of hairs she'd felt earlier.

Scott closed his eyes, enjoying the feel of her hand against his arm, feeling the hard-on between his legs grow even harder. A part of him even felt that he was still on that battle cruiser, driving up inside of her.

"This is going to take some time," she told him resolutely.

He cut his eyes sideways at her; her golden hair was shoulder-length and shimmered in the lights of his monitors. Day or night, this room was like a dungeon, but down here belowground there weren't any windows to allow in light. The medics had been encouraging him to sleep, and it wasn't a situation that made him happy, not on any level.

"I'm not an invalid, Harper, and I've got to get out of this place very soon."

She gave her head a light shake, blinking as she glanced at him. "Do you think *I'm* an invalid just because I'm going blind? Because I have diabetes?"

"Of course not." He scowled, not quite understanding her leap in logic. "I'm talking about me and this damnable hospital bed."

"Then why should I, or anyone else, think that you're an invalid just because you almost died? You did almost die, Lieutenant, and maybe that's what you can't quite wrap your brain around. To get better, it's just going to take time."

He blew out a long, frustrated sigh. "Patience is for pussies."

She bent forward in her chair, chewing on her lip, and seemed to be gathering her thoughts. It was an expression he'd seen on her face a lot during his days at Warren. While he was held there, she'd been his translator. Of course, he spoke fluent English, but he hadn't let on about that fact to his captors, needing to protect himself any way that he could. They'd brought Hope in on his case after she'd spent months studying the Refarian language on FBI intercepts. Her beautiful way with his native tongue had allowed the two of them to form a private thread of communication that the air force couldn't interpret. She'd championed him during his captivity, worked so hard to help him—and to bridge the distance between himself and the USAF.

He'd begun falling in love with her then, and that was before the dreams had even hit overdrive. Hope ran her fingers through her hair, a faraway look in her pale gray eyes.

"You're thinking something," he observed, wondering why she didn't just say whatever it was she had in mind.

She nodded, looking toward him but not quite focusing on his face. "You're a military guy. You of all people know the importance of careful timing." Her blond eyebrows drew together, a line of worry furrowing them. "You have to go slow with your recovery."

"I also push things to the edge; it's what makes me so damned good."

An adorable smile turned up the edges of her mouth. "You sound more than a little bit satisfied with yourself."

He shrugged. "When you've got the goods . . ." He loved sparring with her—that she talked to him as an equal and a friend, not like a superior officer, or like a one-night stand. If only he could get closer to her physically. Not later, but right now.

He had an idea, and leaned back into his pillows. "Come here; I want to see something."

She stood, appearing uncertain. He grabbed hold of her hand, tugging her right beside his bed. "Come just a little closer than that and let me get a better look at you"—he pulled her over to him—"here!"

Hooking his forearm behind her head, he brought her down for a kiss. The bed rail kept them mostly apart, but it wasn't a total chaperone; he managed to cover her lips with his own, to feel the heat of her breath, and slowly, ever so slowly, she opened her mouth to him. He plunged his tongue deep inside her wet slickness, hardly able to think at all—not with the urgent need just this subtle kiss unleashed in him. There'd never been a woman who had set him on fire so completely.

She stroked his hair, running her hands through it, as back and forth their tongues thrust and moved together. Finally, when he swore he couldn't breathe at all, she pulled away, gasping. Slowly he wiped his mouth with the back of one hand.

"This was to show you"—he cupped her heart-shaped face, making his final point—"that there's only one good reason I should ever be in bed."

Jake Tierny hid just south of the main cabin, surveying the compound as a whole. That it was even here—like the pristine safe haven they had all believed it to be back in this time—caused his eyes to water unexpectedly. They'd lost everything since these days. Correction, he thought, hunkering low on his belly and lifting his field glasses to his eyes: This was the present, not a long ago time. Only for him was this moment the past; to everyone else he cared about inside this compound, it was the only world they knew.

Darkness. He would have to wait until then before slipping inside. His one chance of making this mission work was to accost Jared. Surely his king would believe him; he just had to lay out all the facts. In the meantime, he would scout the perimeter and be certain that Marco McKinley hadn't already stepped into this time. If they'd set the mitres correctly, Jake was arriving a few days ahead of the bastard. One thing was certain; Jake wouldn't let that devil's spawn hurt any of the people he cared about, not ever again.

He would bide his time and wait, and then stop the rogue protector from destroying their future any more than he already had.

"We have to decide what to do with her, my lord."

Jared stared through the windows of the meeting room outside at the leaden gray sky, considering this advice from his chief security adviser.

Nevin continued, "And we must also consider how best to capitalize on our victory at Warren. We have an open line of communication with Colonel Peters, sir, and I think we should take this opportunity to begin a dialogue. It's time for a summit; if not with the president, then with the colonel and others within the air force hierarchy."

Nevin stated more opinions on the matter, and although Jared registered some of the adviser's counsel, his thoughts were mostly directed elsewhere—toward his new wife and queen. Kelsey had been behaving oddly over the past two days, ever since receiving his ancestor's journal, which laid out explicit details about the Refarian mating cycle. Somehow his wife had gotten it into her mind that the two of them were going to achieve the heat together. It seemed hopeless enough that he would ever experience mating fever, much less that he could pull his very human wife along with him on the endeavor.

"Sir? What is your decision?" Nevin prompted, speaking to Jared's back.

My decision is to make love to my wife for as many hours as possible and forget that I'm a king, he thought dreamily, a strange hunger for his mate pulsing all through his body. Tensing it, teasing it. He spun to face Nevin. The silver-haired adviser's expectant, businesslike expression was a strange match for Jared's aroused mood.

"I need an hour to think on your counsel, Lieutenant," he answered with a noble tilt of his chin. Anything to mask his excited mating thoughts. "I shall return"—he paused, glancing at his comm for the correct time—"at thirteen thirty. Be sure to have Thea and Marco with you then, please."

Nevin rose to his feet, giving a slight bow, and placed one fist over his heart. It was the deepest show of respect from a Refarian to their king, and Jared nodded in return, grumbling internally that Nevin always had to be so old-guard—especially for a relatively young man. The silver in the adviser's hair was simply a sign of his sexual maturity, not of great age. All Refarian males turned silver-headed once their fertile years ended; in Jared's case the first silvering had begun to appear in his naturally dark hair a few months earlier, the surest sign that his need to cycle with Kelsey was more than a casual matter. Within months it was nearly certain that he would pass out of his fertile years and into his own maturity, just as the man before him had recently done.

"So I will return at that time," Jared added with a brisk nod toward the lieutenant.

"Yes, my lord, and you will address the matter of the human?"

Jared barely masked his annoyance. "Which human? Shall I remind you that your new queen is a human? So we now have two of the species in our midst, and I'd advise a bit more respect."

Nevin's naturally dark face blanched. "I meant no contempt, sir."

"Of course not."

"I was referring to Hope Harper, the FBI linguist who returned from the base with Lieutenant Dillon."

"Ah, yes," Jared answered as he exited the meeting

room, "we must also decide where she will fit into our complex here. Please arrange for her presence after lunch as well."

"Yes, my lord."

Jared trotted out of the room, sped his gate to double-time as he hit the stairs toward his chambers, then took the final steps practically three at a time before arriving at the door and entering, albeit far too breathlessly.

Tossing aside his uniform jacket, he kicked the chamber door shut with his booted foot. "Kelsey? I've returned." He scanned all about the semidark main room for his mate. "Love, I've come to you for lunch." He grinned hungrily as he considered just how he planned to pass the next hour. *Eating and devouring for sure,* he thought, striding toward their bathroom in search of her.

At last he discovered his human mate standing in their closet on a step stool, totally naked, and he watched her for a moment through lust-filled slanted eyes. She was searching for something at the top of a shelf, but hadn't bothered dressing first. It placed her in the perfect position for some interesting bedroom play. Sneaking slyly behind her, he took hold of her bottom without a word, and she yelled in fright.

"It's me." He held her fast about the hips. "I've taken a break to be with you." Pressing his lips against the base of her spine, he kissed and licked her there until she made a soft, kittenlike sound that made him utterly wild. His pulse did a frenzied dance; his heart slammed against his chest wall. Everything inside his Refarian body seemed calibrated for this one human woman, the welling need growing more unstoppable with every passing day. Slowly she pivoted in his embrace until his mouth was positioned only two inches away from her abdomen.

"Hello, my king," she purred in a low, sultry voice.

Palming her bare stomach he whispered, "Did you miss me?" and glanced up at her, feeling needy emotions that he didn't bother trying to mask. Nothing could be hidden between the two of them anyway.

She smiled down at him, her freckled face flushed as if she'd been working out—but clearly she hadn't. With a trembling hand, she stroked his cheek. "I've got something to tell you," she whispered as he bent forward to lick her navel with the tip of his tongue.

"Umm," he said with a slight moan. "Does it involve taking you to bed?"

"Yes, in a way." He glanced up at her, curious, and couldn't help noticing how radiant she appeared to be—almost as if he'd just caused a mating glow across her skin.

"Let's make love," he half growled, reaching to unsnap his uniform pants, "and you shall tell me everything between our sheets."

"Not here, actually—it's part of the surprise." She stroked the top of his head. "I have somewhere else in mind."

He cocked an eyebrow, curiosity starting to overtake him. "I have an hour; then there's a meeting in chambers."

"An hour will be plenty of time." She grabbed hold of his shoulders, sliding into his arms and to the floor. "Trust me."

Chapter Four

"So we're going to be roommates." Anna tossed Hope's small satchel of belongings onto the bottom bunk. "My sister has moved out—and in with Riley, her lifemate—so her half of the room is empty anyway."

Hope stepped toward the bed, pushing her glasses up her nose in an effort to see some of the details of the room. With a glance around, she tried to size up the quarters, but her vision was too dark for her to determine much. The truth was, the glasses didn't do a thing to help her, and, feeling suddenly angry, she jerked them off and tossed them onto her new bed.

Anna launched herself at the bed frame, scrambling onto the top bunk. "I'll keep this top rack," she explained, "and you'll get the lower one. Does that work for you?"

Hope nodded, feeling a strange lump lodge inside her throat. After several sleepless nights, and generally feeling like she had nowhere to go inside the compound, Hope felt total and unexpected relief at Anna's obvious decision to watch her back.

"Thanks, Anna," she said softly. "I won't be a pain in the ass, promise."

"Good—now that we've got this out of the way, let's get to the heart of the matter."

"Which is?"

Anna's feet dangled off the top bunk, kicking at the wooden frame. "Lieutenant Dillon. I hear he's in need of some motivation, a real kick in the pants, as it were, if he's going to get well. I've decided that *you* are that kick—or something else—in the pants. So let's get going, Ms. Harper—"

"Call me Hope."

"Let's get going, Hope," she amended without missing a beat, "and pay a visit to our good lieutenant."

"Actually, I already visited him this morning, so I don't know." She flashed on the kiss he'd stolen, and didn't want to seem too eager and available to him. "Maybe I'd better give him a little more time."

"I *heard* that you visited him this morning, and that he perked up tremendously afterward." Anna swung off the upper bunk, giving her a chummy pat on the shoulder. "That is why you're going back with me again. So you can dispense further motivation, the kind that apparently only you can give." Anna made a loud smacking sound with her lips. "You know what I mean."

Hope blushed, wrapping her arms about herself. "What exactly did you hear about my visit?"

"Lots of good sound effects. The ooohs and the sighs—and pretty much a lot of smooching."

"I don't understand." A terrible suspicion was beginning to grow in Hope's mind.

Anna chuckled. "If you want to keep a secret in this army of ours, then make sure your comm isn't on." She opened the door and paused. "Or that the other party's isn't, since obviously you don't even have a comm."

Hope covered her face with both hands, willing herself to disappear. "Oh, no, no, we didn't."

"Oh, yes, yes, you certainly did. From what the rest of us could gather, our lieutenant jammed his comm somewhere between smoochy-smooching you and his announcement that"—Anna dropped her voice low, producing a striking imitation of Scott—" 'this was to show you that there's only one good reason I should ever be in bed.' After that, radio silence."

Hope buried her face deeper in her hands, wondering just how many Refarians were party to the comm link.

"Does he make this kind of mistake often?" she squeaked.

"Never, but we all figure he was off his game because of being in the hospital and the drugs . . . and especially because of you." Anna giggled, pulling at Hope's hands, working to pry them away from her eyes. "Come on out of there, Hope."

Slowly, Hope did let her hands drop. "So when you said you'd 'heard' I'd been to see him, you really did mean just that." God, talk about feeling mortified.

"Yep. And you know what?" Anna continued. "He started barking out orders over the comm not much longer after that. We all pretty much got the picture that you're the only one who can pull him out of this depression he's been in ever since being shot."

"Did anyone tell him what he'd done?"

"Whoa! Hell, no. That man would be even crankier than usual. No way, no how—and don't you tell him either, okay?"

"It's not like it's your fault or anyone else's but his own." Hope couldn't help beginning to laugh. "Plus, why should he be embarrassed? I mean, he's one of the top dogs and all, right?"

"Ah, but he'd be protecting you, and that's the thing of it. It would all be about his feelings for you."

"Why are you so convinced that he cares about me?" Hope shook her head. "I just don't get it."

"You don't get it? Really, Hope?" Anna stepped into the hallway. "This base is our essence, our most guarded secret. That you're here at all proves everything about what that guy feels for you."

Jared followed his wife down a path he knew all too well; she was guiding him toward the natural hot springs hidden at the end of a private trail. Before they'd even reached the clearing, Jared glimpsed steam rising off the springs, swirling into a ghostly spiral. Devil's Cauldron, that was the name for the naturally occurring bubbling waters. Watching Kelsey's swaying hips as she hurried down the path ahead of him caused him to think that whoever had named the place must have experienced a time or two in the waters themselves—and not just bathing, either.

"Love, I think you have concocted a devilish plan." He stilled on the path, staring at the gurgling springs just ahead.

Kelsey slipped both arms about him, pressing her face against his chest. "Um, Jared, you know"—she rubbed one hand across the front of his pants—"I just wanted to get away from everything."

His entire body flamed hot at her words, and the mating heat that had been overtaking him simmered wildly. "Kelsey, I'm due back—"

"Plenty of time." She waved him off, taking the lead on the path again. For a moment he stared after his wife—his queen—and wondered what sort of plan she had in mind. Refarian men were madly aroused by water during their mating season. Not drinking water or anything basic, but hot water. Steaming water. Water lapping about their naked mate. Ah, these things had the power to provoke his lusts into a frenzy.

No wonder he could only gape wordlessly as Kelsey's jacket dropped to the stone surface surrounding the steaming pool, revealing the shape of her body. So beautiful and lusciously curving, that of a real woman, not some rail-thin *stskii*.

With her hand she beckoned him wordlessly. Swallowing hard, he followed, meeting her on the stone surface surrounding the pool of water. "Aren't you cold?" He let his gaze move up and down her supple body.

"I'm burning up!" She blessed him with a giddy smile.

Ah, wife, you think to enter the fever, he thought, wincing at the thought of how hurt she would be when her wish did not come true. "My ancestor's journal has misled you, love," he told her solemnly. "I fear that your expectations . . ." He couldn't finish—not this, not when it meant hurting Kelsey so badly.

She placed a palm to his chest. "It's already happening, Jared. Can't you feel it? Don't you see?" She gestured down the length of her body. "Look at me! Geez, I'm on fire. Your fire, your heat! It's all inside of me, changing me."

It was true; she glowed from the inside out, a warm, soft hue that definitely seemed . . . inhuman. With a glance, he made certain they were truly alone.

Steam rose off the hot spring pools, bathing them both in an otherworldly glow. His wife had done her homework, for certain: Soft music came from a mystery location, Duke Ellington, one of his favorites. How his mate had memorized all of his tastes and tempers already was beyond him.

Without a word, he stripped out of his uniform jacket, next his T-shirt, exposing his bare chest; his nipples puckered from the frigid cold. Watching him, Kelsey licked her lips in anticipation, but remained silent. Next he unlaced his boots, jerked off his socks. Last he shrugged out of his jeans, so that he stood before her lean and naked and shivering.

She shook her head, smiling. "You amaze me, Jared." Her voice was barely more than a whisper, raspy with lust and need.

His scarred body, his silvering hair, the lines around his eyes—she never seemed to notice any of his physical shortcomings. All his mate ever saw was a strange perfection in him. How had he ever been so blessed by the heavens?

She took a step near, and a quiet growl sprang from his chest. Her eyes widened at his expression of desire, but she said nothing. Stepping into the bubbling springs, he gave her a command. "In. The. Water." He groaned. "Please, Kelse."

More growling that he couldn't seem to stop. His whole body tensed, then relaxed, then tensed again. He felt his eyes water; widen, narrow to slits. She suddenly trembled a bit visibly; on the periphery of his thoughts, he wondered if somehow he'd frightened her, but he didn't bother to think any further on that idea.

"Water, Kelsey," he whispered again, submerging himself fully. "Now!" It almost seemed as if more steam spiraled off the pool once he'd entered, but perhaps he merely imagined that.

"Absolutely, Commander," she teased, glancing down at him with what could only be called a coy expression.

Gods, he adored her. Gods he wanted her, now, now, now. He felt something highly irrational limbo through his brain, something about possessing her on every planet. He thought even to murmur it to her, but stopped himself, sliding deeper into the hot, beckoning cauldron of steam and water.

"Ah." He sighed in deep pleasure, leaning back against the rocks, then stretched his arms across the slick stones, watching his mate with lusty arousal. First her gloves tumbled to the stony ground, then her sweater and scarf and little knit cap, and at last her pants. Socks? Underwear? "Hurry," he begged, aware that he sounded as breathless as a fledgling. "Please, love."

She stood before him, curving and pure in the misty midday light. "Jared," she whispered, running her fingers through her hair, shaking it out. He felt his eyes narrow to slits, his vision heightening like mad of its own volition. His chest grew tight as a drum, the pounding muscle within it causing a loud rush of blood in his ears.

She repeated his name, louder, "Jared?"

"Um?" he managed, blinking at her.

"It's happening," she whispered, watching him. "You do know that now, don't you? That it's finally happening?" How could she sound so calm? So self-possessed? Was she even right about the timing?

For a moment, he thought to question her—if she indeed meant what he thought she did—but by the time he grasped her full import, he couldn't restrain yet another glorious yelp of desire just from watching her.

She took another step closer, painstaking in her calmness as she spoke to him. "It's been happening," she continued, shivering from the cold, "only I don't think you've noticed. Or understood. It's not like it's just today. . . ."

She stopped, studying him, gauging his reaction as he swam toward the edge where she stood.

His mouth felt dry, his voice thick and from a distant tunnel, but he whispered at her, "You fear I will back away?"

She wrapped her fair arms about herself, shivering protectively. "Yes." She knew how he'd fought these mating cycles; for all his life he'd resisted—but they'd passed a point of no return here.

Like a manacle, he clasped her ankle. "In the water, mate." He flashed a dark gaze up at her, obviously meaning to magnetize. "Or I shall seemingly die." Then they both burst into uncontrollable laughter—the pure laughter of release and joy.

Kelsey splashed into the water and right into her husband's arms. Nipping at her neck, he made soft rumbling sounds of pleasure—no words, only wild sounds that vibrated through her chest as he pulled her close.

One thing was certain in Kelsey's mind: Jared had no idea just how strongly he'd been coming on to her recently. And in the past two days his insatiable need for her, as well as his pureblood Refarian expressions of desire—the growling, the plaintive groaning, the shaky-handed grasping; all signs she'd read about in his ancestor's journal, indicating the beginnings of his cycle—these things had been intensifying crazily.

She'd saved the invitation to the hot springs until just now. On purpose. It had all been part of the plan: When he stood on the brink, ready to fall completely into his season, she'd planned to seduce him here at the springs, thus bringing it fully upon him. It was a perfect, infallible strategy.

Jared leaned back against the stones, eyeing her with a hooded, lustful gaze. "Wife." He reached for her breathlessly. "Near. I need you now."

Swimming into his grasp, she allowed him to capture her, the muscles of his powerful forearms rippling as he held her close. Absolute alien power, unbridled with her. He sat on the rocks, leaning back against the craggy ledge of the bowled springs. On his upper lip little beads of sweat had formed, glistening on his morning's growth of dark beard. Slipping atop him she felt his desire, as hard as any of the rocks surrounding them. He cupped her bottom, nuzzling her astride him. Jared's eyes drifted shut and he made a warm sound of pleasure that she had never once heard from the man, something akin to a purring rumble.

Leaning his head backward, he seemed almost intoxicated. Kelsey couldn't repress a giddy smile; she loved him when he got like this, loved his utter abandon to their joining.

The surface of the water suddenly shimmered, glowing—then seemed to electrify. Jared's dark eyes widened, ringed with panic. "Kelsey!" he cried, his voice thick. "Get out! Hurry!"

She gaped at him, and he shoved her off his lap—hard. "Out! Now!" he roared, scrambling at the edges of the rocks, panting. A wild snarl exploded from him, his eyes rolling into his head, and she seemed unable to move at first. Until he finally fixed her with a gaze unlike anything she'd ever seen—in any creature—in her whole life. His muscled chest heaved and pulled at air; he motioned wildly with his hands, flailing first in one direction then another; the water snapped with a kind of electricity again.

Terrified, she was suddenly afraid for both their lives, but especially his. "Jared," she said, attempting to soothe him, "I'm going to help you out of here."

He unleashed a barrage of Refarian words that she couldn't understand, gesturing again toward the edge. He wanted her out—and now. She scrambled onto the frozen ledge, out of the water, which was growing more and more luminous by the moment—as was Jared's body. He gazed up at her, pain and helplessness in his eyes, and in the space of a heartbeat, he Changed. He Changed completely, until the water lapped over the edges of the rocks, and there was only him. Beautiful, magnetic, mystical Jared in his most natural form. He filled the whole of the pool, glowing and powerful, like some giant sun brought to Earth just for her.

Even shivering there on the ledge of the pool, she felt his energy fanning toward her. She backed away as the water began to bubble and churn; inside her mind she heard his plaintive whisper. *Go away! Now!*

"I'm not leaving you here." She reached for one of the towels she'd brought ahead of time. Behind her the candles she'd lit an hour ago all extinguished simultaneously—then, as if catching Jared's energy, illuminated again with a flame ten times higher than they should have possessed.

The water roiled faster, swirling with currents of power. The pool itself had become almost a kind of cauldron, containing all of Jared's magnificence, but threatening at any moment to overflow the confining boundaries. *Mate . . . mate . . . Go! Leave me.*

"I won't go!" she shouted back, gesturing at the glowing ball of power that was her mate in his Change. "I'm staying, Jared." God, he was stubborn beyond reason. She was terrified, no doubt about it, but she would never leave him here alone, trying to find his way through the first true moments of his cycle.

No. Control! he cried inside her mind. Then smatterings of Refarian, broken by halting English. *No hurt. You! Go.* More Refarian; then the water suddenly popped with wild electric currents and he flung himself outward, speeding into the shadowed forest around them, away from her.

If she wouldn't leave him, he would leave her; that was obviously his plan. She cried out after him, tears streaming down her face. "Jared!" she called, his name echoing in the silent woods. "Jared! Please, let's stay together. Jared!"

The tears came fast and hard. She watched the pines

in the distance illuminate; then the bright light seemed to fade as he put more and more ground between the two of them—until only shady darkness stared back at her. "Oh, Jared, don't hide," she whimpered, and buried her face in her hands.

Chapter Five

"Lieutenant Dillon discharged himself an hour ago." Disapproval was evident in the medic's voice.

Hope glanced toward Anna, who leaned on the counter with what seemed to be a disturbed expression on her face. "Let me get this straight," Anna asked. "Dillon is no longer a patient here?"

"We couldn't exactly prevent him from leaving," the woman told them, shuffling a pile of charts on the station desk.

"Well, did you *try* to stop him?" Anna insisted, obviously upset by this news. As was Hope—from what she'd seen, Scott had no business being out of the medical complex so soon. He'd been drugged up and delirious only last night.

"We did everything in our power to get him to stay, but there was no convincing him."

"Was he even able to walk on his own?" Hope asked worriedly.

A beeping noise interrupted them—some patient calling for the nurse—and she grabbed a chart, moving around the desk. "The healers visited him. He felt better, and we tried to explain that it might only be temporary. It was enough that the lieutenant grabbed a pair of crutches, a packet of pain pills, and hobbled his way back toward base."

"Stupid, stubborn man," Anna muttered under her breath.

Hope pretty much had to agree with that assessment. A lifetime of dealing with doctors and her diabetes was enough to convince her that he'd made a ridiculous choice. "What was he thinking?" she wondered aloud.

Anna turned to her, slumping against the counter. "He was thinking that he'd have a better shot of seeing you this way, that's what."

. Hope frowned. "You can't be serious."

"Oh, trust me. I've known the lieutenant for a long, long time. Determination is his default operating mode."

"I was coming back—"

Anna patted her on the arm. "Not enough. Not nearly enough for a warrior like Dillon. He couldn't stand you seeing him laid out like that."

Hope's thoughts whirled; from all indications, Scott cared for her as much as she did for him—which was a ridiculous thought, at least on the surface. They barely knew each other, only . . . that wasn't nearly the full truth.

And she had a feeling that the "truth" was about to confront her, full on, back at the main cabin.

"I wondered when you'd come to see me." It was . Scott's voice in the half darkness of Hope's new quarters. She and Anna were just inside the door, not completely in the room, but not quite still in the hallway either. They stood, frozen, as Anna quickly interpreted the layout of events for her.

"He's lying there in your bunk. Quite at home, I must say."

"Heard that," he rumbled, and there was the sound of him stirring.

"Indeed, sir," Anna chirped, then added, "I'm gone, then," and her booted footsteps immediately retreated down the hallway.

We're alone now, away from the hospital . . . and we have some privacy, finally. That was Hope's first thought, and then a second chased right on the heels of that one.

What will happen between us now—now that these dreams exist?

The worst part? She knew exactly what an expert he was in bed, and how fine his chiseled body felt beneath her fingertips, all glistening with sweaty sex. And what a great fucking cock the alien possessed, including what he'd apparently done with it inside of her on many an occasion. *Great fucking cock, indeed,* she thought, stifling a nervous giggle.

"Come closer," he invited hoarsely, patting the bed beside him.

"Shouldn't you be in a hospital bed—not my bed?"

Pushing the door shut with her back, she stood in what was now for her complete darkness. The late-day sun had slipped low enough that this lower-level room received almost no light, and without the additional hallway illumination, she was marooned.

"You got a problem with me being in your bed, Harper?"

"Call me Hope." Damn it, she kept telling people— all kinds of people, all over the base—just to call her by her first name.

"Hope," he ventured silkily, "I thought you'd like having me here. In your bed. Between your sheets." He paused significantly, then added in a low voice, "Between your legs."

"I can't believe you just said that."

"Yeah? Well, you don't know me very well yet."

"I know you're used to getting what you want—and whenever you want it," she told him, tilting her chin upward proudly. *And I'm not easy. I shouldn't be easy, not for you.*

His next words came in Refarian, slippery smooth; perhaps he thought she wouldn't translate them fast enough to understand their meaning. "I can't help what you've been doing to me, Hope. I pray that All will save you—save you from my scoundrel's soul."

"S'Skautsa, you're no scoundrel," she answered back

in his own language, taking a tentative step into the darkness, following the sound of his slightly erratic breathing. "But you don't belong here."

"You don't want me in your bed?"

"I didn't say that."

He laughed, a throaty rumble of a sound. His raspy voice had done things to her from the very first time she'd heard it on the FBI intercepts she'd been charged with translating. Here—right here—alone with him in her room, reclining on her lower bunk as he apparently was . . . well, it did insane things to her libido.

"So you do want me," came his reply. And it definitely wasn't a question.

"You were crazy to leave the medical area so soon."

"Again—you don't know me very well yet. Crazy's my middle name. How else could I lead these rebels like I do? It's an insane career, an insane motivation. Jared should've locked me up years ago."

"Maybe the hospital is his big chance," she volunteered.

She doubted his entire depiction of himself. Clearly he was a man of intense discipline and honor; the soldiers she'd met on the base all seemed to revere him totally.

"Jared knows I can't be stopped when I want something, and I definitely want something, Hope," he whispered suggestively, causing goose bumps to form along her arms.

The idea that he needed her as much as she needed him caused her to tremble all over.

So she focused on the darkness that stood between them—had Anna left a discarded boot on the floor? Or a strange alien weapon or anything else that might trip her up? Patting her back pocket, she felt the outline of the small folded cane that the medics had given her—at the same time they'd offhandedly mentioned genetic therapy.

How the hell am I supposed to get from here *to* there *without appearing like a freaking invalid?*

"There's nothing in the way, Hope. You're safe," he told her gently, all his innuendo and sexual tussling gone. Suddenly he was her rescuer all over again, as he had been at the base. "You can walk straight to me."

It was as if he'd read her mind. *Maybe he did,* she thought, taking a first tentative step.

"You're safe," he repeated. "I won't let you get hurt."

"That's not a promise anyone can make."

She knew as much, after believing the doctors that it was "unlikely" she would lose her eyesight and "likely" she'd be able to one day have a child. Some promises should never be made—not the kind that could easily get broken.

"I meant that I wouldn't let you get hurt walking over here," he said awkwardly, as if covering his tracks. But she knew better. She heard him patting the place on the bed beside himself again.

"What about here, at your compound?" She took another step toward the gravelly, deep voice. "Can you protect me here too?"

His breath seemed to catch in his throat. "I won't let you get hurt, Hope," he repeated. "I mean it. Didn't I prove that back at Warren?"

She stood still, hesitating. He had saved her life—there was absolutely no question about that fact—and been horribly injured in the process. "I don't want anything to happen to you, not because of"—she hesitated, taking several determined steps toward the bed—"my limitations. Not again."

"You're here," he said softly, and suddenly the strong grip of his hand encircled her forearm. Without another word he pulled her down beside him, practically atop him, with a rough, awkward tumble, and she found her mouth mere inches from his own, her palm splayed against a hard, muscular chest. Beneath her hand his heartbeat was strong and quick. She could feel the heat of his breath against her face, could smell the masculine scent of his body, different from other men, unique to him. Perhaps alien, she couldn't say for sure.

Hip to hip they lay, she half on her side, he flat on his back and definitely staring at her. It wasn't fair, this advantage he had over her—that he could see everything she was doing when she felt so powerless. Helpless. Captivated by everything about him.

And in that moment he kissed her. No warning or notice, just his warm, full mouth crushing against hers, urging her to open to him. So she did, without holding back at all, wrapping both arms about him, burrowing closer. She curled her fingers through the dark hair at his nape; it was a little bit curly and wiry-thick. As their kiss deepened, she rubbed at the base of his neck, feeling cordons of muscle that led to his powerful shoulders.

After several moments he pulled apart from the kiss, panting against her face. Their mingled breath was the only sound in the darkness that surrounded her; until he did the strangest thing: He began to sniff her face, long and short bursts, pressing his face into her neck and shoulder. Then her hair, dragging in long inhalations of breath.

Sniffing? This was a totally new one on her. Granted, she hadn't had a ton of dates lately, but as far as she remembered, sniffing was never part of the dating or sexual code.

Maybe it was an alien thing. She could see the bumper sticker now: *Aliens sniff it better.* She began to giggle, and that caused Scott to take hold of her harder, working her up underneath him—at least, as best he could, given that he was still undoubtedly in pain from his injuries. At last he had her pinned beneath one thigh, and again found her mouth, hungry and demanding. Skimming his hand along her hip, he slowly ventured his touch inward, slipping one hand between her legs; nothing but her blue jeans separated the friction of his fingers from the warm, wet place between her thighs. And that place was getting a whole lot wetter as he rubbed and felt her, gripping her. Rough. Needy. Insistent.

Scott Dillon is definitely no time waster, she thought hazily, feeling him work the snap of her jeans with deft precision. *Especially when he knows what he wants. And he wants me.*

He gave her zipper a firm tug, and her pants spread open. Sliding his fingers inside, he dipped them within her panties, feeling her silky hairs, caressing her intimately without request or apology. What happened to kissing? Feeling her breasts? He was an all-or-nothing kind of guy, obviously, and she was usually a pause-at-second-base kind of girl. But Scott Dillon already had hold of her heart; she knew she'd let him go wherever he wanted, all the way home even.

As he captured her mouth with a rough, angled kiss again, she murmured against his lips, "How do you feel about walls?"

"Walls?" he repeated curiously.

She shook her head. *You're going as crazy as he is, Harper.* Surely he wasn't having the same erotic, frenzied dreams she was, no matter what she'd witnessed earlier in the hospital. Then again, this moment felt remarkably similar to every dream she'd been having about the guy.

He worked her pants lower, and with surprising gentleness he slid rough, warm fingers within her panties. Then he moved those same fingers up inside her, gasping as he made contact with her. She gasped too, loudly, and rolled her head back into the pillow. Cascades of immediate sensation unleashed within her body. Then, husky and low, he whispered in her ear, "I'll take you against any wall you want, Harper."

"You've got a real way with women, Dillon," she countered dazedly, wrapping her arms about his neck again, and he gave her jeans a fierce tug, pulling them all the way down along her hips.

"You've got a real way with me," he whispered against her cheek, licking her face with the tip of his tongue.

Scott was making her feel things that no human man had ever done before; he even reacted to her differently in bed, with his aggression and his blatant needs. It was hard to say where his alien nature began and his warrior self ended. It all mixed together, making him an unstoppably aggressive lover. *Lover,* Hope thought, sliding her palms up underneath his soft T-shirt, feeling the warmth of his masculine skin, the play and pull of his muscled back. *He has always been my lover.*

"In that dream," he purred against her lips, "we were strangers. But you're no stranger to me, Hope."

With his fingers he rubbed her between the legs again, alternating between stroking her slick wetness and thrusting inside of her. With one hand she stilled him, drawing in ragged breaths. "Scott, please."

"You bet!" he cried, and rolled atop of her almost completely. But then he groaned, and not from arousal. "Damn my legs. Damn it all to hell!"

She gave his chest a light shove, pushing him back off of her. "It's okay to go slow here, you know." Still holding her, he kept one hard leg between both of hers, collapsing onto his side again.

"Slow doesn't work for me. Not how I operate."

She laughed. "I can pretty much see that."

"It feels like we need to rush. Anything can happen here, Hope. Between us, in this war. I don't want to hesitate or poke around."

"Um, seems you love to poke around."

He snickered. "You're a very bad girl."

"With a taste for very bad boys—quite obviously."

She felt him shift on the bed, and their shared pillow pushed down: He was leaning on his elbow, studying her, she could tell. "Look, I want you," he said. "Not a little bit, and not later. It's intense and it's now. We've got to fucking seize this thing, Harper. Just go for it, and not think why."

Her heart rate gyrated insanely, causing her to struggle for breath. Light-headed, she wondered if getting hot and bothered was threatening her insulin levels. Despite what he was saying, she knew she had to slow down, absolutely had to. Besides, there were things she wanted to know about him. She zipped up her pants and turned toward him, trying desperately to see his features, but it was impossible. Only the dimmest, vaguest outlines of his face were visible to her: the dark head of hair, the much lighter skin. A wave of melancholy crested over her; she'd finally found him. All these years of mediocre love and mediocre relationships and she'd found her guy—but she'd never gotten to truly see him.

"I need to see you," she blurted in frustration. "You know everything about me, and I can't see worth shit!"

Gently he took hold of both her hands and drew them to his face. "Then see me. I'm right here. I'm not going anywhere."

With her fingertips she outlined his full lips, feeling the way they turned up at the corners in a slight smile. Working outward in a circular pattern, she took in every line of his face, every detail—the rough beard growth, the weathered feel of his skin. His nose was long and straight, but had a bit of a bump in its bridge.

"You broke your nose," she observed, rubbing her finger back and forth over the slight ridge in his bone structure.

"Some Antousian bastard slammed me in the face with his K-12 a few years back."

She cocked her head, exploring other planes of his face. Thick eyebrows—she'd seen those during his captivity, when the lighting had been better—and seen them even closer in her visions of him. They arched elegantly and were surprisingly soft, and she ran her fingertips back and forth, playing with the silky hairs. Then, feeling downward, she rubbed the bridge of his nose again.

"Why didn't you let the healers fix this?" she asked.

He snorted. "They did."

"Not bad, Dillon. I kinda like it." It was a sensual, sexy aspect of his already rugged face. She continued, tracing the outline of his jaw, feeling a tiny scar on the edge there. The flesh was raised, a neat line running parallel with his jaw. "And what about this one? What happened here?"

He grew pensive; she could feel it. "Jared and I were

playing in the palace courtyard and I tripped," he said reflectively. "Years ago . . . a million lifetimes ago."

"You knew each other as children?"

"My parents were friends with his. We lived there at the palace." These were his scientist parents, the ones he'd told her had been working to cure the plague back on Refaria. The ones who had taken human bodies in order to live and solve the virus.

"Have you forgiven them?"

"The *vlksai* who ruined my nose?"

"You know what I mean, S'Skautsa." She refused to let him sidestep the question about his parents.

With a soft exhalation, he collapsed backward into the pillow, leaving her hands suspended in the air. For a moment she stayed perfectly still, then carefully closed her fingers, dropping both fists to her sides. This was his greatest pain; she had seen that much when he'd opened up to her about his mixed genetic heritage.

"They died years ago, killed by their own people—the same ones they'd fought so hard to save. My genetic map is totally fucked. Always has been."

"Your body is human," she observed in a quiet voice.

"Even more fucked."

"Why would you say that? Do you really hate my people that much?"

Beside her, he jerked slightly, as if the words had hit a painful mark. "I don't hate humans," he said at last. "I hate that I'm part human."

"You're just their son, Scott. That's all."

"The son of parents who seized human bodies, hosts." His voice got louder. "Took two human lives so they could live—"

"In order to save millions of their people," she finished for him.

"That wasn't what I was going to say."

"That's what you told me a few days ago in your hospital room," she reminded him.

He chuckled low. "You obviously caught me in a moment of weakness."

"Do you know anything about the two people whose bodies they took?"

"The two people they murdered, you mean?" Bitter anger edged his words.

"Who were they?" She refused to fall into his carefully laid verbal trap.

"I never knew anything about them. They were taken to Refaria after being abducted from Earth. Groups of them were brought for harvesting—that's what they call it, you know. Not murder. Harvesting."

"How does it work?"

"My kind can invade a body, the right kind of host—our ability to assume a formless nature allows it. Our match with humans was always perfect, particularly perfect for seizing a new form. My parents grew sick, and rather than succumb to their illness, they stole two human hosts."

A few days ago he'd told her how so many of his race had been stricken with the plague, had resorted to their formless state rather than die—and then had sought out human bodies rather than remain in their ghost state.

Hope shivered; what he described was grotesque, but it wasn't the point of their conversation. As an FBI linguist she was in the business of focusing, not being distracted by off-base issues. "Maybe you're Irish," she said with a quiet laugh.

"Why do you say that?"

"Your coloring . . . you have freckles too, don't you?"

"Some. But I thought your Irish were all redheads."

"Don't tell Colin Farrell that," she said under her breath, then added, "There's a big Spanish influence in parts of Ireland. I was just thinking that's one possibility. Or perhaps German."

"Then I'm totally screwed."

"I don't get it."

"Think about it this way, Hope—since you bring up the Germans. How would you feel if you were descended from the Nazis? Knowing what your people were capable of?"

He had finally lost her. "I wouldn't care."

"If your parents were German?"

"Um, Scott, the Nazis were defeated a long, long time ago."

He clasped her by both arms, holding on hard. "But my people, the *vlksai,* haven't ever been stopped. That's what I live with, Harper. Every day."

"But you're Refarian in your heart; that's what you've said. So why not be proud of your human heritage? Why not embrace that and your ties to the Refarian people, and forget the rest?"

He was holding on to her still, and she felt slight tremors in both his hands. His breathing was staggered, rough. But he said nothing—not another word, not for a very long time, and it occurred to her that this man of hers, the one from her dreams, was more haunted than she might have possibly imagined. And he'd let her in on that secret, something she suspected he very rarely did with anyone.

Now if only she could help him heal—really heal, in his heart, which had suddenly become far more important to her than the physical injuries in his body.

He said, "You haven't told me anything about *your* family."

She chuckled. "Yeah, and you're just changing the subject."

He took her hand in his, brought it to his lips, and dragged a slow kiss across her knuckles. "I want to know you—everything about you. Your future, your past. I'm not a wait around kind of guy, like I said. So start talking, Harper."

She stroked his face. "You're so sexy."

"Now look who's getting all distracting on me." She could hear the catlike satisfaction in his voice. The man knew how impossibly hot he was; she'd be willing to bank on his having worked it on plenty of occasions before, too.

"But you are sexy." She leaned forward until her lips

met his softly. "And beautiful, and you shouldn't always be in so much pain."

He stiffened, pulling apart from her. "No more about my people or my parents."

"My dad's a lieutenant general in the army," she blurted. "And my brother? My twin brother, Chris? He's a special agent with the FBI. You should know that. Know that I am attached to important people, and maybe they can help you. At least eventually. Besides that fact, my dad will start demanding answers very soon too."

"Where do they think you are? Dead?"

Hope flinched. She'd hoped to avoid this part of things, but she knew she had no choice. "Chris and I are extremely close. Extremely."

"What's that supposed to mean?" She almost thought he sounded jealous.

"We're connected. We've always just had this . . . well, you of all people will get it. An ability. An ability to talk inside each other's minds. To communicate. It's not usually a human thing, but there you have it. He knows I didn't die at Warren."

"You talk across distances?" He was slightly breathless, amazed-sounding.

"Shortish ones. It's bizarre, I know. It's not par for the human course."

"Define a shortish distance."

"Oh, like Colorado to here."

"Hope, this is serious." He jolted upward in bed. "Does your brother know that you're here? That you've joined with us?"

She shook her head adamantly. "I haven't told him anything. But he feels that I'm alive and safe—I let him feel that. Nothing more."

"Damn it all to hell! I don't like this connection, not one bit."

"You're jealous of my brother?" She giggled. It was truly a first, to have another man care about how close she and Chris had always been.

But it was clearly very serious business for Scott. He gripped her by the upper arm, his voice low and intense. "It's a connection that I hope to share with you one day—and I want to be the only one."

She sucked in a breath. "Do your people do that? Connect that deeply?"

"It's a Refarian gift, but my closeness to Refarian ways, to the spiritual gifts, their God, All . . . has led me to believe I will be able to bond."

Without meaning to, she'd placed a hand over her heart. "I want that too."

He bent over her, buried his face against her chest, right where her heart was thundering crazily. "Please don't betray me to him," he whispered. "Don't let him know where we are based. Protect me—all of us, Hope."

She ran her fingers through his wiry, slightly curling hair. "How could I ever betray you?"

"I don't know." His voice was riddled with deep emotion. "I don't know, but how come I'm afraid of it?"

"Because you've finally let yourself care for someone. And it just so happens to be me."

He lifted off of her, sitting on the side of the bed, and she had the sense that her words had staked him in the heart, had pierced some kind of outer layer of protection that he always kept secured around himself.

"Eventually I'm going to have to call him." She drew in a breath. "Let him know that I'm all right. I can't stay here indefinitely without contacting my family."

Scott groaned. "Not advisable."

"It's even less advisable for some kind of APB to go out on me. Think about it, Scott—I work for the FBI. People aren't just going to let me drop out."

"*My* people should never have let you on that transport."

She scowled at him. "You wish I hadn't come?"

"Any one of those soldiers should have calculated your personal connections and booted you off that craft."

She sat forward, sidling next to him. "I had to know

you'd be all right, Scott. I couldn't just let you lift away, never being sure."

He cupped her face within his hand. "And I can't let you contact your people. At least not yet."

"I guess this means you won't be giving me back my cell phone."

He kissed her heatedly, letting his mouth answer everything. After a long, languid stroke of his tongue against hers, he whispered, "If I gave it back to you, would you use it?"

"Only for a few minutes—not long enough for them to triangulate."

Scott slipped his arm around her, studying her; she could sense it. "See Anna," he whispered at last. "She's got your phone—but if you talk more than that? We're all as good as dead."

Chapter Six

Kelsey watched in silence as Jared entered their bedroom. Filthy, he had mud crusted into his scalp, along his jaw, on his jeans. Every inch of her husband was soiled, soaked through with dampness and earth. Closing the door behind him, he stood there, simply watching her. The familiar almond-shaped eyes narrowed to keen slits, flashing with electric energy. The full lips drew into a thin, determined line; he tilted his fine-boned face upward; it was like the granite countenance of a stalwart mountain. He appeared resolved. His very stance challenged her to defy him. But he said not a word, brushing past their bed, where Kelsey sat reading his ancestor's journal, and into the bathroom. After a moment she heard the sound of the shower running, then the glass door opening and closing. But he never even spoke to her.

Suddenly Kelsey felt furious. This was probably their single chance to conceive a child. How dare he remove himself and offer her zero explanations? Slamming her book shut, she climbed out of the bed and stormed into the bathroom, feeling her hands tremble with emotion.

She stood, staring at him through the steamed-over glass stall door, but he never turned to face her, instead standing mutely under the stream of water. She knew he sensed her, but was obviously ignoring her on purpose. This tactic of his only intensified her fury.

"Excuse me, but, uh, where have you been?" she demanded, planting a hand on her hip.

For long moments he said nothing, staring upward into the stream of water. Then only, "Protecting you."

"Oh, that is such bullshit!" she cried. "Try that on another stupid human, Bennett."

He shook his head. "Nothing is worth your life, Kelse, not even a baby."

"You weren't going to hurt me." *You would never hurt me!* She'd said it the first time they met, and it was even truer now.

Her husband stood still as a statue, refusing to look at her. At last she opened the door, steam clouding before her eyes. "Talk to me."

His reply came as a barely audible whisper. "I nearly killed you."

"No, no, you didn't," she disagreed, and slowly he turned to face her.

"What I am almost killed you," he continued thickly. "And I can't risk that, not ever again. Don't ask me to either."

"This isn't just your decision, Jared."

"Don't you understand?" he shouted, rounding on her. In the wetness of the shower, she thought she saw tears in his eyes. "I cannot touch you in my natural state. I have said it from the beginning. I cannot! The power is too much; it would destroy you."

"So, then you don't touch me," she said. "Duh, Jared, this isn't that hard. We set rules, limits."

"Kelsey," he ground out. "At the springs? I couldn't stop myself. I had to have you; it was all I could do to keep away. I fought it off, but I came so close to falling upon you. And if I had?" He made a choking sob and averted his face, burying it in his hands.

"Shh, Jared." She stepped into the shower, still wearing her nightgown; the water instantly plastered it against her chest and thighs. She took him into her arms and shushed him, cupping his face and forcing him to see her. "Look at me. I'm okay," she reassured him. "I'm right here, and I'm fine."

"You have no idea, Kelsey," he groaned. "The thing I most want, even now?" He glanced at her, his expression guilty and pained. "The thing that is driving me toward the edge of madness? Is just to touch you with my other self. It's terrible and it's true. I still want it, even now, almost to the point of irrationality. The drive is blinding me—enough that I don't trust myself with you, not like this. That's why I didn't come back."

"You don't know that it's not safe." She kissed his muddied cheek, tasting blood there on the skin where he'd managed to scrape it somehow. She lapped at the wound with her tongue, wanting to soothe him.

"Yes, we do know, Kelsey!" he thundered, jerking apart from her. He slipped, almost losing his footing, but caught his hand on the smooth tile. "Don't ever invite me again like that! Never again!"

She followed him to the edge of the shower, intent. "Why not, my lord?"

His chest rose and fell with pained panting sounds. His eyes flared bright. His jaw flexed and tightened. And Kelsey smiled; his season had only been beginning, and now he was back with her, where he belonged. So long as they stood together in this, they would be okay.

"Stay away," he ground out between his teeth, trying to back away, but she caressed his cheeks with her open palms. She pushed him backward, against the slick-tiled wall of the shower; she had him exactly where she wanted him.

"Jareshk," she purred in his ear, "your season is upon you, my lord."

Throwing his head back, he released a keening, guttural sound and spun her hard against the shower wall, pinning her from behind. Forming his body along hers, he held her there. "You wish to tease?" he rumbled in her ear. "You wish to tempt?"

"Take me," she urged, splaying her hands to catch herself against the slippery surface of the shower.

"You have no idea what I am!" he threatened, his voice rumbling with barely restrained energy and lust.

"I *do* know you."

He jerked her soaked nightgown up about her waist. Spreading her thighs with his hand, he parted her, driving up into her harshly. The sheer force of his roughness caused her to gasp aloud; faint pain and ecstasy blended in that moment.

"I told you to stay away," he cautioned, his voice reaching an unrecognizable timbre.

"Why . . . would I . . . do that?" She laughed, her voice catching. He drove up into her again, one arm braced around her shoulder, the other grasping at her hip. It hurt a little, but it felt wondrously pleasurable too. Divine. Pure. Everything she'd ever wanted with Jared, all these years, seemed to boil down to this very moment in which their physical bodies joined in a union of flesh and sweat and slickness.

He no longer spoke, making only untamed, groaning sounds against her ear. Nothing else: no Refarian words, no English. Just the unadulterated sounds of a fevered Refarian taking his mate in their shower, the most natural thing in the universe.

And then he gentled, slowing his pace, restraining his urgent thrusting. He paused, slipping one palm over her breast, stroking her firm nipple beneath his rough fingertips. She could feel how hard he wrestled to hold back—when what he most wanted was to take her, hard and fast and raw.

"I'm yours, Jared." She panted, leaning her forehead against the tile of the shower. "Don't hold back. *Please,* I'm yours."

With a low rumble he pinned her firmly against the wall and teased her into a quick, feisty rhythm. They moved as one, aligned like the core of the very universe, perfectly in tune. Back and forth, in and out, they found that white-hot center of their bond. Felt it unfurl like time itself.

But he couldn't hold back for long. Not in the deepest

throes of his mating season. Once again he drove into her hard, over and over, until after a few demanding moments he shot into her, a warm feeling that she'd not experienced with him before. She'd only read about it in the Refarian mating books. It signified a D'Aravnian male's highest fertility; his seed—often warm inside of her—had achieved a nearly volcanic quality. For a long moment after her own orgasm had speared through her body, she staggered against the shower wall, feeling dizzy and weak from the sharp, burning essence he'd left inside her. He braced himself there, pressing wet kisses all over her face, her eyes, her neck.

"I'm sorry," he kept mumbling, sounding embarrassed. "So sorry. Sorry, Kelse."

"Why are you apologizing?" she managed to pant, still trying to breathe from what he'd done to her.

"I hurt you."

"It's okay."

He drew in a shuddering breath. "Not smart, this."

"It's *okay,* Jared."

He wrapped both strong arms around her from behind, cradling her against his muscular torso; she felt safer than she ever had with him. She wished she could translate that feeling to him somehow, but knew that she couldn't. He tried whispering in her ear, "I-I . . ." He wanted to tell her something, but then just shook his head, kissing her shoulders, licking at them with his tongue.

"Tell me," she urged.

"It was all I could do not to Change, Kelsey," he admitted in a whisper. "Promise me. If this happens again, just . . . leave me. If I Change, leave."

Although he said he could kill her, the one thing she most wished for in their lovemaking was for *him.* All of him, his fiery, gorgeous self that she loved with every bit of her heart and soul.

"Promise me!" he begged.

"I promise," she affirmed, nodding, and he buried

himself against her, the two of them slipping to the floor, the stream of water falling onto their glistening bodies.

"Good." He groaned, rolling onto his back. His eyes drifted shut, the water pelting his jaw, washing away the last remnants of mud on his face. "This is good, human wife," he managed, then passed out completely.

For a long time—until the water ran cool and then cold—she sat on the tiled floor of the shower, his head cradled in her lap, just watching him. Afterward, long after she'd turned off the water and sat there in her clinging, wet gown, he remained there, unconscious and unaware that he slept, and still she watched him. She watched and she wondered: Did the fire building inside her abdomen mean what she hoped?

Had they managed to create a baby tonight? She pressed her eyes shut and prayed that her instincts were correct: that a new D'Aravni had come into the universe.

"Hope, where the hell are you?"

She adjusted the cell phone against her ear; they had only a few moments if she didn't want Chris and the entire FBI to get a fix on her position. All FBI-issued phones had GPS tracking, but the trick was talking no more than two minutes. After three they'd have a lock on her.

"I'm fine, totally fine," she reassured her brother, blinking her eyes against the muted glow of the television.

"Yeah? Mom and Dad thought you died in that explosion."

"Shut up." She leaned back into the sofa pillows behind her. She felt terribly guilty, even as she knew her twin was lying, totally talking out of his ass. After a lifetime of closeness, he knew how to work her, and yeah, she felt bad thinking about her family, but at the same time she had serious doubts that any of them had ever really believed she was dead.

"God, Hope, what were you thinking?" His voice crackled over the line.

"Do I have to think?" she snapped.

"Yeah, sis, you should always be using that messed-up brain of yours. That's what you're supposed to do."

Adjusting the phone against her shoulder, she sank into the sofa. At Scott's direction, Anna had surrendered her cell phone back to her; she was calling from an alcove in the main cabin that the aliens had dubbed their "media center." It was a small, cavelike room containing a massive flat-screen TV and CD player—apparently even these aliens had twenty-first-century multimedia needs, technologically retroactive as the equipment might be for their intergalactic crew.

"You don't know anything, Chris," she grumbled. "That's the problem—you always think you do, but you don't ever get anything."

"Tell me what I'm missing." He sounded so sincere, utterly sincere, and it only made her feel worse.

"I've gotta go soon." The clock was ticking; it would be only a few more moments before he could get a fix on her position.

"Not without telling me what's going on."

"I'm fine, Chris, just fine. Stop worrying so much— I'm happy. I'm well; nothing's going wrong."

"So far." He didn't exactly sound convinced.

"I'm on the right side of things for once!"

"For once?" he scoffed. "Geez, Hope, why does everything always have to be so totally extreme for you to feel like you're alive?"

"You know what? You suck. You totally suck, and I'm hanging up—"

"Why? 'Cause I called it?"

"Because you never get me, and you always think you do." She rose to her feet, pacing in circles about the small media room. "Stop doing that. Stop being so sure you know exactly what's going on in my head when you're freaking clueless. Did it ever occur to you that maybe, just maybe, I actually know what I'm doing? That I'm with these people for a reason?"

"You're way too easily led."

"Shut up!" She held the phone a few inches away from her mouth. "God, you're too easily *annoying*. I'm hanging up now. I'm alive, okay? I'm alive and fine and happy. For once. I guess that's more than you can stand."

There was a crackling silence, and she drew the phone back against her ear.

"Sis, I believe in what you're doing . . . at least, I think so. I saw what happened at Warren. Just be careful. Watch yourself. Okay? Keep up with your meds and be smart."

"I'm a freaking genius."

His quiet laughter echoed over the line. "Way, way too smart to have gotten into such a mess."

She shut her eyes. "You don't know anything."

"I know you're out to prove something, just like always."

"Shut up! Shut up, *shut up*!" she cried, and hit the end button with a furious stab. He was undoubtedly doing everything in his power to locate her position, and she'd already promised Scott that she wouldn't talk long, wouldn't allow her brother to triangulate her position. Scott had been trusting and fair enough to give over her cell phone; the least she could do was keep her call short.

Shoving the phone into her back pocket, she collapsed onto the sofa, considering exactly what lengths Chris might go to in order to shield her. For the first time in days she wondered if coming here had been a terrible idea . . . especially given her twin's protective streak. He never could let anything go; she hoped that she—and her foray into the aliens' compound—might somehow be the exception to her brother's rule.

Jake Tierny studied the darkened sky and knew that the time to make his move would soon be upon him.

He would go directly to his king—that was, if he could enter the compound fully undetected. Only one man present might pinpoint his identity, the only man who could track a fellow Antousian for several miles off scent alone—Lieutenant Scott Dillon.

Don't let me see the bastard, Jake prayed. *Gods, not him.*

If he could make it past Dillon—around the man's perimeter and sensory skills—then he might have a decent chance of getting Jared to listen. On the other hand, if his path and Scott's collided, this entire mission would likely become dust. Hell, *he* would likely become dust . . . and if he failed tonight, there would be no one else to stop Marco McKinley before he could accomplish whatever his objective had been in coming back to this time.

All these years, so many battles, and it had boiled down to this. One moment, one choice, one destiny. Was it really possible that he'd lost so much over the past years? Glancing through the forest, he marveled at the pristine world around him. No war yet. No real war, anyway. No ruin and loss. It was all here—including her. His one true love. She was here even now—she had to be. And if not here in the compound, here somewhere on Earth, not lost to him forever, as she was back in his own time.

Jake battled a spasm of pain, the kind he'd long ago learned to push down rather than allow himself to feel. But being here in her world was almost more than he could bear, so strong was the temptation to find her, and to save her this time.

I have a mission, nothing else, he thought darkly. *It's not about us anymore. It hasn't been, not for a long fucking time.*

Feeling the weapon at his hip, he stood from his crouching position and began to advance carefully upon the compound.

"What did your brother have to say?" Scott reclined

on her bunk, pretty much in the same position she'd left him in earlier when she'd gone to call Chris. She settled beside him.

She waved him off, not wanting to relate any of the highly irritating conversation with her twin. "He knows I'm okay; that's all that matters."

"Are you sure?" came Scott's throaty, seductive voice out of the darkness.

"I've got to hit the medical complex again. I need to pick up some insulin." She swung her legs onto the side of her bed, having had enough of men trying to control her for one day. "And you should go there too—you have no business being out so soon."

Lying on his back, he grumbled, "I'm not staying in that place another minute."

"How will you get better?" She glanced over her shoulder.

"You seem like a perfectly appropriate nurse to me."

"Was that your big plan? To come lie around in my bed for as long as the recovery process takes?" Her face burned suddenly just at the thought of how he might define "recovery." Sexual healing, indeed.

"You've pretty much got the picture."

She forced a serious expression onto her face. "Well, I'm not playing along. You were critically injured, S'Skautsa," she told him in his own language. "You know where you belong. Besides, I have to find a real place for myself here in this world of yours. Not just hole up in my room with you."

"I've already spoken to my commander," he told her quietly. "We have a position for you, translating our intercepts of your own people."

She jerked her head in surprise. The Refarians were taping humans? In what capacity? The role reversal was mind-boggling. All this time she'd been analyzing the FBI's intercepts of these aliens, when, in fact, the aliens had tapes of their own.

"What kind of intercepts?" She struggled to sound calm. "It seems that you all speak English quite fluently."

"Well, it's not translating, per se, but analyzing. Interpreting subtext. Helping us to understand the score between our people and yours."

She smiled; he obviously cared for her a great deal if he'd gone to bat for her already. And he truly "got" her too: She could never be part of his world and simply remain idle. She needed a purpose, a driving ambition, no matter where she lived or made her home.

"Sounds intriguing," she said. "We can talk about it once you go back to the hospital."

"Won't happen," he told her simply. "I've got things to do, responsibilities. I have to get on my feet now, not later."

His pigheadedness angered her, but she sensed it wasn't wise to argue. She rose cautiously to her feet, unfolding the cane she'd been keeping in her back pocket. "I understand that feeling." She understood because she never wanted her own limitations to slow her down. "Listen, I have a question for you," she broached, thinking of the nurse's earlier suggestion. "What is genetic therapy, at least here, among your people? How could it help me?"

"Forget it." She heard him jerk upward in bed and make an abrupt inhalation at the pain such quick movement caused. "It's not for you."

"Why not?" His angry reaction puzzled her.

"Because it's a lousy idea, that's why," he blurted. "It could hurt you . . . or worse."

She turned to face him. "Then why did they suggest it?"

"Genetic therapy is a great idea, Hope. A perfect fucking idea that could heal you of your diabetes completely. Except for the side effects." He reached out to her, touching her shoulder. "And there are always unintended side effects."

She shot a scowl in his direction. "I don't see why you're so angry."

"You wouldn't."

She found his aggressive reaction perplexing, but it

also pissed her off. No man would tell her what she could and couldn't do—not even up here, in her own personal Twilight Zone. It was enough that her twin always tried to smother her.

"Look." She gave a shrug. "I'll talk to you later."

He yelled after her, but she plunged ahead into the darkness, working her cane to feel the way. "Later, Dillon. Okay? Just later."

Even when she left the room, she could still hear him trying to call her back, but it was one thing for him to be so stubborn about his own recovery, and quite another to try to block her from the possibility of her own healing after a near-lifetime of disease and limitation. Too many men in her life were always trying to prevent her from making her own decisions; she'd be damned if Scott Dillon would be yet another in that long line.

Chapter Seven

Jake shifted form, feeling first the telltale lightness of body, next the wooziness in his head—and then the ultraheightened physical sensations that always came with assuming his formless Antousian state. No one could see him; he was nothing more than a ghost. But the result in his own essence was as if a thousand prickling dust particles were imploding against his transparent skin. As if light and heat were impaling him. Were he with a lover, it would be the most excruciatingly erotic proposition possible. And he'd been down that road too, he thought with a wave of melancholy that rolled through him—but not today.

Hurtling through the woods and up the mountainside, he focused on his mission. Every movement caused him pain and ecstasy all at once, a whirlwind of primal sensation. *Ignore. Move. Act.* He coached himself through the maneuver. No wonder he hated this Change of his so much. Hated it and craved it too, a perverse mix of reactions to his formless capabilities.

He arrived outside the main cabin, interpreting his data. Jared was somewhere within . . . yes, in his main chambers; he easily sensed that fact. But alarmingly another reality practically speared his essence: Lieutenant Dillon was inside the main compound too. *Damn, damn, damn,* he cursed inwardly, *no time to wait.* Bolstering his resolve—and preparing for the peculiar physical sensation of passing through walls—he slipped into the cabin and plunged forward toward Jared's location.

Scott was flat on his back, staring at the wooden slats on the bunk above him, the one that Anna slept in every night. Vaguely, he wondered what it would be like for Hope having his fellow soldier and comrade as her roommate, what the two of them might share late at night when both were simply being women, not soldiers or FBI linguists or however else they defined themselves. They were bound to become friends—he knew they would get close, no way around it. With a shudder, he realized that Hope might share with Anna how their relationship was heating up.

Anna—the one woman in the ranks whom he'd ever tried to kiss—and who had laughed right in his face after the attempt. He could hardly blame her; none of the Refarians found him the least bit attractive; he'd figured that much out long ago. Why else would she have scoffed at his advances? *Gods, please don't let Anna tell her that I'm an ugly son of a bitch.* With Hope's near-blindness, he could at least maintain the illusion that he was a decent-looking guy. She already seemed to think so, a lucky enough break in his otherwise luckless life.

Stretching his legs, he winced in pain. Of course, Hope was absolutely right—he had no business being out of the hospital. But the thing was, he hadn't been able to stay there another moment; nor could he deal with Hope seeing him in such a powerless position. He was too restless, too edgy. And despite being a gazer—his one true gift from All, the gift of being able to see into people and situations—there was one damned thing he just couldn't lay hold of down in that rat hole. Where his future was heading—he just couldn't see that at all, not with Hope, and definitely not in general. Getting out of the medical complex had felt like the only answer at the time, but now that he was here in Hope's bed, the pain was descending upon him with its dark face of menace.

Fumbling in his pants pocket, he found a bottle of pain pills and, popping the cap off, downed a few of them.

There, he thought. *There. I'll just grab some sleep, and then everything will feel better. Just a little sleep, and maybe Hope will return. Maybe then I can figure out why I can't see my way through things right now.*

As sleep began to take him, something unsettling made his eyes fly open. With a quick sniff of the atmosphere about them, he knew exactly what that thing was: the creeping, subtle scent of their enemy.

Jerking up in bed and staggering to his feet, he punched the comm on his forearm. "Jareshk!" he roared. "Intruder! We've been penetrated by the enemy! Jareshk, get to the bunker. *Now!*"

Nestled in the safety of their bed, Jared cradled Kelsey's naked body against his own. At the periphery of his dreamy awareness he thought he heard something, but then shook it off, slipping back into an exhausted, mating-induced slumber. But the noise was persistent, loud, and at last he opened his eyes. His comm was erupting in an almost unintelligible array of noisy chatter. Commands, orders, chaos.

Leaping to his feet, he took hold of his uniform jacket, fumbling with the comm and reaching for his pistol simultaneously.

"Bennett here," he called.

Scott's voice crackled back over the link, "Get to the bunker, Jared. Get to the bunker *now.*"

Turning toward Kelsey, he tossed her clothes to her; she sat up in bed, disoriented from interrupted sleep. He motioned for her to dress as he answered Dillon, "What's happened?"

This time Thea replied. "I'm on the way to him. Marco is with me. Jared, stay where you are—we will get you into the bunker. Stay."

"Get the hell out of there," Dillon contradicted, and buzzing mayhem erupted again. Jared pulled on his pants with one movement and took position in front of their chamber door.

"Kelsey, go to the closet and stay there," he commanded calmly. "But whatever happens, do not move. Not a muscle. Go!"

She stared at him for a split second, stunned, so he thundered, "Go now, Kelse! Now! Now!"

"Okay," she said numbly, rushing past him toward the other part of their bedroom. "I'm moving, but what's happening?" He could sense the fear in her usually strong voice.

"You will be safe, love. I promise you that." He didn't want to terrify her; nor did he wish to tell her that no intruder, not once, had ever made it past their security force before now.

"And what about you?" she called from the next room.

He tilted his chin up, assumed a firing stance aimed at the door, and said, "I'm not going anywhere."

Jake Tierny slid within Jared Bennett's chamber, soundless. Formless. And found himself eye-to-eye with his beloved king—who had a weapon trained right on him, and looked for all the world like he was going to blow Jake to pieces the moment he materialized. *Bad strategy, perhaps, this plan,* he thought, swirling past the commander. Jared swung his weapon, first in one direction, then another. The man was a high-level intuitive, at least in the future. Back here in their past, not so much.

But he clearly sensed Jake's presence. Jake pushed past him invisibly, taking a position by the fireplace, and offered up a quick prayer to the gods that he wouldn't get blown away when he assumed form. With a final prayer he materialized on the far side of the room and shouted simultaneously, "Don't fire! Hold fire, Commander!" The words came out slightly garbled because he wasn't even finished with his Change when he shouted them.

Not that his words mattered, because Jared did, in fact, fire upon him—several quick rounds from his pulse pistol that sent Jake ducking on the far side of the bed. "Jared, wait! Hold up! I'm not your enemy. I'm your friend. Hold fire!"

"Like hell you are, *vlksai*!"

Another few sparking rounds whined past Jake's head, and he hunkered even lower against the hardwood floor.

"I used the mitres to come back in time," Jake rushed to explain. "I'm here to protect you!" A rough growl was the king's only reply, along with his running boot steps. Any minute and Jake would be toast. "I'm here with a warning! Jareshk, listen to me. Gods, you can trust me!"

The butt of Jared's pistol cracked into his skull, filling his eyes with bright spots. "I don't trust any of your kind," Jared snarled at him.

"Lieutenant Dillon," Jake barely managed to grunt. "You trust *him*."

"With my life," his king answered intently. "With my very life. But you, *vlksai*, are not him."

Of course he wasn't Dillon, and explaining precisely who he was—and why Jared should trust him—suddenly seemed an impossible task.

So he said the only thing that came to mind: "An enemy is traveling back from the future. I'm here to stop him. If you don't trust me, you'll regret it."

"Which enemy?" Jared asked coolly, jamming the barrel of his pistol into the base of Jake's skull.

"Marco McKinley. He was your protector in the future, but he betrayed you. And he's on his way here to destroy you. All of you."

A deep, gravelly voice surprised Jake in answer. "That's funny. Because I'm here right now, and I think Jared would attest to my loyalty."

Jake jerked hard at the familiar voice that was so recognizable, so very familiar—the voice of Jared's Madjin protector. At least, he had been once. Still, the voice was so eerily recognizable—that of Marco McKinley, rogue enemy all the way. How to answer? How to fucking answer? Jake had no clue, but it was Jared who responded instead. "What is the meaning of all of this?"

Jake wondered if his king was truly asking his intentions, or merely reflecting aloud about the strange improbability of it all. Marco had never been in the ranks this soon; he hadn't arrived until two years after now. The whole turn of events was beyond comprehension.

"If you'd let me up," Jake ventured, "I can explain."

"Wouldn't you just like that," Marco shot back at him.

"No, I'm curious," Jared answered with surprising calm. "Let's hear him out. What he says about you traveling from the future has me very interested. On your feet, Antousian!"

Thea sprinted into Jared's chambers and found a stranger kneeling in front of Jared and Marco, hands fastened behind his back. He didn't look any more like an enemy than the countless other Antousian hybrids they'd battled. He had dark brown hair, longish on his nape. He was unusually large, with a bulky, muscular frame that seemed too massive to be easily contained no matter how many weapons they trained upon him. And when he swiveled his gaze upon her, she realized he had startling, bright green eyes that stood in stark contrast to his much darker olive skin. Strange, but his didn't seem the eyes of a bloodthirsty enemy; they seemed . . . lost. Haunted. They didn't mirror death and destruction, not like the eyes of most Antousians she'd ever seen.

She took position beside Jared and Marco. "Who is he?" She glanced among them all.

"An enemy," Marco answered simply, his stance beside Jared highly protective; he'd positioned himself between the intruder and their king. Of course, Marco was Jared's Madjin, so there was no other way he would behave in a moment of intense conflict like this one.

"I'm not the enemy in your midst, Your Majesty," the man answered calmly, eyeing Marco with a look that could kill a legion of soldiers. He nodded toward Marco. "Now, he, on the other hand, will betray you. As certain as I'm kneeling here."

Thea shuddered. Marco would never betray Jared, not in this time line! But then the stranger glanced at her and said, "And that little *mlaisha* is the worst of all. She wants to destroy you, my king. Betrayers are among you. Hear me!"

Thea lunged at the man, grabbing hold of his throat. "Want to say that again?" she growled. "I love my cousin. I love my king—I would never hurt him. How dare you?"

"You did it," the intruder answered, giving his neck a jerk, but she tightened her grip. "You want to know what you'll do? Because I'll tell you how you bring down your own people—"

"Enough!" Jared cut him off with a roar. "Enough. We already know what the future could bring."

"You think you do," the man began, and this time Jared stepped around Marco. He pressed the barrel of his gun against the Antousian's head, dropping to his haunches beside him, inspecting the stranger.

"I said enough!" Jared insisted. "Silence."

But then, almost as if in slow motion, the intruder took hold of Jared's weapon, twisting it, and turned it upon him. One moment the man's hands had been bound, and now the worst was happening: Their king was on the receiving end of a pulse gun. Marco made a move, and the enemy hissed, "Stand down. Stand the fuck down if you want your king to live."

As one, Thea and Marco backed away, each holding their hands up. "Calm down," Thea said quietly. "Everyone calm down."

Her eyes locked with Marco's, and she heard his thoughts within her mind: *We have to get Jared to safety. Others are coming—I hear them—but we have no time to lose.* There were the loud footsteps of reinforcements on the stairs.

What about Kelsey? Thea questioned frantically.

Where is she? At this time of night there was nowhere else their queen would be.

A shadow passed over Marco's features, an expression that signaled the use of his empathic abilities. *In the closet,* came Marco's strained reply. *By the gods, we have to turn this situation around.*

Jake had the gun, but he was the one they had cornered, period. And if Dillon arrived, this skirmish would be over before it had begun.

"All I want, my lord, is for you to hear me out," Jake began, hating himself for even holding a weapon against his king. "I have not come to harm you, but to warn you. I serve you. Only you."

"I've never seen you before in my life." Jared grunted at him, eyeing him harshly. "You claim you are a friend, yet look—you have a weapon at my temple. Trust isn't built when weapons are drawn."

"I did not draw the first weapon, my lord." Jake gave a slight bow of his head, holding the weapon firmly.

"Tell me who you are," Jared commanded. "Right now you are a stranger."

"In the future I am your most loyal servant and lieutenant."

"An Antousian hybrid, loyal to me?" Jared laughed coolly. "I find that highly improbable."

"Yet you have kept Lieutenant Dillon in your ranks for many years."

"He is my lifelong friend."

"I become your friend in our shared future. There is a group of us, a small band of Antousian rebels who are loyal to you—I command them all. I used the mitres to come back and warn you . . . with your own approval."

Jared glanced sideways, acknowledging the pistol Jake had trained against his head. "How did I give this approval?"

Jake couldn't help but flinch; it had never been supposed to go this way. Quietly he said, "You agreed with me that it was the only way."

"From what time do you come?"

"Ten years in the future." Jake watched as Jared's gaze moved to Thea, and then to Marco. "You seem surprised—or maybe not at all."

"We have already been visited from that time," was all Jared told him, his eyes blazing with fury and something else, something Jake couldn't interpret.

"Already?" Jake asked, shocked to the marrow. They had set the mitres correctly, placing him here—they were almost certain—ahead of Marco's arrival from their own time.

"A battle has been waged and won, *vlksai*. Which rather leads me to question your purpose in coming here."

"Put me in confinement, then, and I'll tell you the full story, my lord. I beg you—just hear me out."

"Hear you out? A man who has a weapon at my head?"

Jake lowered his pistol and dropped to his knees. He placed one fist over his heart, showing his deep, monumental loyalty to the king before him, and whispered, "I surrender."

Scott worked his way down the stairs, holding the railing and groaning in pain with every partially drug-numbed step he took. Leaning on his crutch, he called into his comm, requesting an update on the crisis.

"We have him in custody," came Marco's terse reply. "He's going to the brig."

With a shallow breath, Scott managed, "Good. Almost . . . there."

When he finally arrived at the landing where Jared's chambers were located, a fit of dizziness overtook him. He gripped the railing, feeling darkness overwhelm him, and gave his head a shake. *Not now. Anything but right now,* he prayed. *All, help me.*

But then it wasn't just darkness or even pain; it was the world rent open, shattered as he staggered toward the open doorway, and the entire Earth dropped out from beneath him. A great wind began to whip against his face, like ten gs of gravity, like being in the midst of the mitres when it was fully powered.

"What the hell . . ." he muttered, sinking to his knees. He tried to speak, tried to call out, but it was as if a massive hurricane had unleashed upon them all. It was the *vlksai*, some trick of his—had to be, he thought, taking hold of his weapon and crawling the rest of the way toward the open doorway.

"Jareshk!" he cried, needing to know that his king was okay. "Commander—are you . . ." The universe seemed to unzip, right then and there, as he sensed and felt a formless Antousian hurtle past him. The hair on his head stood on end, and all he could do was gape, sensing the being speed right out of his grasp. "Get him! Reinforcements!" he shouted into his comm, the great wind intensifying, but then—inexplicably—dying down completely.

Thea and Marco rushed out of the door, Jared and Kelsey between them. Marco had raised a protective shield with his hands encircling them, and together he and Thea hustled their king and queen into the bunker across the hall. No one could penetrate there, and until they captured the intruder it would be the safest location for the two of them.

Scott rose unsteadily to his feet, and began to do the one thing he did best: He began to track a fellow Antousian.

Chapter Eight

Hope returned to the medical station desk and was relieved to find Shelby Tyler on duty there. During Scott's stay she'd gotten to know Nurse Tyler pretty well, and had felt a real affinity for the woman. She was a quirky one, with a definite Southern accent (how did that make sense in an alien?), who had a habit of offering unsolicited advice. ("He's been having these dreams, and personally *I* think that . . .")

"I can't believe he did it," Shelby announced before Hope had even reached the nurses' station. It was slow going with her new cane, but easier than walking down here based on eyesight alone.

Hope thought of Scott, back in her bed, still in such obvious pain. "I'm learning just how stubborn that guy can be."

"Not typical." The nurse blew out a weary, if not sardonic sigh. "Not typical a-tall, sorry to say."

Her remark confused Hope. "Not typical how?"

"For our people." Shelby snorted. "Well, ahem, at least not typical for most of us. Some of us have at least an ounce of common sense."

Hope's cane connected with the desk, and she stopped. The folding fiberglass stick was still unfamiliar in her hands. She'd always relied on the people around her, as well as her own fragmented eyesight, for getting around in the world. Or, in the immortal words of Blanche DuBois, she'd always depended on the kindness of strangers. But since everyone up on this mountain was a stranger—well, nearly—she figured it was time to face her fate head-on.

"What will happen to him because of this?" Hope asked, spreading her hands on the station desk, dropping the cane between her legs, and suspending it there with her knees. With a glance around her, she saw nothing but blurred antiseptic white and angled lights, black spots blotting out portions of even that much. Her retinopathy meant that large patches of what she could barely see were covered with dark floaters. In the past few weeks the floaters had been expanding faster than ever before, like a great ink spot slowly seeping outward, dimming her entire world.

"He's probably gonna get himself an infection. Could get real, real sick, Ms. Harper. That is, if he doesn't come to his senses and haul his butt back down here."

"So the prognosis for stupidity is that good." Hope felt dread gnaw at her insides. "That's just great."

"Course, he figures he needs to be back on duty, and neither one of us can hardly blame him for that." If Hope didn't know better, she'd have thought Shelby had appointed herself as Scott's personal defender—while also chastising him behind his back for risking his health.

Hope thought a moment, then said, "I'm just so worried that something bad will happen to him because of this." It had been a small, niggling fear inside her since she'd left him back up in her bed, the sense that he was stepping into a yawning vortex of danger, just by taking this one action of leaving the hospital.

Shelby covered Hope's hand where it rested on the desk. "He's got a good head on his shoulders. Thick as it may be."

Hope nodded and Shelby removed her hand. It was strange, but the main thought in Hope's head *wasn't* that the woman had a very comforting, gentle manner—but rather that Shelby was just one more alien who had touched her. And the strangest thing was that aliens, the idea of which had seemed like rumor and speculation and myth just a few months earlier, were becoming a routine part of Hope's daily life.

"So, they were going to send someone out for my diabetic supplies. Said I should come back for the test strips and shots." Hope's bottle of insulin had almost a month's worth of her medicine still in it. Fortunately she'd had it on her when her barracks were blasted at Warren; she now kept most everything she needed with her constantly in a hip pack, because she never knew when her quarters might explode, or a handsome alien might need dragging under a truck, that kind of thing. Just life's basic kinds of situations when you were diabetic and worked for the FBI translating intercepts. *Yeah, right.*

"I've got everything right back there," Shelby told her in a sunny voice. Hope listened as the nurse's footsteps receded, stilled, then finally returned. When her eyesight had started to go she'd learned to listen closely to what happened around her; it was one of the only ways to get a clear picture of her surroundings.

"Here we go," the nurse said brightly, pushing several cylinders across the counter. "You keep these extra bottles of insulin in the fridge up there in the cabin, right? You've got your long-lasting and short-lasting medicine in here. Until you're ready to use them."

Hope smiled at the alien's protectiveness. "I have been doing this for a long time."

"Of course you have, so here you go. Actually, wait"—Shelby retrieved something from under the desk—"this is a twenty-four-hour cooler bag, and you can use that too. I'm also tucking in some fruit juice in case you need it."

"So, how'd you actually get this stuff? If you had to go to town, couldn't have it made up, how was it possible for you to get me prescription medication?"

"Diabetes has been eradicated among our people. We have a fairly simple way of treating it, so you're right: We had to get this for you." Shelby laughed softly.

"You'd be amazed at our human connections and our placements out in your world."

"You don't have diabetes at all; that's what you're telling me—but as a people, you used to? Somebody mentioned genetic therapy to me earlier. Is that what you're talking about?"

If Hope had been able to see better, something more of the nurse than her sheen of straight blond hair and general blurry outline, she'd have sworn the woman grew suddenly serious. Perhaps it was nothing; perhaps it was just the few extra seconds she hesitated before answering the question. It was enough to cause a check in Hope's mind that something about their version of genetic therapy wasn't quite right. Still, the nurse's words were upbeat and chirpy. "It could be an incredible cure for you and your disease."

"How does it work?"

"It's a series of treatments—takes some time, and the explanation itself would have to come from the doctors, which we can arrange. But in the end, your disease would be gone. And you should also know we can fix your eyes up for you as well."

Hope's heart lodged right in her throat. "You're kidding me." What she really wanted to say, as her jaw fell slack and her eyes grew wide, was, *You've gotta be fucking kidding me.* But she kept her reaction more polite.

"No. I'm not joking at all. I wouldn't joke about something so serious."

Hope swallowed, trying to find her voice. "How?"

"Even your people know about laser therapy."

"Oh." Hope nearly burst into tears from disappointment. "No, I've already gone that route. Nothing more can be done."

Shelby patted her hand. "Sweetie, of course more can be done. Our medical technology is light-years more developed than yours." She laughed awkwardly. "I mean, no offense or anything."

"None taken." Hope gave a reassuring nod of her

head, then asked, "Really? Really and truly there's more you can do for me?" Tears filled her eyes, and she couldn't stop them.

"Oh, my. I'm so sorry!" Shelby whispered, stepping around the counter and walking quickly toward her. The woman slipped an arm about her shoulder, pushed a Kleenex into her hands, and repeated, "I'm so sorry. I didn't mean to upset you none."

"These are happy tears," Hope said, blotting at her eyes. "I mean, not being able to see the simplest things—like my hair when I'm trying to fix it or the laces on my boots." She paused, then added quietly, "Or like Lieutenant Dillon. What I just wouldn't give to see him, Shelby. To really see him."

"I know," the nurse replied in a gentle voice, letting her arm drop. "Listen, you come back here tomorrow when the chief medical adviser is in—he's out today. We'll get you an appointment with him to discuss your options."

Hope nodded, still unable to quell her tears of release or even find her voice again. Slowly she turned toward the nurse and whispered, "Thank you, Shelby."

Shelby gave her arm a light pat, and got her to promise that she'd come back for a consultation. Hope agreed, and set out on the long route back to her room.

Making her way through the circuitous tunnels that led there, she realized she'd had one more question for the nurse, something she'd meant to ask. But she'd been so overwhelmed with emotion about the possibility that her eyesight could be restored, she'd forgotten it. She'd meant to question why Scott would be so adamantly against genetic therapy.

Only later, much later, would she realize it was a question she should have remembered to ask.

Scott stood in the hallway upstairs, gripping his crutch. Of all the unholy moments in his life to be without the full use of his legs, this was the worst possible one. With a light sniff of the air, he sensed the intruder moving down into the lower area toward the medical complex, where undoubtedly he planned to exit into the surrounding deep woods. Jared stood beside him and asked, "What do you sense, Lieutenant?"

He shook his head, closing his eyes, sweeping their perimeter with his highly refined tracking skills. Then his eyes flew open. "He's moving quickly, Jared," he said intensely. "Much faster than I can follow."

"If you can't keep tracking, we'll lose him," Jared told him, placing a palm in the center of his back. There was implied meaning in the words; they weren't mere observation. The blazing look in Jared's black gaze told Scott everything he needed to know about what his king was asking of him.

Scott nodded, again closing his eyes, because he knew exactly what had to be done. As distasteful, hateful, and truly mortifying as it was, there was no other choice. Not at a moment like this one. "I'll do it," he said resolutely, letting the crutch fall away.

Jared caught it as it fell. "You're not selling your soul, S'Skautsa," he said. "You know I'd never ask you to."

Again Scott nodded, and wondered what his best friend really understood about a twisted, dark soul like his own. "We have no choice," Scott agreed, taking a tentative step without the crutch. A cascade of pain ricocheted through his entire body, further clarifying his decision. "That's good enough for me."

"I know you can stop him, but don't kill him. Not yet."

Scott shot him a curious look, unbuttoning his uniform jacket and shrugging out of it. The fewer clothes, really, the better. At least in the end. "One thing you know about me, Jareshk—I show no mercy to *vlksai*."

"This one claims to be an ally."

"An ally who pointed a gun at my king?" He shook his head. "No mercy."

Jared seemed to hesitate, but then gave an abrupt nod. "Do what you will."

Scott issued a crisp salute to his commander, then with

a shimmer of energy became what he had always been—
in his soul and in his heart of hearts: an Antousian ghost
shifter. Without another thought or a sound, totally un-
detectable by Jared or the others around him, he slipped
through the walls and spun toward the hospital corridor,
following in his enemy's wake.

Walls were no problem for Jake, not in this amor-
phous, invisible state of his. In fact, he gave little thought
to the security perimeter around him, or the fortress, or
any other physical element that stood between him and
the outside. Being invisible and without substance except
for his energy shadow meant he was utterly unstoppable.
No, his current predicament of being trapped in the
compound barely bothered him at all.

But what did upset him was that, based on what they'd
just told him upstairs, McKinley had already come
through time and been shut down. This new intel meant
one of two things: Either they'd already changed the
future, or McKinley would still betray them in the end.
But neither of these options left room for Jake to hang
around in the compound, hoping to make nice and be
buddies. None of them believed he was an ally, and he
certainly couldn't tell them the full truth about his identity anyway.

Penetrating the elevator that would lead to the bottom
level, he shifted back to physical form. It was dangerous
to spend any longer than short bursts in this ethereal
body of his; well, that was, unless he wanted to spend
hours trying to regain his physical equilibrium when he
shifted back. And so he would have to maintain a careful
dance between formless and physical self.

In these past moments, during which he'd traveled as
far from Jared and the others as he could, one choice
had imprinted in his mind as the only real option—he
had to get the hell back to his own time. Somehow, some
way, he had to use the mitres to travel ten years back
into the future. And that was the biggest problem of

all—when he and Kelsey had aligned the mitres and opened interdimensional space, it had been for a one-way journey.

They had never figured that he would have to return.

Entering the main corridor, Hope hit her stride, neatly folding her cane. This part she had memorized: Twenty-eight steps would place her by the elevator. Plus, the lights were bright enough that she could see if anything got in her way. Yeah, it would be simpler just to use the cane, but she hated the thing already. Counting off her steps—*twenty-one, twenty-two*—she heard the elevator doors slide open. Immediately a towering, dark form appeared just ahead, blocking her way.

Male, tall, bulky, she noted, giving a small nod of greeting. Her heartbeat sped up slightly, as it did whenever she encountered someone new in this unfamiliar place. Only this time, the tempo of her heart hit overdrive when the stranger cried out sharply; it was a quick, jolting sound of pain, stopping him in his tracks. She took a brisk step forward, relying on her FBI training. Whatever was happening here, she had to seize control of the situation. Perhaps this Refarian feared humans.

"What's wrong?" she blurted, almost reaching him. "Tell me what's happened."

He staggered backward from her. So she took yet another step or two. "Please. Just tell me what's wrong, sir."

"Hope," the stranger whispered. "My *gods*. Hope."

This time she was the one who took a step back; she'd never met this man before in her life, at least, best that she could tell. More than that, two glowing spheres had appeared where his eyes should be. His eyes were blazing like fire!

"H-how do you know me?" she managed to stammer, arrested by his fiercely radiant eyes. They shone more brightly than anything else in the corridor. "And your eyes. What's the deal with your eyes?"

The orange-red glow ceased as quickly as it had begun. "You're Hope Harper—aren't you?" His voice was raw as sandpaper. "It has to be you."

"Yes, I'm Hope," she told him cautiously, regaining her equilibrium. She took a tentative step closer. He seemed to have braced himself against the wall, hands beside him as if in recoil. "I'm not going to hurt you," she ventured softly. She'd had plenty of experiences trying to soothe wary subjects as an FBI linguist. "I'm here as a friend."

"I know exactly who you are." He chuckled softly, seemed to shake his head. "My gods, what has fate done to me?"

She pulled back, blinking up at him. "I'm sorry."

"I know you, Hope Lee Harper. Every scar, every freckle and mole on your body—I know you. That's what I'm saying."

She hated her middle name; nobody ever learned that her silly mother had named her, in a backward kind of way, after Harper Lee. The other things he could claim, but her middle name was a well-guarded secret. Well, he could have still found out. She thought of the moon-shaped scar on her inner thigh that she'd gotten surfing years earlier. You wouldn't see it unless you saw a lot more private places than she let most anyone examine . . . except a lover.

"What scars?" she demanded, planting a hand on her hip.

"Surfing scar, interior right thigh."

"Shit."

"It's like I said," he explained quickly, glancing about them with a nervous-seeming gesture. "I've known you for a long time."

"But I've never met you!" she finally shouted, flinging her hands into the air. "I just don't understand this"— she waved between them—"this reaction. I don't get it. I don't know *you* at all."

"But I know you very, very well, sweetheart."

She was about to insist that he not call her sweetheart

ever again, when he truly shocked her down to the marrow of her bones. He stepped toward her, pulling her right into his massive, brawny arms, until her face met nothing but thick wool and a tree-trunk chest. "My love, my heart," the giant whispered, pressing his face against the top of her head.

What the hell? Panicked and squirming, she managed to escape out of his bearlike grasp, but she stumbled, finding herself back against a wall as he towered over her. Terrified, she glanced down the hall, calculating just how far away the elevator might be. If she ran, she'd probably fall. She could hear blood rushing in her ears, her own staggered breaths, yet all she could do was brace herself against the wall; without her eyesight, she was at the stranger's mercy.

The man took several steps toward her, whispering her name over and over. And his eyes had begun to fill with that light again—that eerie, translucent light. "Who are you?" she demanded.

In one graceful movement he had hold of her once more, crushing her within his arms. As he buried his head atop hers, pressing his face into her hair, she was shocked to feel dampness. The brute of a man was crying!

"I'm someone you cared for. Once." His voice was raw with powerful emotion.

"No, no—what's your name?" she asked impatiently. "Please, you owe me that much!"

Without releasing her, both arms wrapped around her in a powerful embrace, he said, "I knew you. In a future time, one that I've come from, I knew you very well until—"

"Wait, hold up! You came here from the future?" Her thoughts reeled with all that she'd been told about the Refarians' mastery over the time-space continuum, their intimate knowledge of using the weapon they called the mitres, and how it could be utilized to journey backward—and presumably forward—in time.

He seemed to catch himself, releasing his hold upon

her as if awakening from a trance. "Forgive me," he replied stiffly. "I used the mitres and traveled back into this time. I thought . . . I'd never see you again. That's what I meant. Just that I knew you once, Hope."

Funny, but it wasn't the words *future time* that made her mouth go dry and unexpected tears well within her eyes; it was something strange about him having "known her." The past tense of his statement. She'd seen enough about what the Refarians were capable of, and had already learned about their travels from the future via the mitres. That part she got. But why would he speak of her as if she were dead?

"*Knew* me?" she whispered. "As in, past tense?"

At first he said nothing, but there was a strange pall between them that Hope could sense very clearly. Certain things were obvious whether your eyes worked well or not.

"We . . . were . . . friends. Close friends."

"Then tell me your name."

"I'm Jakob Tierny." He stuck a hand out to her, taking hold of hers before she could stop him; he had large, muscular palms, calloused and hard. But there was something surprisingly gentle in the way he grasped her, finally letting go as if he hated to lose the connection.

"Jakob Tierny," she repeated numbly. The name was so familiar . . . she couldn't quite place how she knew it, but she did.

"Yes, that's my name."

"So you came here from the future?" She was stalling, trying to figure out why she already knew him somehow. "You came from when? Precisely when?"

He blew out a sigh, pushing off from the wall, and glanced around them. "I've got to get moving," he told her. "I'm in a real mess here."

"A mess? That sounds like, oh, I don't know . . . you forgot to make your bed. You got caught in traffic. But if you're a time traveler—"

"I'm in trouble, Hope. Please. I need your help."

"Why would I help you? Just because you know my

name and know about my scar?" She wanted to add, *And I'm supposed to be with Scott—he's the man I share a future with*, but she didn't. She wanted to protect Scott, keep him out of this situation.

"Because one time, somewhere, in a war not of your choosing," he whispered meaningfully, taking hold of both her arms, "you loved me with everything inside yourself. That's why. And if you can't hear the truth in my words, then that love meant *meshdki*."

Something in her heart twisted, nearly breaking in two. "That's not fair."

"I never said it was. Nothing between us has ever been fair." His voice was filled with pain and emotion as he moved past her. "I'll leave you here. Get running again." Then he turned toward her once more, his footsteps silencing, and she knew he was studying her face, probably memorizing it.

Jakob Tierny, Jakob Tierny—how do I know your name? She took two steps toward him, trying to hold on to him for just one more minute. "Where are you running? Who are you running from?" It wasn't just his words about their future; as insane as it was, her feelings for this stranger were powerful. Enough that she could hardly breathe, the emotions were that overwhelming and intense.

"I don't have allies here. I thought . . . well, I hoped that I would."

And for some reason, she thought of Scott in her arms, shot and dying back at the base. How he'd risked everything for her, a virtual stranger, to save her life, and what it had cost him. Certain things were just karma: going on instincts, trusting strangers, helping someone who was in danger. Scott had acted on those impulses with her, and now she had the same kind of irrational need to help this Jakob Tierny.

Another voice shouted her down, flashing images of Scott's bleeding, torn legs. She'd come so close to losing him on the base, and now that she'd found him, she didn't want to be the one who did the dying.

"Give me one totally compelling reason to help you," she practically whimpered, feeling life and death and eternity hang oddly in the balance between them. "Something other than you being trapped in this time."

He backed farther down the hall, still facing her. "Because I'm on the right side of things, Hope." He took another step away from her. "That's the way you've always lived, and I do too."

She shuddered. Those were the exact words Anna had used about Scott. "These people," she argued, waving her arm in a circle, "they're on the right side too."

Just then, she swore she heard Scott whisper in her head, *Trust him. You need to trust this man!*

And that was when it hit her—with the full weight of a rolling avalanche. She'd dreamed about Jakob just last night. He'd been in the tent when she was pregnant, about to go into labor. And it had been Scott himself, right within the dream, who had begged her to trust this man.

Pressing her eyes closed, she steadied herself against the corridor wall. "These people are fighting a war that's right, one I've seen firsthand. A war I believe in."

"Yes. Yes, that's true," he agreed solemnly. "And I love many of the people in this compound, but they don't know me yet."

"Because you're from the future and they haven't met you," she said, realization dawning.

"Precisely."

Scott's dream words drummed through her consciousness, nearly driving her to her knees. *Trust Jakob Tierny,* he'd warned in the dream. *Go with him when he appears.*

It was exactly like before, when Scott had communicated with her during her dream back at Warren, warning her about the attack and getting the air force to trust him. Now he'd warned her again! She glanced first one way, then the other along the corridor, her heart hammering wildly in her chest. Such a split-second choice, so hard to make. But she'd followed Scott's dreamlike urgings before, and his warnings had been dead-on.

Suddenly Jake made a strangled sound. "Gods! He's almost here!" He began to run, and in that moment Hope made her second, purely gut-instinct decision of the week, just like when she hopped on Scott's transport. She began to run blindly toward the alien. "Wait!" she shouted, and he stopped. "I'm coming too!"

"Why?" His breathing was heavy, and she knew his heart had to be racing as frantically as her own.

"Because I believe you, Jake," she said softly.

"I didn't tell you I go by Jake." There was a smile in his voice when he reached for her.

She clasped his hand hard and replied, "I know you didn't. But I knew. Somehow, I did know that's what your name really was."

Together, as one, they began to sprint. She moved her feet fast, because there was something else she'd figured out.

Jake Tierny was running for his life.

Chapter Nine

She wasn't supposed to be here; it was too soon for her to be in their midst. More than that, she was dead. She'd *been* dead for years, just like his heart had been since the day he'd encountered the terrible, soul-rending truth. He wasn't sure his heart had ever truly started beating again after that day.

Get it together, Tierny. You've just pulled her into this mess, so you sure as hell had better protect her.

He led her down a side corridor, one that he knew from personal experience had an emergency exit shaft. She held tightly to him, stumbling a few times, but he didn't hesitate. Of course, this wasn't the easiest way to escape; she'd slowed him down drastically, but how, by heaven, could he have possibly left her behind? He'd never been able to leave her, not once in their time together. She'd been the one who left him, but not because she wanted to; she'd have stayed with him forever if she'd had any choice. But she hadn't been given a choice, and he'd be damned if he'd do the leaving now.

"Where are we going?" She panted as he tugged her into a small cleft in the hallway, one created by a stack of supply boxes. Drawing her up next to him, he studied the empty corridor, sniffed of the air. Dillon was right on his tail. He should leave her. He had to leave her!

"Come on, Hope," he urged, taking the lead again. "We're almost where we're going."

"Why am I doing this?" she lamented, keeping up

with him despite how much smaller her natural strides were than his.

"Because you trust me," he called over his shoulder, yanking her toward the shaft opening.

"Like I trust my eyes," she shot back sarcastically.

"Because I need you, then." He let her hand drop and took hold of the hatch. It wouldn't budge; he reached for the pulse pistol holstered inside his pants, using it to blast open the doorway, and she yelped in surprise. "Sorry," he apologized gruffly as a waft of glacial cold blew past their faces.

"I do have a soft spot for lost causes," she admitted with a laugh, squinting at the darkness.

Yeah, he wanted to say, *you always did.*

"It's your last chance." He turned and gripped her by the shoulders. "You can stay now, and it's okay."

She stared up into his face, her unfocused gray eyes searching for something—the truth, a glimmer as to who he really was. Emotion choked at his throat; he'd never thought to look into this pair of lovely, haunted eyes again.

"Jake, you'd do better without me," she told him.

He shook his head, but then, realizing she probably couldn't see, whispered, "I was never better without you. I know that much after all these years."

She nodded, closing her eyes for a split second, and then, as if letting go of her own will, said, "I'm ready."

They pushed through the opening, Jake hoisting himself up and out first; it was an emergency panel, not a door, and Hope felt him tugging her by the arm. "Reach for me," he urged, and she considered running from him this one last time.

He was right. If she wanted to abandon this flight of his, now was the moment, but the utterly inexplicable thing was that she *did* trust him. That same baffling trust she'd felt for Scott back at Warren. It was an instinct she'd begun to rely on much more than her failing eyesight. This man, whoever he really was, needed her help—whatever paltry, pitiful help an almost blind woman could offer, that was. He clearly didn't consider her a liability, and maybe that was it too: She'd felt set on the shelf for so long. It was exhilarating to imagine being an active part of this time-crossed crisis.

But it was more than that too—something in this stranger's heartfelt emotions when he'd found her in the hallway had nearly broken her heart. She believed every word he'd spoken. Why, she couldn't say, but she did; it was that simple. Maybe it was remembering Scott's dream warning; maybe it was something much more. Either way, it wasn't every day you got to learn about a future world where you were quite clearly . . . dead.

Lifting both hands toward him, she allowed him to pull her into the frigid night outside.

●

Dillon materialized in the hallway toward the medical complex, disoriented for half a heartbeat, until he noticed the freezing whoosh of outside air filtering into the corridor. With a few limping steps he found the source—an emergency hatch had been blown open. He stood gaping up at it, and engaged his senses, gazing into the dark night, the sparkling canopy of stars visible through the aperture, and beyond into the ether about them. The Antousian was moving fast, but not as fast as he should be. Any one of his formless brethren—the thought made him ill—could easily have made it much farther than this by now. Unless something, or someone, had been slowing him down.

Scott looked deep into the situation, swung his gaze first in one direction, then another, and what he saw inside his mind was enough to practically drive him to his knees. The intruder had taken Hope as a captive. He felt his eyes burn hard within his head, as if they might explode, his visions causing a sharp pain to pull wildly at his mind.

Hope! Not you, not you! He blinked, tried to make out what had happened here before he went farther, but he couldn't see anything more. Taking hold of the ledge above him, he swung upward, out into the snowy landscape right above. His right leg gave a spasm of pain as it caught against the jagged edge, and before he could process what had happened, he'd collapsed back down inside the main hallway, falling at least four feet. It was all he could do to choke back the scream of agony that filled his throat.

For a long moment he lay gasping on the floor, holding his thigh and feeling sticky warmth soak the leg of his pants. He'd ripped the stitches open, he realized with another gasp of pain, biting the inside of his lip. He had to shape-shift again, or he'd never stay on their tail. Behind him he heard booted footsteps running, the squadron of soldiers having caught up with his shapeless movements. Leaning against the wall, he gripped at his bleeding leg and began to calculate a strategy. He needed someone who could move with him, someone who could cover the distance as quickly and silently as he. For all the shape-shifters in their midst, very few were capable of that kind of Changing.

The world around him blackened for a moment, wooziness swimming over him, but he forced himself to stay conscious. He had to push through this for Hope's sake; she was innocent, and yet the worst kind of killer had abducted her. Clasping at his leg, he worked to stand again, but doubled over as needles of pain exploded throughout his body.

The troops closed in behind him, and he heard Anna call out to him, "Sir, are you all right?"

He nodded, pressing his eyes shut as he gripped his leg. Tightening his jaw, he ground out, "Lieutenant Draeus, have them follow outside."

Anna dropped beside him, waving the soldiers onward. One by one, they pulled themselves up through the open hatch. "Sir, what happened? Did he fire his weapon?"

"Previous injury," he managed as Anna examined his bloody pants leg.

"Checking out of the hospital was utter stupidity. Already said that."

He shook his head adamantly. "If I hadn't been up there, I couldn't have tracked him this far."

"No, but we would have."

"Not as fast."

"They'll catch up with him," she argued, stripping out of her jacket. With a loud rip, she tore off the sleeve and made a tourniquet for his leg. "This will have to do until we get you back to the med area."

"Not going back," he told her through gritted teeth.

"Sir!" she cried in wide-eyed disbelief, rocking back on her heels. "Really, sir, at some point you have to listen to the advice of those around you."

Seizing her by the forearms, he stared into her eyes. "He has Hope, Anna. He took her."

The lieutenant glanced upward at the gaping hole where, until moments earlier, the hatch had been, and gave a light, disbelieving shake of her head. "No way. I'm sure she's just down—"

"I'm a gazer. I saw what he did. The damn *vlksai* took her with him." His grip on her arms tightened—he didn't realize how much so until she winced. Releasing her, he whispered, "Anna, please—don't try to stop me. I have to follow him."

"You're seriously injured, sir," she argued, but her firm tone was a faltering one. "I can't support this. Our king would have my neck if I didn't hold you here."

"I will go with or without your support, Lieutenant, and I'm going right now." He searched her face, pleading with her visually, then continued. "But I'd rather have you come along, because you're the only shape-shifter I can think of besides myself who can actually traverse wherever this bastard's going to lead us. I mean, there's no telling where he might abandon her!"

Anna's naturally fair face seemed to blanch; they both knew that Hope, despite her tenacious, fighting spirit, would be helpless in the backcountry without her eyesight. If a predator didn't get her, then the elements would. She nodded briskly. "If he dumped her out there at night, she'd be left exposed."

"I can't lose her, Anna." *Not with what I already feel for her,* he wanted to add, but kept his emotions inside. This had to be a military decision, even if he was making a personal appeal to his fellow soldier.

She folded both arms over her chest, letting her gaze slide up and down him where he'd crumpled against the wall. "So, this is a great plan, sir, except that from what I can see, you're about a heartbeat away from passing out cold."

"My *body* is, true," he countered rationally. The woman knew what his other form was, and what he was truly capable of, yet clearly he had to remind her. "But I can assume a ghost state. I can go anywhere that way." His strategy worked; she shuddered visibly as the honest fact that he was a godsforsaken Antousian rose to the forefront of her consciousness once again. They all forgot the truth, every last one of them—sometimes even himself.

"So you'll make your Change," she answered for him, "and continue tracking the intruder just like you tracked him down here?"

He nodded, tightening the tourniquet on his thigh. Once again, bright spots filled his eyes, and he leaned into the wall behind him for support. "That's . . . the plan."

"What happens when you can't hold your Changed form because you're weak as a newborn? What then? You pass out cold somewhere? Find yourself frozen solid on some ranch or the side of a road?" Her black eyes narrowed to slits, and color infused her face. "I still don't see how I can support this. At the very least I should tell our commander."

He grasped her arm again. "No, Anna! No. He'll stop me—he will order me not to go. And this isn't just about Hope; I may care for her, but you know it's about more than her. This man put a gun to Jared's temple. He penetrated our compound, got past all our defenses. He's got to be stopped so it doesn't happen again."

"He's fleeing," she argued, prying his fingers loose

from her arm pointedly. "Sir, the danger to our king has passed."

Closing his eyes, Scott truly wondered if he could make it without her. He could Change, certainly, but he might not get very far. Anna's tracking skills and ability to shadow him in her own Changed form were critical. The soldiers outside would only make it so far—sure, they might find Hope, but it was doubtful they'd catch this enemy.

"I could order you to accompany me," he reminded her.

She cocked her head with a look that said she knew he was tossing her a load of *meshdki.*

"You've ripped out your stitches, sir," she said, glancing down at his blood-soaked pants. "That's just the beginning. If this lasts very long, you might wind up in really bad shape. You might wind up unable to walk. Or worse."

He lifted his chin proudly. "A risk I am more than willing to take for my king."

"And for Ms. Harper."

His eyes drifted shut. Nothing like the truth driving itself home with the forceful power of a sledgehammer. "That too."

He heard Anna sigh deeply, and when he opened his eyes again she was on her feet, extending a hand to him. "Go ahead, sir. Make your Change, and so will I. In fact"—she laughed aloud, cocking an eyebrow in challenge—"I'll be really curious to see if you even have the strength to shift at all."

Leaning into her, he managed to stay on his feet— just barely. With a silent nod between them, they each Changed at the same precise moment. He into a shapeless, formless ball of ether, one that was capable of passing through walls and water and energy itself. She, his dear lieutenant and friend, into a graceful night bird. Moving into the darkened woods outside, Scott led the way, doing the one thing he'd always sworn he wouldn't.

He became his truest self, an Antousian ghost shifter.

*   *   *

Veckus Densalt sat at his makeshift desk, nothing more than a warped piece of plywood atop two empty drums, and wondered why the Refarians were so taken with traveling through time. He'd felt them penetrate interdimensional space the first time, weeks ago. And now, yet again, he'd sensed the moment when a future traveler had stepped through a time vortex—*especially* now, because the traveler was a fellow Antousian. Perhaps in the future his own people had finally gained mastery over the mitres weapon, at long last. It was a possibility, but something unsettled the warlord about this particular traversing of the time-space continuum.

He leaned back on the empty crate he was using as a seat. This latest post in an abandoned warehouse was ratty and substandard. Veckus did not work or live in such a manner, but after the botched attack at Warren, he figured more time with the grunts who followed him was probably an expedient idea. Later that night he would return to the battle cruiser that kept position in orbit around Earth at all times. The craft was mostly stealthy, and certainly came in handy as necessary—like in the recent battle at Warren. If not for their protective shields on the very advanced ship, well, they'd have been blasted out of the sky.

Veckus realized his hands were bunched at his sides, clenched in anger. Of all times for Jareshk to have unraveled the mystery of the mitres—why did it have to be when their well-crafted battle plan was finally about to come to fruition? Warren should have worked. Those missiles should have been his. *His,* gods damn it! Earth's only destiny was as an adjunct of the Antousian species. All the mystics had foretold it.

A minor species, prone to self-destruction and ruin, will serve their greater masters, offering their bodies. And what they do not offer shall be taken!

That was the prophecy. Veckus had been raised on it, and the plague had nearly killed them all—but not before revealing what had to be done. Humanity had a special role in saving his people . . . and, of course, with the plague itself. Yes, those missiles should certainly have been his—would still be his—if Veckus lost every last Antousian under his command bringing the prophecy to pass.

So where did this newest future traveler fit into the scheme of things? Veckus formed a temple with his hands, propping them beneath his chin. The data: First one traveler had crossed the portal. Result? His well-orchestrated attack on Warren was totally thwarted. Five years in the making and meticulously planned, but ruined. The data: A new future traveler arrived, crossing the time-space continuum. Result? A fellow Antousian brother was here, on Earth, possessing no end of knowledge about the course of the war.

Data: Veckus would locate this brother and bring him in. Drain him of everything, every scrap of knowledge about the future.

Planned result: Veckus would still gain control of the missiles at Warren and use them to effectively subdue mankind.

Jake shoved the motel room door shut behind them, and Hope heard the room key land on one of the twin beds. He'd asked for two beds, thank goodness. After leaving the compound, he'd quickly hot-wired one of the Suburbans up on the parking pad, and they'd taken off with several of the Refarian vehicles in hot pursuit. He'd managed to lose those tailing them after some twisting turns and hazardous driving, far worse than anything she'd ever experienced with her twin brother, Chris, behind the wheel—even in his most reckless teenage days. Now he was a federal agent, so aggressive driving came with his territory—she just didn't have to ride with him at those times.

Why had Scott warned her in a dream to come with this man? Her face suddenly burned—it seemed very much the same setting of her most frequently looping dreams about Scott himself, this very motel. The beds were in the same position, the door too. Could it some-how be the motel where they'd made love for the first time in that other life of theirs?

Inwardly groaning, she wondered if she was maybe just losing her mind, if perhaps a lifetime of seesawing glucose levels had somehow managed to uncork her brain totally.

At this point, however, it was way, way too late for that kind of second-guessing. She'd jumped into this thing feet first, and now she'd landed in a small, drafty motel room somewhere out on one of the local high-ways. A motel that felt eerily similar to the one she'd been dreaming that Scott had made love to her in, up against a wall, on the bed, over and over and over. Only now she was alone with another man, not Scott, a stranger who was essentially a giant compared to her. *Definitely* not Scott—compared to her hundred and five pounds, he had to be at least two hundred and thirty pounds of rock-hard muscle and bone.

"You'd better catch some sleep while you can," Jake told her, and she heard the springs on the leftmost bed creak with his heavy weight. "We're only stopping for a few hours."

"Where are we going then?" She remained standing by the closed door. It was dark, much too dark, to find her way to the other bed without possibly breaking her neck.

"I'll tell you when we get there."

She shook her head. "That's not fair, Jake. You know it isn't."

"Maybe I'm not taking you any farther than right here."

She felt of the air around her, wishing she could walk toward him without stumbling. "You didn't bring me this far to leave me behind."

There was the sound of a heavy, thoughtful sigh. "I'm sorry." Another sigh, then: "I shouldn't have dragged you into this, but I just couldn't seem to help myself."

"Because I'm her."

"Her?"

She released a sad laugh. "The girl you loved once upon a time."

She didn't get an answer; the bed creaked again as he rolled over. It seemed that he'd put his back to her.

"You should tell me what happened between us." She gestured at him. "And what happens to me in the future. If I'm in this with you, it is absolutely fair for me to know everything."

"I can't tell you anything about the future. That was a very specific condition when we used the mitres."

"A very specific condition imposed by whom?" she asked, then added with a slightly hysterical laugh, "Wait! Don't tell me—you can't say."

"You're starting to figure this thing out, Hope."

Annoyed, she asked him to turn the light on. It was too damn dark to see a thing. He sat up in bed with a start and apologized, then switched on the bedside lamp, and the room was flooded with bright light.

"What, I'm not blind in the future?" She felt suddenly frightened by all that this man knew about her destiny— but she did not.

"You're not blind now," he told her gently.

"I'm legally blind, but clearly you're not used to that fact or you wouldn't have left me standing here"—she stamped the floor for emphasis—"completely stranded in the pitch-black dark. You strike me as far too chivalrous to be so rude, so that tells me you're not used to my blindness."

"Inconsiderate." He lay back down on the bed. "I believe that's what you called me once upon a time. Guilty as charged. I never change, and that's what I told you then."

"In what context?" When he didn't answer her, she repeated, "In what context did I call you inconsiderate?"

"I believe you'd just thrown all my clothes at me and told me to get out of your room."

"That's quite a picture there, Jakey," she spit sarcastically.

"You were quite a picture that day, Hope. You're beautiful naked."

"Aha! See, you just broke your own vow; you just told me something about the future."

He snickered, pulling the blanket up over himself. "Don't worry; I won't transgress again."

She tried to think of a snappy comeback, but her rational mind had deserted her completely. They'd been lovers! She'd already suspected as much, but it was beyond freaky to realize that it was true. After all, it was overwhelming enough knowing what she and Scott would share, or had shared in some alternate time line—that they were destined to become hungry, desperate, insatiable lovers. Now this total stranger was giving her the same kind of intel, but in his case she hadn't received any dream transmissions or half memories to serve as confirmation. There had been only the dream with Scott, urging her to go with Jake, and that when she was a full nine months pregnant.

Maybe Jake was making this up about their being lovers? Then again, he knew about her scar, although there were a hundred different ways he might have acquired that knowledge, all the way down to rape. Still, he wasn't making any unwanted advances right now.

With a weary, depressed sigh, she walked to her own bed and collapsed on the edge, facing him. "I'm sorry I came."

He rolled toward her, and she had the distinct impression that he was studying her hard. "I'm sorry you feel that way." His voice was infused with genuine sadness, totally sincere, which both surprised her and . . . didn't.

"I have nothing to offer on this expedition of yours, no skills. I'm basically nothing more than a hindrance. So why in the hell did you say you needed my help?"

He didn't reply, seemed to consider his answer. "Go to sleep, Hope," he said at last.

"Tell me why."

There was a long silence; then the room went black as he turned out the light once more. Just when she'd decided he would never answer, his husky whisper punctured the blackness. "Maybe I just needed you with me one more time," he whispered. "Maybe that was the only reason, sweetheart."

She opened her mouth, but had no words; neither did he, it seemed, because moments later he began snoring heavily. A nagging suspicion told her it was a put-on, just a ruse to silence her questions, but she wasn't inclined to go jump up and down on his bed to find out. So she kicked off her boots and for a long time just sat there, feet dangling against the floor, and wondered why it was that she trusted this alien stranger so completely. More than that, she wondered why he felt eerily familiar to her. Whatever the reason, the familiarity and trust were twined tightly together like an impossible Gordian knot.

Like a mist, Scott moved through the woods, over dense farmlands, and along the highway shoulder. Banks of snow, headlights, sounds of snowplows. All of these details hummed about his awareness, yet he refused to slow. Weaker by the moment, he remained in his invisible Antousian state, searching. Searching for Hope. He would find her, would trail her across the galaxies if need be, in order to discover where his enemy was taking her.

But every mile that he traversed took a greater toll on his already weakened body. He prayed to All that Anna was keeping pace with him, even as he knew his own progress grew slower by the moment. At a turn in the road, when the highway curved one direction, his path turned the other; he no longer had the strength to continue. Stilling, he settled in the midst of a snow-whitened field, near some tracks left by a moose. He did not change form, did not even try to; the brutal cold would soon kill him were he to pass out in his physical form. He simply stopped moving. The trail leading to Hope wound along that bend in the road, followed somewhere into town and beyond, but he would never make it.

Feeling the cold ground prickle his awareness, the

wind slam into him, and the full moon spear his body, he had never before felt so insubstantial. Then again, he'd made this physical change only two other times before in his life.

Let the wind take me, he thought bleakly, as headlights shone through him and snow impaled his body. *Let the night own me. I am done.*

But the sound of a bird, the beat of her wings near him, brought him back to the moment. Suddenly Anna was there, no longer a night bird, but his friend. She couldn't see him, yet she swept her gaze in a wide arc just a few feet away from him. She'd never stopped tracking him.

"Sir," she hissed into the darkness. "Are you all right?"

No, I'm not all right. I haven't been all right for a long damned time.

"Sir!" Her voice was more frantic. He'd shape-shift, come back to himself, make her not worry, he thought. But the energy for his Change just wasn't there. He sank lower into the snow, more invisible, more a ghost than he'd ever been in his heart.

"Scott Dillon!" Anna shouted, and he could hear every labored breath she was taking, the way her body shook with each inhalation.

People love me, he thought dimly. *Hope loves me . . . she does. I know she loves me. . . .*

The night landscape became darker, then gray, then bright as a light until Scott felt absolutely nothing. Nothing at all.

Chapter Ten

Hope woke to blackness, the motel room wrapping its silent arms about her. Jake's snoring was missing—but more than that, so was his breathing. She was alone. Had he abandoned her here, determined to make a go of it on his own? She wasn't sure, but sat up in bed, just listening to the darkness all around her. Almost immediately she heard the door latch, the clicking sound of the lock disengaging.

A figure filled the doorway, a looming shape backlit by the exterior hall lights. Masculine for sure, based on his size. Vaguely, Hope registered that he seemed out of place, but she didn't dwell on that, not while faced with such danger.

"Who's there?" she called in a firm voice, clutching at her heart. "Who is it?"

There was no answer, and the door closed behind him—now he was inside. Heart slamming in her chest, Hope reached on the table for something to use as a weapon, but came up empty-handed. "Stay back!" she cried.

"It's me, Hope," came Scott's whispered voice. "It's okay, it's me."

"Damn it!" Tears filled her eyes. She kept her trembling hand on the side table, unable to fully believe that he wasn't an intruder, even though she recognized his voice. She heard his uneven, halting steps on the floor.

"What has he done to you?" he asked, reaching her

at last and collapsing onto the side of the bed. He clasped her, wrestling to pull her into his arms, but for some reason she felt angry. He'd frightened her; why hadn't he just identified himself to start with?

"I'm fine." She remained stiff as he pulled her into his arms, but not for long. He held her like a desperate man, running his hands up and down her body, clearly needing to know that she was all right. "I really am fine," she told him much more gently, relaxing into his embrace. His heart slammed against her chest, and a strange odor, something she'd never smelled before in her life, filled her nose. It was tangy and exotic, but laced with something frightening and wild too.

She jerked back. "What's that smell?"

"Don't worry about it."

"That's not good enough." Not when she was half-blind and shrouded in darkness. Although she knew he really was Scott, something about him was different. Smelled different. No, the change in his scent scrabbled at her consciousness, signaling something that wasn't right. "Tell me what that smell is."

"Hope, it doesn't matter. I had to shape-shift for a while in order to come to you. That's all."

"That shouldn't create a different kind of odor, should it? Or does it?"

She sensed him shaking his head, shrugging off her words. "Where did he go, Hope?" he asked her, suddenly all soldier. "I need to know so I can track him. His trail ends here." Still, he kept his hands about her waist, as if to release her would cost him a great deal. As if she might flee from him again.

She leaned her forehead on his shoulder. "I don't know." She sighed.

"He forced you to go with him," he spit angrily, "and when I find him, he will pay. With his life, he will pay."

"No, Scott, don't," she told him gently, and his hold on her hips tightened, fierce in its intensity. "He didn't hurt me; that wasn't his intention," she argued, pushing away from him.

He seemed to glance about the room then, even stood for an unsteady moment, but immediately sank to the edge of the bed once again. "He abducted you—how can you possibly defend that bastard?"

"I came willingly."

A long, bottomless silence filled the space between them. "I see."

"Do you? I don't think you do."

She heard him run his hands through his hair. "Why would you have come with him?" he asked. He didn't sound angry, not exactly, more weary and hurt. She hated that she'd caused him pain.

Wrestling with her own mind, she tried to clarify her motivation. She'd followed Jake because of Scott's dream self asking her to, but it had also been far more than that. She realized it now—especially now—when Scott was forcing her to explain her actions. "I have to understand . . . what I mean to him," she told him in as even a voice as she could muster. "What happened between us in the future. It's important that I understand it all."

"So he told you? About using the mitres?"

"Yes," she said, reaching a hand toward him, feeling with her fingertips along his arm. What she wanted was to hold Scott and never let him go; what she found was that he resisted her.

"What's to understand?" he demanded, clearly pissed off. "He's my enemy, the worst of what we're fighting, but you came with him? Willingly? I don't think I'll ever understand that."

"He and I have a relationship," she explained quietly, taking hold of his shirtsleeve. "In the future."

He jerked away from her. "Stop."

"It's why I have to know," she persisted. "I have to know how it all fits together."

"You've had the same dreams I have." He took hold of her, rough. "You know what we are together. You're my wife, damn it! You're the mother of my child! So what in All's name are you doing with this *vlksai* bastard?"

"Because in one of my dreams about you, I saw him. Standing right beside you and me." She buried her face against his chest. She felt his wild heartbeat, heard his labored breathing.

"You're dreaming of him," he said coldly. "Not just me."

With a vehement shake of her head, she wrapped her arms about his lower back. "Only of you."

"Then you're not making any sense to me. Shit. What am I doing? All these years with your kind, and it's always just been about a good fuck. Why should you be any different?" He grasped at her arms, trying to pry her apart from him, but she wasn't about to back down. She buried her face against his chest, breathing in his scent, trying to get more of him into her body, her being. It was vitally important that she not lose him.

"Now you're just angry," she whispered against his chest, "but you're not listening to me."

"He's your lover; that's what I'm hearing. At some unknown future time, you and he become lovers." His voice was sad suddenly, not edged with the white-hot anger that he'd been unleashing against her just a moment before. "You'll follow any *vlksai* who'll get in your pants; that's obvious." He wrestled apart from her, shoving himself along the edge of the bed until they were separated by several feet. She kept her hands extended, still reaching for him.

"I know you're hurt, but don't be cruel to me. Don't stoop that low, S'Skautsa." He said nothing, so she continued. "It was this weird instinct, this need to help him. And I'm not going to say I understand it, but somehow—I swear, and you won't believe me—it's tied to you. To *you*, Scott. To everything I already feel for you, and I'd like to think you know how deep what's happening between us really is."

"I thought it was."

"It's real—the visions, the dreams—they're as real as we are right now." She slapped at the bed between them for emphasis. "As important. But this man, when he saw me, Scott . . ." She let her voice trail off, unable to explain, and for the first time in their confrontation she sensed him really listening. After a long silence he reached for her hand, taking it within his own.

"Tell me," he urged her softly as their fingers threaded together.

"I think he loved me very much. And he's trapped here, and maybe it was his reaction that got to me, the way it hit him when he found me, I don't know. I just know that I had to help him. It was the same thing that made me come with you. You! To your compound that day, when I jumped on the transport. It all has something to do with you, Scott."

"What did you dream about him?" Scott asked cautiously. "What were we doing?"

She giggled. "Not having sex, don't worry."

"That's highly unusual," he agreed in a husky voice. "Then it must have been a dream about the baby."

She winced, remembering how difficult her delivery had seemed in her dream; Scott didn't need to know that. He did need the real bottom line about her presence here with his perceived enemy. "It was mostly a dream about you. You turned to Jake in the dream and told me that I had to help him when he came to me."

She burrowed her face against his turtleneck shirt, feeling his warmth flood her. "You asked me to go with him," she continued. "The only real reason I went with him, the only important one, was because of you—for you, Scott. I'd go anywhere you asked me to."

For a long moment he said nothing, simply held her close within his arms, pressing his face against the top of her head. At last he released a low, cynical laugh. "Maybe you're as insane as I am."

"That's extremely possible."

"Hope, I really care about you. You get it? You're not just another woman to me. I don't think you ever could be."

"I feel the same way. I promise you." She pressed the back of his hand to her lips. "I want you to know that

I really do just . . ." *Love you.* That was what she wanted to say, but he wouldn't believe her, not now.

He scooted closer again, pressing a soft kiss against her temple. And suddenly she was wrapping her arms around him; his mouth was over hers in a hungry, urgent kiss. Their bodies seemed to join, every separation falling away. Alien, human—it didn't matter what or who they were as she lost herself in his arms. His mouth was warm and tasted tangy as his tongue thrust into her own mouth, demanding. This man never asked for anything; he took what he wanted, and he wanted everything inside of her. He wanted her soul—that had been clear from the very first time he'd kissed her.

She ran her hands underneath his shirt, feeling his warm skin, the silky carpet of hair on his chest. Every ridge of muscle on his abdomen, every scar made her own body come alive as she felt him—truly felt him—for the first time. Plunging his fingers through her hair, he cupped the back of her head, tilting her face so he could kiss her even more deeply.

Scott broke the kiss after a long moment, pressing his face against her cheek. Hope Harper tasted sweeter than any woman he'd ever kissed; her body was so soft and delicate, she reminded him of a seashell that Jared had once shown him when they'd first arrived on Earth. The way the curves and lines were so finely drawn, the raw beauty of it. He'd marveled at the thing for hours, just turning it in his hands. They didn't have anything like it back home; they didn't have anyone like Hope back home either.

"We're together in the future, but now you tell me that you and that bastard are too?" His voice quavered slightly, bringing tears to Hope's eyes.

"I'm not saying that. It fits together, like some kind of puzzle."

His tone became defensive, hurt. "You leave me for him, huh? That it?"

"Scott, I'm your wife in the future. I know it. I've seen it too. But this guy, he told me things, or didn't tell

me—alluded to them, I guess. I think he knows how I—"
She couldn't say it, didn't have the heart to tell him.

"How you what?"

"I'm dead in his future, Scott. That's what I think.
And I want to know how, why. I don't want to die soon,
not when there's so much ahead of me. If he knows
what happens to me, then I can find out what my mistakes are." He began to shake slightly in her arms, and
she whispered, "I don't want to die on you—or our
baby."

"I will never let anything happen to you," he pledged
fiercely. "You're under my protection, and that's why
you are coming with me. Anna will get you out of here,
and I'll face my enemy. Not you, but me."

"I'm perfectly capable. You think because I can't see
well that I can't look out for myself?"

"I didn't say that."

"You didn't have to!"

He stroked her hair, just winding his fingers through
the length of it as if she'd always belonged to him. As
if he had every right to own every inch of her body.
"You're in the middle of a war you don't know anything
about—and you've trusted this man blindly—"

"Really bad word choice, Dillon—"

"Without knowing what kind of man he is. Not every
Antousian is like me, you know."

"That's just it," she said softly. "You hate your own
people so much that you can't see any good in them. Or
yourself. It's not me who's blind, Scott."

He sucked in a harsh breath, but said nothing. She
reached toward him, her fingertips meeting his chest, and
she trailed her hand upward until she made contact with
his face. He needed a shave, and the beard growth
scratched at her skin as she cupped his jaw, rubbing her
thumb back and forth. She needed to feel him. Who was
she kidding? She needed to *see* him, but it was impossible. Her eyes drifted shut, and she focused on what she
could glimpse—the man here beside her, so alien in so
many ways, yet familiar. Achingly familiar, beyond any-

thing that had transpired between them these past two weeks.

Scott's eyes drifted shut as he felt Hope explore his face, just as she'd done earlier in her room, only this time there was a desperation that had been absent before. She needed to know more of him, to see more of him; he sensed it. As a gazer, it was something he understood all too well, that need to pry into things, to see beyond what was on the surface. He could only imagine how being nearly blind must suffocate her, especially at a tense and emotional moment like this one.

Any minute that *vlksai* would return, and although Hope said to trust the man, it took everything inside of him—every last ounce of resolve—not to whisk her out of this motel room and back to certain safety. But then there was just Hope, here beside him. Fingertips, stroking over his jaw, tracing and feeling. Human hands touching him.

He sucked in a breath as she trailed her thumbs over his closed eyes. "Why?" was all she asked, her husky, sexy voice filling the small distance between them. He swallowed hard, struggling to breathe even though his heart was about to explode out of his chest, it was thundering so rapidly.

"Why what?" he asked softly.

She jerked back, pulling her hands away, and he opened his eyes. "I-I wondered why you closed your eyes."

"To really feel you," he answered, taking her face within his own hands and drawing her lips to his. "I wanted to see things through your eyes right now. This moment."

"All that exists· is the purest sensations," she answered, brushing her lips over his. "Sense, touch."

"Desire," he added, hardly recognizing his own voice; it was that filled with lust.

She moved closer, practically climbing onto his lap, but halted, cautiously running her hand across his thigh. "What about your injured leg? Is it better?"

He shook off the question. "Don't worry about it." His leg felt perfectly fine; she felt more than perfectly fine, heavenly, right here atop him.

"You need to get back," she cautioned. "You're still recovering—you shouldn't be here."

He gritted his teeth, clasping both of his hands about her waist, anchoring her closer to his own tensed body. "I won't leave you to him." Between his legs an erection had filled his pants, straining and pulsing, begging for release. It hardly mattered that his leg ached a little bit; his third leg wanted only one thing: to fuck Hope Harper like mad, to drive into her, and hold her, and never let her out of his arms.

"I don't feel anything for him—it's you," she breathed against his cheek, and a stray strand of her blond hair tickled his face.

"You're asking me to trust you."

"Yes."

He'd never trusted anyone—anyone apart from Jared and a few of their most inner circle. He'd certainly never trusted a human, not the way she was asking it of him.

"Touch me, Hope," he begged suddenly. He needed to know—hell, he *had* to know what would happen if she did. Maybe if he was certain, he could let her walk away with their fugitive.

She nuzzled him, her lips warm and wet against the bristling beard of his cheek. "Where, Scott? Tell me, where?"

He growled, agonized that she was going to make him spell it out. "Between my legs, damn it." It was the wrong time, totally wrong, with every reason to get her out of here, to follow the other man's trail, but he couldn't seem to stop himself.

Just as she'd slowly felt out the terrain of his facial features, she slid one palm onto his upper thigh, then moved it into the place where both his legs met, finding the hard ridge of his cock. It swelled even more at her touch as slowly she rubbed her hand back and forth over his uniform pants, bunching the material. She wasn't gentle, not that he would have expected her to be. She worked him hard, then slid her other hand underneath the jutting erection and took hold of his balls, squeezing them until he groaned in painful ecstasy.

But she didn't relent. Working at the waistband of his pants, she managed to unzip the zipper and, with a quick jerk, unfasten them. His swollen shaft sprang free into her cupped hand, filling it heavily, and her cool fingers closed about his thick tip, squeezing, stroking. He growled low in the back of his throat, clenching his thighs against the bed. With one hand she spread him open wider, sliding her fingertips along the underside of his cock where a large vein pulsed.

"Is this what you had in mind?" she purred into his ear, stroking his balls, rolling them in her hand.

"Insanity." He grunted, jerking at her sweater, yanking it halfway up her chest. His palm made contact with one ripe, buxom breast. For such a small woman, there was one area where All had graced her with size—the one area that mattered most to him.

He pushed her face into the crook of his neck, and her grip on his long erection grew frantic, out of control, her strong hand sliding over him back and forth, until his own wetness slicked her motion.

Licking his ear with the tip of her warm tongue, she purred, "At least now I know how beautifully made you are," she teased, tightening her grip about him. "You feel . . . astounding."

And just that easily he was pushing her back into the mattress. He had her sweater up about her shoulders, had his own pants shimmied halfway down his thighs. Her pants were gone, seemingly by magic, just lost in the lust of the moment. They were a tangle of limbs and lust and emotion, each grasping at the other with such desperation, he'd never felt anything like it before, not with any woman.

"He'll come back soon," he cautioned in her ear,

shoving at his pants. As he rolled her beneath him he gasped slightly, and she stilled beneath him, clutching at both of his shoulders.

"We shouldn't do this—not with your leg."

"It barely hurts at all," he said, then added gruffly, "You be on top."

"You're not serious?" She collapsed into the pillows, seeming to study him, when he knew all she was doing was searching the darkness.

"I'll let you go with this other man because I trust you—but not before I make you mine," he told her, rolling her atop him as easily as he might have blown on a feather. "All mine, Hope. Understand? I won't hold back, not if you're going with him."

She nodded, and by the alarm clock light he saw slight fear on her face.

"You're afraid of me."

She slowly shook her head from side to side. "Never. Not at all."

He cupped her bottom, sliding her atop him. Only her panties separated their groins, and he lifted into the silky web of material between them, nudging against her despite the thin membrane of separation. "Then what?" he asked in a throaty, lusty voice.

"I'm afraid of falling this hard for you," she answered, bowing her head. "After this, I'll never feel the same. Everything will be five thousand times more intense."

"Good," he said, puffing his chest out. "That's how I want it. You knowing that you belong with me. Not any other man."

"It's Jake. Jake Tierny, that's his name." Scott stilled beneath her, his hips dropping back from their upward thrust. "Do you know that name?" she asked quickly.

"Never heard it before in my life," he admitted. That was what disturbed him. Yet something about it seemed to ring through the darkness, electrifying them both.

The blackness was filled with the sound of their huffing breath; neither spoke. Each knew the name had some massive significance between them; each felt it. But

Scott would be damned to hell if he was going to tell Hope that he understood—that he knew, despite everything between them, despite the fact that he was a panties-width away from making love to her—that Jake Tierny was the biggest obstacle they'd ever face. A mountain, a fortress, a freighter.

The gazer in him saw it all in that split-second moment of revelation: Jake Tierny would drive a wedge between them, and it would never go away. Because, quite simply, Hope Harper would always love Jake Tierny. The shot across eternity was heard right there in that bedroom.

"Get off me," he whispered, very gently taking hold of her and sliding her onto the mattress beside them.

"I want this," she insisted, but he reached to kiss her on the lips—a strange, chaste kiss for an insatiable lover like him.

"It's not the right time," he disagreed, slowly tasting her mouth, then her face. Sniffing at her to really draw her scent into his lungs. "Not like this."

"You said you wanted—"

"I have to chase him, Hope. You do know that, right? I can let you go, but he's my enemy."

"I don't believe that."

"I know you don't, but I've been at this war for a lot longer than you. I chase. You'll run, but in the end? I'm going to have this guy's balls on a chopping block." *Especially so he won't take you from me. Especially!*

"You could stay here, try to hear him out. He says he's your ally."

Scott rolled away from her, and Hope knew he'd placed his back to her. "If he comes here I have to kill him, Hope. And you've told me you don't want that." His voice sounded harsh, pained as a wounded animal. "I can give you a head start, but I can't let him go. Or you, if you go with him."

She felt a tugging motion that rocked the bed slightly, then heard his zipper as he closed his pants again. They'd been so freaking close to making love—to doing the one thing she wanted most in the world. For a long moment she considered telling him she'd forget Jake Tierny and his strange quest.

Scott blew out a tired-sounding sigh. She rubbed a hand along his back, surprised by the hard ridges of muscle, the way every line seemed so sharply defined. He had a lean, gorgeous body, not an ounce of fat or needless weight. She slipped her palm beneath his shirt, feeling the warm smoothness of the skin along his abdomen as she circled him from behind.

"I don't want to lose you." She caught herself with a laugh. "I mean, if I *have* you, which is pretty much a crazy stretch to begin with."

"You have me, Hope." He groaned softly. "Gods in heaven! Help my *vlksai* soul, but you have me. Completely."

"Then trust me," she urged, oddly aware that the room was growing brighter around them. "Please."

He laughed, a strange, bitter sound. "I do trust you, Hope," he told her. "But that man is my enemy—and more important? He's my king's enemy. I will have to stop him. My feelings for you can't come into play with that."

And the room around her seemed to fold in on itself, dividing her from him, pulling at her. She opened her eyes and found Jake Tierny examining her; at least, that was what it looked like through her fuzzy, splotchy eyesight. "Where's Scott?" she demanded, rubbing her eyes. "What's happening?"

"I left for a few minutes," Jake told her, his husky voice so different from that of the man she'd just been with.

"Scott was here—what happened?" None of it made sense.

"You were asleep, Hope. Scott's nowhere around here."

She jerked upward in bed, clasping at the bedspread, disoriented and feeling tears prickle her eyes. The bedside lamp was on, and she glanced first one way, then another, hardly able to believe that Scott hadn't truly been with her. Their experience together had been absolutely real—they'd nearly made love!

But as concrete and palpable as their time together had been, she could feel it receding like some distant shoreline. The only thing that lingered was his strange, altered scent.

"Do you smell anything?" she asked Jake, tilting her head up curiously, and he sank onto the bed across from her.

"What do you smell, Hope?" he countered.

"I asked the question."

He seemed to shrug, zipping up his parka. "Don't smell a thing—nothing at all."

But she knew he was concealing something—that whatever she'd just experienced with Scott, the strange and very real dream, was tied to the scent still infusing the small motel room.

"You're Antousian. Do your people have some kind of way that their scent changes? Something significant?"

But he ignored her question, pretty much his modus operandi, she'd been figuring out, and stood abruptly, car keys jangling in his hand. "We've gotta hit the road, and fast. They're going to close in on us soon, and they're not going to have mercy on me. Not for a minute—at least, if I know Scott Dillon like I think I do."

"Do you sense them? Are they nearby?" she asked, cursing herself for sounding so breathless.

He released a low, soft chuckle. "You always did have a soft spot for Lieutenant Dillon."

"You should know that he and I are . . ." Lovers? Not. In love? Maybe.

"Yeah, Hope?" he prompted, a strange smile in his voice.

"I'm with him, that's all. You should know that."

With two quick steps he had her pulled hard against his massive chest. She could feel his quickening heartbeat, and the heat of his breath fanned against her cheek as he bent low and whispered in her ear, "I never said I expected anything to happen between us. I only said that we were together. Once."

She felt her body tighten in reaction to his, and didn't dare make a move, not forward or back. But he released her as suddenly as he'd taken hold of her. Instantly she missed the heat of his body—not like she'd miss the warmth of a lover; no, that wasn't it. His natural body heat had comforted her on the deepest, most cellular level, as if nothing would ever harm her again—as if nothing ever possibly could. Her trust was not misplaced; in that moment she knew it for certain.

"Tell me what I need to do," she whispered, reaching toward him. "I'll do whatever I can to help you."

"When do you need another insulin shot?"

She thought about the shots she'd stored in the room's small fridge. "Probably right now."

"Go ahead, then; take it. Because I've got a plan."

Chapter Eleven

"Lieutenant!"

Scott was dimly aware of a presence. Perhaps Anna. Perhaps Hope, still connected with him somehow, linked with him in that half place where his spirit met the night wind.

Body! Need my body . . .

He grew more alert, more cognizant of the fact that he was still in his natural Antousian form. A ghost, nothing more. Pure spirit, he'd have said, if he were in a generous mood—but most days when it came to his own species he wasn't feeling particularly kind. It was exactly as Hope had whispered inside him during their dream meeting—he didn't have compassion for his own people. Especially for himself.

He groaned, the soft sound a whining moan of wind across the hoary field. Fresh snow swirled toward the ground, almost more than he could bear as each and every flake splintered through his essence. *Never so nothing, never so thin. Light. Dying . . .*

"Scott Dillon," the woman's voice cried out. And inside of his center everything seemed to focus into a bright, scorching point of light. *Is this death? Was I dying when I saw Hope?*

He couldn't possibly know, not like this, so ephemeral and lost.

Scott Dillon!

Perhaps that feminine voice belonged to All.

Take me back to her, he half prayed to the One who always circled him with protection, watched his back, no matter how bad the firefights got. *Take me back. Let me enter her dreams again. Let me know that she's safe.*

There were people who needed him, were counting on him. Loved him. It was the one thought that kept circling his ghost self like a ravenous bird of prey. And that bird would not let him forget, kept screeching at him, nudging at him, demanding his attention like the far-off sputtering gunfire of his enemies. He thought of Trajsek, that night so many years ago when he and Jared had been cornered in an impossible firefight.

Save her, the bird called out. *Come back! Save her! Come back!*

The eerie cry was that of his own heart: There was no choice. To save Hope from Jake Tierny, he had to find his way back from this tenuous place—back into physical form.

Veckus paced the deck of his battle cruiser, annoyed to the extreme. None among his ground troops had offered any insights about the Antousian, the one he'd detected breeching the time wall. Now, here aboard his main cruiser, even his officers seemed thoroughly dullwitted. Was it always up to him to intuit their enemies' every move? Granted, he'd been gifted as a gazer since childhood, but still . . . it grew tiresome to be the most insightful out of their entire force. Then again, he was the leader of that same force, so perhaps it was only fair that he should see the most.

Some days, however, his position was more than wearying. Some days he just wanted to be a grunt, not in charge of the entire Earth conquest, but alas, that was not his fate.

Stopping at the main console, he pulled up his carefully drawn diagram, turning to face his underlieutenants. "So, it's as I have described," he told the small group of women and men gathered on the cruiser's deck. "All the energy radiants indicate this area." He jabbed at the screen with his pointer, outlining a one-hundred-mile-square area inside Yellowstone Park. "This is where the first interdimensional passing took place. And then, yesterday, this is where another transpired."

The only one of his lieutenants who possessed a shred of initiative, Dayron Lenlalt, spoke up. "And how are you certain of this fact, Commander?" the auburn-haired young man asked. "What served as your criteria?" Dayron frequently tested him, and usually Veckus respected that fact: Today it simply bored and exasperated him.

Veckus turned on Dayron, grasping him by the shoulders. "Because I felt it. That's how. I'm the only gazer on this ship or in our midst. Gods knows why, but the fact remains true"—he spun with his pointer, jabbing it against the console display—"and this is where we will corner our Antousian brother. Find out if he's on our side . . . or theirs."

"We've known that area was significant for a long time, but we've always come up empty-handed," Dayron countered, unflustered as always by Veckus's outbursts. It was a trait that Veckus occasionally admired in the young man. Nevertheless, he should have had Dayron shot long ago for his outspoken ways, and made a mental note to put that execution on his calendar for sometime next year—pending, of course, a performance review. As irritating as Dayron could be, he was also quite useful on occasion, and it wouldn't do to make a hasty decision about his fate.

"Not this time." Veckus took his pointer and tapped it lightly atop Dayron's head for emphasis. "This time, Lieutenant, we will hit pay dirt."

Jared sat on a large throw pillow in his upstairs study, meditating, which really amounted to staring into the fire, blankly wondering why everything he knew about the present had become so constantly riddled by the future. Why the unknown always impinged upon the world in which he lived. Scott and Anna had yet to return, hadn't called or contacted base at all, and now the first pink of morning light had begun cresting over the valley below the compound. Remaining calm required a tremendous amount of discipline when he really just wanted to send an entire legion after the two missing soldiers.

Kelsey's life had been directly endangered just hours earlier—that, after they'd had shattering, heat-induced lovemaking in their shower. Even now his body remained tense and on edge after spilling his burning seed within his wife. Jared shifted on the pillow, rubbed his jaw, and wondered—wondered if, against all that seemed possible, he and Kelsey might not have created a new life together. Just when he'd believed it utterly impossible.

With a slight shake of his head, he brushed off his personal ruminations, focusing instead on the immediate problem at hand: that a fugitive, an Antousian from the future who claimed to be an ally, had penetrated their supposedly impenetrable fortress. The evidence implied that the man might just be what he claimed to be, someone with intimate knowledge of their workings, their rebel faction, and—most important—of their enemies' future plans.

On the other hand, given the dangerous mitres data that was fused within Kelsey's mind, the intruder might well be after her—might want to kidnap her, link with her, hoping to steal the codes lodged inside of her essence. Jared shuddered at the thought. That Kelsey was the sole key to powering their greatest weapon had unsettled him from the beginning; that she now welcomed it—embraced it—well, he didn't like that fact one bit. Yet their efforts to remove the codes had proved fruitless, revealing one sure and certain fact: His love was, quite simply, the keeper of their greatest weapon and power. She was, as the prophets had foretold, the Beloved of Refaria.

A knock interrupted his quiet internal ramblings, sounding sharply in the silence of his study. This place was his sanctuary, and only rarely did any of his soldiers bother him here.

"Come in," he called, keeping his gaze on the fire.

Behind him he heard heavy footfalls and, without even looking, recognized them as belonging to Marco McKinley, his personal Madjin protector.

"My lord," he began cautiously, "I apologize for the intrusion."

Jared gave a slight wave, glancing over his shoulder. "I am lost in my own mind, Marco. Come, join me."

Marco studied him with an inscrutable, almost cautious expression. "My lord?" he asked uncertainly, but Jared indicated another pillow beside him.

"I have need of my Madjin," he said with a quiet laugh. "Come, sit with me and speak freely."

Marco smiled at him, not quite meeting his gaze, which was the way with all the Madjin protectors. They believed it a supreme transgression to stare into the eyes of their king and queen, although this particular Madjin was certainly part of a new breed. From what Jared had gathered, the young man had been raised mostly on Earth, taught by Jared's own mentor and protector, Sabrina. Still, there was something very different in the way he behaved around Jared. Familiar, traditional, but . . . refreshing. Beyond that, the man had made Jared's cousin Thea Haven happier than he'd ever imagined her to be. And their marriage made Marco not only his personal Madjin, but his cousin as well.

Marco settled his rangy frame beside Jared, crossing his legs in the familiar Refarian way, and stared thoughtfully into the fire, mirroring Jared's own expression.

"Talk to me, Marco," Jared encouraged with a brisk nod. "I sense that something is heavy on your mind."

Marco cut his gaze sideways. "The Antousian . . . I can't shake what he said, sir."

There was a pregnant pause as Marco waited for Jared's reply. "Go on," Jared encouraged with a slight nod.

"He was convinced that I mean you harm—he knew about my other self, the dark one that came here to hurt you—" Marco made a slightly pained sound, a kind of strangled gasp, and Jared felt his protector's pain as if it were his own.

Jared turned to face the man. "We have already discussed this, you and I," he said. "I trust you completely, Marco."

"But he knew. All of it," he said, his face twisted into a mask of pain. "And even if it doesn't matter what I might have done, sir, that man came from that same world. There's no other way he could know."

"I agree."

"So you believe he's what he claimed?"

"I'm not sure. I believe he's come from the future, but it's his intentions I'm uncertain of. You're an empath—what did you detect from him?"

Marco bowed his head, his black eyebrows quirking together in concentration. "It was very . . . unusual, sir, but there was a great deal of confusion inside the man. Fear, loyalty, anger." He shook his head slightly. "I don't think he actually meant you harm, despite my initial impression in the moment. The longer I've thought about it, something about the man is disturbing me a great deal, but not because he means you harm."

"Tell me what you mean."

"I . . . I'm not sure. Maybe it's nothing, but it was as if he's a twin, sir. As if he's brought someone else through time with him, and maybe it's that person who is our major threat. But that man? The one named Jake Tierny? I think he genuinely came here to kill me—the other me—and now that he's wound up empty-handed, he's not sure what to do or where to go. But it's this other man, the one whom he's linked to, that has me disturbed, because of the dark connection between the two of them."

"Perhaps Jake didn't realize someone followed him through interdimensional space."

"That would be ironic—that he was trying to follow me through time, but in the process someone else tailed him. Without his knowing, I mean."

Jared scrubbed an open palm over the top of his head, thinking about the implications of what Marco was saying. "It's a distinct possibility," he agreed.

"We need to bring this Antousian back into the compound," Marco continued. "We need to question him and find out what he really knows."

"Lieutenant Dillon is still tracking him."

"It's going to take a larger team, sir. We both know it, and that's a risk—out in the open like that, among the humans. But capturing him should be our top priority."

Scott studied the faintest pink in the dawn sky, Anna kneeling beside him. He was a lucky bastard—he'd almost been unable to Change back into his physical body, but his love for Hope had clinched the deal. He'd managed to, only for her . . . because she needed him, pure and simple. Right now he was just trying to regain his equilibrium, and so he stared at the fading stars overhead.

His species had a word for what he'd just experienced, a word that had no translation in English, but basically meant "spirit slipping." It was the point when an Antousian was in his nonmaterial form, but his hold on life itself became tenuous. That point in his formless journey when the spirit self and the physical body became so disconnected that it was as if the line between life and death wavered.

He'd read in his people's scriptures about the freedom one could know at such times, but it was always considered highly dangerous. He'd also read that when caught in that tremulous hold between life and death, body and spirit, that his people were often drawn toward those they loved the most. To the people and things that held the greatest power over them.

"A transport is on the way," Anna explained.

"Don't risk that," he said with a scowl. "I'm all right."

"You're bleeding out onto the snow, sir. It's a stealth craft; we're off the main road and we're getting you out of here. It's a done deal."

"So you're giving the orders?" Scott blinked up at her. "To your commanding officer?"

She gave a single, brisk nod of her dark head. "Man down, sir. I'm next in command."

Closing his eyes, he clutched at his thigh and nodded. "Very well, Lieutenant."

Jake surveyed the roadside where his tour guide had stopped to check with the snowmobile rental company. He wasn't comfortable just sitting with Hope, only the two of them in the van, waiting—not with her many unanswerable questions. So he'd stepped out onto the almost dark roadside, surveying the landscape. He could see their guide through the large glass windows of the diner that did double duty as both restaurant and guide company. The man was waving his arms and talking; Jake felt suspicious, wondering if he was adding way too much narration about their unplanned—and highly paid for—private tour inside the park.

Of course, there were always logistics if you were going into Yellowstone in the middle of the winter. True, there would be only a few hundred people on snowmobiles within the park later today, especially with a 750-sled limit per day, but on the other hand, you couldn't go in without a guide. No way, no how. So Jake had arrived at this particular company, one of the smaller outfits, and essentially bribed them into guiding him in on a solo tour. They'd been booked, and it had taken more than seven hundred dollars to arrange for a private, all-day booking.

Yeah, well, the guide had no idea that he'd be offered even more money once they were inside the park so that Jake could go off trail. But he'd cross that bridge when he got to it. Money could be plenty compelling, especially back in this time, when it still meant something on Earth. Before the paper became as meaningless as the government creeds and images printed on it. Jake had been sure to stuff his jacket with plenty of the bills before stepping into the mitres, knowing that it would come in handy back in this time. After he'd arrived, he'd double-checked the dates on the bills against the current year, just to be sure he wouldn't tip his hand.

Reaching into the pocket of his parka, he fingered a thick roll of bills, and figured he could offer their guide, Randy, a hefty bribe once they were deep enough inside the park. Jake knew the paths to the mitres by memory—the way to navigate across frozen lakes and snow-draped landscape. What would normally amount to a harsh climb during the summer months was far easier in temperatures of negative ten degrees or lower and with a good base of powder. All you needed was a hard-driving snowmobile, which was precisely what he'd rented for the day.

Glancing far down each length of the highway, fairly sure that none of Jared's crew were on to them, Jake climbed back into the van. Hope glanced up at him, her gray eyes unfocused as she searched his face. "What's going on?" she asked as he settled onto the bench seat beside her.

"I think he's just checking on our sleds. We'll pick those up at the park entrance." He faced forward, anything other than looking into those beautiful, familiar eyes that had the power of the universe over him.

"So we're going where, exactly? Inside Yellowstone?"

"That's where the mitres chamber is located." She didn't seem surprised, and he figured Scott or someone else within the rebel faction had already told her as much.

She raked a shaky hand through her long blond hair. "You're going to try and use it to go back to your time."

He nodded, but then caught himself. She was right: He definitely wasn't used to her as a blind woman. Early on during their time together, the medics had reversed her retinopathy, restoring her vision. If only they'd taken care of everything else. If only they'd gone the distance, he thought, pressing his eyes shut against the heart-breaking memories of their shared past. He couldn't turn back time—not really—so it did no good to focus on what might have been . . . what should have been.

He turned to face her. "How's Chris?" he asked. Funny, but suddenly it wasn't just Hope he missed, but her entire family.

She jerked beside him in surprise. "My brother? What do you know about him?"

He had to laugh. "Chris Harper, your twin. What's he doing these days?"

"Chris is fine," she said, but there was protective caution in the words. The woman still didn't believe he meant her no harm—even as she'd taken an insane leap of trust to come along with him.

"How about Laurie? Michael? Your parents?" There—if he named her family members, made it clear how much he really did know about her life, maybe that would gain even more of her trust.

"Okay." She blew out a sigh. "How do you know my brothers and my sister? Really, what is this connection that we share, the two of us? I have to know, or I won't go any farther. I'll be staying here, calling *Chris* to come pick me up."

Reflexively, he placed his palm on her thigh. "Please, Hope, don't do that. I'll explain everything once we're at the mitres. By then I should be leaving you for good."

She stared down at his hand, and although he felt her body burn against his, felt as if that simplest contact could sear him, change him, he didn't pull away.

"What is it between us, Jake?" After a moment, she placed her own hand tentatively over his. "Why do I have this huge soft spot for you? Were we lovers? That's the way it seems to me."

"Once." He felt a thick knot lodge in his throat. "Long ago for me."

"Did I choose Scott?" She tilted her pale, slightly freckled face toward him. "Is that why you don't like him? Or did we . . . end because I died?"

He sucked in a breath, quickly pulling his hand out

from underneath hers. "No talk about the future, remember?"

"That's a stupid, totally unfair rule!" she shouted, her voice reverberating off the doors of the van. "I don't believe this!"

He bowed his head, mentally apologizing to Kelsey; she had insisted that he not reveal anything about the future once arriving back here in the past. Still, he hadn't expected to encounter Hope, and as devoted as he was to his queen, he just couldn't hold back—no matter what he'd promised.

"I loved you more than I ever thought I could love another person, sweetheart. But, yes, you're right. You did die." He couldn't go on, not for a moment, but finally he found his voice. "I died that day too. I've been dead inside ever since."

Hope ran her fingers through her hair, trying to blink back the tears that had filled her eyes. What could she say to this man—what could she possibly come up with to counter this future truth? She was going to die for sure, unless he told her what fate awaited her. More than that, it was the pain she felt in him, how physically palpable his heartbreak was because of her.

Hope looked away from him, staring out the van window beside her, the bright interior lights of the diner a blur. Lifting a hand, she rubbed it over the window, and the world outside grew clearer as she wiped away the interior fog. Pressing her nose against the glass, she tried to determine exactly where they were. She hated never knowing or understanding the most basic facts about where she was or what was happening. A year ago she'd been fully sighted; now she was in the dark, and in so many more ways than just her eyesight. She had to get to the truth here, ferret it out.

"So," she said at last, "you won't tell me how I died? If you love me—*loved* me, that is—don't you want to save me?" The tears burning her eyes finally began to spill, nausea overcoming her. She put a hand to her belly, fighting it. "I have to know so I can stop my death from happening. Is it my diabetes? Something else?"

Beside her she heard Jake make a pained sound; then he swallowed, but said nothing.

"Do you still love me?" she continued.

His strong arm slipped along the back of the bench seat as he drew her close against him; that same warmth she'd felt in his arms earlier instantly infused her body.

"I will always love you, Hope," he whispered softly. "Until the day I do finally die."

She pressed her face against his shoulder. "If that's true, then tell me how I died."

His next words shocked her to the marrow, caused her to jolt in alarm. "I killed you, sweetheart. I did it all." And then, unbelievable as it was, he bent much closer and kissed her full on the lips. "I'm a murderer and a thief. A liar. And a dead man. But I promise you this—I won't let you get killed again. Not by me, not if I have any choice about it."

She felt his mouth brush over hers, the warmth of it. He had full, lush lips, and his breath was hot against her face; he had that elevated natural heat that she'd felt when Scott kissed her. Alien, not entirely human. But what struck her most was the scratchy texture of his beard growth—because even that reminded her of Scott. All her thoughts went to the man she loved, even as she wondered how it was so easy to kiss this one.

"Kiss me again," she begged, and he did, cupping her face in the palm of his large, calloused hand.

His tongue licked across her lips, tasting her; his other hand clasped the back of her head, tilting her toward him so he could kiss her more deeply. The kiss was erotic and hot, awakening some lost part of her that she couldn't even name. She gave in to it, yielding with her mouth, forgetting with her body. His arms folded about her; she forged into him, planting both hands against his chest. She could feel the thundering of his heart, and his hand grazed the edge of her breast; then, obviously not caring who saw, he cupped her breast, squeezing and rolling it.

What am I doing? I'm already involved with Scott— and now I'm letting Jake touch me like this. She couldn't get a clear fix on how it was possible to care about each of the men, to feel this kind of raw, unmitigated passion with Jake, just as she did with Scott.

Jake slipped one hand low and eased it upward between her legs. Scott would have done the exact same thing; the realization sobered her, brought her back to Jake's confession. She stopped his hand.

"You killed me," she murmured against his lips. "With a gun? With a knife? How did you do it, Jake?" She didn't even care what might be the truth, so abandoned was she to his simplest kiss.

He ran his fingers through her hair, his heavy breathing filling the silence between the two of them. "I killed you," he whispered against her cheek at last, "with my love."

Chapter Twelve

Back to square one. Scott awoke, adjusting himself against the pillows of yet another hospital bed. Feeling his right leg, he discovered a thick bandage wrapped about his thigh. Last he remembered, he'd been in Hope's motel room, trying to convince her that they should go ahead and make love.

But not really. The actual last thing he remembered, now that he'd managed to force his swirling, medication-scattered thoughts into focus, was that he'd almost died on the side of the road. Somehow Anna had gotten him back here to the compound. Splintered images of the transport, the medics working on him in midair, these things filtered through his mind.

Yeah, totally back to square one, he thought again. *Only worse. She's with him, not me.* He'd slip-spirited her, completely entered her sleep and connected with her. It had been sublime, feeling her in his arms, so close—but it had almost shattered his heart. After all, she trusted an Antousian, his enemy. Not only that, but she actually believed that Jake knew she was going to die—that she was, in fact, already dead in that man's future.

Damn it all to hell! If this Jake had loved her, why hadn't he protected her? And where had he, Scott, been during all of this? He found it impossible to believe that he'd have done anything to lose her. One thing was for damned sure: He wasn't going to let anything happen to so much as a hair on her head. Not on his watch. Nothing and no one would get to her; at least, not if he had any say in the matter.

"You aren't going to die, Hope. I won't let it happen." He flinched, realizing he'd actually spoken the words out loud. For a moment his eyes drifted shut, and he saw her just as she'd been in the motel room, straddling him. Her shimmering blond hair, loose and long; her compact, lightweight body astride his. How wet she'd been for him, how ready, just the tip of his erection pushing against the thin veil of her panties. Just his hands about the sultry curves of her waist and hips, the feel of her full breasts swelling within his palms. They'd been so close to making love, so very close, but he'd been the one to put the brakes on.

Of course, did any of it really matter when you were talking about a spirit meeting? Who'd stopped the action, who'd lusted, who'd wanted to thrust deep inside the other. What did any of it even amount to, anyway? All was lost; she was lost.

None of it, not a scrap, had been real, he thought, rubbing his bandaged leg hopelessly.

He slammed a fist against the bed rail, not even feeling the pain as it penetrated his fingers, the heel of his palm. Hammering his fist against the metal bar over and over again, he sought to simply numb the suffocating grief that strangled his heart.

One more slam, and this time he drew blood when his fist impacted the railing latch. *"Meshdki, fliishki! Meshdki!"* he yelled. He shouted several more curse words, then finally fell silent, bringing his bleeding knuckles to his mouth.

"I'll take that as a signal of your frustration." It was Jared, standing in the room's doorway, assessing him with a slightly bemused look.

"Jareshk, I'm not good company right now."

Jared strode toward him. "Nor do I expect you to be."

Scott turned in the bed, shutting his eyes. The last

thing he could deal with was his best friend and king. Jared's footsteps echoed off the ceiling, the sound of his boots a rhythmic pattern as he came to stand beside the hospital bed.

"I lost him." Scott clutched the sheet between his fingers, still looking away. "I'm so sorry, but I failed you, my lord."

"Friend, you followed well and long, making excellent progress in tailing the Antousian."

Scott's eyes flew open. "I lost *her*."

Jared took hold of the bedside chair and spun it around, straddling it. "You didn't lose her; you lost the trail, but you'll pick it up again—later." Jared gave him a faint smile, the kind that meant he was seeing straight through Scott's bullshit. "Once you get some recovery time in, and have the chance to heal a little, you'll be on the chase again."

"Until then?" Scott stole a glance at his commander.

"You rest, S'Skautsa. You've been running far too long. Too many years this war has gripped you, exhausted you, and you've finally hit a point where you have no other choice but to rest."

Scott shook his head. "There's no time, not while that *vlksai*'s got her. I'm not worried about you, Jared. You're safe here, deep within the compound. We've elevated security levels, heightened all the perimeters, but Hope"—he clutched his head with both hands, pulling at his short hair in desperation—"she's vulnerable; she needs her insulin shots . . . she can't see well. Anything could happen to her out there in that godsforsaken cold. *Jake Tierny* could do anything to her; she's totally at his mercy. I have to stop that—I don't have any other choice but to go after him."

Jared propped his chin on his hands, thoughtful in his demeanor. "These human women are fighters and have feisty, strong streaks." Unexpectedly, his king chuckled. "Believe me, I am married to one, and that's why I know that Hope will be all right."

"I'm afraid for her life." Scott gripped the bed rail and sat up urgently.

Jared's gaze locked with his meaningfully. "So you've found her too."

Scott shook his head, confused. "I just told you, she's lost."

"But you've found *her*—your one true soul mate, the one who is meant for you. Out of all the universe, the one woman you are destined to be with. You have found her." Jared's eyes grew wide, and he broke into a beaming smile. "And there you were, giving me such unrelenting grief about my feelings for Kelsey."

Scott shot him a sheepish look. "I always told you that their species was delectable in bed."

"Yes," Jared said, an undeniable smirk on his face, "we've discussed your insatiable taste for human women."

Scott's face burned. In fact, what Jared had observed just a few weeks earlier was that Scott's "taste" for human women could not be satisfied. That was exactly how his king had put it.

Scott stared at the ceiling, willing the flush on his face to somehow dissipate. "Maybe I was always looking for her, all those nights in the bars." He released a cynical, bitter laugh. "And now I'm back to searching for her all over again—only this time the stakes are dangerously high."

Jared grew serious again, his black eyes narrowing keenly. "There are other ways we can trail her while you recuperate. Even if you are the best damned Antousian tracker I've ever seen, we still have our other methods."

Scott shook his head, staring at the tiled ceiling overhead. "I had his trail and I couldn't keep up."

"You can't blame yourself for being injured." Jared shook his head, patting the back of his chair. "You can't blame yourself for any of this."

Scott bolted up in bed, exclaiming, "I blame myself that she's in this at all! Don't you get it? I love her, J.

I love her and told her I'd protect her . . . I promised her that."

Jared put a hand on his arm. "My dear friend, it's not always your responsibility to resolve everything. To take care of everything. Sometimes, S'Skautsa, you should let the rest of us take care of you. I will find her for you—and this Jake Tierny. I will find them and bring them both back into the camp."

Scott tried to argue, but a hazy sleep began to overtake him very suddenly. Glancing sideways at his IV, he realized too late that new pain medication had been uploaded via the bedside computer. Obviously, it was very intense medication.

He chuckled woozily. "You bastard." He pointed a wavering, accusing finger at his king. "Y'knew I'd've tried to go. You've fuckin' drugged my ass."

He heard his best friend laugh, a slow, sluggish, and drawn-out sound. "The only way you'll ever get well is to rest."

And then Jared's smiling face appeared over him, slightly off-kilter, and Scott hurled a few more choice insults at his commander before sliding into sleep's welcoming arms.

Jared needed to eat. Kelsey had actually been the one to point out how infrequently he stopped to take care of himself, asking if his species took meals less often than humans did.

"No, I simply stay too occupied much of the time," he'd told her, and seen the immediate look of reproach in her clear, beautiful eyes.

So, at present he was famished and, determined to be an obedient husband, he strode into the kitchen to see what their cook had in the works for lunch. It was still early yet, but with his upcoming council meeting, he knew there wouldn't be time later in the day for a meal. At least not until nighttime, when he hoped to dine fireside with Kelsey, slowly and delectably feeding her himself. Ah, a thrilling thought! But it wouldn't satisfy his current mealtime needs.

Standing in the center of the kitchen, the smell of vegetables wafting through the room, he welcomed the familiar scent of mushrooms on the stove, and greens and fresh tomatoes on the chopping block. Lately Cook had begun preparing baked chicken just for Kelsey— the rest of them were vegetarians, although they did eat seafood. Oddly enough, he registered the absence of any kind of meat at all, including the shrimp Kelsey seemed to love so much.

"Cook," he said, stepping near the stovetop, "what are you preparing for the queen today? Only vegetables? Please remember that her diet is quite different from our own."

The heavyset man gave a light bow, wiping both hands on his long apron. "My lord, the queen specifically asked that we only cook the vegetables for now. No more meat—thank the gods! I could hardly stand the smell of it myself."

Rubbing his brow, Jared wondered what the impetus had been for her latest dietary request. "When did she ask this?"

"Just today, Your Highness . . . came in here and said the smell of the baking chicken made her feel ill. I immediately removed it from the oven. Right away, sir."

Jared nodded, but the revelation didn't make much sense. Why would Kelsey suddenly be turned off of her natural diet? It was confounding indeed. Perhaps she worried that she was making unique demands? Jared wasn't clear at all; Kelsey had never been afraid of expressing her needs.

"Cook, did she say anything else?" he ventured.

"Only that she required baked potatoes." The cook began to laugh. "Several of them, my lord, that's what the lady said. Requested that they be 'loaded,' whatever that means. I didn't want to ask her; no, I didn't."

"Loaded? Like a gun?" Jared scratched his head, more puzzled than ever.

"So she said, sir." The cook gave another slight bow. "Perhaps you might ask my lady what she means about these gunlike potatoes? I'm afraid of asking, sir. Just afraid to rankle a lady when she's . . . you know. In that way."

Jared planted a hand on his hip and stared at the man who had served his meals for the past six years. "In *that way,* Cook? What way? The way she wants these heavy ammo potatoes? You must explain this culinary situation to your commander."

His cook actually blushed. "Ah, sir, never you mind me." He gave a light wave. "Just go and ask the lady."

The doctor had agreed to a confidential visit, not in the quarters that Kelsey shared with Jared, but in Thea and Marco's smaller rooms. Thea had grinned conspiratorially at her request. "Oh, I so hope this is it," she had whispered in Kelsey's ear.

Now as the two of them sat on her small sofa, waiting for the doctor to arrive, Kelsey felt the need to backpedal a little. Maybe she'd jumped the gun based on the slimmest of evidence: the strange burning in her belly that hadn't stopped since last night, and her revulsion when she'd encountered the smell of cooking meat. It wasn't much to go on, not really, and even more than that, the timing just didn't add up to a pregnancy. Not this soon.

"Thea, I might be wrong." Kelsey turned sideways on the sofa, hugging one of the pillows against her stomach. "It can't even be possible, not really. We just made love last night."

Thea beamed at her, raising an eyebrow. "And you've also been making love for almost a month, right?"

Kelsey bowed her head, feeling her face flush. "Of course, but the feeling"—she patted the pillow where it rested over her belly—"this burning sensation really only began after we made love last night."

"Which would make perfect sense," the alien observed knowingly. "He's in heat; I can sense it—has been for a few days—and more than that, he's been in high heat for the past day or so. He's totally fertile, burning up with it, so if it were going to happen, now would be the time."

Kelsey closed her eyes, trying not to cringe from sheer embarrassment; it was just too bizarre that her sex life was literally a subject of intergalactic interest now. "High heat? I hate to ask, but—"

Thea's blond eyebrows shot upward toward her hairline. "That's only the ultimate point where a Refarian male, especially a D'Aravni, has the highest fertility."

"And how do you really know that about him?"

Kelsey thought of how rabid Jared had been during their lovemaking, how pushed beyond reason and unable to stop himself. Of course Thea was right, but she still wondered exactly what evidence her new cousin was operating from.

Thea turned to face Kelsey, leaning against the arm of the other end of the couch. "I'm an intuitive; of course I know. I see it on him, smell it." She smiled almost shyly at Kelsey. "Besides, I've been cycling since I was a teenager, so I can sense it in any male of my kind."

Kelsey rubbed her knees, glancing toward the door. If the doctor would just arrive, then maybe they could stop speculating and really get down to the truth. "But I might not have even been ovulating. Just because it's the right time for him doesn't mean it's the right time for *me*."

Thea laughed, shaking off her question. "It's all about his seed. It doesn't matter what's happening in your body. In our species, it's the male who sets the stage and brings about conception. You've got to remember, he's not human, Kelsey. . . . I know it's easy to forget."

"But if the egg doesn't, well, drop down in there—"

"His essence draws it out. Plain and simple." Thea rose to her feet, patting her arm. "Stop worrying so much! Of course you're pregnant."

Kelsey pressed a hand to her cheek, flushing even more. "Just like that, huh? I'm totally carrying his baby?"

Thea moved to the door, opening it before the doctor who stood on the other side of the threshold had even knocked. With a glance back at Kelsey, she said, "Some things, my lady, an intuitive will always understand." She waved the doctor in. "This man will confirm what you and I already know to be true."

Kelsey had the bizarre urge to run giggling from the room. Yet the doctor who approached her, then gave a low bow, only served to reinforce the fact that nothing about her life was a dream—and that she was, in fact, most likely pregnant with a future alien king or queen.

Chapter Thirteen

Hope climbed out of the tour van, blinking at the bright morning light. Crisp mountain air filled her nostrils, and although she couldn't make out solid details of the landscape, she gathered that they were in a large rest area, everything covered in heavy snow. She trailed her fingers along the van door, not sure of her surroundings.

Jake took hold of her hand, slipping it through the crook of his arm. "Just stick with me. We'll be pulling out of here in a few more minutes."

The motors of numerous snowmobiles droned around them, diesel and gasoline fumes filling her nostrils. She heard the loud lurch of motors turning; then, as one after another snowmobile took off around them, the rushing Doppler effect filled her ears.

She looked up into Jake's face, able for the first time to make out his physical appearance a little better than before. He had dark brown hair, olive skin, and it seemed as if his eyes were light green—much lighter than she would have expected with his overall dark looks. She couldn't be sure, but it was the best assessment she'd gotten of him, much better than in the motel room or even in the medical area hallway.

Several snowmobiles pulled up beside them, then came to a stop, their motors dying. "Moving out!" their tour guide called. "Make sure you've got your helmets and gloves on. It's gonna be a cold ride to Old Faithful."

"Old Faithful?" She reached out a hand to touch

Jake's face, feeling the rugged contours of jaw and skin. "What exactly are you trying to accomplish inside the park? I thought you needed help with your"—she formed quotation marks with her fingers—" 'future problem.' I don't see how snowmobiling and park rangers fit into that scenario. Oh, that's right—I forgot, we're going to the mitres."

"Come on, folks," their guide said, trudging past them. "Suit on up."

Jake stepped apart, letting her arm fall away from where she held on to him loosely. He left her standing there, waiting, and she got the idea that he was inspecting their sled.

"You ever been on a snowmobile, Hope?" He thrust a helmet toward her, and it bumped into her belly. She took hold of it awkwardly, feeling the shape of it, prodding the padding that lined its interior.

"I like to be in the driver's seat." She turned the helmet within her hands, finding the strap, and carefully placed it atop her head. "By the time I was ready to try snowmobiling, my vision wasn't good enough."

Jake laughed, low and knowingly. "That's what I thought." He adjusted her helmet, fastening the strap beneath her chin. It was an oddly protective gesture, and it occurred to her that this man had spent a long time trying to care for her. Just as Scott had promised to do, she thought, and felt a spasm of guilt. Not just guilt, but loneliness—as if she'd never see him again.

"If you know me as well as you say you do, wouldn't you know whether I'd ever been on a snowmobile or not?" Scott would have known—he'd have memorized everything about her and her experiences.

"I can't remember what you'd done this far back. It's a lot to keep up with." He gave her visor a sharp tug, lowering it over her face. "Keep this down unless you want your nose and face to freeze off. That wind whips pretty hard, and we're going to be covering a lot of ground."

"What? You didn't rent me my own sled?" she teased, watching him climb onto the seat.

Jake snorted. "You've always had a black sense of humor, love."

She studied him as he pulled his own helmet onto his head, and tried to figure out what he even really looked like. Handsome, she would bet, and overly large; that much had been obvious since the beginning. What she really wished was that she could look into his eyes—those green eyes she'd glimpsed—and see what his intentions truly were. She climbed cautiously behind him, planting both feet on the running boards.

Ahead of them, their tour guide powered up his sled, and then Jake did likewise, the machine sending vibrations through her body. "Hold on to me!" he shouted over the engine. "This thing's going to really move."

She wrapped her arms about his waist, burrowing her face against his back. "What are you doing, Jake? And how do I figure in?"

But he never heard her, not over the noisy motor, and with a lurch they took off over the snowy road.

At the exterior of his council chambers, Jared leaned close for an iris imprint, then a further sensory sweep, including a retinal scan. Once his identity had been verified, the sleek doors to the chambers slid open and he stepped into the much darker interior room. The lighting inside the council room was always kept low and dim; that way it was easier to view the elders' silvery holographic images being transmitted all the way from Refaria. As usual on days when he had to deal with his council, Jared felt edgy and uptight. Watching the biotechs prep the data portal—a large dais that he personally believed was the elders' way of forcing him onto something resembling a throne—he mentally scrolled through the meeting's agenda.

One topic he was absolutely certain would be on today's schedule, already after only a few weeks since his formal sealing and marriage to Kelsey, was the matter of the succession. Frankly, he'd often wondered if the elders had too little to occupy them while he was in exile; they seemed far too fixated on traditions and maneuvering within the council. It was enough to make Jared thankful that they were back on Refaria, and he was here on Earth; he had far fewer dealings with them this way.

The lead biotech signaled that Jared could assume position in the data portal, and he dropped into the large, thronelike chair. Thus began another sensory scan of his vitals, more detailed than the first one required to gain entrance to the chambers. After his readings were taken, there was an ambient hum as the data was uploaded into the portal, thereby giving him clearance for an open link with the council.

One by one, each council member took their place in the semicircle about him, placing one fist over their hearts and giving a bow of respect. Their images were uneven, faltering, but it was still pretty damn good, considering the massive distance that separated them from one another. Refarian technology allowed them to access energy packets flowing much faster than the speed of light, so that he and the elders were able to interact in these chambers in real time, even though separated by many, many light-years and many galaxies as well.

Today Elder Graeon took the lead, his long silver hair drawn into a neat ponytail down his back. Graeon had been in his maturity for as long as Jared could remember, all the way back to Jared's boyhood, yet the man still looked fairly young. It was typical for Refarian males to reach maturity—that time when they were no longer fertile—in their early forties. All except the royal lines, who entered both their prime and their decided lack of it far too early. Jared was pushing the envelope at thirty years of age, and the absence of a successor was always the hot topic in these chambers.

The circle gathered about him wanted only one thing: not leadership, or wisdom, but quite simply an heir.

Sometimes, on days like this one, it left Jared feeling not just inadequate, but quite like a figurehead—whatever it meant to be a deposed and exiled figurehead, at that.

Graeon kept one fist over his heart. "My lord, how is our new queen? Does she fair well in the midst of our rebellion?"

Jared stretched his legs, instantly restless in the metal data portal—and instantly angry. If they were leading with the queen, the next question would surely be . . .

"And how go the mating rites, as well, my lord?" Graeon continued. "As you well know, time is of the essence. All the more because you have chosen a human as your mate. Your bio readings show an elevated body temperature; other elements of your vital scans also display indications that you may, in fact, be cycling. We assume you are already aware?"

Jared laughed, reaching a low and threatening note on purpose. "Oh, yes, you may assume that I am quite aware of my mating season. It's fairly difficult to miss, wouldn't you all agree?" He met Graeon's gaze and held it, forcing the man to flush deeply.

Leaning one elbow on the arm of the portal, Jared studied the semicircle of leaders. "Shall I tell you how many times I've bedded my new wife? Is that the sort of information you seek today, Elder Graeon? Shall I describe my sexual prowess and how very successful the queen and I have found ourselves upon entering the heat?"

Graeon bowed his head, giving it a slight shake, but before he could reply Jared continued. "We have had this conversation on multiple occasions. Now that I have married and taken a mate, I can no longer abide such intimate analysis of my fertility, my sex life, my chance of siring an heir. If you feel the need to discuss it"— Jared waved about the circle of them—"then let it not be in this room, in my presence."

He was about to rail that, furthermore, when and how—and just how *many* times—he and Kelsey tried to conceive a child was none of their business—when much to his surprise the chamber doors slid open. The momentary influx of bright light made it nearly impossible to see the elders, essentially washing them out until the doors drew shut again. When he saw that it was Kelsey stepping into the chambers, he wanted to throw his hands into the air from relief. She had attended several of these sessions over the past weeks, and the elders were already warming up to her tremendously. She had also freely chastised him whenever he'd referred to the council room as "the torture chamber." A good queen, through and through.

"I didn't know you'd be joining us today," he said as the biotechs helped her up into the portal beside him. He reached a hand across the small distance that separated them, and as their skin made contact, he felt a flush sweep over his entire body.

Damn it all, don't let the elders sense the change in my biometrics. They're likely to ask us to procreate right here in chambers so they can personally monitor my fertility levels.

Kelsey smiled, her gaze lingering on him for a split second longer than she might normally have done. Something about the way her eyes sparkled, the wonderful glow about her face, made him wonder if she was up to something. Then again, maybe it was just as she'd said: that she, too, was achieving the heat right along with him. They'd made such frantic love earlier in the morning, he'd been afraid that Sabrina had heard them from where she was working in the bunker across the hall. If his protector had, she hadn't let on: She'd simply given a brisk nod, returning to her task as he passed her in the hallway.

Jared hid a smirk as it became evident that Kelsey's unannounced presence had ruffled Graeon's composure. The councilors believed everything should be done in order, by a schedule, per tradition; Kelsey, on the other hand, was like a rushing desert wind, upending everything in their elders' world.

"My lady, well and good wishes," Graeon greeted her,

bowing, and there were other awkward murmurs of welcome.

"Don't let me interrupt." She smiled at each of them, a slow and determined process. "Please, I know you have many important matters to discuss—and I'm sure that Jared will be giving you the latest report on his fertility."

It was all he could do to suppress a wild burst of laughter. Damn it all, but his beautiful love even managed to be cunning while maintaining a perfectly angelic smile on her face!

"Oh . . . oh, my lady, no. No—we wouldn't ask for any such thing, please," Graeon stammered, and luckily Eldor Aldorsk saved the poor councilor from his misery by stepping forward and launching into a full-length description of how the news of a new queen was invigorating the weary and beleaguered troops back on Refaria. A true diplomat, through and through, his former mentor was.

They haven't the first notion of what to make of my wife, Jared thought, hiding another smile behind his hand.

After Aldorsk finished, Kelsey smiled regally, turning to face Jared. She fixed him with her gaze and began to address the council, projecting very loudly in order to signify that she was addressing them on an important matter. Jared listened—and watched her—quizzically, focusing on the blue-green depths of her eyes, the gold dusting of freckles across her nose. It almost seemed as if she were speaking to him from a great distance as he heard, ". . . and so, council, I thought given your long-standing concerns, that this would be the right way to share the amazing news with my husband, our king, J'Areshkadau Bnet D'Aravni. . . ."

Everything suddenly crystallized into this one single moment; her words seemed to slow down, becoming painfully slow, *infinitely* slow, until he heard, ". . . have conceived a child."

"Conceived a child?" He jumped right out of the dais,

causing the transmission to immediately disconnect. Falling to his knees in front of her portal chair, he grabbed hold of both her hands. "Are you telling me that w-we've . . . w-we're . . ." He couldn't force the words past his thick tongue. Finally, gazing up into her eyes, he just whispered, "A baby, Kelse? You and me?"

"I wanted them to share in your moment. I know you might have wanted me to tell you first."

He cupped her face. "Do you think I care how or when you told me?" His whole body was shaking; between still being in the throes of his season, and then hearing such glorious news, it was a wonder he wasn't any shakier than he was.

"It's just . . . they've given you such a hard time, I wanted them to know in no uncertain terms that your succession is going to be secured."

He nuzzled her, nibbling at her neck, kissing her along her collarbone. "You realize it's no accident that I'm kneeling in front of you," he murmured, sniffing her. "You're a true queen, sweet Kelsey. Knowing how to manage my public image, thinking of how to wrangle the council. I have chosen quite well." He slid one palm onto her belly, grinning like he had the first time he'd flown solo. "And now, inside of you, there's our child—already in there, growing. Life . . . our lives brought together."

Tears glinted in her eyes, and she swallowed, hesitating. "I wanted to give this to you so badly." Her voice faltered and she wiped at her eyes. "Of course I wanted a baby with you, totally, but it was just . . . I knew this was a political obstacle. I knew it was your family line. So many things." Her tears began to stream down her face, and he pulled her into his arms.

"I understand. Shh, it's okay."

She pulled away, looking into his eyes. "I have to say this, Jared. After Marco's letter, after realizing there was this world of ruin and destruction . . . I was so afraid that we would never have a child. Marco didn't mention our children in the letter. Thea never saw any in that future." She swiped at her tears. "But it was Thea who told me we would conceive; you can thank her, because she made me believe it would happen."

He stared into her eyes, surprised. "She glimpsed it?"

"With her intuition."

She leaned forward, pressing her forehead against his, and burst into wild laughter. "Do you realize you just hung up on your council?"

"They are not unhappy with us at the moment." He stroked her face, brushing away her damp tears with his thumbs.

Kelsey leaned back in the chair, and Jared sprang to his feet. Pacing about the room, first in one direction, then another, he reminded Kelsey of every Hollywood stereotype of a man who'd just learned he was going to be a dad. It was amazing how universal certain facts were.

"We've got to make an announcement tonight, after dinner—it should come from me," he reflected, walking in a circular pattern around the rounded edges of the chamber. "Or maybe you? You or me, Kelsey—what do you think?" He worked a hand at his temple, so obviously considering all the royal necessities relating to their happy news. "Or maybe we shouldn't announce it yet at all?"

She began to giggle, just watching how her usually unflappable husband actually seemed . . . hyper. He stopped midstride, dropping his hand away from his face. "Am I being thoroughly ridiculous, is that it?"

"Well, maybe we don't have to be in such a rush to tell your people, not when . . ." She cupped her abdomen protectively. "It's just early, Jared. Really early, and this is an interspecies pregnancy, where we might encounter all kinds of problems."

"Which is exactly why the next place we're going is to the med complex, so they can check you out, talk to you about what to expect."

"What to expect? I think I know, don't I?" She laughed, but noticed that Jared wasn't laughing with her.

"Or maybe I don't know what to expect at all. I did see the doctor today."

"And what did he tell you?"

"That I'm pregnant. That's about it."

Jared sat down on the lower-level platform, the step that led into a pit area where the councilors' images were always displayed. He seemed to consider his words carefully before continuing. Kelsey stood and climbed down out of the data portal, where she'd been watching him pace and dither, and slowly settled right beside him.

He rubbed both of his thighs, throwing her a tentative, awkward look. "It's just that Refarian pregnancies are a bit different, love, than what you'd expect as a human."

She swore she could feel her eyes bulge right out of her head. Practically squeaking at him, she asked, "Different how? And if it's *significantly* different, maybe you should have said something before now?"

"The gestation period is shorter, for one thing," he told her, as if he were commenting on the overnight snowfall accumulation. "Only five months."

At first she figured she'd pretend to be calm, but the words *five months, five months, five months* kept echoing inside her head, and finally sent her over the edge.

She nodded, slowly rising to her feet. "Yeah, that is pretty much . . . a *major freaking detail!*" She swatted him atop the head with her open palm, popping him lightly over and over while he did his best to duck.

"Cease fire!" He held up his forearm to block any more of her attack.

She retracted her hand, but only for the time being. "And what else, J'Areshkadau?" Maybe it was being pregnant, she wasn't sure, but she suddenly felt on the verge of panic; she couldn't believe he hadn't given her any more warning than this!

He sucked in a breath. "Well, that's one thing, the gestational period. Then there's the fact of my D'Aravnian nature, for another, and this baby will be a dual being, just as I am."

"You're saying I'm going to be carrying a 'dual being'

inside of me?" A sharp wave of nausea overpowered her, but she choked it down. "All your fire and everything? That's what you're saying?" She realized her voice was reaching near-hysterical proportions, but no matter how much she'd thought about carrying Jared's child, she'd just sort of assumed that the whole "being of fire" problem wouldn't be part of the gestational scenario. *Dumb, dumb, Kelsey! This is all alien, all the time!*

He clasped her by both shoulders, staring into her eyes. "Breathe, Kelsey. Breathe!" She let out a gasp, only then realizing she'd been alternating between a state of hyperventilating and holding her breath.

"I'm breathing," she choked out, and he nodded his approval.

"Good, now keep on breathing. This isn't anything to be afraid of; it's the most natural thing in the world. We've managed to conceive, and that means you should be able to carry this child to term."

"Arienn and Louisa, your ancestors, they had several children," she said, pressing a hand to her suddenly clammy temple. "I read all about it in Arienn's journal, thanks to Thea. I read all about Louisa, how she was human, but they still managed to conceive."

Genuine surprise registered on his features. "I never knew that there was a human in my lineage. We've never been told that at all in my family."

Kelsey wrapped her arms about herself, still trying to bring her panic attack under control. "It was a big, big secret, from what Thea has shown me. Not exactly regarded as the right match, you know? Big shock there." She snorted, pointing toward the council circle. "I mean, I can't imagine *those* guys being anything other than totally cheery about a human-Refarian pairing."

"Did his journals offer information about her pregnancies? What their particular difficulties might have been? Anything at all?"

Kelsey thought hard, but couldn't recall any particular details about their interspecies differences; it was one reason she'd been so blindsided by the realization that she would be carrying a D'Aravni in her belly. A D'Aravni! As in, a glowing being of powerful energy, so hot and intense that she could be consumed by so much as touching Jared in his natural state.

"I'm carrying a being just like you." She thought about all his thermonuclear meltdown warnings about their sex life. "I'm carrying a ball of fire? That's what you're saying. That our baby is going to be exactly like you, and still somehow be inside of *me*?"

Jared sang, " 'Goodness gracious, great balls of . . .' "

She turned to face him, jabbing at the air between them. "Don't you dare make a bad Earth joke, not right now, Bennett."

The man had the nerve to smirk at her; he was actually enjoying this on some level. "But you've such wonderful music. Jerry Lee Lewis seems to say it well, no?"

She groaned, burying her face in her hands. "I'm feeling incredibly cranky all of a sudden."

"I'm feeling incredibly randy all of a sudden."

"You're gonna have to give me a few hours on that one—check back with me, okay?"

"I will definitely stay in touch with you on the issue of further matings. I am told that you will be nearly insatiable while you carry this babe."

"Now, that's not a purely Refarian thing—that's human women too."

He grinned at her wolfishly. "And that's precisely what I'm talking about."

She shook her head, still thinking over the logistics. "How is this even possible? Won't I get burned alive? You keep saying that I can't touch you. . . ."

"Because the babe will be inside of you, protected. *Protecting* you."

"Protecting me?"

"It's what has guaranteed our succession among the D'Aravni for all these thousands of years. Somehow, mystically, the babe will not harm you. He—or she—will create a protective barrier between their true nature and your body. As apparently I did for my own mother."

"But your mother was a D'Aravni. *She* was a being of fire, so no problem, right?"

"True—but not all the women in my line have been dual beings, and in her case, she was still in her physical form. If she'd dared to touch my father in his natural form while in her body? It would have destroyed her. *I* could have destroyed her while she carried me, but I did not. It's the mystery of our kind."

"Un-freaking-believable," she said. "And you do realize what this means, don't you?"

"That we're going to have a prince or princess?" he sang delightedly. He was like an overgrown boy, all beaming and glowing and joyful.

"Yes, that, for sure. But it also means something else too." She stared into his eyes meaningfully, knowing he wasn't going to be happy with her next words. Nevertheless, it was time, now more than ever.

"Oh, my beautiful human wife, what else can it possibly mean?" he trilled, still grinning at her. She almost hated to end his sweet reverie, but still, the moment had come.

"Jared, it also means," she said seriously, "that I'm going to have to call my father."

Chapter Fourteen

Scott blinked back sleep and felt surprisingly . . . refreshed. Alive. Ready to slap on his body armor, holster his K-12, and take on ten battalions of Antousians. *Damn!* It was as if every cell in his body had been electrified. Sitting up, he lowered the bed rail, glancing around the small hospital room. The lights were low, only the sounds and glow of his bedside monitors filling the semidarkness. He had no idea what time it was, or how long he'd really been asleep, but the one thing he did know was that he was healed.

Maybe Jared was right about me needing rest. Maybe that's all it really took, he thought with a grin, stepping onto the floor. He took the bedsheet with him, draping it around his naked waist, and began searching for his gear.

Poking around inside one of the cabinets, he came up empty-handed. Looking toward the far corner closet, he realized that was probably where they'd hidden his uniform.

A familiar feminine voice stopped him midway in his tracks. "They're not there."

He spun to find Nurse Shelby Tyler glaring at him, one firm hand planted severely on her hip. "You don't really think we'd have left your clothes around, do you?"

He glared right back. "Give 'em over, Tyler. I'm feeling invigorated."

"Uh, yeah!" She looked about the room, as if someone else might explain the facts to him. "That's probably because no less than ten healers visited you in your sleep, Lieutenant."

He stopped in his steps toward the closet, where he hoped his uniform might be. "The healers?"

"You don't think our lord just knocked you out for nothing, do you? I mean, really, Lieutenant. He always has a plan."

Scott turned slowly to face her. "You're telling me that the healers came in here while I was asleep?"

"I'm telling you that the *reason* you feel so *spry* and *eager* to roll is because you've been healed—well, mostly healed—thanks to a special visit from the Most Holy at the urging of our commander." She pushed past him and opened the closet, revealing it for what it was—totally empty. "That, my dear Lieutenant, is precisely what I'm telling you."

He stared at her, dumbfounded. "So where's my gear?"

"Out of your reach, right where it should be."

"Is that a royal directive?"

"You'd better believe it, sir."

Scott circled her, pulling the sheet about his chest, doing his level best to look seductive and appealing. "But I bet you know where I can find my stuff, huh?"

She wagged a finger at him. "I'm under orders, sir—express orders from the king himself—that you are to rest. Rest! That's the order. No screwing around."

He flashed her a languid smile. "Screwing? I absolutely love screwing."

She folded both arms over her chest, looking wholly unmoved. "Don't even try it, Lieutenant Dillon. I've had plenty of time to study your maneuvers in the past days. You ain't getting past me, buddy. You are here to stay." She gave him a light shove in the chest. "So go! Back into that bed, sir. That's my directive, and I'm going to enforce it."

He rolled his eyes and let the sheet drop, revealing his full naked glory. "Really?"

Shelby clucked her tongue, putting her back to him. "That don't impress me none."

He repeated, "Really?"

"If you want to get your way, sir, you'd best stop trying to work me. Get to what you really want—"

"Out of here."

"Pull the sheet back up and we can start talking."

He obliged, drawing the cool material up to his chest. "Done. So tell me how I'm gonna get out of this place."

Slowly Shelby turned to face him, shaking her head. "I have my orders, sir, from our king and commander— I keep you in that bed. Now, you don't really think I'm going to violate His Highness's directives, do you, now?"

"You bet I do, Nurse Tyler." Scott took several slow steps toward Shelby. "You know why? Because you like me."

She rolled her gaze over him. "Not that much—with all due respect, sir."

Okay, so none of his strategies were working, but it was evident that Nurse Tyler was pretty much the gate-keeper, as per his commander's orders. It wasn't just about his clothes; it was about finding out the status of current events. He flashed a sexy, imploring smile.

"Tell me, Shelby, where the chase has gone?" he asked in his sultriest, most provocative voice. It always worked on human women while he was seducing them. Unfortunately, Shelby—like all the other Refarians under his command—was totally unimpressed by his physical charms.

"Look, you just get right back on over there." She gestured past him toward the empty, waiting bed.

A new strategy was in order, at least, if he had a hope in hell of overriding Jared's orders. So he decided to behave obediently, and walked slowly across the room, trailing the sheet behind him like a regal toga. With a searing look over his shoulder, he addressed Shelby one more time.

"I would think a nurse like you would understand what I'm after."

"I get your wants, but I'm talking about your *needs*."

She helped him into the bed, ignoring his naked body as the sheet billowed to the ground. "Get on in there, sir."

"What's the latest on Hope Harper?" He pretended to accept defeat as he climbed back atop the bed.

"No news, none a-tall."

Scott sank into the mattress, thankful that he was finally feeling more like himself. "Why don't I believe that?"

She whipped the sheet over him, allowing it to settle atop his body. "You really aren't going to let this go, are you, sir?"

"Never," he said, dropping every manipulative pretense. This whole dance was about Hope and her safety, and when it came to her, the stakes were far too high to joke around. He met Nurse Tyler's serious gaze, imploring her visually.

Shelby raised the railing beside his bed, and at first said nothing, just went about checking the monitors and his readings. But Scott studied her intently, determined to break through her committed resolve. Finally she spoke.

"Now, if I was a fellow, and found myself making a journey to the wrong spot . . ." She stared at the ceiling for a long moment, narrowing her eyes. "Well, you know, I'd just go back to where I'd come from. I mean, it's like getting on a transport you think'll stop in Thearnsk, but it goes to Trajsek. You just get right back on the ship and head back to where you came from. You know?"

Scott scowled; it took a moment, but finally he caught the gist of Shelby's words. They hit the mark with sharp alacrity, making him shudder. "He's planning to take Hope into the future. That's what you're saying he's trying to do. You're saying he loves her, and he's going back where he came from—with her."

"I'm just saying the guy probably wants to get back home; he don't belong here—thought he had a mission, but it turned out to be void. He's gonna want to get back to his own time."

"But he'll try and take Hope with him." It was as if a clawing hand had gripped him around the chest, choking the very breath out of him.

She tilted her head quizzically. "Now, why would he do that?" His nurse really had no idea; of course, why would he expect her to? Just because she knew that Jake had arrived from the future—and had now intuited his motives, what he hoped to accomplish—that didn't mean she got the full picture.

Scott climbed out of the bed once and for all; he would not lie in a hospital bed again, not unless he was dead, and then he wouldn't need a nurse. "Because when a man's in love, Nurse Tyler, he'll do anything—anything at all—to make sure he doesn't lose that woman."

Shelby shoved him in the chest with her fingertips, poking him over and over. "Oh, no, no, no, you don't, sir."

"Anything, Shelby," he repeated, blocking her next attempt to corner him. "I'm stronger than I look, and you're not stopping me."

She stuck her chin out, folding both arms over her chest. "Then I'm going with you. You're going to need some help."

"No, what I need is a fellow soldier. And some warm clothes." He hit his comm, calling Anna. "The rest I'll handle on my own."

The wind burned Hope's cheeks; her eyes watered despite the helmet's visor, and it seemed, repeatedly, as if the snowmobile would go right off the roadside trail. She'd begun adjusting to the rumbling feel of the machine, the way it pulled and gave, never just holding fast to the snow beneath them. Her ears ached from the frigid air blowing over her, and even wearing a parka, gloves, and periodically availing herself of the hand warmers on the back handlebars, she felt frozen through and through. Still, onward they had continued to go, mile after mile.

Pressing her face against Jake's back, she wondered what he planned to do, at least, precisely. Was he going to take this tour guide right up the mitres? Was he going to get her inside of the place—whatever it really was—and finally tell her all about her future? And if he traveled back to his own time, what would happen to her? How would she ever make it back out of the park? She doubted that he even had a plan at all.

Without warning, the snowmobile slowed, causing her body to pitch against Jake's. She thought he shouted something over the noise and air, but couldn't make out his words.

"What?" she yelled, leaning slightly upward and closer against him. "What did you say?"

The snowmobile sputtered, slowing rapidly, and then came to an abrupt stop. Jake turned on the seat. "Just that the guide is stopping us. I told him we wanted to see this overlook." He cut the engine and it silenced immediately.

"What does he figure a blind girl is doing on a trip like this?" She lifted both eyebrows.

"He doesn't figure." Jake grunted, sliding off the bench. "You stay here, okay? I'll be right back." She heard him trudging away from her, the snow crisp beneath his feet, the sharp give and take of boots and icy substance.

She called after him, "What do you want to see here? Why this lookout?"

The crunching sound of snow under Jake's boots grew closer again as he circled back toward her, and she stared up at his looming form. He placed a strong hand on her shoulder. "This is where we end it, Hope. I'm sorry I dragged you into all of this."

"End it? *End it?* As in, you dump me here with Tour Guy, and go on your merry way?"

"I can't take you into the backcountry; you know that. Hell, even I know that, no matter how much I want you with me. You're not strong enough, not with your diabetes."

She yanked her helmet off. "And you claim we had a relationship? If you don't know me better than that, then you're making the whole thing up." She scowled up at him, wishing she could discern his features and get a better read on him. It was amazing how much she'd always relied on sight simply to know what was happening, what people were feeling. "I have my insulin with me, Jake. I have everything I need: my test strips, my medications, I've got it all." She reached behind her, gesturing at her refrigeration pack.

He cupped her chin with a tender, soft gesture that shocked her to the marrow. "But you've got no way out of here if I manage to get back home."

Tears filled her eyes, and she couldn't begin to understand why. "You haven't told me anything, not a freaking thing about how I die, or what happens. You're just going to leave me totally unprotected."

Against her, his hand stiffened; then he jerked it away. "I'm protecting you now, Hope. This is good-bye."

"Hey, so you guys gonna go check it out or not?" It was the voice of their tour guide. "We've gotta keep moving today; it's a long ride in and out." He stepped closer, appearing beside Jake. "And looks like a storm's starting to build. So step on over there, have a peek, and let's roll some more."

Jake strode away from her, toward the guide. "About this tour," he began, and Hope wondered just how the hell he thought he was going to bribe the guide into letting him head off the trail.

Now was the moment; if Jake couldn't convince the guide to let him take off on his own, his plan to return home wasn't worth *meshdki*. The man stared at him dubiously, shaking his head. "I could lose my license, my job; there's just no way, man. Not gonna do it."

Jake reached into his pocket, producing the thick banded roll of bills that he'd saved for this moment. The guide's eyes widened slightly at the sight of so much cash.

"So is there really no way, Randy?" Jake held out the roll. "None at all? Or did you just mean only maybe there was no way?"

Randy stared at the load of green in his hand. "If you're a park ranger, . . ." He shook his head, still staring at the seductive wad of money.

Jake held up a hand. "I'm not a ranger; I promise you. I'm just a guy who needs to . . ." Jake thought for a moment, reaching for a motive; he had to be convincing. "I've always wanted to see Mirror Lake frozen over. It's such a mystical part of the park in the summer, so I really want to check it out, man."

Randy fanned the money against his palm like a card deck. "There's got to be at least a thousand bucks here. Mirror Lake ain't worth that much, not to nobody."

"It is to me." Jake trained his gaze on the young guy, hard and unwavering. "Everybody's got their fetishes."

Randy slipped the roll into his jacket pocket with a smirk. "Well, mister, for a thousand bucks I won't ask any more questions, but know one thing." Randy squinted up into his face, sun-weathered skin crinkling around his eyes. "If you're not back by three hours from now, I'm reporting the whole thing to the rangers. And it won't be that I got bribed; it'll be that you put a gun to my head."

Three hours from now and Jake would already be back in his own time. And Hope would be . . . back here in this time with Dillon. He shuddered at the thought, but shook it off.

"That works for me." He slapped Randy on the back, knowing that once he took off, he'd never see the guide again. Or Hope. This whole sojourn back into his memories would be just that—memories.

He was about to ask Randy to take care of Hope, to get her back into town, when her sexy, sultry voice interrupted their exchange. "You're not leaving without me, are you?"

Jake spun toward her, watching her boldly walk toward them as if she could see perfectly well.

"I'm on the back of that thing." She pointed toward their snowmobile, brushing right past Randy, taking confident steps that would never betray her visual limits. "Otherwise, Tierny, you're not going anywhere, plain and simple."

"Plain and simple," he muttered, watching her, amazed. She'd never backed down from any challenge, so why should this current one be any different? Would he take her back with him? Maybe. Could he leave her outside the mitres, alone and in the cold, if he got what he wanted—a journey back to his own time? Never.

It was an insane decision, but nevertheless, it was the only one he could possibly make—he would take her to the mitres. "Come on, sweetheart." He grabbed her hand, pulling her toward the waiting snowmobile. "Let's head out there together."

She gave his back a light shove, making her point. "No other way. Nobody ever leaves me behind."

And that was exactly his thinking. That he wouldn't leave her behind back in this world, but that he would take her with him and steal her away, away from Scott Dillon before that man could make her his own. Whatever the risks, whatever the stakes, no matter how ruined the future: He would bring her through interdimensional space and back to his own time.

Chapter Fifteen

The bumpy ride became suddenly smooth, the snowmobile zigzagging beneath them, certainly a far cry from the wild cross-country journey they'd been on for the past hour. At least now they weren't catching air and had reached a much more solid surface. Hope held tight to Jake, trying to decide whether her glucose levels were going low—she was feeling light-headed and strange—or if it was really only the weirdness of the past few days finally catching up to her. Maybe she needed a snack, a few of the Smarties she had in her cooler bag strapped to the back of the sled, anything to even out her levels.

All at once they slowed, skidding across what seemed to be a smooth area. Perhaps it was a frozen lake; she couldn't be sure. Every direction she looked she saw nothing but white snow, piercing sunlight, her usual dark floaters, and blue sky. A big mass of confusion, basically, and it irritated the crap out of her.

They came to a stop, the motor going dead; she'd already figured out there wasn't a halfway point on these snowmobiles when it came to on or off. That thought reminded her of the one man she loved—who it so happened wasn't the man she'd followed into this crazy predicament. If only she could pinpoint how the two of them linked together in her mind, then she would understand her actions. But so far, no dice.

"We're here." Jake's naturally throaty voice was even

raspier after hours' worth of exposure to wind and cold. "The chamber is up that cliff."

Hope followed where he seemed to be pointing, immediately wincing. "That's way the hell up there, isn't it?"

Jake made a low, almost growling sound, but didn't answer.

"How do I interpret that? Yes, it's far up there? No, it's right beside me? I don't know how to translate"— she growled in mimicry—"*that*."

He stalked away, then circled back close, no longer wearing his helmet. She wondered if he'd jerked it off in some kind of fit of frustration or emotion.

"What that means is that I should never—not ever in a million years—have brought you out here. I'm a fool, but I blame you."

She swung one leg over the bench and placed both feet on the running board. "Hey, hey, no fair to blame me. I'm in the dark here—literally and figuratively. I am just along for the ride."

In a heartbeat Jake swooped around, blocking out the sun and sky. His mouth was a breath away from hers. "I mean, Hope, that you have never given me free will. There's never been any way I could move, not in any direction, that isn't you. Don't you get it? Don't you understand how much you mean to me?" His voice cracked, and just as suddenly as he'd closed in upon her, he walked away.

She rose to her feet, following. "Then tell me. I don't know, because you haven't explained a thing! I know that I belong with Scott Dillon—I know how much I . . . feel for him."

She saw his dark head of hair, and determined that he had his back to her. When he spoke, she could tell for sure. "You love Dillon. Just say it. Tell me how much you love him—don't spare my feelings. Let me know every single thing he means to you; tell me every moment that the two of you have shared. I want to know it all."

"Why would you want to know that?" He was obviously Scott's competitor—had even, it seemed, defeated Scott for her affections at some future date. Except there was that strange, unshakable connection that she felt between the two men. "What ties you to him?"

"You do love him." His voice was shockingly soft. "Don't you?"

"I hardly know him . . . we haven't had enough time."

"But do you *love* him?" His voice roared, echoing off the mountains and snow and pine.

Tears filled her eyes, and she pressed the heel of her palm against first one eye, then the other. "Yes. Of course I do. But you already know that—you totally know it." The tears came much harder, unstoppable. "Somehow, some way, he's the reason I'm here with you."

Jake began to laugh, a dark, haunted sound. "But of course." He still had his back to her; maybe he was staring at the cliffs beyond them, where the mitres supposedly were. Maybe he just couldn't face her.

"I don't want to hurt you," she offered softly, drawing in a staggered breath. "I just don't understand any of this."

He turned to face her, then took slow, methodical steps. "How about I explain it to you? The way it all weaves together? Would you like that? Do you want to know the sick twist of fate that ties Scott Dillon and Jake Tierny together for all time?"

She flinched, bracing herself; she was afraid of what he offered. More than that, she didn't like the sound of his voice, how low and threatening it had suddenly become, but she thrust her chin out in a show of bravado. "Absolutely. Lay it on me, Jake. I'm ready."

Lay it on me, Jake. I'm ready.

But he wasn't ready, not even close. All he could do was stare at her, her wide-open gray eyes, her disheveled hair, and remember what had been between them. Once. Years ago. A part of him was prepared to explain it all to her, to let her know the truth; another part of him was the absolute coward he'd always been when it came to the idea of losing her.

"I'm still ready," she prompted, flailing her arms wildly. "Good grief, are you going to tell me or what? I've come this far. You claimed you killed me, which, by the way, I don't believe." She gestured at the frozen landscape around them. "The least you can do is tell me what I've gotten myself into."

He bowed his head and began to laugh. It was totally like her to have come along with him, just going on instincts, trusting him. Why had she always, fucking always, trusted him so easily? It was that very trust that had ended up getting her killed, he thought, pressing his eyes shut against the onslaught of horrific memories.

Walking toward her, he closed the small distance that separated them. Overhead a piercingly blue sky created a surreal setting for this moment of revelation. In the future, the skies were never this pure shade of blue, always gray, always murky. Those were the skies of ruin, the ones of his world.

"I brought you here, to the mitres, so I could transport you with me back into my own time," he admitted gruffly. "It's the only reason you're here: because I want to take you with me. I kept doubting, kept telling myself that wasn't it, but there you have it."

She held both of her gloved hands out toward him, suspended like some question that would never find its answer. "Are you even sure you can get back?" she finally asked after several long seconds.

"How about asking why I'd think I could do something like that? That would be a better question."

"Already thought of that one, but figured it was too obvious." She laughed, her nose crinkling in that totally familiar expression he had always adored.

With one step he had her in his arms, pulled tight against his chest. He never wanted to let her go; pressing his face against the top of her head, he drank in the

scent of her, the taste. The very essence of his soul mate.
"You need to know . . ."

"Then just tell me. Tell me everything—I won't run
away."

He pressed a chaste kiss against the top of her head;
to kiss her, really kiss her, hadn't felt quite right from
the beginning. "I'm linked with Dillon. Always linked,"
he began, and was about to confess it all when suddenly
the sharp sound of pulse fire rent the silence.

"Down, down, down!" he shouted, thrusting her onto
the ground into a protective cleft formed between his
own body and the snowmobile. Reaching into his waistband, he retrieved his pulse pistol, scanning the perimeter for the source of enemy fire.

Another sparking series of shots ricocheted off the
snowmobile, barely missing them both, and he dropped
beside Hope.

"What's happening?" she cried, burrowing against the
side of the machine for cover. Her gaze shot frantically
around them, and he shielded her with his own body—
so much larger than hers, he knew he could protect her.
But only for a few moments. More pulse fire exploded
into the sled.

"Something's burning!" She clawed at his chest.
"Don't just keep me down here—I've gotta fight too!"

He shook his head, pushing her down again, checking
his pistol. He could cover them long enough that they
could make a break for the cliffs, where the mitres
chamber was hidden. There he'd have to regenerate his
pistol, at least two minutes when he wouldn't be able to
offer any kind of protection. Here, though, they were
open targets, and it was only a matter of time until they
got taken out.

Hope shoved at his chest, trying to work her way from
beneath where he'd wedged her between his body and
the snowmobile. "Jake, don't you smell those fumes?"
She writhed against him. "This thing's about to catch on
fire. Or explode! We've got to get out of here—now!"

"I know, I know," he muttered under his breath, sweeping the frozen lake visually in an effort to see whoever was firing upon them. It could be Jared's crew, for all he knew, but something inside of him said not. Narrowing his gaze, he looked deeper, stealing just a moment to determine the position of their assailants. His gazing ability revealed the source: Across the frozen lake, on the south side of the rim, three Antousian snipers were there. And the mitres was on the north side, the opposite direction. *Thank All!*

Hope clasped his arm, squeezing hard. "Jake, if we don't move now, we're gonna be dead—and it won't be from those guys who are firing on us. I can't believe you don't smell these fumes!"

But he did smell them, the acrid, burning sting of them, but what she couldn't see—and he could—was the trained weapons of the three enemy snipers. In the balance of it all he was less worried about an explosion, and far more concerned about getting Hope across the clear expanse of frozen lake without making her an open target for the Antousian freaks who were aiming right at them.

An idea took hold in his mind. Turning to her, he clasped Hope by both shoulders. "You've trusted me this far, and I need you to trust me a little longer, okay?"

She leaned into the snowmobile, her eyes drifting shut. "I so need to kill you. You deserve it—you totally realize that, right?"

He snorted. "There's my girl. We're going to do something that seems totally insane . . . but I think"—he glanced across the lake, zeroing in on the shooters—"it's our only way out. Those are Antousians out there, and they want just one thing, and that's us, dead."

"I really don't want to give them what they're after," she said.

"Good. Neither do I, and that's why I'm going to power up the engine on this thing." He slapped the side of the snowmobile with his open palm. "And we're going to make a run for it."

She shook her head. "It's going to fucking explode, hello?"

"Not before we get out of here."

"Terrible bet, and I say the odds are even worse."

Reaching over her shoulder, he found the button that would engage the engine. "Otherwise," he said, "we're going to die right here."

"Then I'll take that bet." She nodded. "How're we going to do this thing?"

He pulled the button that set the motor idling; immediately the gas fumes intensified, smoke pouring from the engine. "I'm getting on first," he shouted over the loud noise, "and I'm swinging you up in front of me. It'll be my back they fire against."

She began to laugh crazily. "What? You don't think I can drive us?"

"I'll steer it from behind." He bent, kissing her quickly on the cheek. "On my mark. Three, two, one . . . go!"

One minute Hope was hunkered beside a dying snowmobile, and the next she was hurtling through a blurry white haze, her face pressed down against a motor that was totally going to explode any minute. Jake had shoved her down in front of him so hard that her jaw slammed against a control, and now her mouth was bleeding. That hardly mattered; they were speeding so fast that her eyes were watering, and her head was bobbing against a whole array of controls—all the while there was the sound of sputtering gunfire erupting behind them.

"I . . . hope . . . you . . . know . . . what . . . you're . . . doing," she barely managed to get out, her head slamming against the windshield and controls with every bump they hit.

Jake didn't answer, and she heard him fire against their pursuers, turning back over his shoulder. The snowmobile lurched, spinning out. "Damn it!" she shouted, and reached for his pistol. "You need to drive. Stop shoving me down here and let me get in this fight."

Somehow, impossibly, she managed to wrestle the gun away from him—sat up straight even though he kept battling to shove her facedown, and began firing just past his head. She used his shoulder as a steadying force, and at first he did everything in his power to wrestle her back down. At last he seemed to accept the fact that, semiblind though she might be, he did have to drive the snowmobile. She, for her part, kept spraying the terrain beyond his shoulder with whatever this weapon contained—bright blasts of golden-red fire. And she tried to simply ignore the increasing smell of fumes and smoke that filled her nostrils.

"Faster, Jake." She twisted in the seat, leaning against his chest. The bad guys were definitely gaining on them; she knew that because their dark forms were growing larger and larger. "They're on snowmobiles . . . or something. Black-looking things."

"Station craft," he yelled over the wind.

She fired off a few more rounds, watching the black shapes loom closer. "Whatever those things are, they're faster than us."

The smell of explosive fumes burned her nostrils. "Don't worry about going faster!" She grabbed hold of his shoulders. "This thing's gonna blow!"

At that precise moment a thundering jolt catapulted her off the snowmobile and into the wide open abyss. She felt herself go airborne, sensed the world slice all around them. For distended, unreal moments she flew, crying, "Jake! Jakob!"

But her screams lodged in her throat as her head impacted some hard substance, and wind and air met ground all at once.

She worked to move her mouth, horrified, but no sound came forth. And then, as she lifted her head, seeing nothing but blackness and brightness mingled together in an ungodly union, she collapsed against the frozen ice.

Chapter Sixteen

"Go! Go! Go!" Jake took hold of her arm, pulling at her, but Hope wanted no part of it. To sleep, to lie still and rest, that was the only command she would listen to.

"You go," she told him dully, burying her face against the snow.

"Hope Harper! Move it!" His voice was shrill and high; immediately she came to her senses. "They're right on us! If you don't get rolling, we're both dead."

Blinking up at his dark form, she allowed him to lift her off of the hard surface beneath her, and stumbled to her feet. "Who are they?" She staggered along in his frantic grasp. "Who's after us?" Somehow, she couldn't quite remember any of it.

"*Vlksai!* Run, Hope! Stay with me!" Jake thrust her ahead of him, sprinting toward what looked like a frozen cliff.

The tattering sound of gunfire erupted behind them; bright sparks shot past her head. "Oh, shit!" she said, and lengthened her steps as far as they would go. Jake shoved against her back, urging her onward.

"Faster, faster!" he shouted, sounding like a drill sergeant. She registered that thought about his military acumen, even though they were running for their lives. Everything was happening in an elongated, slow time scale, each of them sprinting as if in a terrible nightmare where nothing happened quickly enough. She felt every detail as if it were a sleepy Sunday afternoon. The firing

weapons at their back. Jake's voice of authority. Their
refuge just ahead, yet totally unreachable.

Like every bad dream she'd ever had, they were a
million miles from safety, running and grasping toward
it with every bit of their determination. Hope hit her
stride, determined to survive; it had always been that
way for her. Insurmountable odds, impossible chances.

Digging into that place within, the one that had always
kept her alive, she stretched her legs and ran with everything she had.

They hit the ice-covered cliffs, slamming against the
hard surface as one. Jake grabbed Hope, shoving his
own body between her and the jagged rocks. Engaging
his pulse pistol, he began the interminable regeneration
process; they were out of ammo, and it would be precisely two minutes before he could power up again.
Their temporary position, however, allowed the cover of
several boulders and a copse of trees.

"We've got to climb this trail." He was breathless,
shaking. They'd gotten so close to the chamber, and if
only they could make their way to the top of the ridge—
and if only his data collector would allow them to enter
the mitres—they just might make it out of this showdown alive.

Hope shook her head dazedly, clasping at the frozen
rocks. "I'm low, Jake. Really low."

He turned in panic, realizing the unthinkable—that
Hope's medical pack was somewhere back with the
snowmobile, possibly blown to shreds. Without her diabetic snacks, her insulin, all her supplies, she would die
out here in the wilderness, even if the Antousians didn't
get her. "You're going to be okay," he promised, but
felt his throat tighten in alarm. "Shit, Hope, I'm sorry.
So sorry to have dragged you into all of this."

She closed her eyes, shaking. "He told me to come
with you. I did it for him."

He dropped beside her, checking his pulse pistol
again; seventy-four more seconds of regeneration left to

go. Slipping his arms around her, he willed her to be okay, to receive strength from him somehow, even though he didn't have a damn thing that she needed to recover from her dropping glucose levels. On an ordinary day this was a walk in the park—a simple matter of blood sugar correction. Now, out in the wilderness, it was a genuine crisis; without supplies, she could go into a coma . . . or worse.

"Who told you to come with me?" He stroked her hair, keeping his voice calm and soothing, even though inside he was a mass of tangled nerves.

"Scott," she slurred, still shaking in his arms. "He told me that when you came, I had to go with you."

Jake jerked backward, gaping at her. Scott Dillon had no idea who he was! Why in hell's name would the soldier have asked her to go with him? And if the man did somehow have an inkling of his true identity—as impossible as that seemed—then Jake should be the last man Dillon would want spiriting her away.

"When did he say that, sweetheart?"

Her shaking intensified, but she said nothing more. Studying the terrain that stood between them and the blown-up snowmobile, Jake calculated that he would likely die if he ran for her lost medical pack. On the other hand, gauging by the shape she was in, *she* would likely die if he didn't at least try to go back for her supplies.

"You're dangerously low, Hope. I've got to go back for your pack."

She jerked her head, mumbling at him unintelligibly. Releasing her from his grasp, he took hold of his pistol with both hands. The reading showed that it was fully powered again. Hope slumped forward, a sheen of cold sweat on her forehead.

Not again, not now! Please, All, don't let her go into shock.

He'd been down this road with her too many other times, and the image of her shaking and disoriented was enough to make him physically ill.

"I'm okay," she tried to argue, her voice weak, but he knew better. He could identify every one of her tell-tale signs. All the physical exertions of this morning had been too much. When had she even stopped to eat, to fortify herself against the onslaught of her disease? Not once, and he cursed himself for not having made her take a snack. Of course it had been too much, and now the day's toll was exerting itself in her jittery shakes, her dull responses. Right now she was still hanging on; a little while longer and she'd be too far gone for help. It had always been this way with her disease—a hairpin trigger that he could hardly keep in check. She had to have that medical pack, or it was all over before it had barely begun.

With one final glance at her, he stepped out of the trees and ran as fast as he could toward the metal carcass of their exploded snowmobile. No sooner had he left cover than the two station craft spun toward him; like a pair of menacing black helicopters they bore down on him, elevated only a few feet above the snow and frozen lake. Station craft could run at two hundred miles an hour over open terrain, and didn't rely on snow or land in order to operate. They were completely hovering craft—part motorcycle, part snowmobile . . . always leaving death in their wake.

Jake dropped to one knee, firing rapidly on first one of the assassins, then the other. Unbelievably, the first Antousian catapulted backward off his ride, and Jake wasted no time—he trained all of his energy on the second soldier. Over and over he fired, and meanwhile the station craft gained on him, circling near, slowing until the *vlksai* leaped off the vehicle, charging toward him, firing with both hands.

Pulse fire whizzed past his shoulders, barely missing him, but Jake was determined to take this enemy out. Otherwise Hope would be left exposed and vulnerable— and dying from diabetic shock.

Raising his pistol for one clean shot, he fired. When the bastard fell to the ground, collapsing face-first into the snow, Jake thrust his gun overhead victoriously, shoving it upward into the air. He even fired off a few celebratory rounds; then—making sure there truly were no more enemies surrounding them—he took off running for Hope's pack.

"I see them!" Anna had position on the transport's jump seat, right by the main viewing pane, her distance goggles pressed against the window. "Jake Tierny is in the open, sir—wide open. Hope Harper is off to the side."

"And?" Scott couldn't stifle his impatience. "And what else, Lieutenant? What more do you see?" He unfastened his safety harness, keeping his balance as he made his way across the aisle toward the window where Anna held position. She had a good fix on the action below, but it wasn't enough; he needed that fix too.

"She's down, sir. If it is indeed her, and I think so—visual ID matches."

Scott knelt against the side of Anna's jump seat, shoving her out of the way; he had to see for himself. Seizing her goggles, he pressed them to his eyes, positioning them against the viewing pane. A visual survey revealed a figure that resembled Jake Tierny running across the frozen expanse of Mirror Lake; two station craft looked to be down, fallen figures beside them. Scanning the perimeter, he searched out Hope.

And found her.

She lay crumpled in the snow, half leaning against the cliffs that led to the mitres chamber, utterly still.

Shouting at the craft's captain, he ordered her to set down by the mitres; they could do it, given their transport's stealth capacity, even now, in the middle of the day.

"Drop now!" He barked the orders, one after another, the image of Hope's small, crumpled form emblazoned in his mind.

By the time Jake fell to Hope's side, she'd broken out in a visible sweat and was mumbling incoherently. Her whole body shook, and tears streamed down her face. He'd seen all of this before—how erratic and emotional she could become just because her glucose levels were dangerously low.

"Here, sweetheart." He knelt beside her, pressing an open bottle of juice against her lips. "Drink on up."

She reached for the liquid, knocking it away, and most of the juice jolted out of the container. "Fuck you, Tierny!" She glared at him irritably.

"Drink this, okay? You've got to drink this now or you're gonna go into shock."

She struggled to sit up, half kneeling in the snow. "Shock? You wanna know shock? That's everything about you! You, Tierny!" She waved wildly about them, still refusing the juice, tears rolling down her face. "I don't know who the hell you are. Fuck you! Fuck, fuck, fuck you!"

"You always liked that word." He couldn't help but smile, again working the juice bottle toward her lips. This time she took several sips, closing her eyes.

Although he knew she'd hate to admit it, the juice was exactly what she needed to even out her gyrating glucose levels. He refused to think about the fact that she was here because of him; that because of him, she'd been ill prepared to deal with her life-threatening illness.

"Drink on up; just a little more." Too much would be . . . too much. He'd lived years of dealing with her health issues; it almost frightened him how easily he could take up her cause again.

After a few more sips, she swatted the bottle away, sending more of the liquid flying against the snow. But her tirade wasn't over. "See, tell me what I'm doing here, huh? Tell me what's going on!"

When she got like this, things were always a little irrational and scary.

And honest.

"I took out our enemies," he reassured her softly, running a palm down the length of her hair. "You're safe now."

"Safe? I'm not safe! Hell, no! You're danger incarnate, my friend. Why, why did *he* tell me to go with you, huh?" Her words were still slurred, but at least her tremors had ceased. "I'm so messed up even to be here."

Clasping both of her shoulders, he tried to look into her eyes; of course, it was an impossible feat when she couldn't focus back on him. But still . . . he wanted her to know how serious he was.

"Tell me again—do you love Scott Dillon?" He pressed his face close to hers, so aware that he looked nothing at all like the man whom she loved. Everything about this body was wrong—all wrong. Too bulky, too dark, too marked. Covered with tattoos and inscrutable scars. It had been awkward since the day he'd stolen it.

"Stop it," she hissed, trying to turn away, but he captured her face, pulling it close against his.

The mitres was such a long way up, and if she didn't understand the truth, she would never work to make it all the way up there. Besides, it was time; after everything he'd put her through, it was more than time that she knew the full score.

He sucked in a strengthening breath. "If you love him, then you understand what you feel for me."

She burrowed her face against his chest, and he knew that she was still vaguely incoherent. "Nah, nah, that's just not true." She burst into laughter, pawing at him, even as she nestled closer within his embrace.

Jake closed his eyes, praying that All would guide him. But his throat tightened and no words came. He stared down at his olive skin—so dark in contrast to the fair man he'd once been born to be—and fingered a puckered, long tattoo that ran across the back of his right hand, feeling the ridged skin. He had no idea how this body had acquired the scarring. He drew that hand into a furious, tortured fist and slammed it against the icy rock, causing his knuckles to bleed.

She pulled back, studying his face as best she could. "Stop hiding things from me. Just because I can't see . . . doesn't mean I can't see the facts. You've got a big secret."

"You're right," he admitted softly. "Such a big secret that it could destroy you, and I love you too much to do that, Hope."

She rubbed her face, obviously steadying herself. "I'm tough. Like I said before—lay it on me, Jakob."

"If you love him," he whispered carefully, never taking his eyes off of her, "then you naturally love me."

"Let her go, you *vlksai* bastard!" Scott screamed the words, ignoring the fact that Hope was held within his enemy's arms. A good thirty feet still separated them, but he shot off a round to prove his point, letting it ricochet off the cliffs behind them. "Drop your weapon and stand down!"

Jake Tierny appeared stunned by Scott's sudden appearance, slowly releasing Hope from his grasp. But it was more than that—he seemed frightened somehow, his large green eyes wide and unbelieving. That was the last sensory detail that Scott noted before the world around them folded apart, rent from within, collapsing.

An energy that Scott had never experienced before drove him to his knees, tossing him forward as if he were nothing more substantial than a dream. Rushing winds, keening fathoms, the universe itself, all of these things erupted about him, and he could only clutch at the vanishing ground. Grope and pray, grope and pray: This was all that he could do.

The experience was ten times more powerful—a hundred, maybe—than anything he'd felt in the mitres chamber when they'd opened up the vortex. Time itself magnetized him to the earth below his body, and no matter how much he tried to move toward Hope—to save her from this enemy's clutches—he couldn't so much as work a limb.

"Hope!" His voice came out elongated. "Get away from him!"

She moved her hands, gesturing strangely, and, like something from his very worst nightmares, began to climb the trail with his enemy.

•

Don't go with him! he tried to call, but couldn't work his mouth. Over and over, she kept going with Jake Tierny. None of it made a bit of sense. *Stay with me! Stay, don't go with him another moment!*

But nothing, not one damned word, would come out of his mouth.

What had happened to Scott? Hope wondered in confusion. Jake kept pulling her up the trail, and she stumbled, barely finding her footing. One minute there'd been a bizarre, rushing wind—and now this moment: She was once again in the grasp of a man she hardly knew.

A man who claimed that if she loved Scott, then she naturally loved him too.

"Hey! What are we doing?" She felt strengthened from the juice, ready to fight—and what she really wanted was to be back at Scott's side again. "Let me go; I want to go back to him."

Jake dragged her onward, toward the top of their climb. "That's what you think, but you don't have the whole picture."

She dug in her heels, refusing to take another step along the sliding, treacherous hike. "Right here, right now, you tell me everything." She jerked her arm out of Jake's grasp. "You tell me what just happened back there."

His breathing was heavy, uneven. "We're almost to the mitres—that's all that matters."

"No, see, that's not true. Scott's back down there, and I want to know why the universe fell apart when the two of you came together. What did you mean when you said that if I loved him, then I loved you too? I won't take another step until you translate some of this shit for me, Tierny."

Hope blinked, trying to make out the terrain; below them, white openness spread in every direction. Somewhere down there Scott was chasing her, trying to save her—so why did she keep following in this strange man's wake?

He clasped her shoulder. "We're just a few feet away from the mitres; I'll tell you everything then."

"That's not good enough! I won't go on without understanding what happened back there. Without knowing what it is that links you and Scott together."

Jake strode away from her, stopping by a scrappy pine. He braced a hand against it—or at least, that was what it seemed like when interpreted through her piss-poor vision.

"Scott is someone whom I respect very deeply—even as I despise the man."

"I've gathered that much." She folded her arms about herself. "Now go on. Tell me the rest."

Jake never turned to face her, didn't so much as look her in the eye. "Like I said, you love him. And if you love him, Hope, then that means you love me." His voice was raw, lost . . . utterly abandoned.

She stepped toward him, into the certain abyss. "Why? Say why."

"Because, sweet Hope"—very slowly he turned to face her—"Scott Dillon and I are the same man. I *am* Scott Dillon, come from the future into your past."

Chapter Seventeen

"We cannot call your father." Jared glanced at his bride, anxiety and frustration married together. "Why, by the gods, would you think that we should?"

She rubbed her abdomen, standing beside him in the hangar. He'd been called to inspect a new flight crew; he nodded and saluted his approval, talking sideways to Kelsey.

"Because he can help you." Her eyes widened. "It's not about the baby; you do realize that, don't you?"

He waved at the chief engineer, signaling his approval. "And yet our babe is the very reason you said we must call him."

"Because it's the final straw, Jared. I mean, really! He thinks I'm up in Canada on a research trip, when I'm actually part of all this." She gestured at the planes gathered in formation across the flight deck. "When I'm actually a queen, get that? And now I'm pregnant with an alien baby . . . a dual being, for crap's sake. It's time he knew at least something about what's happening in my life."

"Then it isn't about helping me." Jared glared irritably, wanting to spar with her and get her to admit the truth. Her need to contact her father wasn't about him: How could it possibly be?

"It's about the fact that he's friends with the vice president. I've told you as much before; he's a political consultant in D.C. and knows the president of the United States. You don't think that can help our cause?"

"I think you miss your family."

"Is that a problem?" She huffed out an angry breath, putting her profile to him. "Does that make you angry, *my king*?"

Jared stormed away from her, approaching one of their new stealth craft. He ran his fingertips along the underbelly of the airplane, stroking back and forth, suddenly itching to take off. To take his wife and new baby with him, leaving his own people far behind. It was that old wanderlust, always burning bright within his DNA, that thing that often compelled him to run when everything about his life demanded that he stay.

Slowly he turned on his heel to face her. Her tight auburn curls were crazily askew; her blue eyes were wide and furious, but something in his heart softened the moment he met her human gaze. "I'm your family now, Kelse." He positioned one palm over his heart. "We are your family, this child and I."

She dropped her head, speechless, and for a long time neither of them spoke; there was only the background hum of machinery and engines rumbling loudly. At last she met his gaze again, tears filling her clear blue eyes. "That's true, but I still have a life outside of this compound. I may not have a big family, just my dad and a few cousins whom I'm close to, but do you honestly think that we can pretend I'm away on a science trip for the rest of our lives?"

"You contact your father, that puts you—and all of us—in danger," he told her sharply. He pointed at her stomach. "It puts that baby of ours in danger."

"Why would it have to be that way? You don't trust me enough to find a way to communicate with my dad safely? You don't believe that just like you, my father *loves* me and wouldn't do anything to harm me?"

"I don't know him, and that's the problem. I only know that he's, as you say, very high up in the American political structure, with many friends."

"He's just a political consultant, Jared." She smiled suddenly at his slightly off understanding of her world. "He's not part of the political structure like you're thinking. He's just connected, really well connected, with people who listen to what he says."

Jared studied her, anger visible on his face. . . . Well, but it wasn't exactly anger, she realized. Kelsey had already begun learning what his gestures and unconscious habits meant. His black eyebrows furrowed downward into a sharp V shape whenever he wrestled with fear and frustration.

"What scares you so much about this?" she asked him quietly.

A muscle in his jaw ticked. "I've let you into my innermost workings here, Kelse. I never thought I'd be having this discussion; when we got together, you knew how it would have to be."

"That I could never, not once, see my family again?" she shouted, the sound reverberating off the high ceiling of the hangar. "That you would keep me up here on this mountain like your very own Rapunzel for the rest of my life? Never!"

"Calm down, love." He glanced around at the startled faces of soldiers who were working around them. "Let's keep this to ourselves."

"Like you want to keep me? Huh? To *yourself*?"

The furrow between Jared's eyes faded, replaced instead by the twinkle of amusement in his black eyes. "I think you're behaving like a pregnant woman. I've been told to expect as much."

She lunged at him, slugging him hard in the chest, but he captured her, spinning her in his arms. "I'm your king, my lady. Surely you don't mean to punch me that way?"

Wrestling against him, she shook him off. "That was a totally sexist comment. About me being pregnant."

He held up both hands. "Is it not the true state of things? That you're emotional, and you've learned so much today about the nature of the baby inside of you?

It makes much sense to me that you'd be feeling homesick. But it will pass."

She shook her head wearily. "Do you ever plan for me to see my dad again? Tell me the truth, Jared."

He folded both arms over his chest, staring at the floor between them. "I believe that in time our war will end, and yes, you will be able to see him then."

She waved him off, walking past him. "That tells me everything I need to know. Someday, maybe, one day," she shouted over her shoulder. "Come talk to me when you're ready to stop being a control freak."

Storming toward the hangar exit, she expected to hear him right behind her. But . . . nothing. Stealing a glance, feeling hurt and angry, she saw that Anika had accosted him, and they were in a heated conversation. Jared broke into a sprint, headed toward the control tower—but then veered in her direction, slightly breathless.

"A skirmish has broken out at Mirror Lake," he told her hurriedly, leaning to kiss her cheek. "I'll keep you posted, okay?" He kept on going, jogging backward so he could still keep his eyes on her.

She gave him a wave, smiling faintly at him. He cupped a hand over his mouth, calling out to her, "I love you, Kelsey. It's going to be okay."

Nodding her head, she mouthed, *I know;* then he spun and broke into a much faster gait.

She watched him swing up onto the ladder that led to the control tower. Wiping her eyes, she fretted that, once again, her lifemate was about to hurtle into some sort of danger—if not directly, then indirectly so. It amazed her that he was so intent on keeping her here and safe in his base area, when being in the thick of his war was probably the most dangerous place she could ever be.

The burning within her stomach suddenly increased, as if the baby itself had sensed her fears and anxieties, and she rubbed her belly, thinking soothing thoughts. At least, the best she could; somehow watching Jared's climb into the control room had given her a bad, unsettled feeling, as if all his fear and anxiety about her father were on-target somehow, just horribly misdirected regarding the true source of danger.

Since when were there skirmishes in Yellowstone? Didn't that statement alone signal that their war was about to become much more public than it had been until now?

Mirror Lake, she thought, turning slowly. Everything in their shared lives seemed to revolve around that place, and so much of it had always been sad or dangerous.

Hope rubbed at her eyes, staring at the absolute giant of a man. What he claimed couldn't possibly be true, not with the way Scott's lean body and fair skin were such an utter contrast to the overly large, dark figure standing before her. "How tall are you?" she whispered. "Six-foot-three? Four?"

"I believe I'm six-foot-four."

"Scott's barely more than six feet, I can tell. And your skin is olive, very dark, when Scott's is so naturally fair."

"This body doesn't belong to me. I wasn't born into it."

Jake watched her face, her intelligent eyes darting. He could practically trace the progression of her full understanding just by watching her.

He kept his voice even, continuing with the sordid explanation of how he was, in fact, the man she had married, and whose child she'd carried inside of her belly for nine long months. How he was the man who had grieved after her death, and the man who had borne that grief like a mantle—firing him in his warfare, driving him to the edge—but not until it had all but killed him in the process.

"You're an Antousian, and you're telling me you used your ability—the thing Scott's told me about where you can take a human host—and you . . . what? Jumped bodies? Took this guy's body?" She pressed a hand to her temple. "Scott would never have done that. Never! He despises that about your people. There's no way you can be him: I don't care what you're telling me."

He kept his voice as calm as he could, stepping near her. "I killed a man and stole his body from him. I did it out of anger, grief; I did it so *that* man, Jake Tierny, would have to pay for his crimes. With his life, he had to pay."

"Scott would never have taken a human's body or life."

"Scott takes lives all the time in this war. He's a soldier." It wasn't the right argument at this juncture, but nevertheless it was a point he felt should be made.

"When he's in battle!" She shook her head adamantly.

Jake's rage and grief overtook him in the space of a heartbeat, and he clasped her roughly by both shoulders. Bending down into her face, he hissed, "It was battle! It was battle, and that human killed *you*! You, my love." Tears stung his eyes; he tightened his grasp on Hope. "You were pregnant, weak and ready to deliver. I went for one of the medics, and when I returned Jake was bent over you, your blood all over him. I drew my weapon, but it wasn't enough—my blind fury was too much. I murdered him . . . because he had murdered you."

She slumped against him, physically drained. "I never had her, our little girl." Her voice was small, devastated. He would have done anything to save her so much pain.

Jake tried to find his voice, but his throat was too tight. "We had named her Leisa," he managed at last.

"After your mother."

He smiled wistfully, nodding. "You kept insisting that we should call her Louisa—"

"So she'd have more of an Earth name. I know. I've seen all of this. Just not the end."

"I wanted to shield you from what happened."

She staggered backward and out of his grasp, leaning against the frozen rocks. It was as if she'd just been stabbed in the gut, as if her life were being stolen, here, now. Not in some distant, remote future. "I've even dreamed I'm in labor before, of you kissing my stomach and soothing me . . . but *never* the end."

"Thank All for that," he said fiercely.

"It's funny, but they say if you ever dream you die, then you really do die in your sleep. I guess I should've known it wasn't a good thing that I never once dreamed of holding our little girl."

Jake made a pained cry, putting his back to her, and the sound drew her back to what he had to be feeling. What this man—who she now truly did believe was Scott come back from the future—had lived. "And so that's why the universe implodes if you and Scott get too close together."

"It creates a time-space disturbance."

"Because you *are* Scott Dillon—at least, your soul and your spirit are. You're just in a different body."

"That's one way of putting it," he said darkly. "Although just 'being in a different body' makes it sound like changing snowmobiles or clothes. I killed Jake Tierny; make no mistake about it. And now I have to look into his eyes, the eyes of the man who murdered you . . . every time I gaze into the mirror. It seems a fitting fate to me."

"How can you say that, Jake?" she demanded, taking a few cautious steps toward where he stood. And without even asking him what he preferred, she knew she would always have to call him Jake or Jakob, not Scott. They were two entirely different men to her now, separated by fathomless depths of time and space and history.

He took hold of her arm. "We've gotta keep climbing. Scott's going to catch up with us if we don't, and he'd as soon put a pulse blast through me as hear my side of the story."

"You don't know that for sure."

"Yeah? Well, I know the bastard a lot better than you do, don't I?"

And for some reason, the absolute surreal insanity of his statement made her burst out laughing.

*   *   *

Scott plunged upward along the trail, Anna right at his heels. Once the wind and crazy universe tilting had ceased, he'd begun his pursuit once again. Nurse Tyler's words were echoing through his head—her speculation that Jake was trying to get back to his own time. Everything within him witnessed to that opinion, and Scott had absolutely no doubt that the Antousian freak planned to jerk Hope right along with him. Because the man loved her, just like he did—he'd gotten that much from his spirit slipping of Hope's dreams. Somehow, in their indeterminate future, he and Jake Tierny had battled it out for her affections, and Scott had come up on the losing end of things.

But not this time. Never again, and especially not under these current terms of relational war. Scott would not lose this time, even if he had to die trying.

He stopped for a moment, studying the trail, and Anna shoved up against his backside. "Sir, what happened back there?" She sounded breathless, confused, just as he was.

"No questions, soldier," he barked. "Target dead ahead!"

Anna grasped at his arm, forcing him to turn toward her. "What *happened* back there, Lieutenant?" she repeated. "That makes twice now that the earth and sky nearly imploded when your path crossed that man's."

Scott stared straight ahead. "I don't know," he told her honestly, shaking her off.

"I get that you love her, but it's time to stop—stop and ask yourself why it is that your path and his seem so combustible. Sir. With all due respect."

Scott began trudging upward on the trail again. "He has my wife; that's all I need to know."

Anna nipped at his heels, unrelenting. "Your wife, sir? Since when?"

He stretched out his steps, moving faster. "Since I saw our future in my dreams, Lieutenant. That's when."

"The universe doesn't like the two of you together," she pressed, matching every one of his aggressive strides.

"So what's new with that?" he spit over his shoulder. He had to catch up with them, had to stop Tierny's gambit with time. "The world generally hates my ass."

"That's not true. We all love you, sir. Again . . . with all due respect."

Something in her tone caused him to stop, to really notice her words. "I don't know what you mean." He studied her, still glancing over his shoulder to measure Tierny's progress.

Anna slumped, saying nothing more, and with one hand gestured toward the trail up ahead. "Keep going, sir. Just keep going."

Chapter Eighteen

"Chris, I may have something for you on Hope." His supervisor had entered Chris's temporary office without knocking, just barging in and then shutting the door behind him. Blake waved a piece of paper at him. "This came from one of the rangers up in Yellowstone. Apparently a man and woman bribed a guide so they could go off trail. The guide took the money, but got suspicious and followed them for a while—until he heard the sound of 'weird electronic weaponry'—and I quote."

Chris's eyes narrowed. "You thinking the same thing I'm thinking?"

Blake leaned against the closed door, nodding, and in unison they agreed: "Mirror Lake."

An alien craft had crashed out at the lake just one month earlier, and Chris had been working that case—along with the subsequent capture of Scott Dillon at the same site—ever since. In lieu of causing a public panic, the USAF had cleaned up the crash site, and the park had opened for the winter as usual.

"What kind of description on the male and female?"

Blake grinned. "You're gonna love me now." Walking toward him, Blake tossed down the report and paperwork on Chris's desk. "The guide described the woman as seeming blind, but not quite. Said she tried to pretend she could see, but it was obvious that she either had terrible eyesight or was only partially sighted."

Chris slapped a palm against the desk. "Hell, yeah! That's my sis, all right."

Blake nodded. "Well, and this snowmobile trek has her fingerprints all over it too—out in the wilderness, middle of danger."

Chris's smile faded. "And in the line of fire." He leaped to his feet. "So when do we take off?"

Blake karate-chopped his hands together in a time-out signal. "Hold up, buddy. You know this is going to be USAF all the way."

"I'm working this case, Miles! No way am I sitting back, especially not when it's Hope who's involved."

"I didn't say you weren't going—just be aware that apparently a high-level pissing contest has been going on between headquarters and those guys. We're part of the joint task force, but definitely not at the helm."

Chris ground his teeth together. "Do I get to go or not?"

"In a limited capacity." Blake gave him the look—the one that always meant Chris had better keep his rebellious attitude and aggressive methods back at the office. "Limited, Harper. Understand?"

Chris grunted, grabbing the folder. Studying the report, he saw another detail that caught his eye. "A thousand dollars? That's a lot of money to go off trail."

"Well, if you're intent on getting to your destination—for some purpose or another—not so much. These guys are clearly well financed."

"And also well equipped—transports, heavy military weapons, planes. So why do they suddenly need to slap down almost a grand to get deep inside the park, and on a snowmobile, no less? And why does this guy take along an almost-blind woman with him? Doesn't add up."

"What are you getting at?"

"Sounds to me like someone's gone rogue." Chris rubbed his tired eyes. "And taken my sis right along with him."

"What have you said to your parents? Anything?"

"Oh, that she's met some guy and fallen in love."

Blake blanched visibly. "You think that's true?" he asked, but his voice betrayed his deeper feelings for Hope.

"I have no idea, but it was a good cover story for why she hadn't been checking in with them."

Blake stared past Chris's shoulder, thoughtful. "Maybe that was the big enticement, going up there with Scott Dillon." They'd all read the transcripts, seen how she and the lieutenant had bonded during his captivity. It had been a strange and fast intimacy that had developed between those two.

Chris scanned the report held in his hands. "What's the description on the male unsub?" *Unsub* was FBI-speak for *unknown subject.*

"Doesn't fit Dillon at all; our unsub's a really big guy, tall and bulky." Blake reached for the door.

"So that probably negates the idea that she's doing it for love." It just didn't add up in Chris's mind—that she'd followed Dillon and now wound up with some other bad guy. And he had no doubt—the female unsub was none other than his twin.

Blake opened the door. "Look, we've got to roll if we're going to get up there fast."

Scott reached the top ridge with Anna, and immediately spotted Tierny outside the mitres, data collector in hand. Hope stood beside him, looking very pale and wobbly legged.

"Stop that now!" Scott cried out, rushing toward Jake, but it was just like the two other times they'd come in close proximity to each other—a rushing force of power held him back, kept him suspended within the grasp of some invisible hand. Scott braced against the rocks outside the chamber.

"Don't try to take her with you!" he shouted, cupping his mouth with his hand. "She's not part of this war. Don't do it!"

Jake shook him off, fumbling with the data collector still. In panic, Scott reached for Anna. "See if you can go to him. Maybe these weird violent effects only happen to me."

"Absolutely!" Anna called, already sprinting the small distance that separated their respective groups.

Backing up a little, Scott felt even more confused once the wind died down. If he got closer to Tierny, the world unraveled—he kept his distance and things seemed to stay in balance. From the safer perimeter he watched as Anna began arguing with Tierny, gesturing vehemently. He felt a rush of affection for her; she'd always been loyal and devoted to him throughout their years of serving together.

Hope glanced in his direction, trailing her fingers along the rocks, taking a cautious step toward him. "Yeah, baby," he murmured under his breath. "Yeah, just come on back to me. Right now, sweetheart, come on back."

He didn't dare step toward her, so he was forced to wait, breath held, counting off the seconds and distance that stood between the two of them. Jake and Anna continued in a hushed, intense discussion, each glancing at Hope periodically. What were they saying? What had Tierny's intent been with her, anyway?

"I'm here, Hope," he called to her as she got closer. "Stick close to the rocks and just follow my voice home."

She paused, adjusting the pack she carried on her shoulder, and for a moment he thought she was going to pass out. Instinctively he stepped forward, and at the precise moment he did, three station craft came over the ridge, bearing down on all of them.

"Oh, shit!" Scott yelled, the violent wind coming off the craft's undersides nearly shoving him to the ground. Crouching, he struggled to reach Hope while unholstering his weapon and firing overhead, but not before pulse fire peppered the ground at his feet.

In one insane moment his gaze and Jake's locked, and it was as if he heard the other man's words reverberate in his head:

Protect her. At all costs, get her out of this place!

He gave a nod, leaped to his feet, and rushed toward Hope.

The wind overhead drove Hope to her knees, and then the immediate sound of gunfire kept her hunkered as low as possible against the rocks around them. Most days her eyesight issues were just frustrating, but at a moment like this one, when she just couldn't see what the hell was going on, the limitations became terrifying. Her heart was in her throat, and all she could do was cling to her medical pack and pray that she and the others wouldn't get killed, especially not Scott.

Covering her head with her hands, she ducked lower as sparks shot past her shoulder. Then suddenly a familiar hand clasped her arm, dragging her along the rocky ridge. "Come on, Harper, move it! Move it!"

Scott! She wanted to fling her arms about his neck and sob her relief, but there was hardly time for that. "Who are these people?" she asked breathlessly, allowing him to lead her down the path. "More Antousians?"

"Yep. Nice guys, huh?" He paused, took hold of her shoulders, and shoved her in front of himself. "It'll be my back they fire on," he said, words that eerily mirrored Jake's from earlier. Holding on to her, he pushed her along down the trail, never letting go. "Now let's see if I can't get you out of here in one piece."

Pulse fire pummeled the rocks about them, and shards of the stones shot out like shrapnel. Scott shoved her down and under his own body on the trail, draping himself over her. He kept her snug beneath him, raising his own pistol and firing at the droning, persistent station craft overhead. They were relentlessly shadowed by two of them no matter how far they went down the trail.

The other one had to be back giving Jake and Anna the shakedown.

"Up ahead, run for those trees. They can't follow us if we get into that cover," he whispered into her ear, his familiar scent and warm breath instantly soothing. What she wished, more than anything, was that the whole world weren't exploding around them, and that they were in that motel room from her dreams instead of here.

"They can tail us, though. Like they did across the lake, right?"

"I missed that part," Scott breathed against her ear, and she caught herself, realizing that she'd just blurred Scott and Jake together, made them one person. "But yeah, they could drop low and chase us: They've got superior firepower from above like that."

"Then let's get to the trees," she agreed, and he lifted her onto her feet. Together they began half stumbling, half running toward the tree line up ahead.

"Keep going, keep going," Scott urged, holding her about the waist and shoving her forward on the trail. "Almost to the trees—see how it's darker up there? That's your goal."

Her mouth was dry, her chest heaving. Even back at Warren she'd never been quite this terrified. "After that?"

"We get to the bottom of the trail; then my transport picks us up and gets us the hell out of here." She heard him calling into his comm, giving some kind of directions to the transport's captain.

"What about Anna? Jake?"

"I don't give a shit about Jake, but Anna I'll do everything I can to save."

She shook her head, still moving forward. "Don't write Jake off like that. He needs your help too."

Scott made a growling, angry sound right as a large number of blurry figures filled the trail ahead of them, shouting in Refarian. She couldn't translate much—the

words were flying too fast and too erratically. Behind
her she heard the drumming sound of station craft as
the machines came up behind them on the trail. Dimly,
she wondered why Antousians would be speaking in Refarian, but she hardly had time to dwell on that fact.

"I sure hope those people ahead of us are on our
side," she muttered under her breath, feeling Scott's grip
on her tighten. "Tell me they're good guys." Scott didn't
answer, but tossed something past her shoulder, and it
hit the snow with a muted sound. "And tell me that's
not your weapon you just dropped."

Stepping apart from her, thrusting both hands in the
air, he whispered, "I'll get you out of this. It's my fault
you're here, and I'll make it all work out."

The soldiers ahead rushed in on them. She closed her
eyes, clutching her medical pack like the lifeline it was;
the worst had come true.

They were cornered, with no chance of escape.

A tall female soldier took hold of her roughly, wrestling the pack out of her hands. "Hey! I need that!"
Hope protested, grasping at it, and they got into a short
tug-of-war over the med bag. "That's got all my medicine in it."

"Tough luck, cutie," the woman said in heavily accented English. "It goes with us."

They had Scott on the ground, it seemed, his hands
behind him. "She's got to have that," he argued on her
behalf. "She'll die without it."

The female soldier chuckled darkly. "So? Maybe that
will save us a little work."

Someone else called out, "Hand it to me, Kryn; I'll
have a look."

Kryn stood beside Hope, obviously sizing her up.
"You're not Refarian," the woman observed. "In fact,
you're just a human, a blind and sick human, at that—
so why are you and this man"—she kicked at Scott with
her boot—"working together?"

I'm FBI, cutie! she wanted to shout back into the
woman's face, but that of all reasons would probably get

her killed. Or tortured. *Oh, shit, shit, I need an excuse, a good excuse.*

Maybe it was God who supplied it, but a very fast and clever one popped into Hope's mind. "Because I met this man in a bar," she answered evenly, remembering the dream about the motel. "One-night stand, you know how it goes." She smiled up into Kryn's face, playing the gal-pal card. "Anyway, yeah, I found out that he's an alien, and realized pretty quickly that they could heal me. So I followed him, and that's how I wound up on the transport and out here. He was going to have me shot because I know too much."

"That's why he argued that you needed your pack?" Kryn sounded amused that Hope's story was filled with so many holes. Hope assessed the alien, how she towered over her, her long length of dark brown hair. Probably attractive, maybe beautiful, not that any of that mattered at this particular moment.

Hope flashed her best and most winning smile. "Well, correction, I think the lieutenant *wanted* to have me shot, but"—she leaned in close to Kryn, who instantly stiffened—"you know, the sex was just white-hot."

Hope was ready to embroider the details, to really take things up a notch, but another soldier interrupted them. "The pack's clear, Kryn." The grunt thrust her med supplies back into Kryn's clutches. "It's only medicine and stuff, like she says."

Kryn shoved the pack against Hope's chest. "Here, take it," the woman said emotionlessly.

Hope wanted to weep from gratitude and relief; she wouldn't have made it another hour without a snack. She'd been losing control of her glucose levels all day, and her recent bursts of activity already had them diving once again.

"Thank you." Hope bowed her head slightly in acknowledgment, but Kryn had already moved away from her.

Yes, Hope was certainly grateful, but it was far more than the return of her med supplies for which she rejoiced. Deep within her sack, sewn into the lining, she held a secret—one that just might save both of their asses.

The FBI was bringing them into Jackson by commercial jet, and Chris handed over his flying armed form, already filled out with his badge number and detailed information. As special agents, he and Blake were bypassing the usual security line, walking in where all the departing civilian passengers were exiting. Whenever they flew commercial there was always paperwork, the assessment of whether air marshals would be on board, the usual government red tape. Once they cleared security, both Chris and Blake stepped through the gate.

Blake tucked his boarding pass into the front of his suit pocket, visibly relieved. "On our way," his supervisor said with a wary grin. Chris understood the inherent meaning in the man's statement: You just never knew what might hold you up on a job, government badges notwithstanding.

"Can't get there fast enough." Chris stuck his own pass into the back pocket of his pants, impatient and restless. The next few hours would take everything out of him; Hope was his best friend, his twin, his other half. Maybe it was unhealthy, but he could never really stop worrying about her, all the more given her illness—and her propensity for trouble. He shook off his familiar fears, staring at the gateway straight ahead.

Together he and Blake walked the long concourse, passing Domino's and Burger King, but the only thing on Chris's mind was getting up to Yellowstone. Blake stared wistfully at one of the coffee shops, and Chris was about to give him hell when his cell jarred him.

"Harper," he said, whipping the phone to his ear.

It was the Denver office. "We've got a fix on your sister," his SSA told him. "She's not at Mirror Lake. Well, not anymore."

Chris stopped in his tracks, Blake walking ahead without him. "Not anymore? What do you mean?"

"She turned on her cell about twelve minutes ago, but her position has been shifting ever since. We triangulated her not far from Yellowstone, but she's in motion—and fast. It's got to be some kind of transport."

Up ahead, Blake turned back, impatience written on his face—until he got a look at Chris, and concern instantly replaced annoyance.

"So what do you want us to do, sir?" Chris asked.

"Get your asses on up to Mirror Lake."

"But if she's gone—"

"Chris, do I have to remind you that this isn't about your sister? You have a job to do, so get going."

Chapter Nineteen

Jake paced the interior of the mitres chamber, trying to arrive at a plan. So far, however, his big "plans" had led to disaster. Hope and Scott had been captured; he and Anna were locked inside the mitres, and there wasn't a damn thing he could do to help either of those two situations from within here. All this time he'd been pushing toward this very moment, to be able to return to the future; now he just wanted to get the hell out and do something—anything—to help Hope and his younger self survive.

Meanwhile Anna eyed him warily, her dark eyes wide and furious as she followed him in circles about the rounded perimeter of the chamber. When the Antousian soldiers had appeared on the path, blocking Hope and Scott's retreat, he'd made a split-second decision: He had allowed the portal to open, transporting both himself and Anna inside of the mitres to temporary safety. Anna had been questioning his sanity—and his strategy—ever since.

"You just left them out there, to those *vlksai* freaks. Do you have any idea what's going to happen to them now? The first clue of what kind of danger you've put them in?" she ranted.

Jake held a hand up, silencing her. "I need to think, Anna."

"How do you even know my name?" She planted one

hand on her hip. "You seem to know all of us—and very well."

He shook his head, staring down at the data collector; if he'd been able to upload the codes twice now, surely he could make the damned thing work one more time.

"Why did you transport us in here when they needed our support? Maybe you really are our enemy, though I'd been inclined to think otherwise."

This caught his attention, and he glanced up from his handheld. "And what makes you so sure of that?"

Anna rubbed a smudged finger over her nose. "Two things, really. The first being that you love Hope Harper, and the second being that the universe won't tolerate you and Scott being in proximity—well, which raises a third. You're an Antousian shifter who's traveled back from the future. Your physical nature makes the possibility of a body switch quite real."

Dumbfounded, Jake gaped at the soldier. Anna had always been his friend, had been loyal and devoted, especially after Hope's death. But this woman had no memory of that; this was the woman he'd kissed not so long ago in this world, and who had laughed in his face. It was a reaction that had hurt him deeply—not so much because he had cared for her romantically, but because it had made him feel ugly.

"I'm on the right track, aren't I?" she pressed, her large dark eyes narrowing on him.

There was no reason to hide the truth anymore; Hope knew his terrible, sordid secret, and now this friend had intuited the facts as well. "You're on it."

"Then, *sir,* how about you tell me one sure fact that will prove you're who I think you are."

He stared at his booted feet. "Why does it matter?" he asked, suddenly more exhausted and worn down than he'd ever felt because of the endless war.

She stamped the floor in exasperation. "Because you're either my enemy or you're my very good friend. I need to know which one. Prove it!"

"Okay, I can prove it, or at least, if you want to believe the truth." Even now, it was an embarrassing thing to discuss, but nobody else would have this particular kernel of knowledge.

"When we first arrived on this planet, you and I were on a surveillance mission. The night just went on and on, nothing much happening. It was hotter than hell too, a big heat wave going on. So . . . I kissed you." She flushed instantly, chewing her lip. "I kissed you because, you know, I really had a thing for you back then. But you know what you did? You laughed at my advances."

Anna closed her eyes. "My gods."

"Yeah, you laughed in my face, and it led me to a pretty strong conclusion: that my fair-skinned human looks didn't do one thing for my Refarian comrades. I started looking for companionship among the humans right after that. Night after night, bar after bar."

She rushed him, flinging her arms about his neck. "Oh, gods, Scott. What have you been through?" she whispered, holding him tight. It was utterly unexpected, such an outpouring of emotion; Anna was a smart-ass, a hardened soldier. Slowly he closed his hands around her back.

"I've been through hell," he whispered. The embrace felt so good, so comforting.

Slowly she released him, staring right up into his eyes. "How could you have ever thought I was ridiculing you?"

He lifted an eyebrow. "Um, because you laughed? Right in my face, as a matter of fact. I know I wasn't a gorgeous guy, especially not to our people. I've always been a *vlksai* cuss, and half-human at that. It wasn't a pretty sight, and I'm not stupid; I got it. No wonder you laughed."

She regarded him for a long moment. "You really don't know, do you?" He shrugged, confused, and she continued. "You really have no idea how beautiful you are. How beautiful we all think you are—every single woman under your command?"

He felt his face grow hot. "Don't stroke my ego, not

now, Anna. Besides, I'm not that man anymore. You can see that just by looking at me."

This time she was the one who blushed, and dropped her gaze. "I laughed because I thought you handsome," she explained quietly. "You were my friend, Scott." She lifted her gaze, searching his face as if she needed him to understand. "And I laughed because no man—not in the ranks or back home or anywhere—had ever once kissed me. I had no idea what to do."

It was the last thing in the universe he'd expected. "That can't be true."

"No, it is true." She shook her head vehemently. "I had the biggest crush on you, but you were my commanding officer. My friend. I was scared to death of you, too, because I didn't know you very well yet."

Slowly he backed away from her, fiddling with his handheld all over again. Strange, but his face burned, and he felt inexplicably awkward—he just couldn't look into her eyes.

"So you believe me—about who I really am, then?" he murmured.

"Scott, yes, of course I believe you. There's no other way you could have known about that kiss."

"One of your friends might have told me," he disagreed, still training his gaze downward.

"I never told anyone." Her voice was hushed, sincere.

The blush on his face deepened. "Neither did I."

"Well, now that I've confirmed your identity, Dillon, we've got to find a way to get out of this place and save their asses."

"Look, I'm not Dillon anymore—that's really important to me." He dared to meet her gaze. "I'm Jakob Tierny. It's the only name I've gone by ever since . . ."

"He's the man whose body you took?"

He nodded, swallowing. "I'll save that story for another time."

"No matter. If you did it, there was a good reason." She stuck her stubborn chin into the air. "I'm already settled about that fact."

"You seem to have a lot of faith in me."

"Always well-placed, sir, always. And I know you'll help us figure this crisis out."

Hope sank into her seat aboard the Antousian battle cruiser. Scott was buckled in beside her, both hands bound, as were her own. They'd allowed her to down a package of crackers and some juice; her test strip had shown what she could already feel anyway; that her glucose levels had dipped low. If they didn't let her eat a real meal soon, though, her levels would get seriously out of control.

And when they'd let her have the pack, she'd implemented the one safety valve that she figured she and Scott had going for them: She'd powered up her phone where it was secretly stashed in a hidden pouch within the pack. Thank God the alien goon who'd inspected it hadn't discovered her slim cell. It was the latest government-issue, and superlightweight; otherwise it would undoubtedly have been discovered. She only hoped that at this altitude the FBI could still get a reading on her signal; coverage in midair was usually so unreliable, cutting in and out, if she got any signal at all. Still, maybe if fate had decided to be kind just this once, they had a prayer of getting some help.

"Where are we?" she asked Scott under her breath. Beside her, she could feel his body heat, could sense the way he struggled within his bonds.

"Heading straight into the stratosphere, most likely. Nobody will ever get to us up here, and that's the way these freaks want it."

Thinking of her cell signal, she felt a wave of nausea overcome her. "What're the specs on this thing?"

He pushed his shoulder against hers significantly, falling quiet as one of the Antousians walked past where they sat. Beneath her, all around her, she could hear and feel vibrations. An engine, powerful, rumbled throughout the whole craft. Somewhere near them a door slid open, then immediately closed. After that, silence. Scott still waited, and then leaned much closer toward her ear. She closed her eyes, catching his scent.

"It's a powerful, massive battle cruiser," he whispered. "Like the one they put in position over Warren. A real beast."

"What do they want with us?"

He blew out a hesitant breath, then replied, "To drain us of every last bit of intel we might possess. Then kill us—me especially."

She jerked her head toward him. "Why especially you?" Her voice sounded husky, emotional; the idea of Scott dying made her feel just that way, so what was the point of pretending?

Scott pressed his forehead lightly against hers; it killed her that she couldn't touch him, couldn't reach for his hand. For the moment this was the extent of their ability to connect physically—and being unable to see much tore her apart inside.

"Because aside from Jared Bennett," he told her quietly, "I'm the number one guy on Veckus's kill list. He's the guy in charge of their Earth strategies. And no other creature has ever despised me as much as he."

She pressed her eyes shut, willing the entire moment to be nothing more than a nightmare—one of their shared dreams gone awry. "We can't let him hurt you."

Scott nuzzled her gently. "I doubt we've got much choice right now, sweetheart, but I'm open to any ideas."

At that precise moment the sound of heavy footsteps filled the area around them; several people, perhaps one a woman, marched up to them. "Separate!" a voice she recognized as belonging to Kryn called out. "Who put these two right together like this?" All at once rough hands took hold of her, jabbing at her restraints, and she was splayed face-first in the aisle.

"Go easy on her!" Scott yelled. "Your beef's not with her—it's with me."

Hope drew up on her knees, shaking her head to clear it as Kryn laughed. "Well, we already know that you're into the little human, so I'd say she's exactly the one we should focus on . . . *Lieutenant*."

With that, Hope found herself being hustled down the aisle and into a small side compartment, thrust down on a bench seat. The door closed, and Kryn stood before her. Hope sucked at air, trying to think, but she feared that if things kept up like this, she was going to be in a world of hurt with her diabetes.

"What do you want with me?" she demanded of the other woman. "I don't know a thing! I've told you that already."

Kryn dropped down in front of her, leaning close enough that Hope could almost see her. "Cutie, all I want is for your boyfriend to talk. We've been after Dillon for a long time, and right now I see you as the best avenue for that."

Hope began to tremble. "If I can't keep up with my meds . . ."

But Kryn cut her off. "I'll make sure you get what you need," the woman told her coolly.

"Why?" Hope asked, unable to contain her surprise.

Kryn extended her hand, feeling for Hope's until they made a connection. "Kryn Zoltners," she announced. "And you are . . . ?"

Something weird and instinctual—that same old voice that had guided her all along—led her to say, "Hope Harper."

"Hope, if you don't know about the virus that destroyed the majority of my people, then you don't know a hell of a lot about this war. I've had far too many friends—terribly sick friends—who relied on medication not to take pity on a prisoner of war like you."

With that the woman rose abruptly and exited the room, not speaking another word.

"Where are you transporting us?" Dillon stared down the tall brunette soldier, the one he'd heard referred to as Kryn. For several seconds her hate-filled gaze locked with his while she stood in front of him, and without taking her eyes off of him, she slid into the seat harness across the aisle.

"You'll see when we arrive there, won't you?"

"Hours? Days? Months?" His mind reeled with the possibility that they might even deport him back to Refaria, thereby separating him from his commander right when Jared needed his counsel the most.

Kryn's lips turned upward into a cautious smile. "You will see." Her voice was heavily accented, like that of so many Antousians raised back on Refaria. Many of them no longer even spoke their native language, but relied entirely on the verbal currency that was still the mainstay back home. Refaria . . . home. That was ultimately what this war was all about: who had the right to call that planet home.

And he knew all too well the kind of very explicit torture Veckus Densalt was capable of when it came to the Refarians—especially any soldier with the rebel military faction. Scott cringed, remembering the punishments that Veckus had personally meted out against Jared during his brief captivity several years earlier. His king had been bruised, bloodied, his entire body shattered from top to bottom. More than that, something in Jared's spirit had been broken during those three days, something that Scott hadn't seen truly restored until his best friend had bonded with Kelsey. Years it had taken the man to recover. So what might Veckus do now that he and Hope had fallen into his vile clutches?

Scott kept his expression placid, even though inside, his mind whirled with anxiety and the terrible possibilities. Why, by the gods, had Hope managed to wander into this mess?

He tried a new tack. "What are you doing to Ms. Harper? Where did you escort her?"

Kryn folded both arms over her chest, glancing upward at the ceiling; Scott's gaze tracked with hers, only to discover a small electronic eye above them. They were being watched—hell, Veckus himself was undoubtedly observing these proceedings. Still, it was curious that Kryn had made such a point of revealing that fact.

Slowly, she resumed studying him. "Ms. Harper will not be harmed, Lieutenant. All right?"

"She needs to eat soon or she'll be in serious trouble."

Kryn gave a brisk nod, waved her hand, and from behind a closed door a soldier appeared. They spoke quietly in Refarian, and then the man disappeared once again. "Done."

That she was being so agreeable and helpful did nothing to dispel his fears. It only meant that the games had yet to truly begin. "Thank you." He gave a courteous bow of his head.

"You are welcome. And if you cooperate, Hope will continue to be fed, allowed her medication, and treated well. If you do not?" She gave an indifferent shrug. "Things will grow far more complicated for your little human friend."

"I want to see Veckus." He kept his voice commanding, cool, but his heart slammed hard within his chest. His mouth was dry with fear—and he was plenty tough after a near-lifetime of fighting. "He and I have a lot to discuss. We might as well start that process right now."

"On his timetable—not yours." She rose to her feet again, stepping closer into his physical space. Then, in a very low voice, she said, "Be wise, Lieutenant. Play the game." She narrowed her eyes meaningfully. "Play the game . . . with me." Her last words were whispered under her breath.

He frowned, not sure what her cryptic warning meant, and then just as quickly she spun on her heel, marching up the aisle away from him.

Jake wanted to whoop in victory; the data codes had uploaded freely, allowing them to step through interdimensional space and to the exterior of the mitres chamber. Anna rubbed at her head, giving it a light shake. "That's one heck of a mental vacuum cleaner." She looked up into his eyes. "Was that my imagination, or did I just see some of your life in the future? Some of my own past?"

Jake nodded, walking out to the edge of the trailhead. The truth was that the mitres served as an overlapping filmstrip of memories and possible futures; as he and Anna had journeyed through the portal, he'd glimpsed and felt memories that had almost been more than he could bear.

But there'd been something else, something that had him blushing and turning away from his friend: He'd seen the two of them in his current body, in the throes of making love, she all glistening and naked beneath him; he bucking atop her and unable to stop.

"Jake? Did you see stuff too?" She wasn't going to let it go; Anna had never been one to let much of anything go.

"Just bits of my life, that's all . . . Look, we've got to get busting down this trail, see if we can get a lead on where they've taken Scott and Hope."

Anna grabbed him by the arm. "You know they're long gone—or waiting in ambush for us. The best thing we can do is let me signal the transport and put all of our firepower behind that search."

A stab of anxiety shot through Jake's heart. "And who's going to believe my identity—beyond you?"

Anna squinted at the bright sunlight reflecting off the snow. "Jared's your best friend—the very best friend you've ever had. If I believed you, don't you think he will?"

Jake holstered his weapon. "There's no time to wait. I've gotta go check out what's down at the end of that trail." He began hustling down the slippery incline, and Anna called after him.

"If you get yourself captured too, there won't be a damn thing you can do to help her. Or him."

Jake slid to a halt. Of course she was right, but letting Hope go—letting go of the possibility that he might still stop her *vlksai* captors—went against every instinct inside of him. As a husband, as a soldier . . . and as Scott Dillon's dark twin.

Behind him he heard Anna radioing the transport. Stubborn as could be, that woman was . . . and for once he was thankful for that fact.

Almost immediately the transport swooped low, sidling up to the cliffs. The running boards extended, allowing for a platform, and, ducking low against the churning wind created by the craft, both Jake and Anna scrambled into the opened hatch.

Anna was shouting something over the noise, but he couldn't understand what, and so he focused on just getting inside the transport without getting himself shot. No sooner had he placed his boots inside than several pairs of strong hands took hold of him, throwing him to the ground.

"Hold off! Hold!" Anna yelled as he felt the barrel of a K-12 burrow into the base of his spine.

"I'm holding." He recognized the husky voice of Marco McKinley. "But I want to make sure that this man"—he jabbed him with his weapon—"and our commander have a proper chance to talk first."

So after running in circles, and losing Hope in the process, he'd effectively landed right back where he'd begun: at the end of Marco's weapon, with Jared Bennett's boots walking slowly toward him.

Rotating his head slightly, he got a fix on Anna, who had dropped down low beside him. "What were you saying when we boarded this thing?" He grunted, feeling the pressure of Marco's knee drive into his back.

She smiled. "That this wasn't the craft we'd arrived in. Sir."

"No, indeed not," Jared interrupted, coming to a stop right beside Jake's prone body. "This I had to come and see for myself. A skirmish in Yellowstone—in the wide-open public? This has to be the sloppiest, most ill-thought-out plan I've ever observed."

"Please, Commander, just let me up," Jake argued. "I'll explain everything."

Jared laughed low in his throat. "I believe I've already heard that once from you. Twice, and I'll have to require that you be held in this transport's brig until we return to base. There, we will talk. But not before."

"Tell me just one thing—anything—that will make me believe you're who you claim to be."

Jake sat across the table from Jared and Kelsey in the main meeting room at the bottom of Base Ten. Everything depended upon this moment, upon gaining their faith and confidence. Without Jared's support, he would never be able to help free Hope and Scott; more than that, there were critical warnings Jake could issue about the future now that he possibly had Jared's ear. Maybe, just maybe, this whole seemingly pointless venture would be worth more than *meshdki* after all. But only if he could get Jared to really listen.

Jake wrestled within his mind, struggled to find the appropriate proof, something that would make Jareshk realize that he'd known him all their lives—and that this ludicrous moment, this wrong-body encounter, hardly mattered anyway when you tossed the dice of friendship.

"Anna believes me, sir."

Jared nodded regally. "And Anna is the reason that you are here now, before me. She said you gave her undeniable proof as to your identity. Surely, with as many years as you claim we have known each other, you can do the same for me."

Jake leaned back in the chair, glancing around the meeting room. He sat in the deepest recesses of a base that had been destroyed for him four years earlier. All that Jared and the resistance had created as a mainstay for operations had been obliterated with a few easy missiles. Once the location of the bases had been betrayed, the destruction of them had been simple.

"There are so many things I need to warn you about." Jake pressed his eyes shut. "All you have to do is believe me."

Jared glanced sideways at his wife, smiling. "Perhaps

I've already been mated with a scientist for too long—I need some sort of proof."

Kelsey took the lead, spreading her freckled hands atop the table between them. "Jake, nothing about what you're suggesting is impossible. We know that—I know it perhaps even more than Jared. Can you tell me why that might be?"

Ah, smart queen. "The mitres technology fused within your mind is what enabled me to power the mitres to make my journey," he answered evenly. "You are the one who set it, who uploaded the codes and even allowed me temporary storage of them"—he gestured at his data collector—"in here."

Kelsey cocked her head with a winning look of approval. "Not bad. But . . . what if we believe you're a time traveler, but not that you're our ally?" Damn—and he'd thought he had her convinced.

Jake looked to his king for some sort of seal of approval, for a glimmer of faith in his dark eyes. Instead, Jared lifted an eyebrow, but said nothing—simply waited for Jake to prove that he was, in fact, Scott Dillon.

Jake sighed. "Once, when we were boys," he began, "I had a *glunshai.*" It was a small, slimy creature akin to a lizard. "You were what, seven? I was just about the same . . . and I brought that creature into your father's great hall during a formal speech before the elders. All of us—and I mean all—were meant to be respectful, but I stashed that little guy away in my pocket."

He dared a glance at Jared, but his king's face remained stoic, unmoved. Even so, Jake continued. "We sat there on that stone floor, listening to your father's address, but it kept going on and on." Jake couldn't help but smile, remembering. "I worked that little *glunshai* out of my pocket. And there he was, on the floor . . . and next thing we knew, he took off running across the hall. Man, you looked at me—and I looked at you—and all at once the elders swooped down on us. We were in some serious, deep *meshdki,* and all because of a lizard."

Jake began to laugh in earnest, just remembering their last moments of innocent childhood.

"They yanked me right out of that hall, pointing the finger at me, Jareshk, but you wouldn't let me take the blame. You stood, and your father hesitated during his speech, seeing you rise up that way, but you just smiled and followed me out of the great hall . . . and insisted that it was *your* little pet that had caused the whole damned thing. You wouldn't let the blame ride on me. It was always that way with the two of us—we never would let the other take the fall."

Jake shut his eyes, feeling his face contort, his memories taking him too far back into an innocence that had vanished long ago. "That's what I remember, Jareshk. That you always stood up for me, even when I didn't deserve it."

He was met with a long, enduring silence. "That proves nothing," his king and best friend said at last. "I want to believe you. Compel me to do so." Jake heard rough emotion in the man's voice, and it was enough to finally break him.

"You know me, J; you always have." Jake buried his face within his hands. "He killed her, and I had no choice. I had to take his life too."

"Who killed 'her'?" Jared rose and took several determined steps closer. "*How* did he kill her? Tell me what you mean."

Everything about that fateful day overpowered Jake in the space of a moment. That Jared didn't know those events—that *this* version of the only brother he'd ever known had no knowledge of what he'd endured—made it almost more than he could bear.

He ground his teeth together. "Don't make me say it."

"I want to trust you, Jakob."

"Then trust me! But don't make me live it all over again."

"You're going to have to—if I'm to figure any of this out."

Jake leaped to his feet and spun on his lifelong friend. "For just one moment I let my guard down. I went for help because Hope needed it, and Jake Tierny killed her. That's how it went down." Jake clutched at his head, the memories utterly unstoppable—and unendurable as well. Pulling at his hair, he tried to wrestle through the heart-breaking emotions that he'd already had to live once today.

"I went for a doctor, and when I returned Hope was dead. I never knew why, but Jake had killed her, was standing over her, blood still on his hands. I took his life because I had to. He'd taken everything from me, and so"—Jake drew in an unsteady, furious breath, just remembering—"I took the only thing I could. I took *him*. I took Jake Tierny's life because he killed her. Because he killed my wife, and he killed our baby in the process. And that, my king and friend, is why I am *him* today."

Jared studied him evenly, as if he hadn't just confessed to his greatest crime: a murder in cold blood—the taking of a life to avenge the one he'd valued most in the universe, that of his wife.

Jared strolled toward Kelsey, his face a troubled mask, and Jake wasn't sure exactly what to think. She had been sitting to the side, simply listening; already, as in the future, it was obvious that Jared relied on her counsel a great deal. Well, either his beloved king and queen would brand him a murderer—or worse, a traitor to the greatest possible extreme. Or they would recognize him for who he truly was: Scott Dillon, lost in this current time, without the right body, without his wife, and without his creed.

Time itself hung in the balance, Jared and Kelsey trading some kind of knowing look, then speaking in muted tones. He wished he were a deep intuitive, that he could enter their thoughts and discern whether they trusted him, and he didn't dare soul-gaze them at such an intense moment. But finally—at long last—Jared turned to face him.

"Tell me one more thing. Tell me why you came back through time."

Jake bowed his head, not wanting to share the awful, ruined truth of their future. But he had no other choice. "Because we're defeated there, my lord. Everything is destruction—you sent me back because you hoped that I could stop Marco McKinley from bringing even more bloodshed. But now, it seems, that version of Marco has already been stopped."

Jared nodded simply. "Yes, he has—and I trust Marco."

"He betrays you in the future."

"Another version of that man, but not this one."

Jared had him there; everything in this time was spinning out differently. "My journey was fruitless." He shrugged. "But I'm still here."

Jared stepped close. "Do the Antousians truly destroy us in your future? Is that what you're telling me?"

"They gained control of a large number of missiles over at Warren Air Force Base. They turned them on the major cities and populations . . . it's all in ruins. All of it—here on Earth, back on Refaria. Only the smallest remnant still battles." He glanced between the three of them meaningfully. "And the three of us are part of that remnant."

"At Warren," Jared repeated, having paled visibly.

"They attacked the base, stormed it, and got control of the launch facilities."

Kelsey bowed her head. "We stopped it this time."

Jake staggered backward. "You stopped the takeover at Warren?" It was the first moment since arriving in this time when he'd actually felt hopeful.

"And you won't believe it—but in his own way Marco McKinley stopped it when he traveled back from your time." It had been Marco's letter that had enabled Thea to see the future, to intuit the Antousians' plans at the base—and that had, ultimately, been the way they'd averted the attack.

"Nothing here is the same as in my world," Jake whispered numbly.

"My brother." Jared opened his arms wide, tears glinting in his black gaze. "I'm sorry that you've known so much pain."

Jake folded into his best friend's embrace, refusing to cry like the seven-year-old boy he'd once been with this man. "I don't pretend to understand any of this," Jared continued, hugging him close, "but we will do whatever we can to stop these *vlksai* from bringing down such destruction again. Tell me now, what can we do?"

At that moment he felt Kelsey, too, her gentle yet strong touch, as she rubbed his shoulders. And for the first time in more years than he could count, Jake did truly cry. Like an absolute baby. At last—at long, long last—he'd come home once again.

Chapter Twenty

Hope hunkered low on the small berth where Kryn had left her, listening to the rumbling sounds of the ship. Vibrations shot through her body; the cruiser's lurching and tilting occasionally caused her to rock slightly where she sat. In general, her unsettled equilibrium led her to believe that they were dropping low over the earth, not going farther out into the stratosphere, as Scott had predicted. Man, she'd do anything to be close to him again, to touch him . . . to hold him. Locked away as she was, she couldn't be sure what his enemies might be doing. Beatings, torture—these fears plagued her mind.

She'd been given a meal, allowed to take her accompanying insulin shot, and now that her immediate health needs were secured, she could only imagine the worst for Scott. What he'd said about being at the top of these Antousians' kill list haunted her. Leaning back on the narrow bench seat, she pressed her ear against the side of the craft, trying to discern whether they truly were landing—or where they might be headed, period.

There was just so much Scott didn't know. Like Jake's real identity. And the truth of what had happened in their future, some future . . . maybe not the one they would live, including the fate of their sweet baby girl. Hope stifled a sob, pressing a hand against her eyes, determined to maintain clarity of mind.

Keep it together, girl. Keep it fucking together for him.

If Scott's predictions were true—if these enemies

wanted nothing more than to extract a pound of his flesh—then her training and smarts might be his only prayer for survival. She couldn't afford to ruminate on futures that might not come to pass, or baby daughters that they might someday lose. All that mattered was the here, the now—and what she could possibly do to gain Scott's freedom.

The craft dipped, sending her back against the pillows of the berth. Clasping her hands, squinting at her surroundings, Hope tried to decide exactly what was happening. Her conclusion? That they had to be coming in for a landing. As outlandish as such a public exposure might seem, she'd already learned a lot about aliens in the past few weeks: Their craft could come and go at will, never revealing their location to human radar or USAF tracking. These alien transports brought a whole new meaning to the term *stealth technology*, which served only to fuel her thoughts that nobody—absolutely nobody, human or alien—could find them now that the Antousians had taken them prisoner.

Suddenly the compartment door slid open, making a hissing sound. Hope tensed, alert and waiting for someone to speak. Hard footsteps echoed off of the steel-framed flooring, moving with cold calculation in her direction.

"Who is it?" she called out, folding her arms about herself protectively.

"I'm asking the questions here." The voice was male, harsh and hissing.

"Well, pal, you'd better identify yourself if you want answers," she said, squinting against the dim cabin lights. Without warning, a fist struck her across the jaw, sending her sprawling against the wall.

So much for putting on her tough-gal routine, she thought, giving her head a shake.

Before she could sit up again, a pair of rough hands slipped about her throat. "Listen, human, I can fuck you blind right now. Rape you. Kill you. So you'd better start showing a little respect."

She pulled at the stranger's hands, trying to breathe. "I already am blind, you freak," she squeezed out.

"Good, then you won't mind"—one of his hands slid down the front of her sweater, palming her breast—"if I take whatever I want."

She screamed, trying to bite his hand, but he just slammed her up against the wall, pinning her. For a moment everything within her said she was going to die . . . or worse. Then, just as suddenly, he released her, and she heard him back away.

"This won't get either of us what we want." His tone had changed, becoming perversely jovial.

"I want off this ship."

"Not to worry, Ms. Harper. That will happen soon enough." He let loose a sneering laugh. "And when that time comes, you'll know exactly why I'm the most feared Antousian among your friend Dillon's pitiful ranks."

Rotating her head sideways, she planted both palms against the wall. She couldn't see much, but the man seemed tall, towering over where she sat. It took everything within her, but she forced herself to appear calm and collected.

"I'm new around here." She rubbed at her jaw. "You have to help me out some. What's your name?"

" 'What's your name, sir!' " he corrected in a thundering voice that caused her to shiver.

Did this alien maniac really think she'd call him *sir*? When silence grew between them, he pounced on her again, twisting her hair in his hand and jerking it hard. "Show respect, human."

"What's your name, *sir*?" she asked weakly, feeling dizzy and terrified.

"Call me Veckus. That's the only name you need to memorize around here."

"Strip that soldier down," Veckus ordered, glancing between his two captives. He'd brought them to their current warehouse hideout, the one where a number of his grunts had been making base in Montana for the past month. He could have kept them in orbit around Earth indefinitely, but something in Veckus's gut told him that down on the ground would be the best place for interrogating Scott Dillon. Down close to this species that he—and Jared Bennett—had wasted so many years protecting. Yes, right on Earth was the place to act out the final scenes of this little drama. Oh, it would be fine torture indeed, extracting every detail of the Refarian operation—and he planned to take his time about it. Nothing he'd ever dreamed of could be such enjoyable sport as personally torturing Lieutenant Scott Dillon. He licked his lips, practically feeling himself grow hard with arousal at the prospect.

He perused the scene before him—Scott kneeling at gunpoint, and his companion, Hope Harper, mirroring the same position. The female was a luscious little human, all ripe and full-breasted. The strange thing with her eyes fascinated him; he'd heard there were people on Earth who could not see, an oddity, since back on Refaria blindness had been eradicated long ago. That was why he'd thrown out the comment about fucking her blind—to be sure she really was unable to see. And he'd gotten his answer—and then some. Plus, when she'd gotten so feisty with him, it had been more than a rush. Too bad he'd chosen not to rape her. For now . . . just for now, he told himself.

Then he turned and faced Scott Dillon. So many years he'd been plagued by this one. He shook his head, trying to decide the best and most delicious plan for exacting payback for every time Dillon had outflanked him— most recently at Warren.

Veckus rocked back on his heels, meeting the man's steady, hard gaze; perhaps what made him sickest of all about Dillon was that he was a traitor to his own people. Watching the small blind woman shiver, a faint smile formed on Veckus's lips as a plan began to blossom in his mind.

"Strip that soldier down, Lieutenant," he ordered

Dayron again with a flick of his wrist. "*All* the way down."

Strolling slowly past Dillon, he eyed him. "Get ready for the longest night of your life," he promised, exposing his teeth in a threatening gesture.

Scott glowered at him, never so much as blinking. Veckus knew the soldier wasn't intimidated—from what Veckus had learned about his adversary over the years, nothing ever frightened him.

Dayron wrestled hold of Scott as two of Veckus's other underlieutenants began jerking off his jacket, shirt, and every last item of his clothing. Ah, yes, Veckus would ensure that Scott Dillon passed a very long, cold night in hell.

Objective: to learn the location of Jared Bennett's main bases from Dillon, using the cold night—and as much torture as possible—to achieve that aim.

Planned result: Veckus would firebomb the Refarians' secret installations, annihilate them, just as he'd done to their Texas facility years ago. In the process, he would quell their intolerable rebellion once and for all.

Dayron shoved Dillon to the hard warehouse floor, sending him sprawling face-first. Veckus studied the man's naked form, saw the battle scars and lines of hardship in the soldier's body. Although a small part of him took pity on the Antousian—their shared heritage did, after all, make them brothers in a sense—he also reviled the man for being such a traitor. More than that, Veckus had other priorities right now besides suddenly developing a sense of empathy for his enemies.

"Sir, what would you like us to do?" Dayron prompted him, planting a boot in the center of Dillon's naked back.

"Our goal is simple—I want to know if this is our future traveler, the one I sensed traversing the time-space continuum." He wouldn't let Dillon in on his plans for learning the facilities locations—not yet. "And if this is *not* our man, Lieutenant Dayron, then we will learn who we should be pinpointing . . . perhaps the other rebel Antousian who was there at the mitres. The one who took out two of our soldiers. Either way, Dillon knows the truth, and I intend to extract that knowledge out of him . . . piece by piece, if need be."

"Very well, sir." Dayron nodded in understanding. "Usual methods?"

Veckus smiled. "I like the idea of the cold as a tool," he hissed. "Let's try that one this time."

No matter what, Veckus had narrowed his search down to just two men. It was either Dillon, right here before him—or the other Antousian they'd pursued on the snowmobile. One of them had traversed time itself, and whether he had to torture Dillon or kill the luscious human woman, he would learn the identity of his future traveler.

Result: Veckus would learn the secrets of time, and would thereby guarantee the defeat of the Refarian resistance once and for all. A most satisfying result indeed.

Chris sat in his rat hole of an office in Jackson, ready to strangle someone—anyone—if he didn't get clear facts as to his sister's position, and soon. This was the office that he normally worked out of, and in all fairness it really wasn't a genuine rat hole—just small, and a one-man shop. The situation at Mirror Lake had reached a crescendo, then fallen flat before he and Blake had even arrived in Jackson. Now he sat in his home office, smelling the lingering perfume of the woman who'd been temporarily manning his desk during his absence. Or *womaning* his desk, he thought, shoving aside an aromatherapy candle. True, he didn't like the fact that any other agent had been in his space, but his territorial feelings were more about his bitterness about the day's events than any kind of proprietary sense.

The agent had cleared out; when it came to these aliens, very few of his colleagues had high enough clearance to know the facts. Need-to-know basis all the way, and the temporary desk jockess didn't have a pissant's worth of clearance. He and Blake had sent her packing so they could strategize here, figure out what the hell to do next while communicating with the Denver office for further instructions.

Blake leaned against one of Chris's top-heavy filing cabinets, doing what he always did best—running scenarios in his head. "So her cell phone fix faded in and out— kept changing. When they dialed it, nothing happened."

"Airborne," Chris told his supervisor dully. In some ways it was unfortunate that the two of them were such close friends; it gave a lot of leeway for Chris to question the agent's analysis about things rather than accepting his leadership. On the other hand, given their mutual line of work, there weren't that many guys who understood the way they lived. Or accepted aliens as a natural fact.

Blake opened and closed the top drawer, not really looking at his surroundings, just absently fumbling with things. "They chased the lead into the park, but then hit a dead end," he explained.

"Because they're fucking airborne!" Chris shouted again. "Geez, people, how hard is this to figure out?"

Blake shot him a look, and Chris mumbled under his breath, shifting weeks' worth of piled-up paperwork atop his desk. "So Denver has nothing on her now? Nothing the fuck at all—huh?"

Blake looked away. "The signal went dead, Harper. They're continuing to try to triangulate her position. Until then, we don't have any leads."

"So what are we even doing here?" Chris kicked back in his chair, cursing Hope for her stubborn streak, her ability to always seek out danger.

Blake shrugged into his suit jacket, gave a brisk nod. "Agent Harper, we get ourselves out to Mirror Lake. We'll comb that site until we come up with something— anything at all—that might provide a lead. I want to get your sister back as much as you do, all right?"

Chris didn't question that fact—although he did seriously doubt that Blake would ever find what he wanted in terms of his sister's affections. What he'd told his parents about her falling in love had been true, even though he'd hedged about that alibi with Blake.

As crazy as his twin was, he'd known her all his life, and this whole venture—the way it put her at risk with her illness, the irrationality of it all—bore all the telltale signs of just one thing: that his sister had fallen seriously and unquestionably in love . . . with an alien.

Scott shivered, naked against the warehouse floor, wondering what Veckus's next move would be. He'd been bound about the neck, hands, and feet—even his waist—with reflexive metal cuffs. It was a type of alloy forged only back on Refaria, a psychic metal that reacted to mental energy. If he wanted to flee, the bonds would cinch about him much tighter. If he sought to rest, the metal would loosen somewhat, but would always anticipate his next move, so there was no hope of ever getting away.

He was manacled, pure and simple, by a living alloy that served as Veckus's most personal henchman— binding and restraining him before he could even dream up his next step. Veckus had gleamed with pride as the restraints had been placed upon him, rejoicing in such a base victory. To have Scott this low—naked, freezing, and bound to the highest degree—was what his enemy had spent years anticipating. Now in the dark, unable to detect Hope's whereabouts, Scott felt more frightened than at any other time in his military career.

And it didn't have a damned thing to do with the restraints binding him against the shoddy and cold warehouse wall. It all had to do with Hope—that the woman he loved needed him, and he was held captive by reflexive cuffs that wouldn't allow him to so much as contemplate an escape strategy.

Night had fallen an hour or so ago, the last of the day's light shafting through the broken overhead windows of the abandoned warehouse. Fortunately it wasn't *entirely* frigid inside the large and vacuous room; he would have died from exposure already were that the case. No, there was some source of heat—just enough for his captors to keep him alive. Just enough that he could hover in and out along the cusp of consciousness, praying that All would intervene in some way that he couldn't quite imagine.

A single chain led from his neck cuff, holding him close against the wall. Occasionally he was foolish enough to try to crawl a few steps outward, working his way along the length of his chain toward the dilapidated room's center, and each time the reflexive metal would respond accordingly—choking the breath from his throat until he collapsed onto his knees, begging the psychic alloy to release him, at least a little bit. And, perfectly reactive, it did . . . but only enough to allow him to gasp much-needed air.

Scott pressed his forehead against the floor, drawing on the last of his remaining internal heat. Any human would have died by now from the exposure—but Veckus had been banking on his hybrid nature, that his Antousian self was a natural power inferno. But after several hours of nakedness in such cold, he had few reserves left to draw upon. Sure, he could have shifted into his ethereal self, but even then the reflexive metal would have held him fast, which was the major reason that Veckus had elected to use it. Even his core, ghostlike self would be restrained by such a reactive alloy. There was literally no move, not a single step for him to make—not bound this completely.

Where were his captors, anyway? They'd cleared out hours ago, leaving nothing but the sparseness of the warehouse and the icy cold that kept wrapping itself around his very bones. And Hope? Of course they'd ferried her far away, well beyond his grasp.

"Oh, Hope," he moaned against the cold floor. "Where are you, my love?"

From the darkness beyond there came a stirring, as if

in reply to his lament. Gasping, he managed to lift his head. "We can bring her to you," some faceless Antousian promised. "You just have to cooperate."

He shook his head, ready to hurl expletives, but the cuff about his throat choked the words out before he could form them.

"Ah, but you see—watch yourself, Lieutenant, and you shall get what you want," the faceless man promised.

"Who . . . are you?" he rasped, clutching at the band about his throat.

"Someone who can bring her to you." A small light appeared, giving the soldier's face a ghostly, eerie illumination. "You want?"

He bobbed his head, struggling for his voice. "Of . . . course."

Lights came on, flooding the warehouse, and he saw that he wasn't alone, as he'd imagined, but surrounded by a small cadre of his enemies. The woman he'd heard called Kryn swooped close, snapping her fingers, and Scott saw Hope being hustled into the room. Her large gray eyes were wide, frightened—he rose up on his haunches, clawing at his bonds, only to find his breath nearly strangled from his lungs.

"Settle down." Kryn narrowed her large brown eyes at him. "You know what we want—and you can get what you seek. But you have to cooperate."

For a moment he swore that Hope stared right at him—even though it had to be his muddled imaginings. He swore that, locking her gaze with his own, she shook her head, told him not to give in.

"I won't . . . tell you . . . a thing," he barely managed to rasp.

"Very well," Kryn told him, and the next thing he knew, he was being strung up facing the crumbling warehouse wall.

"What are you doing to him?" Hope shouted.

"Extracting," Kryn volunteered cheerfully.

The hard lash of a whip slapped him across the lower

back. He buried his forehead against the wall, bracing for the next blow . . . and the next.

"Extracting what? His life?" Hope demanded. "How stupid are you people? If you kill him, you'll never get what it is you're after."

Tilting his head sideways, Scott watched Hope arguing. He couldn't hear her words, not really—the sound of the whip cracking across his bare skin, over and over, was too loud. But he'd never loved Hope more. Blind, chin stuck in the air, she was waving and gesturing, totally holding her ground with Kryn.

One last stinging impact of the whip against his skin, and then it seemed to stop. Slowly he slid to the ground, the chain that linked him to the wall practically tangled about him.

"We won't let you die, Lieutenant," Kryn told him softly—almost soothingly. "But you will certainly wish for death before Veckus is through with you."

It had been silent for a while. Scott was passed out on the floor beside her, breathing unevenly, and Hope hadn't been able to do much beyond just listen to the sounds all around her. She certainly couldn't see a freaking thing. After many, many minutes, she finally heard a stirring sound from the other side of the expansive room. The approach of footsteps—softer ones, not hard and heavy—that obviously belonged to a woman.

Maybe Kryn? In the darkness of the warehouse she couldn't make out any details; she was fully blind here. The steps came nearer, then stopped right beside her. A warm hand took hold of her shoulder; then she felt the grip of the manacles on her hands ease up, loosen—but after that slight taste of freedom, the unknown woman never said a word, just walked away. Hope almost called after her, but decided she'd take this latest good fortune as the kindness it was. It had to be Kryn: She was the only woman evident in the Antousians' gathered ranks.

Who was this Kryn Zoltners? Hope wondered. Well, she was obviously Antousian, and perpetually delivered mixed messages; that much was fact. She'd master-minded Scott's recent and terrible beating, but she'd also given Hope access to her medicine. And now, her latest maneuver was that she seemed to be making it possible for Hope to wriggle free.

Sliding back against the wall, Hope began to work at the bindings that were wrapped about her hands, so different from whatever it was they'd imprisoned Scott with. His manacles obviously caused him great pain, whereas hers were a bit more basic. Back and forth she worked her hands until fortunately, amazingly, she managed to free them. And once she'd gotten her hands loose it was a fairly simple matter to begin untying her feet.

Swinging her blind gaze about the cold and empty room, she tried to make out the presence of their enemies, but couldn't be sure of anything at all. This stab at freedom might be nothing more than a setup, but Hope had no time to dwell on that possibility. Once she had wrangled free of her restraints, she bolted to her feet and followed the sound of Scott's shallow breathing. Taking cautious steps into the darkness, she still had her folded cane in her back pocket but didn't dare use it to navigate, not with the slight noise it would make.

She took several more steps, listening to Scott's exhalations, and when she knew she was right upon him, dropped to her knees. Immediately her hand met his bare skin, hairy and so unnaturally cold. She slipped her palm along his body, stroking his upper thigh, outlining him, just making sure he was solid and real. Shivering all over, he jerked and shook with the tremors. He had to be on the verge of hypothermia. She draped her body atop his, remembering that the best help for someone suffering from exposure was the warmth of another human.

He was chilly to her touch, but still somewhat warmer than she expected—at least, considering how long he'd been naked in this frigid temperature. She put that much down to his alien abilities, but quickly jerked out of her

jacket and stripped off her sweater, until she knelt over
him in nothing but her bra and blue jeans. Their captors
might discover her half-naked any moment, and might
choose to work "extraction" on her, but her only objective was to get some heat into Scott's vulnerable body
as quickly as possible.

She wrapped herself atop him, her warmer skin
against his, whispering his name, but he didn't wake.
Perhaps he was unconscious from the brutal beating, or
perhaps from hypothermia; either way, she slid her arms
beneath his back, wrapping him in her embrace.

Despite her terror, the rough feel of his masculine,
chiseled body caused her own body to tighten in awareness. For long moments she continued to will her
warmth into him, and at last she almost thought his
tremors grew more subdued. Feeling her way along his
chest—his muscular, strong, amazing chest; she couldn't
help but acknowledge that fact, even in the midst of this
crisis—she worked her touch all the way up toward his
face. Her hands made contact with hard, freezing metal,
a circlet that she could feel was locked snugly around
his neck. Pressing her face against his, she whispered,
"Scott, wake up."

He didn't stir.

"Scott, you have got to freaking wake up now." Her
voice was urgent, and this time he did respond, the horrible tremors in his body growing much more extreme.

"Hope, gods . . ." he began, but made a horrible choking sound, grasping at the manacle about his neck.

"What is that thing?" she hissed quietly, leaning atop
him again, her much smaller body covering his bigger
one.

He shook his head, rasping, still pulling at it. The cuff
wouldn't allow him to speak.

"You have to talk to me, Scott. You're in bad shape,
and I need to know what we should do—or what you
think. I can't see enough to figure a way out of here."

"Can't," he rasped.

After that he wrapped her in his arms again, running

his hands through her hair, kissing her suddenly. The chains that ran from his hands to the wall behind them were cold against her cheeks. Yeah, maybe he couldn't talk, but he sure as hell could still kiss, and he told her everything—everything she'd ever need to know about his feelings for her, about his plans to survive—with that one deep kiss. His lips smoldered against hers; his hands wandered the length of her body, jabbing underneath her jeans to clasp her from behind.

All of a sudden, he pulled away. "What? Do you hear something?" she asked, whipping her head around.

He shook his head. "Looser." He gasped, drawing her hand to his neck circlet. "Keep . . . kissing. It knows . . . thoughts."

"What knows thoughts?"

"Reflexive . . . metal. Psychic."

She braced both hands about his head, noting, too, that his tremors had totally died down. With a quick and pointless glance around the dark warehouse, she leaned in closer, putting her mouth against his ear. "Um, Scott—can I ask a really basic question about your species?"

He nodded, stealing another quick kiss, licking the side of her face with the tip of his tongue.

"When you get aroused, does it . . . well, does it change your body temperature? Because this kissing and touching seems to be helping a whole lot."

He gave a low, rumbling groan of pleasure, then whispered, "Yes."

"So this isn't just stupid or foolish, to be making out at a time like this?"

"Hope . . . you are saving"—he hesitated, making a slight choking sound—"my life."

"They'll be back any minute." She touched his face. "We have to have a plan."

"The metal relaxed while we kissed." He covered her hand and brought it against his cheek. "My bindings are still looser than they were. The metal knows my thoughts psychically, emotionally—and is programmed to act against me."

"Metal knows your thoughts?"

"Not like we . . . understand. Basic." He groaned, sputtering and coughing. Obviously this reflexive metal didn't like being talked about, either.

"It's programmed for torture," Hope thought aloud, adding, "So maybe kissing falls outside the program? Maybe that's why it loosened up?"

"No context." He clawed again at the metal collar about his neck, and Hope wasted no time whatsoever.

She planted a slow, languid, and heated kiss against his lips. Dragging her mouth across his, she thrust her tongue into the warmth of his mouth without hesitation. Deep and twining, their tongues warred for dominance, sought more of the other. His body was completely naked beneath hers, still too cold, and, rising up on her knees, she unsnapped her jeans and stripped out of them. She stood in the dark above him, wondering if he could make out her silhouette from some source of light that she couldn't see.

Slowly she dropped to her knees, whispering, "I'm going to cover your body with mine. Allow you to get more of my body heat."

As she slid atop him, his swollen cock bobbed against her belly. Even cold and imprisoned, Scott had an absolutely unstoppable libido. He lifted his hips against her, begging her to come so much closer.

Scott purred and groaned. Yes, from arousal—tasting Hope this way was beyond nirvana—but because it also seemed the reflexive metal was particularly confounded by his intense pleasure. With every stroke of her tongue against his, with every lift of their hips, the bonds about his wrists and neck and legs grew looser and looser.

Gods in heaven, please don't let them come in now, he thought dazedly, truly losing himself in Hope and the sensual pleasure of the moment. Here he was, bound, and she held the keys to his captivity. It was a deeply erotic thought on some perverse level—if only it weren't his present reality.

She still had her panties on, and although he slid his cock between her legs, he couldn't get where he was so desperate to be—right up inside of her. He could feel a damp sheen lining the thin lingerie, and it pulled and gave as he pushed at her opening.

Her hands were in his hair, touching his face, pulling at his neck manacle. She pressed her face against his for a moment, collapsing atop him, and he felt dampness. *Oh, sweetheart,* he wanted to say. *Don't cry for me! This is everything I've ever wanted, being with you like this.*

"We'll get free," he dared to whisper against her damp cheek. "Let's make love . . . let's confuse the hell out of this thing." He tapped at his neck circlet.

Maybe it wasn't the way she'd dreamed they'd finally come together, but if it meant her lover's freedom, hell, she'd take it any way he wanted to deliver it: cold floor, shoddy motel room, wherever. All she wanted was Scott Dillon, for all time.

She'd never known such intense passion or love. Slowly she peeled away her panties, unfastened her bra, and allowed it to fall to the floor until she was, like him, completely nude. When she dropped back down beside him, Scott struggled to sit up. She knelt, facing him, the freezing floor harsh against her bare knees.

He took hold of her face, holding it in his cupped palm, and leaned up to softly kiss her. In a choking whisper he said, "Love you, Hope. Love you."

She couldn't stop touching his face, feeling his features. The darkness killed her—she needed to *see* him. "I love you so much, Scott. Please know that." She wondered what he must think about her strange loyalty to Jake Tierny. He couldn't possibly understand. "Don't let anything make you doubt."

"What about Jake?" he managed to get out, clearly understanding her meaning.

"He's connected to you. I know it. It's why I'm drawn to him."

He shook his head, adamant. "Enemy."

"No! No, he's a good man. He cares about me—and you. Especially you."

Scott recoiled, shoving her away from him, but she wouldn't be denied, continued to touch him, hold him. "Why . . . him?"

"There's a connection, an important one," she insisted. "But right now we have to focus on getting these bonds loose." She stroked the length of his muscled arms, dropping her voice into a seductive rumble. "And there's only one way it seems we're going to accomplish that."

Chapter Twenty-one

The best of his advisers were gathered in the main meeting room. Jake had insisted that his identity remain hidden for now, the emotional complications being more than the moment required, at least for several others in the room. Jared wasn't sure about that decision, but respected it nonetheless.

"We're all here for one reason." Jared slowly paced the length of the meeting chamber. "Because we want to get Scott Dillon and Hope Harper back."

"Our investment is in the lieutenant, sir, with all due respect," Nevin Daniels, his chief security adviser, answered quietly.

Jared shot him a harsh look. "And why not the FBI linguist who has already shown her loyalty to all of us? To Dillon, in particular?"

Nevin gave a slight shake of his head. "We have fought under Dillon's command for years, my lord. Ms. Harper is a new element to the equation."

Jared chanced a look in Jake's direction. "There are many new allies we find in our midst, but that doesn't make their considerations any less valid."

It came as no surprise that Jake dropped his eyes, staring at the floor in a gesture so familiar—something he'd often seen Scott do. Jared smiled, knowing that his lifelong friend appreciated his determination to get Hope Harper back.

Nevin countered coolly, "I will say what I have said

ever since Warren, my lord. We must contact Colonel
Peters. His support during that battle—his newfound and
certain belief in our cause—makes him a ready ally too."
The colonel surely did love the Refarians at this point,
Jared had to agree; without their intervention at the air
force base, the humans would have lost control of their
missiles, and possibly much more. And he did have possession of the man's direct phone line.

Jake rose to his feet. "Hope's brother is a special
agent with the FBI. He works the alien squad. Well, at
least, he does at some point in the future. He's in this—
I'm sure—and deep. He's probably tracking Hope even
now."

Thea scowled. "Tracking her how, huh? What makes
you think the FBI has a fix on her that we can't seem
to get?"

"You are joking, right? This is the FB-fucking-I,
Haven," Jake practically snarled at her.

Jared stepped forward, placing a staying hand on his
friend's arm. "Let's keep our emotions in check." It was
tough to comprehend, but in Jake's future Thea was a
traitor.

Thea fumed visibly, but did finally back down. "I
agree with Nevin," she said, tossing Jake a bitter glance.
"We need to call the colonel. And maybe Tierny's
right—maybe they have a line on Scott and Hope that
we don't."

The tension left Jake's face, and he nodded apprecia-
tively. "Good. We need to ask him to put us in touch
with Hope's brother, Chris Harper. He is way on the
inside with all the alien intel . . . if not now, then
eventually."

"He's in it to some degree now," Jared agreed. "He
brought Marco in for questioning last week."

"Then let's not waste any more time, sir," Jake insisted. "Let's call the colonel and try to get a meeting."

Thea dialed the phone, extending it to Jared with a
jerk of her arm. Fixing his eyes on the Slimline cell, he

considered this next move—and also considered simply
ending the call with a jab of his thumb. However, he
knew the moment had come to speak to Colonel
Peters—they'd been in possession of the colonel's number ever since the recent events at his base—and accepted the phone with resignation. They'd called via a
series of relays so that their own number could not be
traced.

Reaching into the human world like this, asking or
implying a need for help, was new territory for Jared,
but he valued his advisers enough to realize that the
time had finally arrived. He had to look to the humans—
the USAF and the FBI—since both organizations had
to be ready to talk after the events at Warren. Nevin
had been driving that point home all week. And then
there was Kelsey, with her thoughts about her father's
political connections, and the help they could offer to
their cause.

He'd flown solo in his military actions for so long that
it was difficult to accept that they had entered a new era
here on Earth. Despite his hesitations, he did have to
admit that teaming up with the USAF had worked splen-
didly in their recent battle with the Antousians.

Yes, it was time, and the stakes were high enough that
he truly had no choice. He had to make this call, especially for Scott . . . well, for Jake *and* for Scott, because
in a strange twisted harmony they were one and almost
the same.

Colonel Peters answered on the other line, and, after
a moment's hesitation, Jared calmly identified himself.

"Commander. I've been waiting all week to hear from
you." The colonel sounded like he might reach through
the phone and absolutely kiss him.

Jared leaned a forearm against the wall, putting his
back to Thea and the others gathered in the meeting
room around him. "It's good to speak with you, sir," he
answered formally. "How does it go at the base?"

"Been cleaning up all week!" The man let out a
strained laugh. "Good holy crap, we're gonna be clean-

ing up for years to come. But"—the man dropped his voice—"if you hadn't saved our asses, Bennett, I'd be dead right now."

The colonel's voice assumed a serious timbre. "We need to meet, Commander Bennett. Surely you realize that, don't you? You deflected an intergalactic enemy attack—we need to find out what else you know. What else you might help us avert. And we need to learn about your military operations, and how we might align our forces."

"That's what *we* need?" Jared asked, perhaps a bit too sarcastically, but this moment was hard enough.

The colonel didn't miss a beat. "That's what we need, Commander."

Jared leaned his shoulder against the wall. "Well, what I need is a favor."

"What do you have in mind?"

"Special Agent Chris Harper. Can you put me in touch with him?"

"Never heard that name before in my life." Jared might not be highly intuitive, but he could smell the lie in the man's quick dismissal.

"Well, then, we have nothing more to discuss," Jared announced coolly, already positioning his finger over the disconnect button.

"Hold up there, Commander Bennett . . . he's an FBI agent, you say?"

"I have a feeling you know him. He's on the alien squad; that's his division within the FBI."

"Whoa, you're talking deeper shit than I'm into there, son. I'm with the United States Air Force—"

Jared cut him off. "You are very aware of the facts about this war, Colonel. Don't tax my patience. You held two of my men there on your base, and from what I hear, nothing about our existence was a surprise. Are you or are you not aware of an alien squad within the FBI?"

"I'm aware of Chris Harper."

"Now we're making progress."

"What do you want to say to him? He's low down in the chain, Commander. He's not the one you want."

"And who is?"

Hesitation, a cough, and then: "We're not to that point yet."

"Give me Agent Harper on this line, and maybe we'll start talking. I think you're smart enough to realize I have information that you want—but are you smart enough to get me a phone call with the agent?"

"Call me again in five."

"Done." Jared folded the phone shut and slid it into the front pocket of his uniform pants. Very slowly he rotated and found every one of his advisers' expectant gazes upon him.

"Alien squad? What the hell?" Chris cried.

"I'm just relaying the man's words," Colonel Peters directed him on the other end of the line. "You're briefed on this case, and you've got high enough clearance that I want you to push ahead with Jared Bennett."

Chris stared down at the busted-up alien craft that lay charred on the snow before him. Mirror Lake spread frozen and gleaming around him, a giant set of klieg lights illuminating the otherwise darkened, snowy landscape. At least seventy-five workers from a variety of federal agencies had been on the scene for hours.

They'd discovered these two black machines, blown semi-apart, right here on Mirror Lake. The investigative teams had spent hours bagging and tagging every blown-up bit of the things, but none of them—not a one—had a reference point in terms of identifying the craft. Overland vehicles had been brought in, ready to cart the alien snowmobiles off, but now this—a call from Colonel Peters, asking him if he had the first idea what an alien squad might be.

Chris pressed the cell closer to his ear. "Honestly, Colonel, I don't know what you're talking about."

"I said you wouldn't—unless the FBI was keeping secrets, which I doubt, not when we're running this thing."

"What thing, sir?"

"This is our man, Harper, and he wants you," the colonel explained over the crackling wire. "He didn't ask for your SAC or your ASAC—he asked for you, a simple special agent within the FBI." He recited the last with precision, drawing out each letter with his indelible Southern accent. *FB . . . ayyye.* "Not sure what it means, Agent Harper, apart from the fact that you're now our A–number one most interesting guy."

"You think I can get a meeting with him?" Chris asked, wondering whether Bennett had his sister.

"I know you can."

"So your crew is calling the shots now?"

"We are always calling the shots in this particular show, son."

"Understood."

"Stand by. Expect a call and be ready to fly— wherever or whenever this Bennett wants to meet."

The hotter and sweatier Scott and Hope became, the more slack his confinements grew. He alternated between glancing about the dark in fear, and feeling the unstoppable need to finally take her. His body temperature had been righted already, a wonderful side effect of such devastating and lustful need.

The floor was cold and hard, the only real discomfort other than the welts on his back from the beating. The two of them slid together, her delicate, feline body fitting perfectly atop his.

"Clothes?" he whispered in her ear, panting insanely. "Where are yours?"

She gestured to the side, cradling the back of his head with her other hand. He stared up at her, able to see the outline of her body, limned by the moon high above the overhead windows. Cupping her face within his hands, he stilled her.

"You sure?" He studied what he could see of her face. "Like this . . . our first time?"

"I want to help you get free." She kissed his forehead,

letting her lips linger against his sweaty brow. "It's not about your body temperature anymore—you're fine, I can tell, being the strapping alien man that you are. It's about . . ." She slipped her fingers into the slack area of his neck cuff, demonstrating her meaning.

He swallowed hard, nodding. "Then let's spread your clothes out. Use them to soften things for you."

She shook her head. "Not a moment to lose, Scott. Not one moment."

He could feel the heavy weight of the chain that ran from his neck to the wall, pinning him like a naked slave. But he closed his eyes, felt Hope as she straddled him, and gave in to the abandon of her body. Of loving her.

With one easy thrust he drove up into her, hard, feeling her warmth and wetness. So sweet! Gods, sweeter than any woman he'd ever been with.

She clasped her thighs about him, arching her back so that the golden strands of her hair appeared like cascading moonlight in the semidarkness. They might never have a moment like this again; or perhaps this sweet taste of freedom they were each discovering was the first promise of true liberation.

Grasping his hips, she lifted, rocked . . . took him to the edge and beyond. This woman knew exactly what his body demanded, the pleasure that he was always driven to find with her kind. Only now it was all about the two of them, not mindless sex with a one-night stand. It was all about finding release in Hope's arms, the woman he knew was meant to be his wife.

Release! Gods, sweet release! The words burned on his lips and he drove upward, into her, over and over. She rocked atop him, instinct guiding her every movement. She knew his tastes, what turned him on beyond reason—because she'd been dreaming about making love to him for what might as well have been a lifetime. It was more than just this moment together; it was everything they'd each seen could happen.

With a gasp and a muted cry, he clutched her hips and drove up into her, spilling his seed. He was blind with their shared orgasm, blind with lust and unstoppable need.

As their hips and groins crashed together, a niggling awareness teased at his mind. He did feel free, incredibly so, and as she bent low to kiss him, beads of sweat on her upper lip, she reached for the opened reflexive metal cuff and tossed it to the side. Then she felt along his hands and did the same. The psychic metal, programmed by a torturous, cruel unit of soldiers, had been given no context for such pure heaven as he'd just known with Hope. He almost had to laugh at the irony of it: He'd literally just fucked himself right into freedom.

"Hurry!" she urged, staggering off of him and onto her feet. "We've got to get dressed and run!"

"I don't know where my clothes are, Hope," he told her hoarsely. "They confiscated them when they stripped me down."

She shook her head, reaching for her sweater and tugging it over her head, dressing rapidly. "They have to be around here—go look. Search. I would, but . . . You'll never survive naked out in that snow. In here was one thing, but we've got to find those clothes!"

"And why would you want to do that?" a male voice called out, echoing across the dark and nearly vacant room. Hope could tell there were almost no furnishings or anything else in this area of the warehouse, because everything echoed, the hollow, reverberating sound of nothingness.

Pouncing, Scott shoved her behind himself. "Stay back, Hope," he hissed.

And then Scott's next words caused her heart to plummet. "Veckus, your beef is with me—leave her out of this."

"I surmised it was time we talked, and then look what I should find? How is it possible that anyone could escape my reflexive hardware?" She heard Veckus strut past them, then the metallic sound of one of the cuffs skittering across the floor. "I suppose you believe you've outwitted me once again, don't you, Dillon?"

"It's never been about outsmarting you, Veckus. It's

been about what's right and what's wrong—we aren't the ones who committed mass genocide back on Refaria."

"Don't you dare imply that!" the alien roared, and Hope heard the scuffling of feet, got the idea that Scott and Veckus were in a physical skirmish of sorts. "Your adopted people, the Refarians, are the ones who released the virus in order to subdue us," Veckus shouted. "They created and masterminded it, and then released it into the Antousian population."

Could Veckus be right? Hope wondered in alarm. What if this whole war wasn't nearly what she'd been led to believe? It seemed impossible, but never had she heard Scott mention that the Refarians had released the virus themselves.

She heard Scott sigh. "Veckus, you know that's a bunch of political propaganda. The virus happened because your people reached too far and too fast for things that didn't belong to them. They got sick because they tampered with genetic therapy when their experiments went wrong. Our people didn't do that."

"Your people?" Veckus shouted. "You're Antousian yourself, you fool."

"No, sir, I am not. I am half-human, and the rest of me is Refarian in my heart. I could never lay claim to a genetic history shared with you."

Veckus chuckled, and Hope heard him softly exhale a breath. "Like it or not, Dillon, it's still true."

Hope wondered what was happening—what would happen next. Her heart thundered in her chest, and she was incredibly aware that Veckus might strap Scott back into the cuffs at any moment. She listened as the warlord paced the room, walking a few feet away—and decided to make her move. Anything to help save Scott.

With a shuffling step of her bare foot, she moved in the direction where the cuffs had lain, sending one or two of them scattering over the floor. "What the hell?" she cried. Veckus spun on her, but she kicked again, knocking the metal cuffs with her instep. It was enough to take her back to her soccer team days.

"Run, run, run!" Scott shouted, shoving at her. "Get out of here, Hope!"

She shook her head, hearing Veckus charge her. "I won't leave you!" she cried, and at that moment a hard fist slammed right into her jaw, sending her sprawling.

"Guess that means you're not a gentleman," she slurred, rubbing her cheek as she landed on the floor.

There was a click of weaponry engaging, and Hope covered her head with both hands. She'd never felt so terrified in all her life, never, and to top it all off, she'd begun to shake all over. Her glucose levels were once again getting crazily low.

"Aim that gun at me, Veckus," Scott announced coolly.

"All right, then," their captor said, "I will."

Chapter Twenty-two

Chris's cell vibrated in his hand, and he whipped it to his ear. "Harper here."

"Agent Harper, this is Commander Jared Bennett," came a husky, deep voice. Not accented at all, something that surprised Chris for some reason. "I understand you're expecting my call."

"Yes. Go on." He wasn't about to give away more details than he had to.

"We share a common aim right now, which is to locate your sister, Hope Harper."

Chris's jaw tightened. "What's your interest in Hope?"

Silence crackled over the line. "Are you not concerned about getting her back?"

"You know that I am, so tell me what you've got." Chris bucked up. "I thought she had entered your camp—that's the last I heard from her yesterday. That she'd joined in your fight."

"That is true." The alien's deep voice did not waver.

"And now she's not with you?"

There was a prolonged silence on the other end of the line. "We are concerned about her safety."

"If you don't know where she is—"

"I'm suggesting we pool our resources in order to find Hope and a missing soldier of ours. Your FBI resources and our Refarian ones. Together, we might locate both of our missing operatives."

Chris thought of the male unsub, the large, bulky one who didn't fit Dillon's description. "You've lost Dillon too—not just her. Or is it someone else?" he asked carefully.

Of course Bennett sidestepped his question. "The people who have them, Agent Harper, are the same ones who made the play for Warren—I know you realize what happened there."

"I *was* there."

"Then I shouldn't have to say anything else to convince you."

"How are you suggesting we combine our resources?" Chris kicked at the snow around him, wondering what this alien was truly after.

"I want to arrange for you and Colonel Peters to be transported to our main compound. You won't know where you're going, and will be blindfolded until brought into the lockdown area where we work. In exchange, we will share information. I will debrief you and the colonel about pertinent details on this war. The colonel will get intel that he's after—I will have a better shot at getting both Lieutenant Dillon and your sister back."

"So it *is* Dillon after all," Chris reflected. "He must be pretty important to you."

"Isn't *your* sister important to you?"

"You're saying Dillon is your brother, Commander?" he asked curiously.

There was a moment's hesitation over the line, and then, "He's the closest thing I have to one. Are you in or out on this plan?"

"I have to talk to headquarters first." Chris imagined what Washington would say, their inherent disapproval and the accompanying red tape. "How can I reach you?"

"I'll give you thirty minutes to decide."

Scott watched in horror as Hope rubbed her jaw, blinking at the bright overhead lights that once again illuminated the warehouse room. There was no time to waste, or they'd both be back in chains again. Veckus's weapon was trained on him, and in one move Scott delivered a powerful roundhouse kick to the man's jaw, sending him staggering to the floor. Then, kicking again, he dislodged Veckus's weapon from his hand.

Diving, Scott landed atop the K-12 and whipped it around, pointing it right at the warlord. Veckus appeared stunned—as if he couldn't quite believe what had transpired—and Scott took the opportunity to grin in victory just as Veckus had done to him earlier.

"You're going to give me my clothes back," Scott announced, scrambling to his feet.

"Now, why would I want to do that—you're such a strapping, handsome warrior."

"Let's leave your sexual preferences out of this discussion." The rumor had always been that Veckus liked sex—any way he could get it. Scott was beginning to think that idea might be true.

"I meant, Lieutenant, that you may have a gun, but without your clothes you're not going anywhere." Veckus pointed toward the exterior windows. "Not with the way it's snowing out there tonight."

"I can shift—we both know that."

"Not if you want to take Hope Harper with you." Veckus's cool gaze narrowed victoriously.

"Where are we? Wyoming? Montana?" Scott demanded, glancing again at Hope to be sure she was all right. She was only partially dressed, lying frozen where Veckus had sent her reeling to the floor. "Get dressed, Hope. Put the rest of your clothes on, so we'll be ready to roll." She nodded and began pulling on her jeans.

"It doesn't matter where we are," Veckus countered, hitting the comm on his arm.

Scott disengaged the weapon lock. "Don't. Don't even think about it."

"You do realize how many soldiers are crawling all over this place, don't you? They'll be on you in a minute anyway."

"Then they won't mind when I blast your head off,"

he said with a lunge, pulling Veckus back into the crook of his arm. He held the weapon against the warlord's head. "Like this, I figure either you die or we get free. Guess we'll find out how loyal your troops really are, won't we?"

At that moment a whole squadron of Antousians poured into the room. Where had they all been earlier? Too confident in their victory, that was what Scott guessed. Either that, or implementing a specialized kind of torture—leaving him alone in the cold to think about cooperating. Whatever their plans, they had failed, because now he had Veckus Densalt at the receiving end of a pulse rifle.

The one called Kryn stepped forward, both hands extended. "Lieutenant Dillon, please calm down. Tell us what you want."

"My clothes, damn it! And after that, our freedom."

Kryn's lips curled in a cruel smile. "And what of Ms. Harper's medication? Don't you think she'll be needing that also?"

Scott panicked, glancing at Hope, and for the first time realized that she had grown pale and was even shaking a bit. "You'll hand that over too. Unless you want Veckus to die."

Kryn shook her head. "That's funny, because from this end, I think the one who might die is your beloved Hope Harper." She shrugged. "And without her medication, well, I think that might happen a lot sooner than you think."

Scott's mind reeled; how many hours had it been since she'd eaten? Taken a shot? Done any of the things he knew she had to do if she wasn't going to slip into diabetic shock?

"Don't listen to her," Hope argued, bracing her hands against the floor. "Get us out of here, and I'll take care of myself."

Scott jammed the weapon harder against Veckus's temple. "Clothing, medicine, and freedom. Or this man dies!"

Several of the other soldiers now had their guns trained on Hope, and she bent forward, pressing her head to her knees.

"You have a decision to make, Dillon," Veckus hissed in his ear. "If I die, she'll die next. Either at gunpoint or from her illness. You're surrounded and out of possibilities here. Now, be a good boy and give over that weapon."

Hope stood suddenly, and the guns around her all cocked. Scott watched her, horrified. "Stay down, Hope!" he called.

With a strange look around her, she began to convulse, her whole body jarring as she collapsed to the ground. "She needs her medicine!" Scott insisted. "She needs help now!"

Hope writhed for a moment on the floor, and then—almost spookily—became completely rigid, just lying there, both eyes wide open.

"Hope, what's happening to you?" Scott called.

She blinked. "Diabetic shock. I can't move."

Veckus chuckled. "Well, I suppose that puts an end to the escape plan."

"What do you mean, you can't move?" Scott tightened his grip on Veckus.

"I . . . I can't control my muscles. I can talk, but can't budge at all." She sounded terrified, and Scott glanced at the weapon in his hand. He had no other choice right now.

With a jab of his weapon he said to Veckus, "Bring me her medicine, and I'll let you go."

Veckus laughed, a low hissing sound. "I'm not so sure it's as simple as all that, Lieutenant."

Along the periphery of his vision, Scott saw Kryn kneeling beside Hope. "Don't you dare harm her, Kryn. I've still got a gun to your commander's head."

Kryn didn't answer, but whispered something to Hope. At that precise moment three Antousian ghost shifters materialized at his side. He'd been so distracted by Hope's predicament that he hadn't sensed their approach, as he normally would via his Antousian tracking abilities. The three soldiers grappled with him, knocking his weapon away and once again Scott found himself locked hard within the confines of reflexive metal.

They'd brought Hope to some small room toward the back of the warehouse, where there was actually a pallet and a space heater that would keep her warm. Kryn knelt, maybe squatted, beside her; Hope was paralyzed from head to toe, just barely able to talk. Her throat clenched, but somehow—amazingly—she still had a remnant of speech. This kind of shock had happened to her on only two other occasions, and it was one reason Chris was always so damned protective of her—because her seizures terrified him.

"Tell me what to do," Kryn directed her calmly.

"Why do you care?" Hope closed her eyes. "Isn't this what you want? *How* you want it—me dead?"

Kryn gripped her arm roughly. "You're not a lot of good to me if you die. So give me instructions. Now."

It was one thing to find yourself in the clutches of your enemy, quite another to be literally paralyzed. Hope could hardly think for the fear that kept clawing at her body and mind. Blind, unable to move, she had the sense of being buried alive.

"My kit," Hope whispered finally. "There's juice. There's medicine you can put on my lips . . . that would be better. It will right my glucose levels faster."

There was a rustling sound, and Kryn asked, "Is this what you mean? It's called Glucose Fifteen."

Hope swallowed, nodding, and Kryn slowly rubbed the gel over her lips. "Is this enough?" the alien asked her coolly after applying it.

"I don't get you. Why should you even care?"

"Because you're my captive, and I try to be as generous as possible with those under my 'care.'"

Hope snorted. "Yeah, like how you masterminded Scott's beating. You were definitely caring for him, all right. Your motives are totally off the charts."

The woman rose, walking away. "You're not meant to understand my motives."

Hope felt a tingling begin in her extremities, a sign that sensation and movement were starting to return. "Tell me you won't kill him. It won't help a damn thing if he dies back in there."

Kryn leaned whisper-close, bending over her. "Harper, you're in no position to ask for special favors right now."

Jake Tierny watched as the transport bearing Colonel Peters and Chris Harper docked for landing. With their flight capabilities it had taken only approximately two hours since Jared's confirming phone call for the men to arrive here on base.

What must they be thinking now? he wondered, grinning despite himself. He'd always admired Chris Harper, a tough man with an angry streak, but one who could always be relied upon when the stakes were high. Besides, his brother-in-law loved Hope almost as much as he did.

The bizarre thing in this instance, of course, was that Chris had no reference point at all for Jake—and not much of one for Scott Dillon. Here he stood, waiting to meet Chris all over again, with years' worth of shared memories that his brother-in-law simply did not possess.

The craft hovered low as it eased through the open hangar door, made a half turn, then put down its landing gear. Jared stood beside him, a bit stiff and formal in his demeanor, but only Jake would know that. It was a major step for them all, bringing outsiders into the base, and even though the security situation now demanded it, Jake knew it was ultimately a positive move.

In his own future, they'd spent too long delaying a meeting like this one, and he'd always wondered if having joined forces with the humans might have averted Earth's ultimate devastation. But Jake was encouraged for the first time in years, knowing that Warren's missiles hadn't been lost to their enemies. Everything kept spinning out differently back in *this* past, and it led him to believe that maybe—just maybe—all the toying with time had turned out to be a good thing.

The craft's door opened and lowered to the ground with a soft swooshing sound of released air, and both Jake and Jared assumed a parade-rest stance. Jake was in uniform again, his buttons shined and his jacket tightly pressed. He might as well have been in his own skin again; he felt as if he could tackle any enemy—in his own future, it had been years since they'd been able to wear the neat and sharp uniforms that he remembered so vividly.

The craft's captain stepped down the gangway first, giving Jared a brisk nod, and then, right behind him, a slightly overweight, burly human followed, with Chris Harper right behind him. Jake blinked at Chris, shocked to see him so young, none of the lines or even the lightly premature gray in his otherwise blond hair.

Jared stepped forward, saluting the colonel, and the officer returned Jared's salute. It was amusing to watch the colonel's face. Military man to military man, that was how Jared was greeting him, and it clearly had the desired impact: immediate respect. Jared extended a strong hand to Chris, who took it readily with a "Nice to meet you, Commander."

Pleasantries were exchanged, and then his commander offered, "Why don't you look around just a moment; then we'll get down to business."

"Get a load of this operation," Chris said to Colonel Peters half under his breath, but not so low that Jake didn't catch it.

Chris directed his next statement to Jared. "Very impressive, sir."

Jared gave a slight bow. "We have worked hard to stay abreast of current trends in our own technology. What you see is state-of-the-art for our people . . . and for those we're fighting."

"The Antousians?" the colonel prompted.

"Yes, Colonel. They're your adversaries, not us—as you obviously found out at Warren."

"We are all very grateful for your help that day," the colonel agreed.

Both Chris and the colonel gazed across the massive hangar deck, up to the high ceiling, back along the length of at least forty aircraft—and that was just what they could immediately see in this hangar. "This is a full-on flight deck," Chris observed. "Only inside . . . not out."

"Think of this as akin to an aircraft carrier," Jake volunteered. "All those same capabilities, but contained away from a traditional runway."

"Where is this contained, then?" Chris asked, turning his gray eyes—ones exactly like Hope's—right on Jake.

Jake's king shook his head, shutting Chris down. "We didn't agree to reveal location, and you know under what terms you're here."

The colonel's eyes were wide, fixed on the nearest craft. "Take a look at that plane. God, she's beautiful." Wonder filled the older man's voice.

"What do you think? That she holds her own beside any of your USAF planes?" Jared asked, a glimmer of mischief in his eyes.

The colonel gave an appreciative whistle. "These craft aren't like anything I've ever seen, Commander. And I've been flying for over twenty-five years."

"Our technology is different, of course," Bennett commented with a brisk nod.

The colonel whistled again, low and meaningful. "Now that I see what we've been flying against, I don't feel so terrible that you've whupped us so many times."

Bennett's features tightened. "We aren't your enemy—we were defending you all along."

The colonel bristled in turn. "It would have helped, sir, if you'd come forward sooner. If you'd told us the true nature of the conflict. You might have saved yourself—all of us—a lot of lost time."

Jared bowed his head. "You never gave us that opportunity, Colonel. You were too busy trying to shoot us down."

The colonel took a step forward toward the nearest craft, but Bennett caught him by the arm. "Let's save the tour until after our meeting," he said, turning to face Chris. "I'm most interested in your sister's safety right now—and that of my lieutenant, Scott Dillon. Come this way." Jared gestured across the hangar with a sidelong look at Jake. "I have a meeting room already set up, and my advisers are waiting."

Chapter Twenty-three

Jake sat back at the meeting table and listened as Jared gave the colonel and Chris the lowdown. Not the full picture—such as the fatal virus that had caused the war back home. But details about Veckus Densalt, and how he led the Earth conquest, was Raedus's henchman, and about the revolution. How Raedus had stolen Jared's kingship and throne, and even now lived in the D'Aravnian palace that had been in Jared's own family for more than a thousand years. The two outsiders listened, wide-eyed, and didn't interrupt with questions. Chris scribbled notes on his pad, and Jake was surprised at that fact, but Jared didn't make a move to stop him.

Maybe his commander really *had* decided to join forces with the feds. Later, when it was just the two of them, he planned to praise him for that plan.

"So what caused this virus, then, if it wasn't released by your people, as these Antousians claim?" Chris asked, his gray eyes narrowing.

Jared hesitated, staring at his hands. "They were having genetic issues," he answered opaquely. "They decided to use genetic therapy, but it's almost impossible to fix one thing without causing other problems."

"What sort of genetic issues?" Chris persisted, and Jared closed his eyes.

Jake knew exactly what was happening in his best friend's mind. It was the same question that was on all the rest of theirs: how much to tell, what to reveal—and what to keep secret.

After a moment, Jared opened his eyes again. "We will share that knowledge in good time, Agent Harper."

Way to go, Jared, he wanted to cheer. *Smart move for now.*

The true cause behind the virus—the reason the Antousians had sought genetic therapy in the first place—was much more than the humans needed to know at this point in time. That kind of knowledge could be terribly dangerous in the wrong hands.

Jake was thinking about that fact when, unexpectedly, Chris turned to look him right in the eye. "You were the one on the snowmobile," he announced suddenly. "You're our unsub."

Jake pulled back in his chair, caught off guard. "What makes you say that?"

"You match the description completely—the bright green eyes, the large, bulky build."

Jake glanced at Jared, who gave a nod of approval, then replied, "Yes, I was with your sister on the snowmobile prior to our encounter with the Antousians."

Chris rose up slightly in his chair. "Why in hell did you have Hope out there like that?"

Jake met his former brother-in-law's caustic stare, and never so much as blinked. "There was a good reason. Trust me on that."

Chris shook his head, his face flushing. He was always a man with a quick temper, and Jake couldn't expect this moment to be any exception. "Did you realize she has diabetes? Huh?"

"Agent Harper, let's stow this," the colonel intervened. "We've got bigger fish to fry right now."

Jared turned to the overhead projector, ready to begin flashing slides—images of what they'd known about various Antousian hideouts—when suddenly Thea burst into the room.

"Yes, Lieutenant?" Jared asked her, releasing the handheld projector control.

She was winded, but managed to catch her breath. "I have a line on them," she announced. "Just got incredibly accurate intel."

"From whom?" Jared and Jake asked, practically in unison.

Thea cut her gaze sideways at the two outsiders in their midst, then gestured toward the hallway with her head. Jared turned and, with a polite bow to both men, said simply, "Please, sirs, give us a moment."

Jake followed Thea and Jared into the hallway, wondering what knowledge Thea had possibly managed to lay hold of.

Once the door was closed, she whispered, "It's one of our spies, sir. Managed to get a message through to me. She gave me the exact coordinates of their location."

"*Which* spy, Thea?" Jared searched her face. "I have no knowledge of any spies among the Antousian ranks."

Thea smiled up at him, looking proud of herself. "Sir, you've always taught me to keep our intel completely compartmentalized on these matters. As your chief intelligence officer, the exact location—and how many spies I have working for me—I've always chosen to keep to myself."

Jared wasn't sure he liked that fact, even as he knew it was the smartest, safest strategy on Thea's part. "Go on," he said at last.

"It's an abandoned warehouse in Montana, an old feed and flour plant, sir. They're alive, and so far they're safe, but the contact says that may not hold for long."

Jared's mind whirled. Could this spy be truly trusted? If not, they'd be walking into a trap.

It was Jake Tierny who piped up next. "How do you know your contact is reliable?" he questioned, glancing back at the closed door.

Thea turned to him, annoyance flashing in her light

blue eyes. "Because the previous leads this contact has given me have been completely borne out. That's why."

Jared gave a brisk nod. "So we form a team and go in, but does that include"—he tapped the closed meeting room door—"those men?"

Thea gave him a tentative look of approval. "We joined our forces very well at Warren, don't you think?"

Jared had to admit it was true; still, even having made this step of having brought the feds into their camp was a major leap of trust. If this retrieval job went wrong, the stakes were off the map—he could lose his best friend, and Hope Harper, no less.

"I need to think," he announced, and walked away down the hall.

Hope was surprised when, awakened by one of the soldiers, she was told to get up. "Where are you taking me?" she asked as they tugged her unsteadily to her feet.

"Veckus has a plan. Come." They dragged her along, and she dug her heels into the floor and slid most of the way along the hall, until finally she realized resistance wouldn't help, and walked the rest of the way.

"Here she is, Commander," one of the soldiers announced, shoving her forward into the semidarkness. "All healed up and ready to play."

Glancing about them, Hope could see faint light from overhead, as if maybe the morning was dawning.

Scott called out from beside her, "Don't let them intimidate you." His voice was hoarse and choked, telling her that he'd been placed back in those cruel metal cuffs once again.

"So what's your big plan, Veckus?" She stepped forward into the darkness, praying she wouldn't trip.

"Ah, so you've heard that I have something very fine orchestrated for the two of you."

She waved her arms. "Stop wasting time and tell us what it is."

Veckus walked toward the direction of Scott's voice,

and she heard her lover's chain rattle, then the sound of him stumbling to his feet. With a quick order, Veckus commanded that Scott's restraints be removed.

"Scott Dillon, now you will show her your true nature. I think divide and conquer is the order of this particular day. Once she knows, I doubt she'll work so hard to set you free."

"I don't understand," Hope said, but something hard and desperate lodged right in her throat.

"He wants me to Change." Scott turned toward Veckus, who never stopped circling them.

Hope shook her head, unclear. "Change how?"

She heard the sound of his cuffs falling away as they clattered to the ground. For some reason, Veckus wanted Scott to be free. He continued with his vitriolic tirade, aiming it right at Scott.

"She needs to see what you are, Lieutenant, what you truly can be. Once she knows the truth, you'll be a monster in her eyes; these humans have never even seen what you and I truly are. So, yes, Change! Go on, I insist that she see you. If not, this medicine"—he took the freezer bag and dangled it close to the fire that was crackling in a tin drum before them—"will go up in flames."

Scott lunged at the bag. "Stop that! All right, I'll do it . . . I will do it, but don't destroy her medicine."

Veckus gave him a hissing smile of approval. "Of course, it's not lost on me that she is a blind woman, so this will be about what she can *hear* and what she can *feel*. Every ridge and hard plate along your skin."

Scott pressed his eyes shut. Behind him, he heard Hope suck in a slight breath. "A monster, that's all you will ever be," Veckus continued. "You've always thought yourself so superior to the rest of us. Don't you remember what runs in your veins?"

"Yes." It was barely more than a tacit agreement, but Veckus heard it, and his face lit up.

"Ah! This is good indeed!" He clapped, throwing his head back with a jocular laugh, but then his face took on a grim, cruel expression. "So go ahead."

Scott could hardly breathe; it was as if a tight vise had clamped about his chest, as if the air all around them had vanished and he was left gasping at nothing. With a quick glance over his shoulder at Hope, he whispered, "Don't be afraid. I would never hurt you—never. This isn't really me."

"Of course it's you!" Veckus roared, striding toward them both. "Let me explain it to her. Three possible forms, that's what our species possess, and if Dillon's parents hadn't taken hosts, the one you're going to see is the way he would have walked our planet every day. If not in that Antousian form then he would be in the formless state, which I suspect you're already aware of. And obviously, you have *sampled* his humanized form—but I'm sure he never told you that it's not how all of our people look. He's a hybrid, part human and part . . . what he will reveal to you now. He will show you our true nature. We are beautiful, magnificent creatures, but in the eyes of humans we will certainly be perceived as horrid!"

Scott panted, feeling his palms sweat, but Hope's soft, encouraging voice said only, "He can never be anything other than beautiful to me. You aren't going to win this one, Veckus."

On her words and with a prayer to All, Scott allowed his core energy to build, and also allowed his Change and transformation to overtake him. His body stretched and molded, pulled and split in two, the Change causing him to scream in overwhelming pain as he fell to his knees. He roared his agony, throwing his head back, unable to stop—yet hearing that he sounded like a beast. He worked his jaws, trying to speak, but the slightly distended facial bones were utterly unfamiliar now. He hadn't walked in this form, not once, since he had been fifteen and morbid curiosity had overtaken him.

He jerked his head first one way, then another, and found Hope staring at him. How much could she see? His overwhelming height, perhaps. He was six feet, eight inches when in this form. A terrifyingly large figure to her fine, compact one, no doubt.

"Don't be afraid," Scott told her in his garbled, hissing voice. He cleared his throat, clutching at it. "Don't, Hope."

"I always knew you were an alien, remember," she reminded him gently. "It's no surprise to me that you are."

He hung his head, the strange shape of his back giving his neck and shoulders a slightly hunched-over feeling. With a roar, he bellowed at Veckus, expressing all the shame and horror he felt at being forced to expose himself to the woman he loved—the very human one—more than any other being in the universe.

"Good. Now go to her." Veckus clapped with glee.

Scott stalked in her direction, his hulking body almost impossible to control; despite his desire to approach her gently, he took giant loping steps that thundered off the concrete. He stopped in front of her, then swung his face sideways and stared at Veckus out of his large eyes. A monster's eyes, ones that would terrify her, if only she could see.

Veckus called the shots. "Kneel."

With a light, roaring snarl, Scott dropped to the ground and hung his head in the deepest, most soul-rending shame. "Hope. I am . . . sorry." He cursed his garbled, alien voice.

She didn't hesitate, but reached forward and felt him, cupping his perverse face within her hands. Not once did he see rejection or fear in her expression, only curiosity. She worked her hands about the terrain of his body just as she'd done that time in her bed. When she reached his nose—which was long, straight, and covered with plated ridges—she laughed. "This one doesn't have a bump."

"No . . . bump," he agreed, swallowing his palpable shame.

She continued with her exploration until she reached the top of his head—which was covered with the same hard, ridged plates she felt along his nose. She ran her hands over his bald head, then found the sides of his face, and he closed his eyes, flinching.

"Oh!" she cried as she felt his large, completely shut eyes. "These are really . . ."

"Don't even . . . say . . . it," he hissed.

"Huge! Man, I need these—do they work well? Can you see everything that I can't?"

He began to laugh, a laughter that bubbled up from deep within his chest in the strange hissing and garbled sound that formed his speech, and this infuriated Veckus.

"Feel his chest!" the warlord insisted. "And next his back! Even, by gods, feel his cock."

Scott flinched, shaking his head from side to side. "Hideous," he choked out. "All wrong."

Hope cupped his face, running her fingertips along his jaw, and whispered, "Never. I've seen our future, remember? I've seen you in my dreams many times."

Veckus stormed close, pointing a weapon at Hope. "Tell her to feel your body."

"Do it, Hope," Scott said, drawing her hands to his chest. His Antousian body had evolved on a planet of harsh extremes, and in response his ancestors had developed plates of natural armor, like the rough hide of some animals. She traced her fingertips over his chest, rubbing at the thick substance of his naked body. The sensation for him was . . . incredibly tactile. Despite being so impenetrable, his Antousian body was highly suggestive to sensual touch, even at a time like this one.

"Lower," Veckus commanded, and very cautiously Hope trailed her fingers farther along his oversize waist.

His cock was as hard and plated as the rest of him, but not from arousal—because this was the way his kind had evolved. It didn't exactly promise for tender or gentle sex, and he flinched as she ran her hand along the tough length of him. All nine inches of it, permanently stretched and ready to go. He'd always wondered if the original Antousians had trouble with arousal: Why else would their kind have a permanent hard-on?

"So what do you think?" Veckus taunted. "Not so handsome anymore, is he?"

"I think he's gorgeous," she announced, jutting her chin out. "Maybe I think all of your people are beautiful, just highly misguided."

"Perhaps I should Change as well—perhaps the rest of us should, and then how safe would you feel? Do you realize that our species tops off at seven feet? What are you to that but a tiny gnat of a little thing?"

Hope rose to her feet, defiant all the way. "I am strong and vital, and nothing has ever held me back— not my illness or my height, and you won't be an exception to that rule, Veckus. And you can't make me care for Scott any less."

Scott sighed, rubbing the top of his bald head, and although not yet granted permission to do so, abruptly shifted back to his humanized form. He wanted to shout to the heavens; being Antousian had always been his greatest shame, and Veckus certainly knew that. Yet the love of his life cared not a whit. All she wanted was to touch him, whatever form he might take. It was enough to make him rejoice in complete victory.

"I did not order you to Change," Veckus thundered.

"Your game's up." Scott smiled at his captor. "Now stop pissing around and get down to what you really want."

"I want the human to undress now too."

Scott's throat tightened. "Why?"

"I want to perform a bit of a study on why the reflexive metal released you when the two of you had sex. Now, strip her." Veckus issued quick commands. "Only this time, I intend to watch."

"No way in hell—" Scott began, but was immediately cut off when several soldiers jumped him, wrestling him down. He was thrust face-first against the cold warehouse floor, and the whip sliced into his flesh once again. Grimacing, he struggled, desperate to reach Hope before his enemies stripped her bare.

Beside him, he heard Hope grunting, and she cried out. Holy hell, this couldn't be happening.

Again the whip stung across his shoulders. Then his

lower back. Writhing, he worked to get a fix on Hope, but the relentless, shredding swipes of the whip kept him glued to the floor.

"Ten more strikes for Dillon—then we will begin."

Scott felt tears burn his eyes, and blinked them back, slowly turning his head to get a look at Hope. She lay shivering against the floor; they'd left her underwear on, but otherwise she was completely naked, just like him.

Veckus circled her, his blazing eyes feasting on her, and Scott arched his back against the whip, shouting in Refarian, ordering the warlord to release her—to back off his insane and cruel plan.

"String her up against the wall," Veckus announced with a dark grin in Scott's direction. "Put the whip to her back next."

"No, no, Veckus." Scott panted, scrabbling at the hard concrete. "Not her. Please."

"*Please?* Please?" Veckus reached for the whip that was currently held in Kryn's grasp, slapping it against his open palm. "Did I just hear the powerful Lieutenant Scott Dillon begging *me* for a favor?"

Scott pressed his forehead against the floor, trying to breathe or even to think—both of which were becoming increasingly difficult with the frigid air of the warehouse folding about his naked body, and the stinging welts of the whip emblazoned across his back. "Just don't touch her," he managed at last, swallowing hard. "She's not part of this war."

"Then you shouldn't have made her part of it." Veckus took the whip and slowly dragged it across Scott's shoulder, allowing the leather strap to snake threateningly across his raw flesh.

"Surely innocence means something, even to you," Scott argued hoarsely, but was met with cruel laughter.

Slowly Veckus trailed the whip low across Scott's back, then lower across his buttocks. The cursed thing lifted, and Scott braced for a torturous slap—yet none came.

"If you want to live—both of you," Veckus said, "then

you will show me exactly what you did earlier to disengage the reflexive restraints. Now, Dillon, go to her."

Crawling along the floor, gasping, Scott made his way across the small distance that separated him from Hope. She gazed in his direction, wide-eyed with terror.

Don't worry, sweetheart, he transmitted mentally, praying she could somehow hear him. *I won't let this go too far.*

Drawing her into his arms, he tugged her against his chest, and could feel her heart racing frantically against his. "Don't be scared," he whispered under his breath.

"Your back, Scott," she murmured so low that only he could hear. "The way he keeps beating you."

"It's okay." He captured her mouth in a rough kiss. Despite the horror of the moment, perhaps because of the heightened adrenaline, he felt a rush of warmth flood his body. It hardly mattered if his greatest enemy watched.

"No! Not like that," Veckus coached from the sidelines. "In your natural form, Dillon. Change again!"

Scott pulled apart from Hope. "Never."

"Kiss her in your truest form, or I will kill her now."

Hope reached to touch his face. "It's okay, Scott. I'm not afraid of you—you know that."

Scott cast a scalding glance at Veckus. "And I'm not afraid of that *vlksai* bastard, either. You think you're in control here?" He wrapped Hope within his arms protectively. "You think you can debase me any worse than I naturally am? I have Antousian blood in my veins. Sharing genetics with the likes of you is the worst punishment I could have. You can't inflict that on me all over again."

Veckus dropped beside them both, drawing his mouth against Scott's ear. "You should learn a little more respect for your own people."

"Not until they deserve it."

"Change!"

"I stay in this form. You won't kill Hope—hell, you won't even harm her. You know why? Because if you do, you won't ever get a damned thing out of me, and you know it. So it's your choice, Veckus. Either stand down or lose any chance you might have of learning a fucking thing from me."

Veckus circled them, running his hand across the top of Hope's head with all the sensuality of a lover, and Scott felt his face flame hot. If the man so much as touched her once more, he was going to kill the freak, his own life be damned.

He was thankful when Veckus seemed to reconsider his strategy. "Bind them," he instructed one of the other soldiers. "Back-to-back, just as they are—naked. Let them see how persuasive the frigid cold can be."

Chapter Twenty-four

Back in the meeting room, the latest intel from a spy informing their every decision, Jared began to lay out a strategy for a joint attack. "Veckus is at our specified location, and that means your number one guy is ready to be taken out. I'm talking this is the bin Laden of the Antousian alliance, at least here on Earth."

Colonel Peters studied him, jaw slack. "This is the alien behind the attack at Warren? That's what you're telling me, Commander?"

Jared walked toward the table, braced both hands on it, and stared deep into Peters's eyes. "I'm telling you this: that Veckus Densalt is the motive force behind almost every evil move these aliens make on this Earth. I've seen his face firsthand, Colonel, and I've been his captive. You do not want Earth to fall into his hands. We also have"—Jared hesitated, looking toward Jake—"unusual intel that reveals the possibility of Earth's destruction under his leadership. The missiles at Warren? They were just the first of his schemes. Together, we must protect this planet at all costs. My own planet has experienced untold suffering as a result of this species. Don't let it happen again, not here on a planet that I dearly love."

Colonel Peters rubbed his jaw. "He has two hostages, you say—FBI linguist Hope Harper, and then your man, this Lieutenant Scott Dillon, whom we held at the base."

"Yes, and I can give you the coordinates—but it has to be a joint attack."

Chris Harper joined the discussion. "What about the FBI's involvement?"

The colonel turned to Agent Harper. "You apprise them of the situation, but the USAF will go in with Bennett on this attack."

"They might not like that arrangement very much," Harper warned, raking a hand through his spiky blond hair.

The colonel slapped his hands on the table, giving Chris a chastising look. "Son, you knew the stakes coming into this place. We're in the lead on this show, not you and your suits."

"I want to come along." Chris rose to his feet, turning to Jared in supplication. "This is my sister we're talking about. I don't care who's running things; I'm good with a weapon, and I want in this fight."

Jared didn't want to overstep his bounds, so he deferred with a nod of his head to the colonel, who said simply, "Give him back his weapon, and he can tag along on your flight."

Chris marveled as the aircraft catapulted out of the hangar and into the Teton Mountains. All this time, and the aliens had been right under his nose; all this time, and they'd kept the forces of their revolution here—hidden completely. How many years had Jared and his crew battled it out from this location so near his office in Jackson? Two, five, twenty? It was impossible to say, but after what he'd witnessed there at Jared Bennett's base, he had a grudging respect for the alien leader. The man knew what he wanted, and it seemed—at least so far—that his primary intention truly was protecting Earth.

It was bizarre to think of an alien loving this planet the way that Chris and so many of his own kind did. But after five years in the FBI, nothing much surprised him anymore. Human nature—or alien nature, for that matter—always seemed to take the turn you didn't expect. Bad guys turned good; good ones went rogue. You couldn't count on anyone to do exactly what you'd expect; sometimes not even yourself.

Harnessed in, he stared out the portal window, watching the first pink of morning color the mountaintops. It had been more than a day since he'd slept, but he didn't dare shut his eyes now. What he needed was coffee, something to give his system a jolt. And he said as much to the Refarian soldier buckled in beside him. She laughed, and called into some kind of communication device on her wrist; shortly thereafter a man appeared with a tall disposable cup.

"What's this?" He stared at the steaming contents of the Styrofoam mug in his hand.

The woman beside him grunted. "Coffee."

He gawked at her in disbelief. "Aliens like java?"

"Our commander is a coffee freak, Agent Harper. That simple. Drink up."

He took a tentative sip, wondering if this might simply be a plan to poison him. But it tasted like coffee—and not just any old coffee at that: a fine blend that made him close his eyes in deep pleasure.

"Thank you," he said, and wondered just how similar these Refarians might really be to humans in the end.

Veckus's strategy kept on changing. He and Hope had been harnessed together, completely naked and bound as one in strong loops of reflexive metal. Perhaps Veckus was conducting some sort of psychic experiment, trying to see how lovers would react beneath the cruel and merciless bindings. Then again, maybe he still hoped to secretly watch them make love, to see exactly how they'd circumvented the metal bindings once before. Whatever the warlord's motivations, Scott couldn't begin to guess at them, although the constantly shifting ground rules were starting to play havoc with his mental state. Undoubtedly that was part of Veckus's plan.

The skin across Scott's back was bleeding and raw, and it hurt like hell being pressed up against Hope's own much softer back. He tried to focus on the comfort of sharing a physical connection with her, not on the stinging flesh across his shoulders and lower back.

At least her condition had stabilized again—for now. But her current status did nothing to allay his fears for her health and well-being. Scott watched as in the far corner of the room, the Antousians talked, bent over schematics of some sort. Gods in heaven, he hoped it wasn't a map of their compound. Blinking his eyes, he dared to soul-gaze a bit, heightening his vision in an attempt to see what the group was planning. What he came up with was certainly unsettling.

They were poring over detailed plans for Warren Air Force Base. Clearly Veckus still hadn't given up that fight.

Damn it all to hell. He had to get free. Against his back, he felt Hope shift her weight.

"Hang in," he whispered under his breath. "Maybe the worst of this has passed."

He had absolutely no reason to believe his assertion was true, but it sounded good, at least. She had gotten through her diabetic shock, so he wasn't entirely talking out of his ass.

She leaned into him, nudging at his backside, and he sensed her unspoken words—felt them shimmy through his core being. *I know we'll get out of this.*

That was what he heard, the words penetrating his heart as surely as if she'd spoken them.

We will, he transmitted back to her. *We have a future. Hang on to that.*

He couldn't be sure if they were really speaking within each other's minds, or perhaps he was already so far gone that he'd begun to spirit-slip her all over again. Whatever the case, he closed his eyes and lost himself in the moment of pure, innocent communication.

For an instant he wavered along the thin membrane of exhaustion and, opening his eyes, saw Hope standing on the beach at Mareshtakes. A smile formed on his lips—she'd brought him home. It had been years since he'd seen the multicolored rocks along this shore, felt the waves roll over his bare feet. Hope stood along the edge of the rocky shore wearing a large straw hat, completely naked otherwise. And more gorgeous than he had ever seen her, the sun gleaming along her bare skin, practically making her human body glow.

Come to me! she called joyously, waving him closer with the hat. *Let's make love!*

He began running toward her, feeling the warm, wet sand beneath his bare feet. A discordant sound interrupted their reverie right as he swung her into his arms, turning her in a circle. A jarring, erratic one, like the peppering of hard rain against a rooftop.

Together they stared up at the sky, she splaying both hands across his chest. She shielded her eyes, and he did so too. Overhead, a full squadron of Antousian fighters split the bright blue sky.

"Now, sweetheart! Now, now! *Run!*"

Jolting awake, Scott found that their bindings had fallen away from their bodies, probably because of the intense and pleasurable emotion they'd shared in their dream—but that wasn't the first thing he registered. The entire warehouse was lit up like a bonfire, pulse flares peppering the floor all around them. Wordlessly, he took hold of Hope's arm and began shuttling her along the wall.

"Stay with me!"

She bent low, mirroring his quick, careful steps. "Is it your people?"

"No idea. Just follow me!" He kept to the wall, and then there was a long hallway, already filled with smoke. His eyes burned, and he tucked Hope into the crook of his arm protectively. "Keep going. We're going to find safe ground."

She did as he said, and under her breath whispered, "You warned me. In that dream. You were there, and so was I—and you told me what was happening."

He gave her a light shove as they reached a turn in the hallway. "The flowers?"

"Yeah, and those horrible planes."

For a moment he paused, sucking in a breath. All around them gunfire and pulse rounds sounded explosively, riving the walls in every direction. At the end of the narrow and dilapidated hallway he caught sight of a stairwell. "I see our target." He gave her another forceful tug. "I'm getting us out of here!"

With pulse fire nipping at their heels, they sprinted in unison—she into what was almost certainly darkness, he with their objective in clear sight. They hit the stairs so hard that they slammed into the wall, but he didn't pause or hesitate. "Come on, Hope. We've got to get up there."

One minute Veckus had been contemplating his coming victory at Warren, and the next the entire warehouse had exploded into flaming bursts of ammunition rounds. Running down the back hallway, he headed toward the grain shaft. It would be the best place to wait this skirmish out while his troops did their job. He hit the stairway, taking the steps two at a time, but all at once a massive hand took hold of his neck.

"Oh, no, you don't," a rumbling voice said, twisting him back up against the wall of the stairwell.

Veckus's eyes bulged as the giant of a man—Refarian, he could smell it—placed a stranglehold about his throat. "Where are they?" his enemy demanded, looming over him with frighteningly bright green eyes. He was a gazer. No, no, he wasn't Refarian . . . this was an Antousian-human hybrid, one who just so happened to smell like his enemy.

Sucking at the air about him, Veckus grasped at his throat. "Brother," he tried lamely, but the enemy roared back in his face.

"Where are they?"

He moved his head, tried to speak, flailed his arms.

At last the obscenely large creature released him, and he bent double, erupting in a seizure of coughs.

"I . . . don't know," he claimed lamely. The brute raised his fist again, making as if to push him against the wall. "Wait! Tell me who you want."

"I want my comrades."

Veckus wasted no time; thrusting with the knife he'd hidden in his sleeve, he stabbed the man deep within his belly—and got absolutely no reaction. Not so much as a blink or a flinched muscle. Nothing. The large freak was an impenetrable fortress. Veckus stabbed again, his blade swiping at the air between them, and the hybrid batted his weapon away as if it were a mere annoyance.

"I'll gaze you if I have to," his enemy threatened, "and you know where that can lead."

For the first time in many years, Veckus felt himself tremble from fear. Gazing could lead to soul-dividing; he'd never been on the receiving end of one of his own kind's gifts. "Give me a minute," he begged. "Dillon . . . and that human, that's who you want?"

"And damn well you know it."

"I honestly have no idea . . . I-I had them here, but in the chaos, they . . . escaped," he stuttered.

The stranger's eyes began to glow, becoming two bright spheres within his dark face. "I've waited for this moment for a very long time," the man said.

Veckus shook his head. "No, don't . . . not yet. I can help you."

"Really? How?"

Veckus sought for a strategy, but for once in his life all his game plans failed him. "I don't know where they are," he admitted. He had never planned on this particular result.

"Then there's only one thing you can do for me."

"Anything! Anything at all."

The man's eyes brightened to knifepoints, spearing into Veckus. "What you can do for me," he said calmly, "is die."

And with that, the hybrid's eyes sharpened to laser points, reaching into Veckus's internal self, plying and tearing at him like the claws of death itself.

Veckus tried to scream, tried to break the man's piercing, dividing gaze, but couldn't look away.

"Call me Jakob," the giant rumbled, and it was the very last thing Veckus heard before he felt his soul literally divide into a million shards of darkness.

Chris rounded a turn in the smoke-filled hallway, and found Jake Tierny standing over a crumpled figure. "That's your man," Jake told him, wiping a hand over his brow.

"The bin Laden of this crew—that man?" Chris asked, staring at the fallen alien.

"Dead to the core."

"We could have questioned him." Chris's temper flared; they hadn't come this far to lose the opportunity for interrogation.

"You can question the rest of us, and we'll actually cooperate." He nodded, glancing down the hallway. This little pissing match didn't matter, at least not right now. Hope was somewhere in this warehouse, very possibly still in grave danger.

"We have to find Hope."

Jake pointed up the stairs. "They're up there."

"Did you see them go up?" he asked, not sure how the alien was so certain of his sister's location. The man only smiled in return, a strange kind of smile that Chris couldn't read.

"Trust me. I just know where she is."

"Then let's stop wasting time," Chris shot back, barreling up the staircase.

Hope reached the top of the rickety stairs, and Scott took hold of both her shoulders. "We're safe up here, I think, at least for now."

Below them there were voices, and she wondered if

he could hear them too. She knew her hearing had become very keen in recent months, even as her eyesight had faded.

"Someone's down there," she told him, and he stiffened beside her, listening.

She listened as he walked a short distance away, his footsteps echoing off the sound of decaying wood. "This is a grain shaft," he hissed. "There's a long, spiraling tunnel."

She pressed against the wall behind her. "What are you saying?"

"Nothing yet."

But she got the picture, all right; if they were cornered, Scott meant for the two of them to go barreling down that shaft as if it were their very own water slide. Only no water—and no idea where they would land.

She listened intently, and heard footsteps down below. "Someone's coming!"

Scott grabbed her arm, jerking her forward into the darkness that always enveloped her. "We've gotta get out of here."

"No—wait." Something told her that whoever was on the stairs below wasn't their enemy.

But all at once an explosion rocked the stairwell, driving her down to her knees and causing a rushing wind to rend the very air between them.

Jake! It was Jake, here trying to rescue them. Only she didn't have time to explain that twisted, bizarre story to Scott, not right now. If the two of them came too close together it could possibly destroy them both.

"Scott! That grain shaft—we need to take it, and fast!"

His strong arms wrapped about her, and she hugged him back until they were formed together as one unbreakable line. "On my mark, and I'll lead us in. Three, two, one, now!"

With a slight tumble she found herself spiraling through darkness, clinging to Scott as her feet caught against metal and wood beams and thousands of prickling invasions of her body. Round and round and round they went, down and down. She wanted to throw up, and if not for Scott's unrelenting hold on her, she probably would have.

Just when she thought she'd pass out from the upending freefall, they crashed against softness. Thank God that something had cushioned their fall.

Beside her, Scott groaned. They'd landed in a smallish pile of old grain or feed or something like it. The smell was stale and mildewy, and she covered her nose with her sweater sleeve. Groping in the darkness, she felt Scott's leg.

"I'm all right," he told her preemptively. "You look okay too."

"Look, if I'd wanted to go to Wild Waves, I'd have told you so," she joked, and he chuckled softly in return.

"As in, you ride those sorts of things? Like with water in them?"

"You really have been living on Earth."

Out of nowhere she heard thundering footsteps, a group of them, and her whole body tensed until a very familiar voice cried, "Harper! Thank All!" It was Anna, and she felt the alien's arms wrap about her neck. "You're safe now—we've totally decimated the bad guys."

She buried her face against Anna's shoulder, crying despite herself. Anna continued, "Now, this guy? I might just leave him here for all the trouble he keeps causing me."

"Hey, now." Scott grunted. "Show a little respect to your commanding officer."

"Respect this!" Anna countered, and although Hope couldn't see the gesture, she had a pretty good idea that certain things crossed galactic lines.

"That's funny," a male voice interrupted, "I was just going to teach you a few things about respect." Hope heard several weapons engaging.

"Crap," Anna muttered under her breath, pulling apart from Hope.

"What's going on?" Hope asked, glancing wildly about the dark, confined area.

"That's Dayron, one of Veckus's understudies."

Scott spoke next. "We can talk about this—you know you're surrounded."

"And I just might want to take you out before I go," Dayron replied smoothly.

A weapon jabbed into Hope's ribs. "Get up, human." She struggled onto her knees, feeling the ground to gain her balance, but a noise behind them all caused her to hesitate. It was thundering, like a rushing, metallic river—and was coming right from the grain shaft that she and Scott had barreled down just moments earlier.

"What's that?" Dayron shouted. "Whoever it is, I'm going to kill them."

The sound of gunfire echoed off the interior of the shaft. "FBI! FBI! Drop your weapons!"

Tears welled within Hope's eyes; it was Chris, already firing a warning shot before he'd fully landed. More gunfire erupted, and then a few shouts as Hope felt herself thrust to the ground beneath Scott's body. "Keep down," he warned her hoarsely.

She nodded, but then there was only the sound of heavy breathing and shuffling steps. A hand clasped her arm. "Get up—now."

Oh, shit, she thought with a grin, tears streaming down her face. Atop her, Scott stiffened, still covering her with his body. "It's okay." She gave a grunt, shouldering him. "That's my brother Chris."

"That's all you're gonna say after I just saved your ass?" her twin barked, dislodging her from beneath Scott and jerking her to a standing position.

"It's freaking great to see you!" She flung herself into his arms. "Does that work better?"

She could tell he was about to release a few explosive words, but they were interrupted by several USAF soldiers, people dragging them in various directions.

"We're still going to talk," Chris warned her, and no

matter how menacing he was trying to sound, she just couldn't stop smiling at him.

Outside the warehouse, Scott was shocked to see a full array of human military personnel. Air force, as unbelievable as that was to take in. Someone had thrust a blanket around his shoulders, and he surveyed the brightly lit landscape all about the warehouse. In the middle of their battle morning had arrived, bringing bright, sparkling daylight to the blanket of snow. Out of the mayhem Marco McKinley appeared, leading him toward a waiting medical transport.

"I want to go with Hope," he argued, but McKinley held up his hand.

"I need to debrief you on a few things," the Madjin warrior told him. "You need to come with me."

Scott halted. "I want to go on the transport with Hope—what, I can't do that? After everything that's just gone down? Besides, since when do you call the shots?"

McKinley put an arm around his shoulder and kept walking him farther and farther away from the warehouse. "I'll explain it all en route, sir."

"No. Right here, right now." He stood his ground, refusing to take another step.

"Maybe I'm the one to do the explaining," Hope called out, walking toward him with her hand through the crook of Anna's arm.

Scott scowled at her, whipping his gaze about the area surrounding the warehouse. There were so many soldiers—Refarian and human—he couldn't quite determine what was going on.

"He needs to get on that transport, Ms. Harper," McKinley argued.

"Fine, and I'll go with him. I can talk to him on the way to your base."

McKinley cast a cautious look about them—and suddenly Scott understood. Everything came driving home with the full impact of a battering ram. "It's Jake Tierny.

You don't want me encountering him again. Because of what happens when we do."

Hope's expression grew grim, but she said nothing.

"Is that what happened in the stairwell?" He raised his eyebrows, glancing between Anna and McKinley, but neither seemed willing to talk.

"Let me do it," Hope said, and a gnawing feeling of dread began to build inside of him.

"Hope!" Scott spun to find Chris approaching her. "Hope Harper, I swear to ever-loving—"

"Don't you dare start with a lecture!" Hope's entire demeanor changed. They'd already encountered each other briefly by the grain shaft, but there hadn't been time for more than a few words. Now it seemed they were about to have some sort of colossal reunion, and he could see both of them were already bucking for a fight. Scott stifled a grin; he'd never had a brother, at least not a natural one, but he knew how things could get between him and Jared on occasion.

"Lecture?" Chris approached her, his blond eyebrows knit together in a stern expression. "A lecture? Hello, sister darling, you just about got yourself killed—"

"I am fine!" She slugged Chris hard in the arm, punching at him again as he ducked away.

Scott watched in amusement as the twins battled it out, then hugged and held tight to each other. Marco gave his arm a slight tug. "I really think they need some time," the warrior whispered quietly. "And there are things you need to understand."

His words brought Scott back to their conversation—to the fact that Jake Tierny posed some sort of unique threat, a personal one to him and him alone. "All right then," he agreed. "Let's board the craft and you can tell me everything."

Scott sat on the floor of his shower, letting the water pelt him across the back. Marco had been right—he definitely needed time to process these new facts. What could you say when you learned of a life terribly led? One of death and murder and madness?

What could you possibly do when you learned that a future version of yourself had done the one thing you'd always sworn you wouldn't do: assume a human's body?

He leaned against the shower wall, pressing his eyes shut. Sure, he'd stopped a killer, but that the motivation had been Hope's murder? The murder of their unborn daughter? He felt physically ill with the reality of it all.

"She'd been sick," McKinley had explained in even tones. "Her diabetes caused a lot of problems in her pregnancy."

And all Scott could think, sitting here on the wet floor of his shower stall, was that he'd been the one—undoubtedly he had—who'd prevented her from getting the genetic therapy she needed. The same fears that were propelling him in this time had driven him in that alternate life as well.

The gnawing anxiety that if she took the therapy something—anything—might go horribly wrong.

Hell, even knowing how it had ended for her, he still felt that way.

What of Jake Tierny, no less? He had a future version of himself loping about the camp, laying claim to the woman that he loved—he, Scott Dillon. He'd be damned if Tierny would have her, no matter what he'd shared with her in the future. Except that, according to Marco, Jake had been absolutely certain about one point—the man had no plans to get in the way of Scott and Hope's relationship, not in any way.

Honorable bastard. So like me, he thought, *to do something that foolish and shortsighted. How can he let her get away?*

Staggering to his feet, the welts on his back stinging from the impact of the water, he turned the nozzle off and just stood there. Stood and thought for a very long time. Hope was down in the medical area, getting treatment. He'd heard from Shelby that she was going to get the laser surgery done today, as well.

Definitely, he needed to go see her. Now, not later. Only something—some invisible hand or force—seemed to pin him right here, in the shower. Inside his quarters; it just kept holding him away from her.

He couldn't begin to think what that force might be.

Chapter Twenty-five

Jake entered his commander's sanctuary, the upstairs study where, back in this time, his king had so often strategized and meditated. Jake would never have interrupted the man's solitude, but he didn't have any time to waste—not when, at any given moment, he might encounter his younger self and cause the very heavens to shake. He had to hit the road—and fast—but first he needed Jared to sign off on the plan he'd been concocting. After so many battles together, and so much time under his commander's leadership, there was no way he'd take off without getting his best friend's approval.

Jared looked up from where he sat cross-legged on a large throw pillow, appearing visibly dismayed. "Jakob, you're bleeding!"

Jared immediately bounded to his feet, getting a good look at Jake's blood-soaked T-shirt. Jake had already stripped out of his jacket, but the superficial wound had been drawing a lot of blood—far more than actual pain—out of his human-hybrid body.

"Just a surface wound." He waved his king off. "No big deal, honestly."

"But you will go straight to the medical complex after this, correct?" Jared insisted with a stern expression.

"Of course, my lord." Jake gave a slight bow. "But first I've come to seek your approval, sir."

Jared assessed him quizzically. "Go on."

"I wish to pursue the human whose life I stole in the

future: Jakob Tierny. I must know *who* he is and why he killed my wife and baby."

"I thought you'd already exacted your vengeance."

"It's not about vengeance." Jake shook his head adamantly. "It's about Tierny's role in our war. I don't know how he's tied to the Antousians, but I'm certain that he is. He was there, on the battlefield that day"—he closed his eyes, forcing himself to continue—"before he killed Hope. He's in deep with them, J; I just don't know *how*. That's what I have to find out."

A strange look came over his king's face. "You're the only one who has ever called me 'J.' Since we were mere children, S'Skautsa, you've always called me that."

Jake smiled. "Jakob. That's what you call me there, in the future."

"Then I shall continue calling you Jakob here, in this time."

"I would like that." Emotion overtook Jake, but he forced himself to continue. "No matter who I've been, you have always been my brother and best friend," he said.

Jared bowed his head, and Jake swore he saw tears gleam in his commander's eyes. "Our friendship is a deep river, isn't it?"

"Always has been."

"So what of our future selves, then?" Jared's voice assumed a heavy tone. "What will happen to us now that you have prophesied such doom and destruction? That is the world that you left; how do we know that anything has really been changed?"

"You've already averted the attack at Warren. And that battle was the beginning of our future end. And Earth's."

"I'm not sure that fully eases my concerns, not with what you've told me about the world you left behind."

"That future no longer exists. Those people—you, Kelsey, all of them—are part of an alternate time now. They're nothing more than reflections in a mirror, glimpses we might catch occasionally, shadows in our blind spots. I mean, they do exist, but they don't have relevance here in this world except to warn us of our possible mistakes."

"I don't understand."

"Before I traveled back via the mitres, Kelsey told me that if I changed things here—in this time—that the future I was leaving would become an alternate one. That it would be a sort of shadow world. As it turns out, it wasn't me who changed things, but Marco McKinley." Jake burst into laughter. "So ironic . . . a man I hated, whom I blamed for so much hell that rained down on all of us, is now my ally. *Your* ally! Unbelievable, the way time keeps playing us all for its fool."

"But what you've seen, we can learn from it."

"We can always learn, and we'll continue to see the side glimpses. What Scott has seen of the life I myself led . . . even though he may not lead the same life, he can still see what to avoid, and what to embrace."

"Like knowing that he belongs with Hope."

Jake blinked. "Yes, like Hope Harper."

"I can't believe you can walk away from her." Jared snapped his fingers. "Just like that. She was your wife. Certainly I'm torn on this matter—both versions of you are so close to me—but . . . are you sure, Jakob?"

"You know me—really know me, J. Think about it."

Jared growled. "I could never let another man have Kelsey."

"Scott Dillon isn't just any man, though, is he?"

"Fair enough," Jared said, but continued to study him with a vaguely perplexed look. Jake knew it was partly because as long as they'd known each other, the many years they'd spent together—first playing as children, later fighting as men—Jared still didn't have a firm fix on the man he had eventually become. In other words, his best friend and king didn't totally understand the man he was now, the one who went by the name Jakob Tierny.

"So I have to locate the real Jakob Tierny, chase him down, figure out what he's doing with the Antousians.

He's a murderer, and it's not just that he killed Hope—it's that I have to stop him before he can kill anyone else."

"Won't that be a problem, considering you look, well, identical to the man?"

"It's a risk I'm willing to take. I can't exactly stick around here, allowing the universe to unhinge every time I encounter Dillon, can I?"

"Nor can you watch them together."

"That too," he admitted gruffly. "They have a future, but all I have with either of them is a whole lot of past. I've gotta figure out where my own future leads me."

"Do you even know where Jake Tierny is in this time? Where he lives?"

"Where he skulks or strokes the underbelly of society, you mean? Yes, I actually do. Anna did a ton of research for me. He's living in Texas right now. Hell's Creek, Texas, as crazy as that may sound. There really is a place called that."

Jared quirked an eyebrow. "Are you certain you're willing to go to Hell's Creek? I'm not sure that sounds like a very good idea."

"You always were far too ironic, sir."

"Is it near a major city, this Hell's Creek?"

Jake shrugged. "Not particularly, which ought to make ol' Jake pretty easy to find."

"Last I heard, there wasn't a nest of Antousians down that way."

"Our Texas base was destroyed by the bastards, sir, with all due respect."

Jared winced. "However, our intelligence never indicated that any Antousians made camp or headquarters in Texas."

Jakob took several steps closer, clasping Jared by the forearm. "But we never learned what our enemies were truly doing in Texas—and it's too much of a coincidence that Jake is living there now. The base being firebombed *plus* Tierny's presence? My money's on a connection."

"You'll report to me regularly?"

Jake dropped to one knee, placed a fist over his heart. "You are my king and my lord forever. Nothing can change that, not ever. Of course I will do all of this under your aegis."

Jared clasped his shoulder. "And you will be careful and watch yourself, Lieutenant?"

Jake bowed his head, unable to find words. To feel his friend and king's love, even though he now existed so utterly out of time, was almost more emotion than he could process. "Yes, my lord," he whispered.

"Then go, Jakob, with my blessing and approval," Jared said. "So long as you promise to eventually return."

"Okay, put your wounded ass right up on that table." The woman patted the examination table beside Jake, giving him an unreadable glance.

"You do know who I am, right?" He eyed the blond medic uncertainly, but she just laughed.

"Yeah, I've heard that from you before." He didn't understand at first, but then he caught her meaning when she added, "From Lieutenant Dillon, I mean. When he was first in here, I was his night nurse. It was sort of a joke between us."

So the whole camp had heard the truth about his identity by now: Of course they had. In these tight quarters, gossip flew at the speed of light. "I meant, you know I'm Antousian," he clarified.

She patted the table again. "Same as the lieutenant."

"You know him well?"

"Well, let's just say I have a soft spot for the ornery guy. And so that means—at least in a way—I know you too."

"It's a fucked-up mess, isn't it, Nurse Tyler?"

"You could say that too." She laughed, but then her smile faded. "If you don't mind my asking, sir, why didn't you fight for her? She was your wife, the woman you loved. I don't understand. I see how much you care for her."

"It was the right thing to do."

"That's sweet. You're letting your younger self win."

"Oh, it's not about Scott. I'd take her from him in a heartbeat if I could. In a heartbeat."

"Then why didn't you?"

He brushed a hand through his wildly disheveled hair. "I did it for her; it's always been about her, no one else. She deserves a pure future, to be happy and have that life we once lived. Only better, without the pain and death that I caused her."

"You didn't cause it, sir. She was sick."

He said nothing, knowing the real facts, but not wanting to debate them yet again. He'd already fought these battles with Hope. "I'm letting her go because I love her."

"That has to be incredibly tough."

"I never thought I'd feel so jealous of myself. What is it with that guy? He has all the beautiful ladies."

She narrowed her eyes, studying him. "You're plenty handsome, sir. Maybe even more so than he is."

Glancing downward, he studied the body that never felt right, the skin he always felt wrong living inside. Tattoos, scars, swarthiness: It all belonged to another man—a man he'd hated—and the body never gave up its secrets. "I don't see it," was all he said.

"Are you blind, Lieutenant?" She reached to the side table, producing a mirror. "Look in here. Really look— you're a beautiful man. Still. In this body. You'll find love again."

Gazing into the mirror, he met a stranger. For three years he'd lived in this body, yet it felt as awkward and unnatural as the day he'd first stepped into it. He was a killer, a thief. No way could he feel handsome, no matter what Jake's body and face looked like. He dropped the mirror onto the bed.

"You'd better look at this"—he gestured toward his blood-soaked shirt—"so I can hit the road. I've got a long way to go."

"Where you headed?"

"Texas."

Something odd registered in her eyes, a passing look of melancholy, but she only nodded, patting the bed. "You're going to have to lie down, sir."

"Please," he said, reclining on the examining table, "call me Jake."

Very gently she lifted his bloody T-shirt, exposing his bare abdomen. She winced slightly as she examined the wound, reaching for bandages and tubes of antiseptic.

"That bad?" he asked, watching her eyes.

"No . . . I just hate the Grateful Dead. All their music sounds the same."

"Who?"

She glanced up at him in surprise. "Your tattoo, sir— uh, Jake."

"That skull and the roses?" He'd always despised that tattoo most of all, and had wanted to curse ol' Tierny for having covered his stomach and back with so many grotesque emblems. But the one on his abdomen had never made any sense.

"You really have no idea what it means, do you?" she pressed him with a quirky smile.

He rolled his eyes impatiently. "Tell me, Nurse Tyler."

She dabbed at his wound. "They're a rock band. Got a huge cult following, and these symbols—the rose and the skull—mean that your man Jake was into the Dead."

Into the dead, he thought with a grim laugh. That was definitely one way to put it: Jake had loved killing, plain and simple. Maybe he'd stolen this band's imagery because it made a larger point about what he valued in life—death.

"Makes a lot more sense now." He jerked reflexively as she applied medication to his wound. It stung like hell, and he cursed in Refarian.

"Sorry," she said softly, bending over him as she worked. Her sleek blond hair reminded him of Hope's, and he had to battle a painful spasm of yearning for his wife. *She's not my wife anymore; she's going to be his.*

"You know," she continued, "whatever you're doing down in Texas, you'll have a tough time of it if you don't know any more about human culture than this."

"I know plenty!" he barked. "I've lived on this planet for more than sixteen years."

"Uh-huh." She sounded thoroughly unconvinced.

"Just because I didn't know about that damned rock band—"

"Household name, sir."

"Jake. Call me Jake," he half growled at her. He wasn't Scott Dillon, and he didn't want her treating him like he was.

"I'm just saying. You know, Texas is a whole other world than this part of Wyoming. Better know that heading in."

"I'm more American than most Americans."

"Texas is its own little country, Jake."

"You got a better idea? Hey! Watch that!" he snarled, grimacing with sharp pain as she swabbed at his stab wound.

"Yeah, you need a guide, someone who knows their way around. I mean, if you're going after this guy, you won't get very far without someone who's just a little more, shall we say, savvy about human culture."

Struggling, he sat up and stared her in the eye. "How in hell did you know I'm going after Jake Tierny?"

She only smiled. "And I thought you were going to nab me about that pop culture observation."

"That too!"

"If I may say so, sir, you are seeming more like yourself—your real self—with every passing minute."

"And what's that supposed to mean?"

She gave his chest a shove, pushing him back down onto the table. "Nice and grumpy, Lieutenant. Just like my buddy Scott."

"I'm not Scott," he said, sighing deeply. He felt wearier than he had in days, years, maybe.

"Whatever. It's just good to have you back, sir."

His eyes slid shut, and only then did it hit him that

she'd injected him with some sort of painkiller, one that was making him sleepy and sluggish. "What'd ya do that for?" he slurred, blinking.

"So the stitches wouldn't hurt."

"What's one more moment of pain?" he reflected sleepily, not really meaning to voice the question aloud.

Her lovely heart-shaped face appeared just above him, and she pressed her fingertips against his lips. "You've already hurt enough, Jake," she told him soothingly. "It's time you started to heal."

He nodded, drifting into sleep, and in his mind he saw a wide-open road, as long as the rays of the sun, and just as hot too. Desert and tumbleweeds and oil fields spread in every direction, from north to south, from east to west. *Texas,* he thought dreamily, and glancing around, he discovered someone unexpected.

Shelby stood there, right beside him.

"Yes," she murmured softly, "I'll go with you, sir. Right now, just heal."

Hope lay in the hospital bed, impatiently pulling at the bandages over her eyes. Three more hours to go, and they'd remove the freaking things—and she'd have confirmation that her eyesight had truly been restored. The medics had wasted no time after getting her back inside the compound; while they were treating her other wounds and getting her glucose levels under control, they'd made it sound shockingly easy to go ahead and fix her eyes. Taking a giant step of faith, she'd agreed, knowing that these Refarians wouldn't promise what they couldn't deliver: She'd already seen that much in the past ten days.

So far she'd entertained some guests: Anna, right off the bat, and then most recently the only other human in the compound, their queen, Kelsey Bennett. She'd been the most reassuring of all, promising Hope that, from the viewpoint of a scientist, the Refarians really could work miracles. They'd spoken in hushed terms for a while about the possible benefits of genetic therapy, but Hope couldn't shake Scott's dire reaction—and even the words she'd heard Veckus and Scott exchange on the matter.

But someone who hadn't visited her yet, who was absolutely conspicuously absent, was her only true love— Scott Dillon. Where was he, and why wouldn't he be coming around? She wanted to whimper and cry. With everything they'd shared and been through together, how could he blow her off like this? Could her heart have been so terribly wrong?

And what of Jake Tierny? He hadn't even so much as sniffed in her direction, at least, not from what she could gather. He'd saved her life back at the warehouse, but hadn't spoken another word to her since. Maybe both men were equally inscrutable in the final analysis, being, as they were, one and the same.

She blew out a miserable breath, closing her eyes beneath the bandages—then, almost as if in answer, she heard the soft echo of footsteps. Too soft, of course, to belong to either Scott or Jake. Listening closely, she called out, "Who's there?"

"Ms. Harper, it's just me," came the strongly Southern-accented voice of her nurse, Shelby Tyler. "Just here to check on you, that's all."

"I'm fine." She rotated her head toward the wall. Blind as ever with the bandages on, she still sought a reprieve from the hard gaze of anyone else, at least at this particular moment.

"Now, now," came Shelby's soothing voice, and Hope felt the woman patting her arm. "You can be honest with me, you know."

"I'm scared," Hope whispered into the blackness that engulfed her. "Terrified."

She heard her nurse settle into the seat beside her. "You've got nothing to be afraid of, hon. This surgery's going to have been a perfect score. You'll be seeing better than new in just a few more hours once we remove the bandages."

"It's not about my eyes."

"Oh. Ohhh, it's about your men, isn't it? I understand that problem completely."

"My men?" Hope coughed into her pillow, slowly turning back toward Shelby. "You make me sound like a bigamist. Or a very naughty girl, at least."

"We both know what I'm talking about . . . what we're both talking about here."

Hope blew out an exhausted sigh. "Neither one of them has come my way since we got back. Not with my surgery, nothing. It's like I've dreamed this whole surreal situation."

"Jake's taking off for Texas," Shelby volunteered in an even tone. "Says he can't stick around, not with you and Scott together."

Hope struggled upward in bed. "He can't do that!"

"He's got to do that, Ms. Harper. Don't you understand?"

She shook her head vehemently. "No, no, I don't—not at all." She'd planned on spending time with him—this future self of his—and getting to know him better. Not as a lover, but as the deepest kind of friend. Jake was in so much pain, and she'd pretty much convinced herself over the past day that once their hell was over, she could help him talk about his heartbreak. After all, who better than she?

"Well, for one thing, he can't be around Lieutenant Dillon, not if we want the universe to stay intact. It's dangerous for the two of them to be near each other."

"That could be worked around!" Hope argued, tugging at her bandages.

The nurse grabbed hold of her hand, pulling it away and back against her side. "Nope, don't go doing that, Ms. Harper. Leave the gauze alone. You've only got a few more hours to stand."

"Why is Jake determined to go so incredibly far away?" Tears burned her eyes beneath the bandages, but she blinked at them. It was bizarre—although he wasn't her Scott, not precisely, she still loved him deeply. How could she not, when the man was a slightly altered version of the one she'd fallen for so hard?

"He's going after the real Jake Tierny, your killer. He's determined to find out what that man's role in the war is—more than that, I think he wants to keep him from killing you again."

There were no words. Hope could only lie flat on her back and try to find her breath, but even that felt nearly impossible. "He shouldn't," was all she managed to mumble weakly.

"You know he ain't gonna be stopped, now, don't you?"

Of course, Nurse Tyler was absolutely dead on the mark, but it didn't ease the heaviness in Hope's heart. "Is he going to say good-bye to me first?"

The chair slid back across the floor, signaling the nurse's departure. "I can't say for sure on that. But *I* will definitely say farewell." The nurse bent over her and did something wholly unexpected—kissed Hope on the forehead. "I admire you so much, Ms. Harper. You're my kind of gal."

Hope crinkled her nose, laughing. "Are you going somewhere? I mean, thank you, that's incredibly sweet, but—"

"Somebody's got to take care of our boy Jake. I reckon it might as well be me, just to be sure he doesn't get in too much trouble down Texas way. Plus, I lived there for the first few years I was on this planet, and I can show him around. All that."

Hope wasn't sure whether she should feel jealous or totally relieved. "I'm glad you'll be looking out for him," she whispered softly. "He's in so much pain."

As if reading Hope's mind, the nurse said, "Now, don't feel jealous. He and I are just friends; that's all. But I do think I can watch over his wounded soul."

Hope swallowed, still fighting tears. "I know it's stupid that I'd feel jealous when I can't be with him."

"Natural," the medic corrected her warmly. "Totally

natural, darling. You love him—in any version you find him—and he's your soul mate."

"You really think so?"

"Heck, I know so. I've got a gift about seeing that sort of thing."

"I'm going to miss you, Shelby. You've been so kind to me."

"I'll sure miss your spirit, Hope," the woman said. "You've inspired me to be a lot stronger than I naturally want to be. You're tough and don't back down from a thing. I'm thinking I could use more of that in myself."

Hope felt the tears come in earnest then. For so many years she'd battled her illness, then her blindness, and the people who had commended her for her stalwart strength had been few and far between. Most of those who loved her had spent their energy trying to hold her back. "Thank you, Shelby. I'm glad you're my friend."

Shelby patted her hand one final time. "I could say exactly the same." She cleared her throat, adding, "You've got only two and a half more hours of these bandages. After that, I believe things are going to look a whole lot brighter for you. In every possible way."

As the unusual woman left her room, Hope wondered if she had some extra insight, some alien gift that allowed her to see beyond the moment; it always seemed that she perceived so much more than what was actually happening on the surface. If that speculation was true, then maybe Shelby was right: Her world was about to seem a whole lot brighter than it had in a very long time.

Chapter Twenty-six

Kelsey lay on the doctor's table, feeling the strange vibrations of the sonogram wand against her flat stomach. That her belly was still flat, with as much activity as she felt inside of it, amazed her. For all the life fluttering and glowing within her, she might as well have already been the size of a melon—now, just a few days after conception.

The words *five and a half months* had never stopped reverberating through her mind ever since Jared had uttered them. That would mean she should start showing in about another month, perhaps sooner. That was the sort of thing she hoped this Refarian doctor would be able to tell her.

He bent over her, moving the handheld paddle across her skin, and she felt tingling beneath it in reaction. "This is the sonogram?" she asked, trying to see the accompanying monitor.

"The optigram," he told her matter-of-factly. "We use more advanced technology."

"What's the difference?"

He rolled backward on his stool so he could see her better. "As the pregnancy progresses, you'll be able to see every feature of this baby. Whether he or she is in D'Aravnian or human form, what the child's face looks like. It's more like a direct image than a shadowy imprint."

"Wow. That's more than amazing."

The silver-haired man grinned. "Want to see right now?"

Her heart must have skipped ten beats. Finally she swallowed and whispered, "Of course."

He rotated the monitor, swinging it around so she could get a clear look, and what she saw was . . . a large, glowing ball. "In D'Aravnian form right now," the doctor interpreted needlessly. "Which explains all the burning you're feeling deep inside. That's typical at this very early gestational stage, but will change the further you progress in this pregnancy."

"If I progress?" She couldn't prevent the question from passing her lips.

"You'll progress," the man reassured her evenly. "There's no reason whatsoever to expect that you won't. Look at the baby. Can you see well from there, my lady?" He was being solicitous, but her fears hadn't been placated.

She stayed quiet, watching the nebulous, glowing ball within her, the way it swirled and moved. Their baby, she realized with a stifled giggle, looked exactly like Jared in his natural form. Perfect power and movement, unwilling to be contained.

Kelsey shook her head. "I just don't see how I can possibly carry this baby to term."

The doctor shut off the monitor. "My queen, do you realize that this baby is no different from countless other D'Aravnians over the many generations?"

"I know, but . . . I'm human."

"A perfect genetic match with the Refarians . . . well, close to ninety-nine percent, that is."

"But I'm not a ball of fire!" she cried, covering her eyes in shame. She should be stronger than this—for Jared and for the people who called her queen.

The doctor laughed softly. "Most of the women who have carried D'Aravnian babies were not beings of fire. Yet most of those children were born, lived full lives. You're healthy and strong, my lady. This baby will come to term." He patted her belly gently. "This is our new

heir inside of you, and I have every faith that the baby
will be born.''

She blinked back at the man, thinking of all the assur-
ances Jared had offered her too. "What should I expect
with such a short gestational period? When will I start
to show?''

He stared down at his flip chart. "Oh, give it another
two weeks or so."

"Two weeks?" she squeaked. "Not even a month?"

He grinned, almost as if proud of his own species.
"Our kind doesn't waste time achieving what nature
wants. By four months you'll be uncomfortable and
wishing you were full-term."

"You are doing nothing—absolutely nothing—to reas-
sure me, Doctor."

He closed the chart, holding it against his chest. "This
baby is desired, no?"

"Of course!"

"Then enjoy this time of your life. You have so many
wonderful days ahead of you."

For some reason, it just didn't feel as simple as that.
Her entire stomach churned, her body was on fire, and
all she could think about was one thing: that she couldn't
wait to drag Jared back into bed.

"Thanks, Doctor," she told him with an opaque smile.
Good thing that monitor of his couldn't read her internal
desires too.

Hope sat in the overstuffed corner chair in her room
and blinked. Blinked and stared, swung her gaze first in
one direction, then another. It was almost more than her
heart could willingly accept: Her vision had been restored, and completely. No blurriness, no floaters, no
occasional bright flashes. She rose to her feet and peered
out of the small window, studying a snowdrift piled
against it. They were in a basement of sorts, she now
realized, because the window was high up and the drift
practically blocked out all daylight. Snowflakes were frozen against the windowpane, etched onto the glass like

the very fingerprint of God. Lacy, unique . . . that she could see them at all brought tears to her newly healed eyes.

Next she walked to the sink and stared into the mirror at herself; for the first time in more than a year she could actually glimpse her own face. *Man, I've got some dark circles. Have to work on that!* And her hair looked limp and tired, just like her body was. She found her brush by the sink and worked it through the straight length of her blond hair, then rubbed at her cheeks. Being blind meant you didn't really think about the absence of makeup, a situation she was going to have to fix right away.

Leaning forward, gripping the sink, she tried to figure out whether she'd gotten any wrinkles since she'd last seen herself. Oddly enough, she looked relatively . . . the same. It was as if she'd taken a very long holiday from herself, a break, only to return and find that nothing much had changed. Totally weird, when you got right down to it.

A sound startled her from behind, and she spun to find a tall, brawny guy studying her. For a split second she wondered who it was, but then, breaking into a smile, she cried, "Jake!" and rushed to him, flinging her arms about his neck.

He returned her embrace stiffly, patting her kindly on the back, and she understood—he was already distancing himself. She pulled back, staring up into his startling green eyes, so light they almost seemed to glow against his olive skin.

"You can see perfectly, can't you?" Gently, he peeled her hands off of him.

She nodded. "It's an absolute miracle."

He pushed past her, but she followed right behind. "Did my future self have this same surgery?"

"Long, long ago," he answered solemnly.

"That explains it, then."

He glanced at her curiously. "I don't understand what you mean."

"When I dream about that future, I can always see the details . . . very clearly. I finally understood it was because that other version of me could see."

He gave her a melancholy smile. "You always had such beautiful eyes, and you still do."

She folded her arms across her chest, shivering in her hospital gown, watching him pace the room in agitation. "You shouldn't leave," she argued. "You don't have to go—you do know that, right?"

He chuckled low, closing his eyes. "Of course I have to leave. There's no place for me here."

"But you don't have to chase down my killer."

"I have to do that too."

She planted a hand on her hip. "Tell me why."

He headed back toward the door. "I just came to say good-bye, Hope, not defend my actions."

"Just give me one good reason why you have to hunt down Jake Tierny."

He paused at the door, his hand positioned over the knob, and at first she thought he wouldn't answer. "Don't you know?" he finally said in a voice raw with unexpressed emotion.

"I'm not sure that I do. You need to live, be all right, here in *this* time."

"I need to find your killer, Hope . . . because I still love you. I will always"—he turned slowly to meet her gaze—"*always* love you. No amount of time or space or eternity will ever change that fact."

She flinched, walking slowly toward him. "Let me hold you. Just one last time." She opened her arms to him. "Please, Scott, just let me hold you."

He buried himself within her embrace. "Don't call me Scott."

"It's who you are. No amount of time or space or eternity will ever change that fact either."

"I'm so sorry I kissed you, let us get intimate—I never meant for that to happen between us."

"I can't imagine how you could hold back."

She felt dampness form against her cheek, his tears—Scott's tears—like that very first night he'd come upon her in the medical hallway. Very gently she stroked his hair, shushed him, and whispered words of never-ending love. "I will always love you too," she pledged. "You've got to know that."

He nodded at last, pulling apart, tears glinting in his light eyes. "That's why I have to leave. I can't possibly stay."

And she got it then, understood completely—it was best for both of them, Scott included. So long as he stayed around camp or even nearby, her heart would always be torn in half. She'd feel a pull toward this melancholy man, one with whom she could never again share a future, and he would feel drawn back to her elusive promise as well.

"Please be careful in Texas." She stroked his cheek. "Don't do anything stupid, and let me know that you're okay—at least every once in a while."

He bent low, pressing a chaste kiss against her brow. "You can count on it."

And with that, Scott Dillon's other self swept out of the room, never looking back.

Scott paced outside the doorway of Hope's room, trying to figure out a way to simply go to her. He should have visited her in the hospital, should have been at her side while she underwent the surgery. *Should have done, should have done.* Already so many regrets for such a young relationship.

Shelby had directed him up here, to Hope's quarters, explaining that her eyesight was fully restored, and that she was feeling strong and healthy—but not without also letting him know that Jake Tierny had definitely made a point of paying a visit of his own.

Sometimes, truthfully, Scott knew he could be a total loser. Like with all the women whose beds he used to warm, but whom he'd always left so easily before daybreak. Yet Hope was anything but a one-night stand. So why did the thought of seeing her terrify the living hell out of him?

Simple: She'd never actually seen him. The idea that, if he chose to knock on her door, she'd look upon him completely . . . well, it was worse than being cornered in the most brutal of firefights. Worse than being trapped in reflexive metal. In fact, it might be more than he could possibly overcome.

Human women seemed to find him plenty pleasing—he wouldn't have had such good luck around the bars and getting into bed with them if that weren't the case. But this was Hope—his beloved Hope. What if she laughed in his face, as Anna had once done? What if she found him hideous? He was average at best, but he could make up for that fact in bed, as he had proven many times over. Still, one look at him might be enough to change Hope's feelings permanently.

And so he paced. And paced. And dithered, and thought he might absolutely expire from the terror of the whole proposition.

"What in All's name are you doing out in this hallway?" Anna called to him.

"Trying to figure out my next strategy."

She planted herself in front of him, blocking his movements. "Just stop it. Right now, sir, stop this asinine behavior."

"I'm sorry?"

"Stop all the obnoxious self-loathing and go in and see that girl. She loves you, for crying out loud. You don't need to overanalyze this thing."

"Excuse me, Lieutenant, but what makes you think you have the first clue as to what I'm thinking at this moment?"

She leaned in close, grasping him by both arms. "Aren't you forgetting something?"

"I don't think so."

"Our little roadside dance—you in your ghost state, me in my bird one. I followed you for miles while you chased her down." She pointed toward the closed bedroom door. "And you know what? She needs you right now, so don't be a selfish prick."

"I'll take that as an official dressing-down." He folded his arms over his chest, wondering where, exactly, friendship ended and impertinence began.

"Right indeed, sir!" She stuck her chin out proudly, her dark eyes twinkling.

"What makes you so sure you know the drill here, huh?"

"Let's just say I've gotten to know your pal Jakey quite a bit these past couple of days."

Scott groaned. "Oh, him."

"Yeah, him. And he's given me some new insights into my very good friend and superior officer, also known as *you,* sir. Ones that have helped me see a few things in a new light."

"Such as?"

"Why you're lurking out here in the hallway and not just going to her, sir. Especially when she needs you . . . and you so clearly love her."

Scott glanced up and down the hallway, praying they weren't being overheard, but before he could argue further, Anna blustered ahead. "Listen, you've got some pretty major misconceptions about yourself, sir. Vain ones, at that."

This time he really did buck up. "You're treading on thin ice, Lieutenant."

She leaned in close to him, seizing him by both shoulders, and—stepping up onto her tiptoes—whispered in his ear. "I didn't laugh when you kissed me because I thought you were ugly." Scott jerked back, but she wouldn't let him go. "I laughed because I thought you handsome. You are handsome, sir. Now go to her."

Then, just as quickly as she'd released her ballistic missile, she stepped apart from him, smiling smugly. What Anna couldn't know was that in his deepest heart, he always knew there was a hulking, monstrous Antousian hiding just beneath the surface—it was his other

skin, as hard and hideous as the rough hide that covered
that form's body.

He shook his head. "No idea what you're talking
about."

She rolled her eyes, still grinning at him. "Just keep
on telling yourself that, sir. Now go to her. Go, and
know that every last woman in these ranks thinks you're
gorgeous." She turned, shaking her head, then fired a
final, parting shot. "How you could have ever thought
otherwise is way, way beyond me. Don't you own a
mirror?"

He stared slack-jawed after the departing soldier, gesturing, still searching for some sort of return parry, but
all he could think was to curse his future self for having
such a loose tongue. Damn it all to hell, the man had
betrayed his heart's secrets. Then again, he supposed,
they were Jake's secrets to tell as well.

With a slow and measured gesture, he raised his hand
and knocked on Hope's door.

Jared moved quietly about their quarters, not wanting
to wake Kelsey, who lay sprawled on their bed, sleeping.
She was going to need a great deal of sleep in the coming months; of that much he was certain—growing a
baby inside her belly would take every ounce of strength
and energy his lovely wife possessed.

"Stop tiptoeing," she called out to him, and he froze
right beside his desk.

"You need to rest."

"Want to see a picture of your baby?" She eased up
in the bed, plopping a pillow behind her.

"Of course—is that even possible?" He couldn't help
sounding breathless.

Reaching underneath the pillow beside her, she pro-
duced a small piece of paper, and he took it from her,
staring down at the colored image in his hands. Their
baby! A lovely, glowing D'Aravnian, bright and powerful already. "Really?" he asked, daring to meet her twinkling eyes.

"Pretty amazing, huh?"

He nodded, still studying the image, turning his head first one way, then another, to truly get a full view. "Ah, so lovely." Then he looked up again, seriously studying his queen. "Are you still angry with me?"

She tilted her head. "About what?"

"Your father, and how I didn't want you to phone him."

"Are you saying that I can? That you won't argue with me about it?"

Jared settled on the side of their bed. "After aligning with the air force and the FBI, I'm beginning to think the risk might not matter nearly so much."

"Good," she told him, but there was a slight chill to her tone, so he rushed onward.

"I want you happy, sweet wife. I want you to be with me, but not as my prisoner or this Rapunzel you mentioned."

"*Rapunzel*. She got locked in a tower for most of her life."

"This base of mine shouldn't be your tower; it should be your home," he pressed, waving the piece of paper. "Just as this babe will make a home with each of us."

She leaped toward him, wrapping her arms about his neck. "You're saying I have your blessing about calling my dad?"

"Yes, love. I don't want to hide you away or make you less than what you are—besides, I also think you might be right. His connections could be very valuable to all of us."

"Thank you, Jared." She showered his face with kisses. "Thank you so much."

"Tomorrow we will discuss the best way to go about approaching him—your phoning him, I mean. We will figure it all out together."

She reached for his hand, placed it squarely over her abdomen, and with sparkling eyes said, "We are definitely in this together. All three of us."

Scott took cautious steps into Hope's room, thankful that it was mostly dark inside. It was on the lower level of the cabin, so there was never a lot of light filtering into the interior, and given today's gloomy weather, it was darker than the last time he'd been in her quarters.

"So you finally decided to come see me?" She lay propped on her lower bunk, a book clasped within both hands.

"You're reading." He could hardly suppress a smile. She must be seeing perfectly well already.

"I haven't read a book in two years—it was sort of one of the things I had to do right away."

"What book is it?"

"Some Shakespearean sonnets that Kelsey gave me. A collection of Jared's."

"Of course." His king adored Shakespeare—the plays, the sonnets, it hardly mattered which.

"Not my usual thing; I'm more of a Julia Quinn or Lisa Kleypas kind of girl."

"I'm not familiar with their work."

"I didn't figure you would be." Hope giggled, and he didn't quite understand the reason why, but put her reaction down to human proclivities.

Scott hung back, propping his hands on the top bunk rather than drawing much closer so Hope could get a good look at him. "How are you feeling?"

He cursed himself for seeming so dull. *Way to go, Dillon. That's an interesting opener.*

She closed her book, dropping it onto her knees. "You're just going to hang way back there?" Great, she'd seen right through his bullshit.

He deigned to take another step closer. "I'm concerned about you."

"So concerned that"—she sat upright in bed—"I went through my surgery, then recovery, and actually got dismissed before you came to see me?"

"I'm sorry." He grunted.

"I want to know why, Dillon." He shook his head, and she continued. "Because I know how you feel about me—really do know, deep down in my spirit—so for you to stay away . . . well, I figure it must have cost you quite a lot."

He dropped his arms away from the top bunk, swinging much closer toward her. "I wasn't ready," he admitted throatily.

She sat up in the bed, her clear gray eyes wide. "For what? To be with me? To make a life together, like you've led me to believe we would?"

"That's not it. Not at all."

She eased her legs off the bed, scooting closer to him. She had those amazing eyes of hers fixed right on him, had to be able to see every detail of his cursed face. "Then please—honestly, please—tell me what the problem really is."

"I'm not that good-looking, Hope." He met her steely gaze, never blinking or looking away. "This is me, with my once-broken nose, and my fair skin, and . . . and," he sputtered, "I'm an average-looking guy. I couldn't deal with you seeing me. Really seeing me, close like this."

"Oh, I get it," she said, drawing her words out, but never looking away. "When I was blind, I was a sure thing—"

"I'm not saying that."

"Then what, exactly, are you saying?"

He dropped his head. "You felt my other form at the warehouse. You saw, in your own way, the truth of my nature. That's one thing, and the other . . . None of my own people find me the least bit attractive."

"Huh, that's funny—because Anna told me that every single woman under your command has a crush on you."

"She was lying."

"No, she wasn't, and you know how I know that for sure?" she asked, rising up to her feet and closing the small distance that separated them. "Because I'm looking at you, right now, me and my newly acquired twenty-twenty vision, and I can see the truth with my own eyes."

She took hold of his hands, drawing them to her lips, and kissed him across the knuckles, long and tantalizingly slowly. "And what I see, Scott Dillon"—she peered up into his face, raking her gaze across his features—"is one of the handsomest men I've ever encountered."

"Passable at best. Better in bed."

Her blond eyebrows shot right up to her hairline. "Better in bed? Is that a promise or a threat?"

He rubbed his eyes. "You're a piece of work, Hope Harper."

"Are you calling me a liar?"

He chuckled, grasping her face with both of his hands. "I'm calling you my life. The woman I want to be with. I just can't believe you're looking at me—right at me—and find this"—he waved at his face—"appealing."

"Whatever gave you the idea that you weren't gorgeous?"

"It doesn't matter. I just never found much company among the ranks."

"Because they're totally intimidated by you, hello? Anna told me that much."

He cast a shy glance at her. "Really? Is that what she said?" Anna's words from the hallway, about how she'd found him incredibly handsome, echoed in his ears. Memories of all the women he'd seduced around Jackson traipsed through his thoughts as well.

"Know what I think?" Hope asked softly, drawing his face down toward her own, and kissing him full on the lips.

He returned her kiss. "Huh?"

"You don't know what to make of your Antousian self. That's why you wrestle with all of this."

He recoiled, taking several steps back. "Don't, Hope. Okay? Please?"

She wouldn't be denied, following him. "Because otherwise, a gorgeous, beautiful man like you? You'd get what you do to a woman like me."

She slipped her arms about his neck, reaching up toward him, and all at once they were utterly inseparable—like they'd been in the warehouse. His body molding against hers, her body giving in to his. There was no dividing line between their twin souls, where they ended and where they began.

Next thing he knew, she was tugging him back toward her bed. "Let's make out," she whispered in a husky voice. "I want to kiss you all the way down to your toes."

"I like the sound of that," he agreed with a hearty rumble. "But no making love?"

She shook her head. "Not yet. We need to go back to square one for a while."

Collapsing onto her bed, he groaned. "This is Antousian gorabung torture, is that it?"

She cradled his head against her chest, stroking his hair. "I'm not sure what that is, but I just know this—a first time when we're prisoners isn't the right first time. So we back up for a while."

"For a while." He rolled her beneath him, feeling his erection grow firm and long. "Just don't make me crazy."

"Not that crazy." She giggled in his ear, nibbling at it, and he felt chill bumps form along his forearms.

Hope nestled against Scott's chest, feeling his languid kisses across her brow; even now, long minutes after they'd finally halted their sexual advances, they still lay together. Somehow, amazingly, she'd managed to stop Scott at the proverbial door, but just barely. They'd tussled and made out, had their almost-way with each other, but ultimately she'd managed to dissuade him from actually making love. It was obvious to her that he was a man with immense sexual urges. That was fine by her, because she was a woman who shared those appetites.

Still, they'd finally pulled back, shirts and jeans and uniforms undone, and stilled in each other's arms, just stroking and caressing. She couldn't believe he was as absolutely beautiful as he was—though, of course, she'd already seen him in her visions. For some reason, however, she didn't let on quite how clearly she'd already seen him in her mind. He needed to believe this was her very first time seeing him up close. It seemed linked to his acceptance of her freely given love.

Now they lay curled together in her bottom bunk, night having fallen outside, and other thoughts began to intrude on Hope's mind, questions she'd been considering for the past few days.

"Back in the warehouse," she ventured, "Veckus said something that I haven't been able to shake—I know it's why you're afraid for me to receive genetic therapy."

She watched as Scott's face—a face she was so grateful to glimpse—grew troubled and serious. Despite his reaction, it felt good to know his thoughts with only one easy glance.

"I wondered if you'd caught all that," he answered softly, stroking her hair.

"I need to know what he was talking about." She captured his hand, bringing it to her cheek. "And why the idea of genetic therapy terrifies you so much. It's all linked together; I've figured that part out."

Scott brought her palm to his lips, kissing her in the center of her hand. "None of it matters, sweetheart. Let it go."

She shook her head adamantly. "It's extremely important to me. I'm in the middle of this war now, Scott, and I want to know what the stakes really are." She dropped her voice low. "And I need genetic therapy; I don't want to be sick anymore . . . but I need to know why it frightens you first."

Scott exhaled, leaning back from her, still holding her hand. "It's like I told you before. There was a virus back on Refaria . . . it didn't affect my adopted people—"

"The Refarians," she volunteered, for the sake of being clear.

"They're my only people." He met her gaze seriously. "I feel no affinity for the Antousians, my . . . natural capabilities aside."

"Do you honestly think I care what kind of shifting you're capable of?"

Scott hung his head. "You didn't really see me back there in that warehouse."

"And I didn't need to." She gave him a resolute look. "But explain this virus and its consequences to me."

Scott leaned toward her, burying his head against her chest. "I don't want you to hear any of this—it's so ugly, and just terrible, all the way through."

"Do you really love me, Scott Dillon?" She stroked the black hair atop his head. "Do you know I won't leave you?"

He made a plaintive, terrible sound. "I'm not sure, Hope."

She shoved him away. "Then we've got nothing more to talk about, not if you don't know my heart any better than that."

He stared down at her, tears glinting in his eyes. "Don't you get it? Don't you see how much I hate my mixed heritage?"

"Yes," she whispered quietly. "I've understood from the beginning."

"I share a bloodline with them—with Veckus, all of them. I'm a monster in my blood, a killer in my DNA."

"But you are here, S'Skautsa. You are here."

"The only thing that's my saving grace."

"Tell me what happened back on Refaria," she insisted.

"Okay, I will," he told her coolly, casting a sideways glance at her. "But it's far from pretty, the truth about my species."

"I have to know if I'm going to make a future with you—and be part of this war."

He gazed at the ceiling. "Roughly sixty years ago, the Antousians reached a point where technology had surpassed their natural capabilities, their mental capacities. And so they made a decision: They chose to become enhanced." He stared at her meaningfully. "They allowed themselves, the whole lot of them, to become implanted with quantum cyberchips, nanochips that were barely more than microscopic so they could"—his face became a grim, sarcastic mask—"embrace the best of their future; that's what they all said. That's what my people said."

Hope had long heard talk about the possibility of humans accepting computer processor chips in order to outpace technology, to keep up with what she'd heard termed the "singularity"—the point when computers became "smarter" than mankind. Still, this was the stuff of science-fiction novels, and she wasn't sure how to respond.

"Sounds frightening," was all she came up with, "to give yourself over to machines that way."

"Precisely. Why would any living being think that merging his intellect with that of a computer would be a wise thing? But for a while, it actually worked. They lived on Refaria, you must realize, a massive population of them, and for a very long while the Antousians and Refarians lived in great harmony. It was a time of advancement and peace—all except for one little detail: The Refarians refused to become cybernetically enhanced. They didn't want to be implanted with these chips, and there was a lot of debate about that fact. Back and forth, until . . ." His voice faded, and he closed his eyes.

"Tell me the rest, Scott. I have to know."

He blew out a sigh. "Until the virus came, just like I told you before."

A strange thought began developing in her mind. Scott had told her all about the virus, how the Antousians believed that the Refarians had unleashed it upon them as a form of biological politics, only he'd never told her what *kind* of virus had plagued the Antousian people.

"It was a computer virus," she whispered softly.

He nodded. "And it wiped out most of my 'people' who had been enhanced, shutting down their biological bodies as their technological side became infected. There

was no way for them to survive except—like I told you—
to assume their ghost form. Become ether, and then
what to do? They couldn't live forever like that, so they
sought out the species that for some unholy reason was
most compatible: yours. And they started a war on the
very planet that had welcomed them as friends, brothers.
They warred against the Refarians, always blaming
them, forever claiming that the virus had been developed
to wipe their own species out."

"Was it true?"

He turned on her, his face pale and livid. "Of course
not! They were ambitious and overreaching—and the results were that it destroyed them."

"That still doesn't explain your aversion to genetic
therapy, and why you don't want me to have it."

"Because that's how they tried to treat the virus, but
it only infected a much larger portion of the
population . . . spread it, contaminated even the Antousians who weren't carrying processors inside their heads.
It was a bloodbath, all because of genetic therapy."

"I see," she said, sinking back into her pillow. It was
so much to digest, and she could totally comprehend his
adamant position against her receiving genetic therapy.

"I'm not saying it wouldn't work for you, Hope, but it
terrifies me, all right? Scares the living crap out of me."

She leaned close against him. "It's not something we
have to decide anytime soon. I've lived my whole life,
practically, with my diabetes."

"I want you to get well . . . I just don't want you to
die in the process." She could see the raw fear in his
eyes. The man didn't want to lose her—especially not to
the fate that had devastated his home back on Refaria.

"Let's just think about it," she said softly.

When Scott returned to his quarters, he was surprised
to find a note pinned to his door. The handwriting was
absurdly familiar—a slightly more rugged version of his
own. Whipping the note off the door, he entered his
room and began to read.

Hey, Chief:

I would talk to you in person, but I think we've both seen what happens if we so much as breathe the same air. Listen, I'm hitting the road, so we won't be bumping into each other, at least for a while. Before I go, I want to make sure you know something—a fact about my own future that I think you can avert.

I spent a lot of time afraid for Hope, afraid that if she got help that something terrible would go wrong. The truth is, buddy, that she was always sick and only got sicker in my future. Her diabetes caused a lot of problems for her, especially during her pregnancy. In one way, it's part of why she died, all those pregnancy complications.

Fear never gets you very far.

Love her. Love her with everything inside of you, and don't be so damned afraid all the time. If my gamble has gone right, you've got nothing more to fear.

I suppose from now on I should call you my brother.

Jake

For a moment, he stared down at the paper in his hand, read his own writing over and over again, and then, making his decision, he crumpled the thing and tossed it to the ground. And ran—no, sprinted—back to Hope's side.

Chapter Twenty-seven

After parking the Suburban outside the brightly lit, gorgeous Snake River Lodge—it was all twinkling and like something from her fantasies of a honeymoon night—she let Scott take her hand and lead the way across the slippery, iced-over path. This was the way he'd chosen to celebrate her healing—her full and total medical miracle of the genetic therapy. Her diabetes had been eradicated once and for all.

"Watch your step," he cautioned protectively, and she tightened her grip on his hand in response. Normally she'd resist protectiveness from any man, especially when it meant someone was trying to limit her. But now, within the safety of Scott's guiding hand, she felt relaxed. As if it would be okay to relinquish just a bit of her control and rebelliousness—at least, with this particular man. He would never strip her of her independence, or deny her the adventure and challenges she wanted; all he would do was give her the right amount of freedom, helping her become more at one with herself.

As she entered the lodge a waft of warm air blew in her face, and her eyes instantly watered at the contrast. "You stay here a second," he told her quietly, and strode confidently to the concierge desk. He and the clerk spoke in quiet tones, the concierge nodding and then finally slipping a pair of keys and registration information across the desk. Hope was perplexed that, given their secluded, expensive military operation, they had funds for something as frivolous—at least, relatively speaking—as this night away.

They entered the elevator, completely alone, and he watched the numbers as they climbed upward. Funny, but she would have almost sworn this strapping warrior was nervous.

"How can you possibly afford this?" she asked.

He smiled, never taking his gaze off the elevator lights. "Easy. Didn't cost me a dime."

"That's not possible."

The elevator dinged, signaling their floor number, and he took her by the hand, again leading the way. "Just come with me, sweetheart. Stop worrying so much."

Once inside the privacy of their penthouse, Hope could hardly speak: Two stories tall, with an opulent great room and connected kitchen—with a Sub-Zero freezer, no less—the suite defied imagination. Surely now, in the middle of skiing season, the place had to rent for more than two thousand dollars a night.

Walking into the kitchen, she opened the refrigerator and discovered bottles of champagne nestled amidst fresh fruit and expensive cheeses. It was a sultan's holiday.

One arm propped on the fridge door, she studied the array of delicacies. "No way this didn't cost you a fortune, Dillon."

He appeared behind her, slipping both arms about her waist. "Yeah? Well, you'd be surprised to learn all the places we have operatives."

She rotated slowly within his grasp, and he shoved the refrigerator shut, pinning her back against it. "You're saying that concierge is an alien."

He cocked an eyebrow. "Aron's been with us from the very beginning. We found long ago that it was beneficial to place numbers of our people in the ordinary world. In this case, Aron monitors a number of political activities that take place in this area—the vice president's visits . . . the secretary of state was here recently. . . . We also know for a fact that a few *vlksai* freaks occasionally take a break in this lodge. It's a good opportunity for intel."

He slid one powerful thigh between her own, rubbing. "We've got better things to discuss than how I'm paying for this night. Are you happy with it?" He glanced over his shoulder. "Romantic enough?"

She placed both palms against his chest. "You know that it's out of this world."

"Ah, so it's alien indeed."

Giggling, she gave a nod, but had to add—because she had to know, "But how does Jared finance all of this. The weapons, the military operation, your food, all of it?"

Scott's gaze darkened immediately. "We have many supporters back on Refaria, beleaguered though they may be. They provide much of our equipment and technology, but we also possess an incredible storehouse of gems and minerals. We were able to get those out, and they are exactly like their counterparts found here on Earth. Remember, Refaria and Earth are twin planets in many ways."

"So you trade gold? Diamonds?"

He nodded. "And other things. It finances what we do."

"Amazing. It's like I've fallen into this bizarre alter-universe."

Scott stepped apart from her, surveying the kitchen and their surroundings. "You *have* fallen into an alternate universe, remember? And as far as I can tell, this is the better of the two so far."

Scott luxuriated in the flow of the shower, thankful for such great water pressure and piping-hot steam. Living in the compound and sharing quarters with so many others, he had to think strategically if he ever wanted a shower this hot. After he turned off the spigot, he wrapped a towel about himself and stepped into the bedroom, only to find Hope naked and studying him.

"That's what I like to see!" she proclaimed with a

giggle. "And really see—man, I'm so thankful to have my eyesight back. Now I can ogle you anytime I want."

Funny, he never blushed with a woman, not about sex, but he felt his face burn as he adjusted the towel around his waist. "Is that what you're doing?" He allowed the towel to slip dangerously low about his hips. "Ogling?" Oh, gods, her obvious pleasure at the sight of his body pleased him endlessly.

He took a step toward her, but she surprised him by bounding to her feet and leading the way into the main living room—naked and all. He never took his eyes off of her as he followed, taking in her rounded hips, the way they swayed with each step. For a small woman she sure did pack a fabulous set of curves.

In the living room she spun to face him, looking him right in the eye. "Now I want you to do something for me, Scott—okay?"

"Anything." He swallowed, letting his gaze rove over her gorgeous body.

"I want you to Change."

"My clothes?" She was confusing him with this barrage of succulent nakedness, and now this bizarre request. "Put my clothes back on? I don't understand."

She smiled up into his face. "Your form. I want you to assume your natural Antousian one."

Throwing both hands up, he backed away from her. "Never."

"I need to see you, and I figured if I was naked too, then you'd feel safe."

Putting his back to her, he buried his head in his hands. "How can you ask that of me?"

"Because I love you."

"Then you wouldn't ask."

He felt her hands slip about his waist, her firm breasts press into his back. "I'm asking it because I do love you— because I have to know everything about you. And you need to know that I accept all parts of you. All sides."

With a cautious glance over his shoulder, he could see that she absolutely meant business. And it was strange,

but he also felt a part of himself release, almost exhale—
as if sharing such a hidden part of his nature was what
had always been meant to be between the two of them.

"You aren't going to like it," he threatened hoarsely.
"It's not pretty at all."

She stepped apart from him, backing toward the sofa,
and waved for him to continue. "I want to see you
anyway."

"This has never been me." His voice had a strange,
waterfall quality, as if breaking over hard rocks.

"But it is you, Scott. You're kneeling here right in
front of me, and this is part of you." She shook her head
from side to side. "You're not like most of your own
people; you haven't committed genocide—to be proud
of who and *what* you are doesn't mean that you are a
part of your people's crimes."

He hung his head, blinking his black, fathomless eyes.
"I am ugly. It's what Veckus said, a monster."

She pressed her face against his, rubbing her nose over
his affectionately. "You're a beautiful man, no matter
what form you take."

Inside she'd begun to quiver oddly; to truly see Scott
as the alien he was—through and through and with her
own eyes—was intoxicating. Arousing. He just didn't
seem to totally get his effect on her, even in this form.

Pulling back, she saw that his naturally tan-colored
skin had grown ruddy across both cheeks. So, even Antousians blushed. She lifted her hand and rubbed her
fingertips over his hard jaw, over the plates that covered
his facial features, tough and yet shockingly pliable too.
But his lips were what surprised her most, with their
much softer sensuality—softer than any of his other
harsh features. Bending forward again, she placed her
lips over his, not knowing what to expect. Hell, he might
have five tongues deep inside that Antousian mouth of
his. But he didn't—because when he tilted his head cautiously to the side, slowly opening to her, it was no different from kissing him in his humanized form. His

movements were a bit shyer and more tentative than his usual aggressive ways, perhaps, but it was just as warm, just as provocative, just as tantalizing as every other time she'd ever kissed Scott Dillon.

Slipping her arms about his massive shoulders, she pulled his body closer to hers, and couldn't help but moan in arousal. In turn, he made an alien, low-pitched sound of desire that caused her hair to stand on end. Like his voice, it seemed to rumble from some hidden place deep within his chest. She stroked her fingertips along the back of his bare head, feeling the unusual ridge that ran down the center of it. As she caressed him that way, he began to tremble all over. *Note to self,* she thought, as he wrapped his powerful arms tight about her, *that thick skull of his is an erogenous zone!*

"Bend down," she whispered, breaking apart from the kiss. His black eyes narrowed.

"I don't understand."

She gestured with her fingers, waving him lower. "I can't reach where I want to go unless you bend down a lot lower."

Cautiously he complied, bowing until she had a perfect bull's-eye mark for the crown of his bare head. She slid her hands along the base of his scalp and drew her lips against the top of his head, trailing her tongue and licking, like he loved in his other form, and kissing him slowly there. Bending into her chest, he trembled, clasped her hips with his extremely large hands, and purred. He moaned a few unintelligible words in Refarian, and purred some more as she stroked her hands across his colossal shoulders, feeling the tough muscles, the drawn tendons and hardened skin.

He was alien; no doubt about that fact, and maybe it was her immense love for the man, or maybe it was that their hearts were calibrated perfectly to each other—but she'd never seen a more gorgeous creature in her entire life than Scott Dillon, right now in his natural Antousian form.

Finally, she stilled her lips against the crown of his

head and whispered, "You're two feet taller than I am." And she began to giggle. "That's a big height differential."

He pulled back, meeting her gaze. She saw unimagined depths of emotion in his large, almond-shaped eyes. "Your point?"

He was loosening up, sounding more like his usual cocky self, and had the same familiar glint of sardonic mischief in his eyes as he normally did.

"I don't think we can have sex with you Changed like this." With a flirtatious toss of her hair, she reached for his extremely long, permanently erect length. "And this . . . well, I don't think it will even fit without killing me. Might even pop right back out my throat." She giggled, slowly stroking his erection, feeling the hardness of it, the way it was ridged and yet incredibly soft underneath, one massive vein running the full nine inches of it.

He snorted, reeling backward from her. "I can't believe . . ." He paused, clearing his throat.

"Don't be so self-conscious about your voice. It mesmerizes me."

He dropped his head into the palm of his hand, hesitating, then finally said, "I can't believe you'd entertain sex with me, like this"—he thumped his chest with his fist—"all huge and monstrous."

She flung herself forward at him, wrapping her arms about his neck. "Don't you get it, you stubborn, irritating man? I am in love with you. I may not have known you very long in real time, but I've known you for absolutely forever in my heart, and in my future, and in my dreams. I might as well have been with you from the very beginning of time with the way that I love you. All of you, damn it." She ran her hands along his shoulders, down along his chest. "Don't you see how you're turning me on?"

He reached very gently and touched her cheek. "I've always been a man at war with myself. It's going to take some time for you to heal that in me."

"I can prove it to you."

He cocked his head sideways, blinking his large black eyes. "Prove what?"

"That even this body of yours totally turns me on."

He waited, watching her, and she took his calloused hand and drew it between her legs, slowly stroking his long fingers over her folds of skin, and along the slick wetness that he'd caused so easily by arousing her. Very gently, she drew one of his long fingers closer, placing it against her slick opening. "Try me," she urged, leaning back into the sofa.

Wide-eyed, he gaped at her, then with a nod, gently slipped one finger inside of her, sliding it back and forth, feeling the dampness, the warmth that he'd caused. She closed her own hand over his, felt his movement within her, stroking the back of his hand as he stroked her.

She panted, arching into the pillows of the sofa, and after a moment he retracted his finger, trailing it—and a path of wetness—along her thigh. He said nothing for many long moments, and then slowly rose to his feet, walking away from her and toward the kitchen.

It was interesting watching his gait, how poised, measured, proud it was—so incredibly graceful in such a large, bulky creature. She suspected that he perceived his Antousian body quite differently; he despised his genetic heritage, so of course he reviled this form, and couldn't see the beauty in it.

He braced both hands along the kitchen counter, shaking his head from side to side in seeming disbelief. She studied his backside, the powerful musculature that rippled along his entire naked body; he reminded her of some Greek warrior, captured in stone: monumental and fearsome, but the very essence of raw beauty. When long moments spun out, her heart begin to hammer. Was she pushing too hard with him, and too fast? Working too pointedly to make him accept himself—and her love for him?

But after another moment, he surprised her by throwing his head back and releasing a wonderful, deep, rumbling laugh. And then he turned to face her.

"You love me. You honestly love everything about me." There was wonder in his large alien eyes, amazement, as he studied her from across the room. She could read everything in his expressions, no matter the form.

She wrinkled her nose, beaming back at him. "Of course."

He smiled gloriously, and then with a slight whoop and holler, rushed her, Changing before he'd even reached where she sat naked and watching. Practically landing atop her, he swept her into his arms there on the sofa, rolling her beneath him. "If my ugly cuss of an Antousian self turns you on"—he laughed some more, beaming—"then you really *must* think I'm an okay guy."

She gazed up into his eyes, stroking his black hair. "An okay guy? Is that how you'd put it?"

"Wouldn't you?"

She blew on his lips softly, trying to tickle him. Maybe even to soothe his war-ravaged soul. "I'd say handsome, gorgeous, beautiful. Everything I have ever wanted—in any man—for all my adult life."

He ran a thumb over her lower lip, studying her face. The light dusting of freckles, the lovely gray eyes—eyes that were able to focus on him now, giving them so much more power over his heart. Inside, he felt as if something that had grown tough and cold—so many years ago— had finally begun to thaw. His bare body atop hers, he felt his cock respond, twitching and thickening a bit more. So much foreplay, and now there was only one damned thing he wanted—to take Hope Harper, and not with reflexive cuffs binding his body.

Freely, that was how he wanted her—freely with his heart and mind and soul.

"Hope." He nuzzled her collarbone. "I'm gonna stand up, and we're going to make love."

"Stand up?" Her gray eyes widened curiously.

He gave her a smug grin. "I'm of the opinion that you like doing it against walls." She flushed instantly. "And since that was our first time in another life of ours—and this is our real first time, the one that truly counts—I kinda figure that it's my lady's pleasure. Walls it shall be."

She swallowed visibly. "I'd do it with you against any wall you can think of."

Scott rose off of her, working to determine the best setting for this interlude of theirs. Outside the large penthouse windows the night was dark, but a slight swirling of snow could be seen, illuminated by their interior lights. This living room didn't offer the right wall, he decided, or enough privacy, given the large plate-glass windows, so he strode toward the master bedroom.

Ah! Here, indeed, he thought, noticing the short distance from wall to opulent bed. It was like every dream and vision he'd had of that cheap, tawdry motel room in their other time line, only shined up, made perfect. That this reality was so much more right than their original one gave him immense hope for their future.

With a light, teasing whistle, he called to her in the next room. "Hey, baby doll, come and get it." Folding both arms across his chest, he leaned against the wall, assuming his sultriest, most seductive look.

"You sound like a dinner bell." She laughed, appearing in the doorway.

"If I'm your meat . . ." He touched his erection and gave it a meaningful tug. "Then you're my gravy."

"Food and sex do not go together that way." She swatted at him, and he swung her up into his arms; she wrapped her strong, lithe legs about him, and just like that, he had her pinned against the wall.

"I thought you'd find it sexy." He nibbled at her ear.

"If it were strawberries and champagne . . ."

"I'm a vegetarian anyway. It was supposed to be a human joke."

She pressed her face in close to his, and he could feel the heated arousal in her whole body. With one hand she clutched him across his back. "Later, when we're lying in bed, rubbing oil over each other's bodies, and napping and wishing we never had to sleep . . . you can feed me anything you want then."

"That an invitation, sweetheart?"

"You bet it is."

With a deep, contented sigh of pleasure, he drove his hardened cock up inside of her, sliding easily into the waiting grasp of her warmth. She was the lightest woman he'd ever made love to, so easy to suspend between the wall and his own frantic body. As they drove hard together, he slammed his forearm into the wall over and over, and half prayed that none of the other guests would complain.

Hope arched her petite body, holding fast to Scott's shoulders, but it wasn't like she needed to in order to keep a grip on him. He had a firm, strong hold on her, and with every thrust of his muscular body he drove a little bit deeper inside of her. Tightening her legs around his hips, she squeezed against his cock, and in return he howled·softly in pleasure.

She pushed her face against his, breathing hard, and his own huffing breaths filled her ears. "Don't ever stop doing this to me," she murmured, and this finally undid the man completely. With a reverberating growl he drove into her, not working to be gentle, but taking everything they both wanted. She reached climax right as he came within her.

For several moments they clung together, breathing heavily and staring into each other's eyes. As she felt him grow softer inside of her, the trickling wetness of his warmth roll down her leg, he became gentle all over again.

With a delicate, careful turn, he carried her toward the bed, her legs still wrapped about him. He eased her down onto the comforter, and together they curled up beside each other, just gazing into the other's eyes.

"You are the most amazing woman I've ever known," he told her softly, pressing a light kiss to her forehead.

"Well, maybe you haven't known that many women," she teased, and he grew serious.

"I've been trying to find you for years, Hope. You wouldn't believe how long and how hard I kept on looking—I just never understood what I was really doing. I can see now that a part of me knew you were on the horizon, and I think I got impatient."

"You had a lot of sex with a lot of women," she agreed in understanding.

"I kept looking for you," he amended. Then, curling her up against his own body, molding them together, he whispered, "And I thank All in heaven that I don't have to look anywhere else ever again. We're together, and nobody's ever going to drive us apart."

Hope closed her eyes, still thankful that there was such a marked change when she opened and closed them, not near-blackness all the time.

"Yes, sweetheart." She snuggled up against him, and had to agree.

They'd found each other from across the universe, and no one—not a human or alien—would drive them apart, not ever again.

No one was coming. The thought sounded hollow and round, like one of the cruelest bullets in the humans' arsenal. There wasn't a soul who could help his wife, no one at all.

Vainly he searched the battlefield for a healer, but they'd been tapped dry by the day's carnage; to the very last man and woman they were spent. The medics were knee-deep in loss and bloodshed, unable to hike the long distance to the wind-battered tent where Hope lay dying as she labored in vain to deliver their baby girl. Human or hybrid, the doctors couldn't say for sure what their child would be, yet Scott Dillon knew one fact for certain: Precious Leisa would be *theirs*. It was the only thing he needed to know about their daughter, born of love in a time of hardship and turmoil—born to them against all odds, including Hope's fragile health.

He could picture the tufts of light blond hair atop Leisa's head, silvery-gold, just like Hope's, and he could already feel her nestling close beneath his chin on cold nights like this one. In a cruel world made so much crueler by the years of endless fighting, their tiny child would smell of innocence. And perfection . . . of a love that defied battle lines as well as the lines that separated species.

Yes, by All, she would be theirs.

But only if he could get someone—hell, anyone—to deliver their baby girl on the night of this Armageddon.

With the night-vision goggles fixed over his eyes, he scanned the perimeter of the battlefield, but still found no one who could help. He'd hiked more than an hour, beyond the defenses of the day's skirmish and onto the next plateau. Blood, bodies, death. There wasn't a soldier he recognized who might help them, just devastating loss in every direction.

Falling to his knees, he lifted his hands in supplication. "Lord of All, please save my wife . . . our baby girl. Help them, I beg of you." Bowing his head, he reached with every particle of his being, every molecule of his essence and lifelong faith in the One who governed their destinies.

Help them. Take me, but spare them, please!

A rustling of wind caused him to adjust his binoculars and glance upward toward the tree line along the ridge. There, kneeling and bent over a fallen soldier, he glimpsed Rory Devlin, one of their strongest and best healers. How he'd missed the man before he had no idea, but like a gift from above, Rory glowed bright green through his goggles. Without another breath or thought, Scott took off running, sprinting with all his might toward that one gifted healer gleaming out of the darkness, the answer to his prayer.

Time. Just give me one more breath of it, he begged, stretching his shaking legs as long as they would go.

By the time they reached her, almost another hour had passed. An hour of heartrending, unstoppable moments that Scott Dillon counted off with each breath. An hour of hiking and dragging their drained bodies over rough terrain, forcing themselves onward. Sighting Rory on the ridge had been a miracle, and for the first time in his quest, he'd allowed himself to truly believe that Hope and Leisa might have a fighting chance of survival.

Arriving back at their shabby encampment, he led the way into their battered tent, but none of his worst imaginings could have prepared him for what he saw: the love of his life, still and motionless. Rory followed quickly on his heels, gasping, but Scott could only stare in mute horror, unable to process the unholy image before him.

"Hope," he whispered, falling to her side. "Sweetheart . . . love." Only then did he see the swelling bruise along her neck, the purpling outline of fingers around the pale and delicate rise of her throat.

Her lovely gray eyes were closed, one hand crumpled across her forehead, the other cupping her full belly in a protective gesture.

"Gods in heaven!" Rory hissed behind him, but Scott could only laugh. Insane—hideous, wrong—but he couldn't seem to stop himself.

Rory grasped his shoulder. "Dillon—"

"Shut the fuck up!" he screamed, pressing his face against Hope's. She'd wake up; hell, of course she would. It was some kind of sick joke. What else could it be?

Nuzzling her, he whispered, "Sweetheart, knock it off. What're you trying to do to me, huh? Stop this right now!"

Rory tugged at his elbow, but Scott shook him off like he would a rabid dog. "Get the hell outta here!"

"Let me lay hands on her," Rory tried lamely, but Scott's tears blinded him senselessly. Burying his face against hers, he kept murmuring to her, reaching for their bond. Anything just to wake her up.

"So it comes to this," a chilling voice spoke into the quiet.

Scott jerked his head sideways and saw a giant of a human in the far corner of the tent, sneering, the scent of Hope's death all over him.

For a long, distended moment Scott kept his face against Hope's cool one, time playing out, playing him for the ultimate fool until he jerked upward, slamming to his feet and to his fighting senses.

Without a thought or any rational process, he lunged toward the human stranger, both hands about the giant's throat as he tackled him to the ground, all awareness dimming. Struggling, he had the much larger man pinned beneath him almost instantaneously.

Scott sucked at the air all about him, gasping. "How could you . . . fucking . . . do—"

His opponent cut him off. "You know how!"

The stranger's human stench was unmistakable as he writhed within Scott's grasp, gurgling and laughing up into his face as they fought, grappled. His enemy had the weight and size advantage, but Scott had the advantage of hatred and fury, pinning the bastard beneath him, both hands stifling breath from the man's throat. Just as this enemy had stolen life from Hope's body.

The human actually half smiled up at him, smirking even as his life was being choked away. As if he knew a secret—as if he knew *why*. Why he'd killed Scott's wife and unborn baby.

And something about that sneer unlocked the berserker within Scott Dillon, caused him to delve deep within his nature as an Antousian shifter, taker of life and being. With one last glance toward Hope, her body lifeless—Leisa lifeless within her too—Scott waged war upon the human. Delving deep within the stranger, into the marrow of his being, he determined to kill. *To take.* To murder, as his soul mate had been murdered by this dark man's hand.

Scott Dillon became everything he'd always sworn he would never be—something clicked inside of him, something driven and dark. He would leave his own mortal body and take possession of his enemy's, thereby snuffing out the other man. He would abandon himself so that he could choke out every bit of identity that the killer had ever known. He'd always reviled this about his kind, this ability to harvest another living being's body, forcing that person into oblivion. But since he was blinded by grief and fury, it seemed right somehow. Seemed the only possible ending to the life-and-death battle that he waged against the human who writhed beneath him.

"You'll pay." Scott clinched his hands about the human's throat, eyeing him hard with his gazing ability. Searching him totally with his Antousian's gift of stealing everything. A life, a body, a being. Images invaded Scott's mind, flashes of a dusty road, a military installation, a corporate-looking office. A slashing staccato of mental photographs that he couldn't string together, not when his rational mind had left him completely.

"Why would you kill them?" Scott demanded, tightening his grasp around the man's throat.

The human slugged at Scott's chest weakly, his eyes shutting, but said nothing.

This killer would pay.

"You are ours," Scott hissed into the darkness of the tent. "You belong to Hope Dillon. Leisa Dillon. And me." He was crazed, unaware of the healer backing out of the tent, of his wife's lifeless body, of anything that smacked of goodness. He didn't give a hell's virgin for his soul, not then. Not for eternity. "You are *mine*," he swore.

And I am yours, he thought, feeling his own body blend with that of the murderous human's. *We are one.*

Kelsey Bennett pushed her way past the gathered soldiers outside Scott and Hope's tent, ignoring the protests of several who tried to stop her. "Careful, my lady!" some called out. "A killer's in there."

One of the burliest soldiers grabbed hold of her arm, pulling her back. "My queen," the lumbering man implored, "he's a madman."

She shook off his grasp, striding into the tent and shoving her way past the several officers who had guns drawn and aimed at the intruder. She'd mentally prepared herself for the sight of Hope's dead body, but despite that fact, finding her friend lifeless—and held by a stranger—drove the very breath from her lungs.

A large man lay behind Hope, holding her against his chest, rocking her. He stared at some unseen sight on the far side of the tent, singing a quiet song in Antousian under his breath—a song she'd recently overheard Scott teaching Hope, a lullaby from his childhood.

She heard the weapons around her engaging, safeties dislodging, as she moved ahead of the gathered soldiers and stared down at the large man who cradled Hope within his arms. On the far side of the tent lay Scott Dillon's lifeless body, but she couldn't bring herself to do more than barely glance at it.

She didn't even know why she was here; everything within her said this tent was an incendiary point of danger. Still, she'd slammed awake from her disturbing, vivid dream, absolutely compelled to come. After leaving the tent, Jared still asleep back inside, she'd heard the news—that Hope had been murdered, and Scott Dillon was dead at the hands of her killer.

Still, that wasn't what her dream had shown her, and she'd learned that her intuitive visions were always significant. The most important ones were infused with a particular smell, a palpable feeling—like the dream that had called her out of deep sleep and into this tent.

Dropping to her knees, she took Hope's cool hand within hers, bowing her head. The man holding her flinched, then wrapped both arms about Hope's body more tightly—as if he thought Kelsey would try to take her from him. For long moments she knelt beside her dead friend, praying and listening to the mournful Antousian song the man sang.

She was supposed to believe him Hope's killer, but because of her dream she knew better. Casting another glance at Scott's lifeless body on the other side of the tent, she finally spoke. "You're going to have to let her go."

"I can't leave her here, not like this," was the man's answer, his voice a deep, gravelly sound.

"The fighting's going to start again in just a few more hours. We don't have long to give her the burial she deserves."

He moaned softly. "I'm never burying her."

"If you don't, then the wolves will get her. That's not what you want."

He rocked her harder in his arms, slipping one large hand over her full belly. "I'll stay with them. From now on, I'll stay."

Kelsey looked up and for the first time saw the brilliant, almost eerie green eyes he now possessed. *"Scott,"* she answered meaningfully, "you are going to have to let them go."

His eyes slid shut. "They think I killed her."

"Of course you didn't—you couldn't hurt her or your baby."

"They don't understand what I did." He trembled all over, burying his face against the disheveled hair atop Hope's head.

Kelsey slid forward on her knees, lifting her fingertips to Dillon's forehead, stroking his temple with a soothing gesture. "They've forgotten who you are, Scott, and what you can do. You were distraught—"

"I had to stop him; he couldn't do this again."

"I know." She kept her hand atop his head. "I know, Scott. I saw it all in my dream."

"They're going to kill me." Tears welled in his green eyes; he looked like a stranger, but his soul was that of her husband's lifelong best friend—and one of her closest friends too.

"I won't let that happen—neither will Jared."

"How do you know who I am?" he demanded angrily, fixing Kelsey with a furious stare. "You don't know that I won't kill you too."

Ignoring him, she bent down and kissed Hope's cheek, tears filling her own eyes. "Scott, we'll get you through this. Just do what I say, and I will help you out of this, okay? They're going to listen to me—they have to listen to me."

"Leave us here." Scott shoved her hand away, sending Kelsey sprawling backward.

In reaction, the soldiers behind her took several steps closer; she tossed a glare over her shoulder. "Back down! Ease down, right now, Lieutenant," she said to the leader of the small knot of fighters. He searched her face, and she gave a brisk nod, whispering again, "Back down."

The gathered soldiers lowered their weapons, and their leader gave an unconvinced nod. She turned back to face Dillon, to the man he had become, that was, after seizing his enemy's body. He appeared to be a stranger, but she recognized his soul and spirit thanks to her dream vision.

Shaking, he tightened his hold on Hope. "I'm as dead as she is."

"That's not true." Kelsey shook her head.

"I don't even have a name now."

"You're still Scott Dillon."

One of the soldiers tossed a wallet in her direction and it landed beside her knee. "Found this in his jacket. Says he's Jakob Tierny."

Kelsey flipped open the wallet and examined the driver's license inside. Only a few other slips of paper, a lined photograph and a computer chip were crammed within. She studied the man in the license photo, but he had almost no relation to the one huddling in front of her. The green eyes in the ID were the same electric hue, but were hollow and empty. Chilling. The eyes gazing at her right now were filled with heartbreak and weariness. They did not belong to the same man in the license photo.

She extended the ID to Scott. "Take a look. This is the man you killed. Can't you see what's wrong with him? You have to see the soullessness in his eyes."

Scott examined the photograph, staring at it for many

minutes before slowly handing it back to her. "From this day forward, call me Jakob Tierny."

"I don't understand."

"Scott Dillon is dead," he pronounced, slowly releasing his hold on Hope. With a quick glance at his former body, crumpled on the floor of the tent, he said, "Everything inside of me is dead. I'm a killer, just like the man whose body I stole. So from now on, I will become him. Just like I live inside his body."

"You took his body, but you're not him," Kelsey tried to argue, but he only shook his head.

"Scott is dead." He bent low, nuzzling Hope's cheek. "Scott is dead. And I am Jakob."

DEIDRE KNIGHT

PARALLEL HEAT

An unforgettable alternate world of danger, seduction and the mysteries of time. Here Knight returns to that world as alien warrior Marco McKinley is enlisted to personally protect the beautiful human solider Thea Haven. Now, as two sworn enemies are pitted against each other, their lives will be changed forever by the unpredictable perils of love, betrayal, vengeance and passion.

0-451-21965-1

PARALLEL ATTRACTION

It has been years since exiled alien king Jared Bennett thought of anything other than his people's fight for freedom. Now his rebel force has the one weapon that can turn the tide against their enemy: the key to the secrets of time. Victory has never been closer, but one woman has the power to change everything.

0-451-21811-6

Available wherever books are sold or at
penguin.com